USBORNE READER'S LIBRARY

TALES OF REAL ADVENTURE

USBORNE READER'S LIBRARY

TALES OF REAL
SURVIVAL

Paul Dowswell

Designed by Nigel Reece

Additional design by Fiona Brown

Illustrated by Ian Jackson, Sean Wilkinson,
Janos Marffy and Guy Smith

Contents

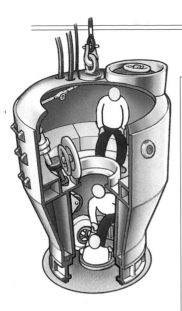

Survival essentials

The stories in this book are about people who stared death in the face and lived to tell the tale. Many of them – explorers, military personnel, mountaineers – were already in extraordinary circumstances when disaster struck. But others – passengers, workmen, tourists – suddenly found themselves quite unexpectedly fighting for their lives.

Good and bad fortune

What separates the living from the dead when catastrophe strikes? Often it is simply a matter of chance – for example, those on the deck of a sinking ship have a greater chance of escape than their shipmates below. But once the immediate danger has passed, sheer determination can become the most important element in the struggle for survival.

The crew of *Apollo 13* survived a catastrophic explosion on the way to the Moon because they kept cool heads in appalling conditions. Every single one of explorer Ernest Shackleton's Antarctic expedition returned home from the icy polar wastes, because their leader was determined to get them all back alive.

Useful skills

Certainly, expertise can be useful. Paramedic Eric Larsen survived his tussle with a shark because he told rescuers what to do to stop him from bleeding to death, but the key to successful survival seems to be the sheer will to live. You can read about these dramatic stories, and other exciting accounts, in the following pages of Tales of Real Survival.

Dive to disaster

Lieutenant Oliver Naquin, 35, stood face to the wind and spray, on the conning tower of his submarine *Squalus**.

Squalus was brand new and undergoing sea trials before she joined the US Navy as an operational submarine. Now, at 8:40am, on May 23, 1939, she was to carry out a practice crash-dive – an emergency procedure where a submarine under attack on the surface submerges as quickly as possible.

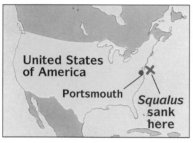

The site of the *Squalus* disaster.

Crash-dive

Naquin ordered his radio operator to report their Atlantic Ocean location to the submarine's home port of Portsmouth, New Hampshire, USA. Then, satisfied that all was well, he hit a button on the bridge which sounded the crash-dive alarm, and hurried below to the control room, closing upper and lower tower hatches as he climbed down.

Inside the submarine a klaxon alarm reverberated around the narrow vessel and men stood alert by dials and instruments, immersed in an intricate sequence of commands. "Secure all vents. Rig sub for diving. Flood main ballast tanks one and two. Open valves – bow buoyancy tanks. Main tanks three to seven – stand by."

Beside Naquin was chief officer Lieutenant Walter Doyle, eyes glued to an instrument panel known as the "Christmas tree". As all outside vents and hatches were closed, a set of indicator lights changed from red to green, showing that the ship was sealed against the sea.

As the ship's ballast tanks filled with water, *Squalus* swiftly sank to 15m (50ft). Less than a minute after the alarm had sounded, it was as if she had never been there at all.

Flood

As *Squalus* settled underwater, Naquin and Doyle congratulated themselves on a successful operation. But then a fluttering in Naquin's ears caused him to startle, and he knew immediately that something terrible was happening to his ship.

Inside an American submarine much like *Squalus*, a crewman stands beside the diving controls. The "Christmas tree" instrument panel, which indicates whether or not the vessel is sealed for diving, is immediately in front of him.

Lieutenant Oliver Naquin.

An instant later, a wide-eyed sailor looked up from an intercom and shouted that the engine room was flooding. Naquin ordered his craft to come up immediately. Compressed air hissed into the flooded ballast tanks and the stricken submarine began to rise. Although *Squalus*'s bow broke surface, tons of water were now cascading into the rear of the vessel. The weight dragged her stern down sharply and she was swallowed by the sea.

Undersea chaos

Inside was mayhem. In flickering light, tools, fittings, plates and forks, even torpedoes unhinged by the steep angle, rained down on hapless sailors as they tumbled along the ship and into the bulkheads that separated each compartment. In the flooding rear section, soaking men struggled to escape before heavy steel doors were slammed to block off the rising torrent, but many were overwhelmed by the deluge.

Sea water entered the network of interconnecting pipes that

---

4   * Squalus (pronounced Skway-lus) is a Latin word meaning "shark".

ran throughout the submarine, and jets of water spurted over men and equipment from bow to stern. Oliver Naquin could only pray that when they hit the bottom his ship would not split open like a bursting balloon.

Battery bomb

But as *Squalus* sank, an equally disastrous fate threatened to overwhelm her. In the forward battery room, ranks of batteries which powered the vessel when she was underwater, were threatening to explode and blow the submarine to fragments.

Acrid blue sheets of flame and spitting white arcs of electricity crackled from terminal to terminal. With extraordinary courage, Chief electrician Lawrence Gainor thrust his arm into the guts of this electronic machinery and shut off the power supply, plunging the submarine into a terrifying darkness.

Four minutes passed before *Squalus* hit the bottom with a jarring thud. But the hull held firm. Several flashlights had been brought to use, and small cones of light now pierced the pitch darkness. Those still left alive began to appraise their situation. Water had entered via an open air vent to the engine room. The "Christmas tree" had indicated that all vents were closed to the sea, so a fault must have developed within this equipment.

In the ghostly glow of a flashlight, crewman Charles Kuney, who manned the intercom connecting all sections to the control room, tried to contact each separate compartment. His calls to the rear of the ship met only with ominous silence.

It soon became clear that all sections behind the control room were now flooded and 26 men there

75 days without a bath

Conditions on board submarines such as *Squalus* were very basic. Men slept in bunks next to torpedoes or among the machinery of the engine room. Although

Squalus could spend 75 days at sea, there were no showers or laundry facilities for the 56 crew. Some submarines did not have a lavatory and the crew had to use a bucket.

had been trapped and drowned. In the forward section 33 men remained alive, some bruised or bleeding, but none seriously injured. They were 73m (240ft) below the surface.

Naquin knew their only option was to wait for help, although no submariners had been rescued from this depth before.

When she hit the sea bottom *Squalus*'s depth gauge read 73m (240ft).

Squalus was due to surface around 9:40am and radio a report to her home base. When no report came, a rescue operation would begin. Meantime, *Squalus* began sending up emergency flares, which floated to the surface and then launched themselves into the air. A marker buoy was also sent up from the submarine, with a telephone link to enable any rescuers to communicate with the submarine's crew. It carried a sign saying

       Submarine sunk here.
         Telephone inside.

Having survived so far, the biggest threat to the lives of the crew was now suffocation. Not only did they need a supply of air to breathe, they had to ensure they were not asphyxiated by poisonous carbon dioxide, produced by every exhaled breath.

The ship's batteries presented another grave danger. Chemicals within them could react with sea water to produce deadly chlorine gas.

To conserve their air supply, Naquin ordered his men to remain as inactive as possible, with no talking or moving around unless absolutely necessary. Soda lime, a powder which absorbs carbon dioxide,

was scattered around and the men curled up in corners, scarcely illuminated by the one or two lamps that now lit the interior, and waited.

Extra air

All hands were issued with a Momsen Lung. This was a crude form of aqualung which resembled a rubber hot-water bottle attached to a breathing mask. The idea was to give a sailor enough air to breathe while he tried to swim from the submarine escape hatch to the surface. *Squalus* was probably too deep for these devices to work effectively, but they could be of momentary use to the men if the air inside the vessel became too foul to breathe.

Momsen rescue

On shore, *Squalus*'s failure to contact her home base had been noted and a rescue operation was gathering momentum. By 1:00pm, underwater rescue expert Charles Momsen (the inventor of the Momsen lung) and a team of divers, had been summoned up from Washington. *Squalus*'s

Charles Momsen.

sister ship *Sculpin* and several tugs were all dispatched to the site to assist in the rescue. In New London, 320km (200 miles) south of Portsmouth, the US Navy rescue vessel *Falcon* prepared to join them. *Falcon* carried a McCann Rescue Chamber – a newly invented diving bell based on an idea of Momsen's. This had never been used in a real-life rescue before and training exercises had been at shallower depths, but without the chamber any rescue would be impossible.

Sculpin arrives

At 2:00pm, after a five-hour wait, the crew of *Squalus* heard the dull drubbing of propeller blades above their ship. The *Sculpin* had arrived. Contact was quickly established via the telephone in the marker buoy.

Sculpin's captain took details of the depth and location of the sunken submarine but, before any more could be said, the line snapped, cutting *Squalus*

Air vent for engine. Water came in here and sank the submarine.

This faulty valve failed to close when *Squalus* dived.

Squalus carried a crew of 56. On the surface she was powered by a diesel engine, which needed air to function. Underwater, electrical batteries supplied all power.

Engine room

Half the submarine was flooded.

Watertight door. The submarine was divided into watertight sections.

off from the outside world. It was 7:30pm that evening before the rescuers located her again, when the tug *Penacook*, after trawling for four hours, hooked a grapple onto a railing on *Squalus*'s deck.

Aboard the submarine the temperature had dropped to 4°C (39°F) and dank, dripping condensation filled the already waterlogged interior. Naquin ordered blankets to be distributed to his weary crew, waiting silently in the dark. The stale air though, made them drowsy and, despite their fear and cold, many whiled away the waiting hours in an uneasy half-sleep.

Above, another tug, *Wandank*, had arrived and was attempting to make contact with *Squalus*, using an oscillator. This device sent a high-pitched tone under water and could be used to transmit Morse code* signals.

The piercing ping of the oscillator offered further hope to the survivors on board *Squalus*. Naquin dispatched two men to the conning tower to reply. They hammered out a response with a small sledge hammer, passing on the grim news that only 33 of the crew remained alive.

Contact

Falcon, and her rescue chamber, arrived at 4:20 the next morning, along with Allen McCann – the chamber's chief designer. By 9:30am, she had anchored herself directly above *Squalus*. A diver was then lowered into the ocean and was able to attach a thick guide cable to her escape hatch.

Everything was in place and, for the first time, the McCann Rescue Chamber was to be used in a real rescue. Momsen picked two of his best divers to go down in the bell, which was winched over the side of *Falcon*, reaching *Squalus* 15 minutes later. Steel bolts anchored it in place over the submarine's escape hatch.

"We're here!"

As *Squalus*'s hatch swung open, a blast of foul and freezing air rushed into the chamber, and a collection of dull, drawn faces looked up at their rescuers. The divers, expecting at least a cheer or welcome, were stunned by the silence that greeted them. "Well," said one, rather lost for words, "we're here!", and began to pass down soup, coffee and sandwiches.

Rescue chamber

Once guide lines had been attached by a diver, the McCann Rescue Chamber could be winched down to a sunken submarine.

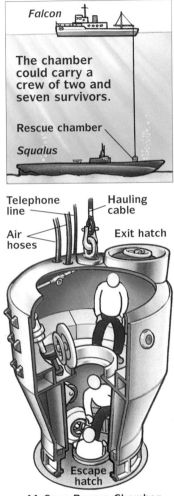

The chamber could carry a crew of two and seven survivors.

Falcon

Rescue chamber

Squalus

Telephone line

Hauling cable

Air hoses

Exit hatch

Escape hatch

McCann Rescue Chamber

Escape hatch. McCann Rescue Chamber docked here.

Conning tower

Control room

Forward battery room. Fumes from here nearly choked the survivors.

Forward torpedo room

Torpedo tube

92

192

*See page 60

The McCann chamber remained attached to *Squalus* for an hour, as fresh air was pumped down from the surface. Seven men climbed inside, and after a slow ascent the chamber surfaced and was hauled aboard the *Falcon*.

Momsen and McCann were jubilant – their invention had worked. They could see no reason why the remaining 26 men on board *Squalus* should not be rescued, and the chamber was readied for a second dive.

Choking gas

But inside the submarine all was far from well. Thick, choking clouds of chlorine gas were rising from batteries contaminated with sea water. Naquin had to act quickly, before his crew were poisoned by the gas, and led them through to the forward torpedo room. The bulkhead door to the battery room was sealed. Confined to an even smaller space than before, the men resumed their cramped, huddled positions, and waited.

Reel jam

On the surface, the diving chamber had been readied for its next descent. But once in the water the cable reel jammed and the bell had to be hoisted up for a second attempt. This time nine men were rescued. A third successful trip followed, after which only eight remained in the sunken submarine.

By the time the divers were ready for a final descent, dusk had fallen and searchlights illuminated the chamber as it entered the water. Once again the docking was faultless, and the remaining eight men climbed aboard.

At 8:40pm the ascent began, but halfway up, the down-haul cable jammed. The two divers operating the chamber hit it with their fists, then kicked it with impotent rage. But they were still stuck. There was only one thing left to do – the bell would have to return to the sea bottom, where a diver could attempt to sever the jammed down-haul reel.

When this was done, the *Falcon* began to winch the chamber to the surface at a

Below. The scene at the Isle of Shoals, May 24, 1939. *Falcon* recovers the rescue chamber after a successful dive.

steady 1.5m (5ft) per minute. But the sea was reluctant to give up its victims. In the stark light of the searchlights, men on board the *Falcon* noticed strands in the cable begin to snap and unravel.

Momsen once again ordered the bell to descend to the sea bottom. Another diver was sent down to fasten a new cable, but he was swiftly overcome by exhaustion and had to be pulled back to the surface. Then a third diver was sent down, but he too failed to fasten a new cable.

There was now no alternative but to haul the chamber back to the surface with the frayed cable. Fearful that the steam pulley which usually hauled it in would snap it at any moment, Momsen and McCann decided the cable would have to be pulled up by hand.

Freezing haul

So, in a freezing wind and after an exhausting day, a team of sailors, hauling and relaxing the rope with the swell of the sea, began the laborious task of dragging the chamber to the ocean surface.

After 10 minutes the threadbare section of cable emerged from the sea – as thin as a piece of string. Momsen, watching with wide-eyed trepidation, found himself bathed in sweat, despite the cold.

With incredible delicacy a clamp was attached to the cable below the break, and once this was done the danger was over. Winched onto the deck at 12:30am, the final survivors of *Squalus* staggered out of the Rescue Chamber after nearly 40 hours trapped underwater. No submariners before them had been rescued from such a depth.

Hindenburg's hydrogen hell

The huge airship rose so gently into the evening sky that those on board only realized they were taking off because the waving figures on the ground appeared to be getting gradually smaller.

Standing at the windows of the observation platforms on either side of the ship, or at their stations within the huge metal and canvas framework, the 42 passengers and 55 crew on the *Hindenburg* could not fail to feel they were aboard the most extraordinary aircraft ever constructed.

Brass band departure

To mark the ship's first Atlantic crossing of 1937, from Rhein-Main World Airport, Frankfurt, a brass band in blue and yellow uniforms stood on the runway and played the German national anthem. Then, when the ship reached 90m (300ft), huge wooden propellers began to turn as four diesel engines roared into life, drowning out the band below. With a thunderous drone, the airship vanished into the night. As the landscape of central Germany unfolded beneath them, many of the passengers spent a pleasant evening watching the gleaming beacons of small towns and villages, and huge pools of city lights, roll leisurely by.

Liner of the sky

Hindenburg was the size of an ocean liner and almost as opulent. The dining room offered such delights as Bavarian style fattened duckling and roast gosling. A lounge, complete with lightweight aluminium piano, and a bar and smoking room, provided further luxury. Passengers slept in 25 cabins lined with pearl-grey linen, each with hot

Passengers aboard the *Hindenburg* enjoyed a champagne lifestyle. Such luxury did not come cheap; in 1937 a round trip across the North Atlantic cost $810 – around the same price as a family car.

Left. *Hindenburg* preparing for take off, Germany, 1936.

and cold water. Like any exclusive hotel, they could even leave shoes outside their doors to be cleaned overnight.

Zeppelin veteran

In the forward control cabin sat *Hindenburg*'s captain, Max Pruss, World War One Zeppelin* veteran and seasoned airship commander. It was his responsibility to ensure the ship remained stable, a tilt of even two degrees could send wine bottles crashing from tables and play havoc with food preparation in the galley.

With Pruss in the cabin was Ernst Lehmann, director of the Zeppelin Reederei – the company which built German airships and ran the Atlantic crossings service. Business was good, and flights were now fully booked for the whole year.

Both men had every faith in their magnificent craft, but neither could fail to be aware

of the fate that had overtaken almost every other huge airship during the previous few years. In 1930, Britain's *R101* had crashed in flames, and almost all on board had been killed. The USA had been no more successful at mastering these aerial giants. Two similarly huge craft had both crashed within two years of their maiden flights.

Hydrogen bomb

Despite the problems other nations faced, in six years of successful passenger flights Germany had built an enviable reputation as the only country capable of flying airships without disaster.

But even the *Hindenburg* had one potentially fatal flaw. The lighter-than-air gas that lifted it into the sky was hydrogen – the same element that burns so fiercely on the Sun. If a gas cell leaked, a mere spark could cause a blazing catastrophe.

The airship's designers

had taken this into account. All meals were cooked with electricity, rather than gas. The bar, which had a smoking room, was equipped with electrical lighters and had a double door to insulate it from the rest of the ship.

Across the Atlantic

So the *Hindenburg* flew confidently on, her passage a succession of wonderful meals, washed down with the finest German wines. Flying over Newfoundland, Pruss took the airship down low, to give his passengers a good look at the beautiful icebergs that lined their way.

The flight reached New York on May 6, three days after leaving Frankfurt, and flew so close over the Empire State Building that passengers could clearly see photographers snapping away as they crossed. Strong winds delayed the trip by half a day, but otherwise the journey was uneventful.

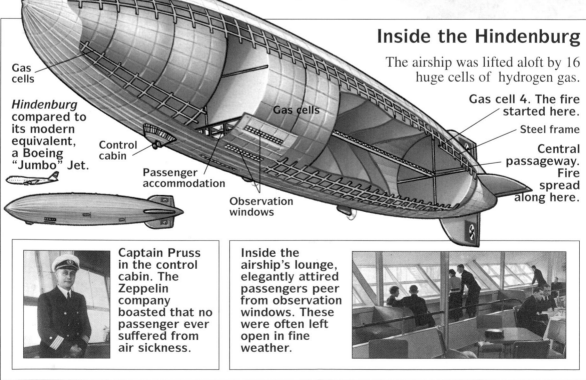

Inside the Hindenburg

The airship was lifted aloft by 16 huge cells of hydrogen gas.

Gas cells

Hindenburg compared to its modern equivalent, a Boeing "Jumbo" Jet.

Control cabin

Passenger accommodation

Observation windows

Gas cells

Gas cell 4. The fire started here.

Steel frame

Central passageway. Fire spread along here.

Captain Pruss in the control cabin. The Zeppelin company boasted that no passenger ever suffered from air sickness.

Inside the airship's lounge, elegantly attired passengers peer from observation windows. These were often left open in fine weather.

At 6:00 that evening, the *Hindenburg* approached its final destination – Lakehurst Airfield, New Jersey. Passengers gathered with their luggage in the ship's main lounge, ready to disembark. Below, over 200 ground crew readied themselves for the complex task of restraining and anchoring the huge vessel in blustery conditions.

Documenting disaster

A large crowd, including newspaper and radio journalists, had also gathered to watch her land. Among them was radio reporter Herb Morrison, broadcasting live for a Chicago radio station. His report began peacefully enough, as the airship loomed out of the evening sky and drifted down to her mooring mast...
"Here it comes, ladies and gentlemen, and what a sight it is...a thrilling one, a magnificent sight. The mighty diesel motors roar."

Blood to ice

But death was waiting for the *Hindenburg* at Lakehurst. Inside the ship, just forward of the mighty tail fins, two crewmen noticed a sight that turned their blood to ice. Lurking in the middle of the number four gas cell was a bright blue and yellow ball of curling fire.

On the ground, observers could see a faint pink glow inside the ship, which gave it a curiously transparent quality. One even likened it to a Japanese lantern. Then, within a second, the entire cell exploded with a muffled WHUMP, and fierce flames burst out of the silver canvas covering. A huge orange fireball erupted into a gigantic mushroom of smoke and flames, and began to devour

the still airborne vessel. Wide-eyed with horror, Herb Morrison watched aghast, his voice turning from cool appreciation to hysteria. "It's burst into flame! Get out of the way! Get out of the way, please!... This is terrible. This is one of the worst catastrophes in the world! The flames are 500 feet into the sky."

Garish glow

Most of the passengers and crew were in the front section of the *Hindenburg*. Their first inkling of the disaster was seeing figures below scatter in panic over the wet ground, which had suddenly taken on a garish red glow. Within seconds the ship was lurching wildly and flames engulfed the passenger decks.

In the control cabin, the explosion was so muffled one officer thought a landing rope had broken. But then frenzied shouts of "Fire" alerted them to the true situation.

As hydrogen gas at the rear of the *Hindenburg* was consumed it sank rapidly, bottom down. As the stern fell, the bow rose, and passengers preparing to jump from the open observation windows saw the ground, and their chances of survival, falling rapidly away from them.

Fire from a volcano

The sharp angle of the *Hindenburg* turned its central passageway into a chimney, and a huge tongue of flame shot out of the nose "like fire from a volcano," according to one witness. Crewmen in the forward section clung hopelessly to metal girders but, scorched by the heat, lost their grip and fell into the swirling inferno. But as the fire from the rear spread throughout the structure, and gas burned off

more evenly, the ship began to settle and landed on the ground with a ghastly hiss.

Herb Morrison could only take so much:
"Oh, the humanity! Those passengers. I can't talk, ladies and gentlemen...Honest, it is a

The *Hindenburg* was reduced to a burning carcass of twisted metal in 32 seconds.

mass of smoking wreckage... I am going to step inside where I can't see it. Listen folks, I am going to have to stop for a minute because I have lost my voice."

Walking miracle

Then, to the amazement of onlookers, people began to stumble and crawl from the raging conflagration. With extraordinary bravery, ground crew, who seconds before had been running for their lives, turned around and plunged into the burning wreck, "like dogs after rabbits," said one eyewitness.

Those who survived owed their lives mainly to where they were on the ship. The crewmen in the tail who had seen the fire start, dashed to safety when the stern hit the ground. Flames and heat always rise upward, so those under the explosion were in the best position to make a successful escape.

Acrobatic escape

Some passengers used their wits to save themselves. One, a professional acrobat, hung from a windowsill as the ship rose and fell, only jumping when he knew he could survive the fall. Another, finding himself lying on the ground surrounded by burning rubble, burrowed under the wet sand to safety.

Others were just lucky. One dazed, elderly woman simply walked down the ship's retractable steps, which had been broken open by the violent landing. One crew member survived the flames when a water tank burst above him, momentarily dousing a clear path away from the blaze.

One passenger, Leonhard Adelt, realized the airship was ablaze when it was 37m (120 ft) from the ground. As he contemplated jumping, the ship suddenly hit the ground with a tremendous impact which threw him and his wife against the floor. Tables and chairs piled up and blocked their exit, so they leaped 6m (20ft) from the open windows onto the soft sand below. Then their whole world went black as the airship crashed down on top of them.

Surrounded by burning oily clouds, they clawed through the white-hot metal struts and wires, feeling no pain as they struggled to find a route through. Adelt remembered, "It was like a dream. Our bodies had no weight. They floated like stars through space."

Another passenger, Margaret Mather, remembered that when the ship stood sharply on its stern she was thrown into a corner and several other people landed on top of her. Then flames, "bright red and very beautiful," blew into the passenger area. Mather

The blazing nose section of the _Hindenburg_, containing the passenger area, comes to rest.

watched others jump from the windows, but she was too stunned to move, imagining she was in "a medieval picture of hell". Then a loud cry brought her to her senses. "Aren't you coming?" shouted one of the ground crew who had dived into the flames, and out she ran.

Last to leave

In the control cabin beneath the ship, 12 officers and men were the last to leave. As white-hot metal crashed around them, they forged a path through the inferno.

Captain Pruss, attempting to rescue a trapped crewman, burned his face badly. Ernst Lehmann's injuries were more severe. He emerged from the wreckage a human torch. Onlookers beat the flames from his burning clothes as he mumbled, "I don't understand it." The future of his company had literally gone up in smoke. He died early the next morning.

The whole incident had taken a mere 32 seconds. Because the _Hindenburg_ was a world famous phenomenon, and because newspaper reporters, broadcasters and newsreel staff had been present at Lakehurst in abundance, pictures and stories of the catastrophe quickly flashed around the world, and people everywhere were stunned by the tragedy.

But perhaps the most extraordinary aspect of the disaster was that 62 passengers and crew were able to walk out of the blazing wreckage and live to tell the tale.

"Breadfruit" Bligh's boatload of trouble

William Bligh, captain of the *Bounty*, began the morning of April 28, 1789 tied to a mast on the deck of his ship, surrounded by surly mutineers. The day ended with him, and 18 of his crew, adrift in a small boat in the vast, uncharted Pacific Ocean.

Fletcher Christian, his former friend, and second in command on the *Bounty*, had led a mutiny against him, shortly after a lengthy stopover in Tahiti, on the way to the West Indies. The harsh life at sea made an uncomfortable contrast with the beauty of the island and its friendly inhabitants. The mutineers wanted to return to the life they had all enjoyed ashore in Tahiti.

Bligh was partly to blame for his circumstances. He was an honest man with a strong sense of duty, but he also had a terrible temper. He subjected the ship's officers, especially Christian, to public and withering contempt, often for very minor misdeeds.

Lubberly rascals

In the days before the mutiny, his unthinking persecution of Christian intensified. He had also become unpopular with his crew, who he once addressed as "a parcel of lubberly rascals", and many of the mutineers wanted to kill him.

William Bligh, irascible captain of the *Bounty*, was a brilliant seaman and navigator.

Five days' food

Bligh was ushered off the *Bounty* with a bayonet to his chest and a musket in his back, and squeezed into the ship's launch. Here, 18 loyal members of his crew awaited him, together with five days' food and drink and a handful of navigation instruments.

In this 1790 painting, Bligh (in white) and 18 of his crew are cast adrift by *Bounty* mutineers. Fletcher Christian (standing tallest on stern of the ship) looks on.

Breadfruit cargo

At the time of the mutiny, the *Bounty* was transporting a Pacific island plant known as breadfruit to slave plantations in the West Indies. Breadfruit tastes like bread when baked and slave owners thought it would provide cheap food for their slaves. Bligh was nicknamed after the plant by his fellow officers.

Cast adrift

The journey the castaways faced was daunting. Although their boat was equipped with oars and a sail, it was too small for the open ocean and so full that no one could lie down. The men on board were cold, wet and very hungry, they could not sleep, and had to bail water constantly to keep afloat. On top of all this, Bligh was resented by many of his fellow castaways, who felt he had brought the mutiny on himself.

But Bligh knew better than most the dangers ahead. He had sailed here with Captain Cook, the famous Pacific explorer, who had been killed by hostile islanders. He also knew the nearest safe haven was a Dutch trading colony on the island of Timor, where they could rejoin a British ship and make their way home. But this was 6,300km (3,900 miles), and maybe 50 days, away.

Tofua Island

Bligh decided their first priority would be to find food for the journey, so, despite the dangers, they landed on nearby Tofua Island, which the *Bounty* had passed by the night before the mutiny.

After a day or so, islanders arrived. They were friendly and traded food for the men's uniform buttons and beads. But when they realized they were dealing with castaways, rather than a party from an armed ship, their attitude changed.

Stone warning

Bligh's men were anxious to go, but keenly aware that their departure might provoke an all-out attack. More Tofuans had gathered at the beach and began to knock stones together in a sinister manner. Bligh had seen islanders behave like this shortly before Captain Cook was killed.

As night fell, the boat was slowly filled with supplies. Bligh's men edged toward the shore, telling the Tofuans they would sleep at sea but trade with them again in the morning. They headed for the boat, but the islanders all stood up and again began to knock stones together. As the castaways entered the water, stones rained down on them and the islanders charged.

The castaways traded beads and buttons for food.

The ship's quartermaster, John Norton, bravely turned to face their attackers and was struck down and killed, although the rest of the party managed to reach the launch. Bligh and others distracted their attackers by throwing clothes overboard. As their assailants stopped to pick these up, the boat sailed out of reach to the safety of the open sea.

Survival rations

Many other lush, green islands lined their route back to a safe European-held haven but, after such a narrow escape, any thoughts of landing on them were quickly abandoned.

Bligh realized that, to have any chance of survival, he would have to ration their provisions very carefully. Aside from the few coconuts they had brought from Tofua, the ship carried a rapidly decomposing supply of biscuits, a few pieces of salted pork, 12 bottles of rum and wine, and several barrels of fresh water.

Standing at the stern, Bligh addressed his weary boatload. Their supplies, he told them firmly, would have to last 50 days. Each man could be given only one ounce (28g) of biscuits, and a quarter pint (0.1 litre) of water a day. Then he made each of them swear before the others that he would accept the rations given to him, and not ask for more.

Hot pursuit

Something in their captain's manner must have reassured the crew, because they sailed from Tofua in good spirits. But two days later, the sun rose red and fiery – a sure sign that a storm would soon be upon them.

That morning an even more immediate threat presented itself. As they passed by the island of Waia, two sailing canoes set out after them, causing great alarm in the launch. The castaways were certain that, if caught, they would be killed and eaten.

Howling wind

Bligh ordered six men to the oars, and they rowed for their very lives. For three nerve-racking hours the canoes gave chase, only abandoning their quarry in the early afternoon. But no sooner had the crew recovered from their escape than a howling gale and torrential rain tore into the fragile boat.

The men endured a miserable, sleepless night and in the gathering light of dawn the storm showed no sign of abating. But Bligh had two remedies to comfort his crew, and they were both surprisingly effective. He instructed his numbed companions to dip their sodden clothes in the sea, which was warmer than rain, and then gave each man a spoonful of rum.

The *Bounty's* launch, from an 1824 account of the mutiny. When the wind was low, the boat could be rowed along.

Four-hour routine

Sailors cast away in open boats often succumb to a state of listless apathy. They curl up motionless, as static as their changeless circumstances. Bligh was determined to prevent this happening. He divided his men into two groups and while one group sailed the boat the other lay in the bottom and rested. These two groups switched every four hours, and this routine gave shape to what would otherwise have been a shapeless day.

Ration ritual

Bligh turned the highlight of each day – the handing out of rations at 8:00am, noon and sunset – into a lengthy ritual. The daily amount for each man was weighed out on a scale made from two coconut halves. A couple of pistol bullets served as weights and the whole process of preparing each portion kept the entire crew entranced. Biscuits were always on the menu, but Bligh kept the pork as an occasional surprise, delighting the boat by handing out tiny strips. Bligh invited his men to make their paltry ration last as long as any ordinary meal. He always broke his bread into minute morsels, and ate it very slowly.

Maps and prayers

He also entertained his men with stories about earlier voyages and encouraged them to share their own adventures. He drew maps to show where they were going and told them all he knew about the route. Every night he led the boat in pitiful prayers – "Bless our miserable morsel of bread, that it may be sufficient for our undertaking" – and tried to lift their spirits with seafarers' songs.

Bligh also instructed his crew to sew together a patchwork Union Jack flag from bundles of signal flags which had been thrown into the boat.

The daily ration of biscuits was weighed out in coconut shell scales.

Who shall have this?

Occasionally, Bligh and his crew caught a bird. This was divided among them all in a navy custom called "Who shall have this?". One man points to a morsel and another who cannot see him calls a name at random. The piece goes to that man. In this way arguments about who has which part of the bird are avoided. In his log Bligh wryly noted the "great amusement" in the boat when he was given a beak to eat.

They would use the flag to identify themselves when the launch reached Kupang. It was a shrewd move. Making it kept the men occupied, but it was also a symbol of hope for the end of their ordeal.

Hunger and rain

For 15 days the tiny boat pushed on through an unbroken spell of bad weather, and the men were constantly drenched and freezing. Bligh recorded that "Our appearances were horrible. I could look no way, but I caught the eye of someone in distress. Extreme hunger was now too evident. The little sleep we got was in the midst of water, and we constantly awoke with cramps and pains in our bones".

Even worse was to come. Twenty-one days into the voyage, Bligh realized their biscuits were not going to last. The ration would have to be cut from three to two portions a day. Although the men took the news without protest, the decision, he wrote, "was like robbing them of life".

After almost a month at sea the crew began to notice signs of land. Not island land, which they had to avoid, but the huge continent of Australia (then called New Holland), where they could replenish their supplies and rest for a while, hopefully undetected.

A broken branch floated by. Many birds now wheeled around the launch. Best of all, clouds, which always form around the coast, could constantly be seen on the western horizon. When they heard the sea roaring against the rocks they knew they would soon be standing on solid ground.

Australian landfall

On May 28, the small boat passed gingerly through the Great Barrier Reef, just off the Australian coast. Although this was still unknown and hostile territory to European seamen, the men were euphoric when they landed on a deserted offshore island. Many were so weak they could hardly stand, but others tore at oysters on the rocks, guzzling down as much as they could eat.

Later that day, in a copper pot taken from the *Bounty*, a delicious stew of oysters, pork and bread was cooked, and each man had a whole pint (0.5 litre) of it to himself.

Curses and beatings

Bligh cautioned his men not to eat the fruits and berries that surrounded them. All were

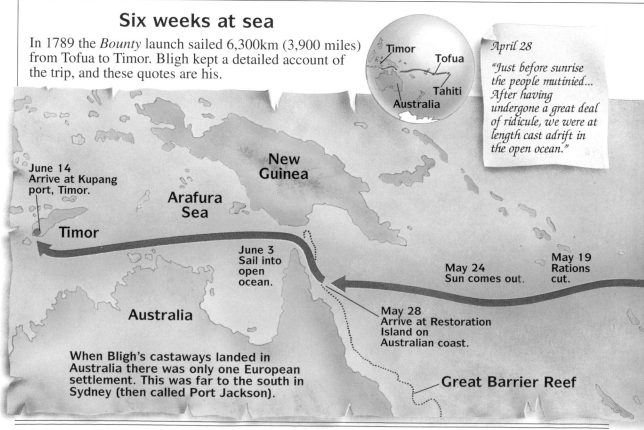

Six weeks at sea

In 1789 the *Bounty* launch sailed 6,300km (3,900 miles) from Tofua to Timor. Bligh kept a detailed account of the trip, and these quotes are his.

Timor
Tofua
Tahiti
Australia

April 28

"Just before sunrise the people mutinied... After having undergone a great deal of ridicule, we were at length cast adrift in the open ocean."

New Guinea

June 14
Arrive at Kupang port, Timor.

Arafura Sea

Timor

June 3
Sail into open ocean.

May 24
Sun comes out.

May 19
Rations cut.

May 28
Arrive at Restoration Island on Australian coast.

Australia

When Bligh's castaways landed in Australia there was only one European settlement. This was far to the south in Sydney (then called Port Jackson).

Great Barrier Reef

unknown to European botanists, and some were bound to be poisonous. But his warning was ignored. On board the boat Bligh's expert seamanship commanded a grudging respect from his resentful crew, but on land this relationship withered and bitter quarrels broke out.

Bligh felt it was his duty to return everyone safely to England. The only way to do this was to share everything between them. But other men felt that everyone should look after themselves, and be able to eat what they found, rather than contribute to a common share.

Sensing his command was slipping from him, Bligh took desperate measures. "I determined [decided] either to preserve my command or die in the attempt," he wrote in his log, and drew his cutlass on one seaman who had spoken to him rebelliously.

The do-or-die approach restored order, but it was a wretched, quarrelsome party that set sail again, on the second leg of their journey to Timor. Despite the stopover, their health soon deteriorated and by the time land was sighted, after another 10 days at sea, most men were too weak even to cheer.

When the boat arrived at Kupang port in Timor, on June 14, 1789, Bligh recorded "Our bodies were nothing but skin and bones, our limbs were full of sores, and we were clothed in rags. In this condition, the people of Timor beheld [looked on] us with a mixture of horror, surprise and pity."

Kupang arrival

From Kupang they sailed to Java and then homeward on a Dutch merchant ship. The journey to

This contemporary engraving shows the *Bounty* castaways landing at Timor.

England took nine months, and several men, weakened by their ordeal, died on the way. The quarreling continued too. Bligh had two of his crew imprisoned aboard the ship for daring to suggest he had falsified expense forms. But despite his obvious faults, and against extraordinary odds, irascible William Bligh had ensured that 11 of his crew would live to see their families again.

May 3
"We walked down the beach in a silent kind of horror (then) stones flew like a shot."

May 4
"We bore away across the sea where the navigation is but little known (and) not a star could be seen to steer by."

May 21
"We were so covered with rain and salt water, that we could scarcely see."

May 24
"For the first time, during the last fifteen days, we experienced comfort from the warmth of the sun."

June 14
"It appeared scarcely credible to ourselves that in an open boat and so poorly provided, we should have been able to reach the coast of Timor in 41 days..."

Pacific Ocean

The *Bounty*

April 4
Bounty leaves Tahiti.

Tahiti

May 7
Chased by canoes from Waia Island. Storms begin.

The launch

May 6
Pass by Fiji.

April 28
Mutiny occurs.

May 2
Launch arrives at Tofua.

Susie Rijnhart's Tibetan trek

It had not been a successful expedition. Journeying into Tibet, Canadian Protestant missionary Susie Rijnhart and her husband Petrus had met only disappointment and tragedy. They had made few Christian converts. Their servants, fearful of the bandits that infested the mountainous countryside, had deserted them. Most of their pack ponies had been stolen. When their 11-month-old son died in the Himalayan mountains they almost gave up in despair, but worse was to come.

Petrus sets off

On a frosty September morning in 1898, in the Tanggula Shan region, Susie Rijnhart bid farewell to Petrus as he set off to a nearby village on the opposite side of the mountain river bank where they had made camp. Two more ponies had been stolen and he was going to inquire if anyone knew what had happened to them.

As daylight turned to dusk, Petrus did not return and Rijnhart began to feel uneasy. The dark, desolate stillness of the mountains filled her with foreboding and she could not rid herself of the thought that something terrible had happened, and she was now totally alone.

Rijnhart the missionary

Rijnhart, a Canadian doctor of medicine, was drawn to missionary work in the Far East in her early thirties, and soon mastered several languages, including Chinese and Tibetan.

Tibet, where the principal religion was Buddhism, was an unwelcoming place for missionaries, especially women.

Rijnhart dressed in Tibetan fashion to make herself as inconspicuous as possible. Europeans were almost unknown in the region she visited, and practically everything she carried, from spoons to towels, was an item of curiosity that could be traded for other goods.

Susie Rijnhart in Tibetan costume.

The next day passed, and a gnawing suspicion that her husband was dead grew deeper.

Armed party

Another night came and went. Next morning, as Rijnhart stood scanning the horizon with the telescope she always carried, she heard shouts behind her. Thinking it was Petrus, her heart leaped with joy but, instead, a party of armed Tibetans approached.

Curt greetings were exchanged and questions asked. Where was her husband? He had gone to a nearby village she told them and would soon return. Was she not afraid to be alone? No, she carried a revolver.

Rijnhart produced the gun and explained it could fire six shots before a bandit could fire one. Each bullet, she told them, could go through three men. As a stranger in dangerous territory she was aware of the need to appear confident and powerful and the horsemen trotted off, suitably impressed.

Looking for help

Convinced now that the local villagers had killed Petrus, Rijnhart decided to go to the next settlement, to try and find

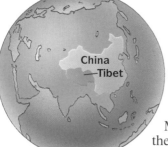

Mountainous Tibet

In 1898, this icy, mountainous country was part of the Chinese Empire. It was a dangerous, lawless place. The few Chinese officials who ruled the region depended on local chiefs to keep order. This was a very informal arrangement. Most Tibetans led a nomadic life, taking their tents and cattle wherever suitable.

help. Loading her belongings on her horse, she walked along the fierce-flowing river until she saw a cluster of tents on the other side. She shouted to attract attention, and waved a *khata* (bright ceremonial scarf) as a lure, but this was an inadequate bait. Only when she waved a piece of silver did someone agree to help, and she was ferried across the river on the back of a yak (a hairy mountain ox).

At first the villagers were suspicious and unfriendly, but after a couple of hours they warmed to Susie Rijnhart. She spoke their language, was respectful of their customs and kind and courteous. They were sympathetic when she told them about Petrus, but were too afraid of the nearby villagers to offer her any help.

Trip to Jyekundo

Instead, they suggested she travel to Jyekundo, where there was a Chinese official who might send soldiers to punish her husband's killers.

Jyekundo was 10 days' travel by horse, or 15 days away by yak. Rijnhart did not know the route, so she hired three villagers to act as guards and guides. Without them she would soon be lost in the bleak mountainous terrain or assaulted by ruthless robbers.

Bandit territory

The men accompanied her for five days, but the farther they got from home, the greater was their fear of attack, and eventually they turned back. But before they left they found three more local villagers for

Rijnhart's revolver was her only protection in a hostile world.

her to hire. These men were pleasant enough, but knew Rijnhart had little money. She suspected they were making deliberately slow progress, so that when she could no longer afford to pay them, they would only have a short journey home.

New plan

Stranded in such hostile territory Rijnhart knew her chances of survival would be slim, and she was determined not to be left alone. As they trudged through the mountains a large, imposing chief's hut in the valley below caught her eye, and she headed there intent on negotiating the use of new guides. She also wanted to hire horses, as these would be much quicker than the yaks they were using.

The chief was reluctant to help, but Rijnhart managed to convince him that if she died on his territory, Chinese officials would blame him for her death and punish him, so he grudgingly agreed to provide guides and horses to take her to Jyekundo.

Telescope deal

The chief was particularly taken with the telescope Rijnhart carried and was desperate to buy it. But rather than sell it, she promised to send it to him as a gift when she reached Jyekundo. This way it would be in the chief's interest to ensure she got there safely.

That evening she was introduced to her two new guides and began to wonder if the telescope was such a good guarantee for her safety after all. Both seemed sullen and, although one looked ordinary, the other, who had a shaven head, looked quite evil.

Cruel companions

They took to the road the next morning and her misgivings were thoroughly confirmed. During the day they furtively stole from her small supply of food, and that night they suggested she sleep with them. Rijnhart was revolted by their crude proposition and told them that if anything disturbed her in the night she would reach for her revolver. The men laughed cruelly and told her to be careful not to shoot their dog.

Next morning they treated her with disdain, even telling her that they were ashamed to be seen with her. But then they changed their tone.

They asked her kindly if she would like them to carry her heavy telescope. Rijnhart declined. She suspected their chief would kill them if they returned without the instrument, and that they would leave her to fend for herself as soon as they got their hands on it.

She was walking a tightrope, and could not afford to antagonize her disagreeable companions too much. Only her telescope kept them with her, and only her revolver stopped them from killing her.

Marsh retreat

As daylight faded to misty darkness, the party reached an immense marsh. All evening their horses waded through the sodden ground. Eventually they stopped on a spot of solid earth so remote that Rijnhart wondered if any human had ever been there before.

The guides were wearing their pleasant faces that night and, as they built a fire, they told her that here they were safe and she could sleep soundly with no danger from robbers. They curled up around the fire, men on one side, Rijnhart on the other, and a deadly waiting game began.

Weary prayer

Although she was exhausted, Rijnhart knew she was in great danger. If she fell asleep in this isolated spot she would be murdered, and no one would ever know what had happened to her. Revolver in hand she prayed for the strength to stay awake.

As the fire burned to a few glowing embers, the Moon and stars shone bright in a cloudless sky, bathing the three recumbent figures in a ghostly silver light. Six times during the night the men called softly to her, and each time she answered swiftly and sharply, and received no further reply.

The party set off at dawn with the guides in an especially foul temper. Susie Rijnhart was not the pushover they imagined her to be and their patience was running out.

This photograph, taken in the 1890s, shows two typical Tibetan nomads by their tent.

They waded out of the marsh and returned to the beaten track, reaching a fork in the road by the middle of the morning. One of the guides went to nearby tents to ask for directions and returned with the distressing news that Jyekundo had been hit by a smallpox epidemic.

Both immediately refused to continue, as they were very afraid of catching the disease. Rijnhart reminded them that their lives depended on returning home with her telescope, but they replied that they would rather be killed among friends in their own village, than die among strangers in Jyekundo.

Faultless logic

Logic like this could not to be argued with and put Rijnhart in quite a predicament. Someone had to take her to Jyekundo. Besides, if she dispensed with their services they would kill her on the spot. She needed time to think and suggested they stop to rest.

Searching for a compromise, one of the men suggested they take her to the town of Rashi-Gomba on a well-used trade route, and make sure she met up with a party of Chinese merchants. She could travel to Jyekundo with the merchants and they could take the telescope back to their chief.

His companion evidently disagreed with this plan. A fierce argument broke out between the two guides and swords were drawn. With exemplary Christian charity Rijnhart persuaded them to put down their weapons, promising again to hand over the telescope as soon as they met an obliging Chinese merchant.

Beauty and beasts

They pressed on, the men in a sullen sulk, Rijnhart exhausted but ever vigilant, and made

camp that night in a beautiful green valley, teeming with flocks of birds and grazing yaks. But further dangers awaited. After talking to the locals, the guides returned and told her there was a *lamasery* (Buddhist monastery) ahead where there was an intense hatred of foreigners. If she was spotted they would all be killed. Everything she had that betrayed her nationality would have to be destroyed.

More heartbreak

Rijnhart was not a conspicuous figure. She was dressed from head to toe in Tibetan clothes and her skin was burnished brown. She could hide her European features behind a large hat and scarf. Almost anything she had that was European had now been traded or stolen. But she still carried her husband's bible and diary, which she had kept with her since he disappeared, and now she faced the heartbreaking task of burying these precious mementos at the bottom of a nearby stream.

The next evening, as they camped high in a rocky promontory, a voice called to them out of the dark. The two guides rose to meet a stranger who had been sent from the *lamasery* to investigate them. He immediately pointed to Rijnhart and asked who she was. The guides had their story ready, and it was a good one – their companion was a Chinese man who spoke no Tibetan, so there was no point talking to him. Rijnhart's hat and fur collar concealed most of her face and nothing in her appearance gave the stranger cause to doubt this story.

Safer territory

The next day was bright and sunny. As they passed through verdant countryside a light breeze rustled the leaves of the evergreen trees around them. Rijnhart felt happier for the first time since Petrus had disappeared, and the nearer she got to Rashi-Gomba, the safer she felt.

When they reached the town the guides took her to the house of a *lama* (Buddhist priest) where a Chinese merchant stayed. Their part of the bargain completed, they snatched the telescope with a grunt and a sneer and made off, leaving Rijnhart overwhelmingly relieved to have survived their company.

Kind and helpful

This Chinese merchant was kind and helpful, and arranged for her to be presented with an official permit which guaranteed her guides and horses from any local chieftain on her way back to China.

After several weeks' travel she came to the Yangtze river, whose waters eventually flow to the Pacific Ocean. Although she was still many thousands of miles from home, she felt comforted to be by a river which reached an Ocean that shared a distant shore with her Canadian homeland.

She never was able to persuade any officials on her route to investigate Petrus' disappearance. His probable death remained a mystery.

Safe hands

Six weeks later, workers at the Roman Catholic Mission in the Chinese town of Da jian lu answered an insistent knocking at their door. Before them stood an apparently native woman – exhausted, half-starved, her clothes in rags. She seemed close to tears and all she could say was "I am Dr Rijnhart".

In safe territory, Rijnhart soon recovered from her ordeal, but she was haunted by her last glimpse of Petrus. Wading across the river which separated their camp from the village, he had turned in the sharp autumn light and shouted something she could not hear, and then vanished forever.

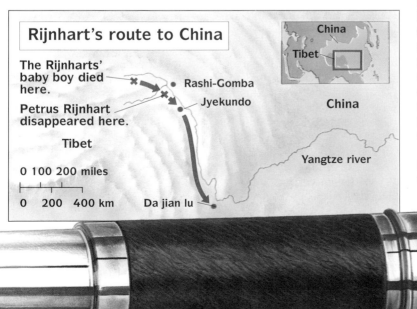

Rijnhart's route to China

China
Tibet
China

The Rijnharts'
baby boy died
here.

Rashi-Gomba

Petrus Rijnhart
disappeared here.

Jyekundo

Tibet

Yangtze river

0 100 200 miles

0   200   400 km

Da jian lu

Mirage misery for St-Exupéry

Outside the cockpit window, beyond the wing lights, the two men could see nothing but pitch black, unfathomable darkness. They were four hours out of Benghazi, en route to Cairo, and completely and hopelessly lost. Blinking away exhaustion, Antoine de Saint-Exupéry offered his copilot André Prévot another cigarette.

It was December 30, 1935. The two men were attempting to fly from Paris to Saigon* faster than anyone before them. If they broke the record before the end of the year they could claim a prize of 150,000 francs.

Saint-Exupéry, known as Saint-Ex to all, knew their lives were now in serious danger. Below lay the Sahara desert, and, with fuel rapidly running out, it was vital that they found something – a river, a city – that would give them a clue to their whereabouts.

Saint-Exupéry (right), and copilot Prévot (left), were flying between Benghazi, Libya, and Cairo, Egypt, when they crashed.

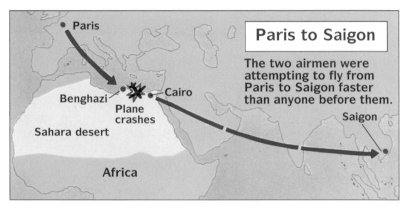

Paris to Saigon

The two airmen were attempting to fly from Paris to Saigon faster than anyone before them.

Paris · Benghazi · Plane crashes · Cairo · Sahara desert · Africa · Saigon

Crash landing

Then, both at the same time, the two men spotted a lighthouse blinking in the darkness. They must be by the sea! Saint-Ex took the plane down low, hoping to spot a suitable place to land and ask for directions. But an instant later the plane smashed into the ground, shuddering violently as it plunged across the desert. Inside the cockpit, the flyers braced themselves for a fiery, violent death. But no explosion came, and the plane rapidly screeched to a grinding halt.

Scarcely believing they were still breathing, the two men tumbled out of the cockpit and fled for their lives.

Safely away, they ran trembling hands over their bodies, checking for broken bones. With extraordinary luck, neither had injuries worse than bruises. Looking around, it was clear why the plane had not exploded when it hit the ground. They had landed on rounded, black pebbles, rather than sand, and their aircraft had rolled along, as if it were on ball bearings.

Phantom lighthouse

So far so good, but where were they? A quick look around confirmed that the lighthouse had been an illusion – maybe an instrument light reflected in the cockpit window. The sea was nowhere to be seen.

Checking the supplies, they found the plane's water container had burst, its contents instantly soaked up by the arid ground. Between them they had a small flask of coffee, half a bottle of wine, a slice of cake, a handful of grapes and an orange.

Specks in the desert

Saint-Ex and Prévot crawled back inside the plane and waited for the dawn. Neither could sleep, their situation was too desperate. If they had crashed on a recognized flight path they might be rescued

*Now called Ho Chi Mihn City, in Vietnam.

within a week. But they were completely lost – specks in a huge, sprawling desert. A search party could spend six months looking for them without success. In the heat of the day their supplies might last five hours, and Saint-Ex had been told that in such an environment a man could live less than a day without water. Both began to wonder if it would have been better to have died when their plane hit the ground.

Black pebble world

The dawn brought no relief. All around, rising and falling in dunes and hillocks, black pebbles stretched to the horizon. Not a single blade of grass grew from the ground. Their surroundings were as lifeless as the Moon.

Saint-Ex took a map from the plane and studied it forlornly. Even if they had known where they were, it would have offered little comfort. The vast emptiness of the desert was punctuated by the occasional symbol for a well, or religious institution. But these were few, and far apart.

Desert reconnaissance

It was too early to give up hope. Perhaps an oasis lay nearby? They wrote their plan for the day in huge 10m (30ft) letters in the ground, in case anyone should find the plane when they were gone, then they headed east, scraping their boots behind them to leave a trail back to the plane.

They soon forgot to mark their route, and after five hours of wandering, began to worry they would not find a way back. As the sun rose, the fierce heat drained the strength from their bones and mirages began to torment them. A faint shape

on the horizon could be a fort or town? The dark shadow to the west could be vegetation? Lakes glistened in the distance, but all vanished as they approached.

Tormented by thirst

After six hours, the need to drink became the only thing that mattered, and when they stumbled over tracks left hours before, they made their way back to the plane, and the last of their supplies. The coffee and wine were quickly consumed and the two men then set about building a fire, dragging a piece of wing away from the wrecked aircraft, and dousing it with fuel.

As thick, black smoke rose into the cloudless sky, both men stared into the flames. Saint-Ex imagined he could see his wife's face looking up at him sadly from under the rim of her hat. Prévot too thought of his loved ones – and the grief his death would cause them.

Animal burrows

There was one ray of hope. Saint-Ex had found some animal burrows. Something had managed to survive in this sterile wilderness, so perhaps they could too. That night they set traps over a couple of burrows.

Next morning, they woke determined to beat the desert, and began the day by wiping

Desert maps are as empty as the areas they depict. Saint-Ex's map was useless, as he did not know where they had crashed.

dew off the wings of their plane with a rag. Rung out, it yielded only a spoonful of liquid – a sickening mixture of water, paint and oil.

New plan

Prévot decided to stay with the aircraft, where he could light a fire in case a search plane flew over. Saint-Ex would go into the desert and forage. Although his traps were empty, there were tracks nearby. Judging from the three-toed palm imprint in the sand, the animal was a desert fox. Saint-Ex followed the tracks until he came to the animal's feeding ground – a few measly shrubs, with small golden snails among the branches. The snails were probably poisonous, and there was no water to be had from the shrubs, so Saint-Ex pressed on.

Hallucinations

Thirst was taking its toll, and he was having terrible trouble deciding whether the images he could see were mirages, hallucinations, or for real. First there was a man standing on a nearby ridge. That turned out to be a rock. Then he saw a sleeping Bedouin* and rushed to wake him. This turned out to be a tree trunk. It was so weathered and desiccated it had turned to smooth black charcoal.

*Desert tribesman

Then he saw a desert convoy of Bedouins and camels moving along the horizon, and called out to the empty desert. A monastery, a city, the sound of the sea, all followed in succession. Saint-Ex was a philosophical character and, rather than be tormented by these illusions, he allowed himself to be amused. In his dazed state he staggered around happily, laughing at his circumstances.

Despair at dusk

Darkness fell, and the mirages faded. Despair swept over him. Saint-Ex cried out desperately, his hoarse voice no more than a feeble whimper, and returned empty handed to Prévot, who had lit a fire to guide him back. But in the flickering light, Saint-Ex saw something which made his heart leap. Prévot was talking to two Bedouins – they were safe! Contact had been made with people who could guide them out of the wasteland! But the two strangers vanished as he approached. Saint-Ex had seen another cruel hallucination.

Water from the air

That night, the two men tore a parachute into six sections and laid it on the ground, covered with stones to stop the wind from blowing it away. This would catch the morning dew and provide them with much-needed water. They shared an orange and slept an exhausted sleep.

Soon after dawn next morning they wrung out nearly 2 litres (4 pints) of water from the parachute fabric into the only receptacle they had – an empty petrol tank.

Unfortunately the water was horribly contaminated by both the lining of the tank, and chemicals used to treat the parachute. It was yellow-green and tasted quite revolting. Both men spent the next 15 minutes retching into the sand.

Walk into the unknown

Prévot and Saint-Ex realized that no search party was going to find them. To stay with the plane was to wait submissively for death. There was no other choice but to walk into the unknown and hope they would find something or someone who would save them.

Heading east, for no particular reason, they trudged stoically through the sand, baked by the scorching sun, heads held down, to avoid the tormenting mirages. Saint-Ex felt as if he were pursued by a wild beast, and fancied he could feel its breath in his face.

Too thirsty to swallow

By dusk they were so thirsty neither could swallow, and a thick crust of sand covered their lips. But as the sun set, Prévot saw a lake glistening on the horizon. Saint-Ex knew it was not real, but his friend was sure this hallucination was genuine, and staggered off to investigate.

Lying on his back, Saint-Ex began to daydream about the sea. Time passed and still Prévot had not returned. He stared at the Moon, which now loomed unnaturally large above him, then he saw lights in the darkness – a search party! – and shouted after them. A figure loomed out of the dark. It was Prévot. The lights were another illusion. The two men began to bicker at each other's stupidity, their frustrations boiling over into unreasonable impatience. Then they stopped. "I guess we're both in a bad way," said Prévot.

Desperate drink

Desperate for a drink, Saint-Ex's thoughts wandered to the small bottles of alcohol, ether and iodine* they carried in their medicine box. He tried the ether, but it stung his mouth sharply. The alcohol made his throat tighten alarmingly. One whiff of the brown iodine stifled any further experimentation.

Cold night

Although deserts are very hot during the day, at night they become intensely cold, and fierce winds swept over the two men. For the last three nights the plane had protected them, but now they were out in the open. Nothing in the desert offered any shelter and, having been roasted by the sun, they were now in danger of freezing

Saint-Ex and Prévot were so desperate to drink, they tried the poisonous liquids in their medicine box.

*These are used as ointments and are very poisonous.

to death. In desperation, Saint-Ex dug himself a shallow trough and covered his body with sand and pebbles, until only his head stuck out. As long as he stayed still, the cold did not cut into him.

Grave reminder

For Prévot, a hole in the ground was all too reminiscent of a grave, and he tried to keep warm by walking around and stamping his feet. He also built a feeble fire with a few twigs, but this soon went out.

The night seemed to go on forever, and when dawn finally came there was no dew. But at least they could still speak. When people are dying from thirst and exhaustion their throats close up and a bright light fills their eyes. Neither man was in that state, so they hurried off, determined to travel as far as possible before the sun got too hot.

Ceased to sweat

By now, both men were so dehydrated, they had ceased to sweat. As the sun rose in the sky, Saint-Ex became weaker and started to see flashes of light before his eyes. A French folksong, *Aux marches du palais* ("To the steps of the palace"), played constantly in his head, but he could not remember the words.

As they struggled on, their legs began to buckle beneath them and the horrible taste in their mouths was a constant torture. The urge to lie down in the soft sand and sink into an endless sleep became overwhelming.

But then a sixth sense told them life was nearby. A ripple of hope passed between the men "like a faint breeze on

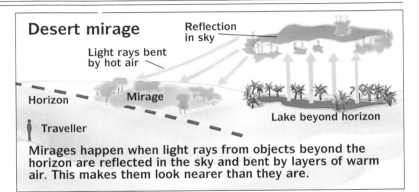

Desert mirage

Reflection in sky

Light rays bent by hot air

Horizon

Mirage

Traveller

Lake beyond horizon

Mirages happen when light rays from objects beyond the horizon are reflected in the sky and bent by layers of warm air. This makes them look nearer than they are.

the surface of a lake," as Saint-Ex later recalled. Ahead were footprints! They could hear noises! Saint-Ex saw three dogs chasing each other, and pointed joyously to them. But Prévot did not see them. They were another illusion.

Then they both saw a Bedouin on a camel. They began shouting and waving, but their voices were too feeble to be heard and the apparition disappeared behind a sand dune. But then another Bedouin appeared, and this time he saw them. To the delirious men he looked like a god walking toward them.

Great good luck

The Bedouin who found them knew exactly what to do with survivors who have been marooned in a desert without water for three days. Placing his hands on their shoulders he made them lie in the sand. He unstuck their parched lips with a feather

and gently rubbed mashed lentils into their gums, to moisten their mouths.

Only then did the Bedouin bring them a basin of water, but he had to keep pulling their heads back to stop them from drinking too quickly.

Prévot and Saint-Ex were lucky to be found by these desert wanderers and not to have stumbled on some source of water on their own. They would have drank frenziedly, and the insides of their parched mouths would have split open.

The two exhausted airmen were placed on a camel and taken to a nearby settlement. Against all expectations they had survived for three days in the fierce heat of the desert.

After his rescue, Saint-Exupéry revisits the scene of the crash.

Beware the savage beast

Killer's rubber feast

The great white shark is one of the most feared creatures in the world. So perfect is this ocean killer that it has ruled its domain since the days of the dinosaur.

The great white usually hunts fish and dolphins in the open ocean, but occasionally it will follow prey into shallow waters.

On a cool summer morning in 1991, surfer Eric Larsen, 32, sat astride his surfboard. Alone in the coastal waters of northern California, he noticed a huge, ominous shape drift effortlessly by. Within an instant his left leg had been seized by a great white shark.

Massive jaws

Larsen, who was wearing a wetsuit and gloves, instinctively thrust his hands down to wrench open the massive jaws. He was an exceptional athlete, and his great physical strength was now invaluable. The jaws inched apart, and Larsen freed his leg, only to have both arms snapped into the jagged mouth.

Pulling for his life he managed to wrench his shredded right arm free, and smashed his fist into the shark's belly. The startled animal released its grip and launched itself at Larsen's board. For a few frantic seconds, the unfortunate surfer, tethered to his board by a short cord, was heaved through the water. Then, the shark was gone.

Larsen's injuries were severe. His left leg and both arms were torn to the bone, and he was bleeding badly from the main artery in his left arm. But he was a skilled paramedic and knew exactly what he must do.

Fighting to stay calm, Larsen struggled to mount his board and headed for the shore. The temptation to paddle as fast as possible was overwhelming but Larsen knew this would make his heart beat faster and he would bleed more. Moreover, the extra blood in the water might coax the shark into another frenzied attack. His measured pace paid off. He reached the safety of the beach, and began to drag himself to houses nearby.

During an attack, the great white changes the shape of its mouth.

Snout lifts up.

Upper jaw protrudes from mouth.

Sharks have the biggest teeth of all fish. No other animal has a more formidable bite.

Out of the water, Larsen clamped his right hand firmly over the spurting gash of his bleeding artery and held his left hand above his head. Wounds bleed less when blood has to flow against gravity.

As he dragged himself toward the nearest house the world spun around him, and he collapsed. But two local residents had heard his cries, and ran to help.

Larsen explained exactly what they needed to do. His shredded leg needed to be raised above his body, to slow the flow of blood, and he showed one of his helpers where to press down on his arm to restrict the blood still pouring out of him.

Local emergency services arrived soon after, and an hour later he was in hospital. A blood transfusion, five hours of surgery, and 200 stitches saved his life.

Despite his brush with death, Larsen soon returned to surfing. He credited his escape from one of nature's most ferocious predators to the unpleasant taste of his rubber wetsuit.

Honeybee horror for truck driver Shane

Most animal attacks on people are ferociously swift, but the ordeal that truck driver John Shane faced was agonizingly slow. In May 1992, Shane, 46, was delivering 250 beehives to a beekeeper in Florida. Shortly after midnight a collision with an oncoming car overturned his truck, leaving his bruised body covered in shattered glass and trapped in twisted metal.

There were five million bees aboard the mangled truck and they soon started to swarm. In the dark interior of his cab, the trapped truck driver began to feel hot, pin-like jabs on his neck and face, as the angry insects instinctively attacked the nearest living creature. Shane was used to working with bees. He knew that stinging bees released a scent which encouraged other bees to sting. He also knew that few people were strong enough to survive more than 200 successive stings.

Police and fire crews quickly arrived, but their flashing lights and sirens seemed to make the swarm even angrier. Two firemen began to try to free Shane from his cab. They too were persistently stung, and progress was terribly slow.

Useful advice

After a while, a local beekeeper arrived and was able to offer the rescuers useful advice. All lights were turned off and the truck was sprayed with a constant jet of water, which seemed to calm the frantic bees. But Shane knew the swarm would grow angrier as dawn broke, and he still seemed to be hours away from being freed.

His desperation grew as a bee crawled in and out of his ear, and his patience finally snapped. He called to the cutting crew and persuaded them to hand over their equipment. He would attempt to cut himself free. It was worth a try and, after a long struggle, Shane was able to cut away the steering wheel which pinned him to his seat.

As a faint glimmer of light played on the eastern horizon, he was pulled from his cab and rushed to hospital. He had been trapped and stung for a horrific 196 minutes, but apart from multiple bee stings, his injuries were confined to sprains, cuts and bruises.

Ali's treetop tiger tussle

When Subedar Ali, 29, an elephant handler at the Corbett National Park, India, was attacked by a tiger in February 1984, he felt his last moments had come. Ali, foraging for animal fodder with his colleague Qutub and two elephants, was up a tree a short distance away from his workmate when the tiger pounced and pulled him to the ground.

The animal grabbed the back of Ali's neck, then bit off the top of his scalp. As it chewed at the morsel, Ali tried to scramble away, but a swat from the tiger's huge paw pinned his leg quite firmly to the ground.

Ali knew that nothing he could do would make matters worse. Inches away from the huge animal, and enveloped in an all pervasive catty stench, he grabbed its tongue. The cat looked perplexed and then promptly bit his hand. Howling in agony, the elephant handler began to beat at the tiger's head with his other hand.

Dragged into forest

Rather than killing him instantly the tiger merely swept a magisterial paw across Ali's face, and then sank its teeth into his back, dragging him into the forest. It dropped him and paused. It seemed puzzled by its rebellious prey.

Ali seized this moment to call for help, but his companion Qutub dismissed his desperate cry as a practical joke. Fortunately, at that moment, his elephant caught the tiger's scent and reeled in terror. Qutub, atop his mount, lumbered toward Ali, shouting angrily at the savage predator. Alarmed, it backed away, allowing Ali time to call for his own elephant, who bent down low to let him crawl to safety on its back.

Ali's encounter with the tiger cost him six months in a local hospital, but its encounter with Ali cost the tiger its freedom. After the attack it was captured and spent the rest of its life in an Indian zoo.

Space catastrophe for unlucky 13

On the evening of April 13, 1970, on a flight that began at 13 minutes past the 13th hour of the day, an oxygen tank inside the American spacecraft *Apollo 13* exploded violently. In the ship's tiny command module the crew heard a loud bang and felt the ship shudder. A shrill alarm filled the capsule and control panel warning lights began to flash, indicating vital power and oxygen supplies were fast ebbing away.

The astronauts, on their way to make America's third Moon landing, had been trained to keep a cool head, but their first radio message to NASA* headquarters in Houston, USA, sounded distinctly edgy. "OK, Houston, we've had a problem." They were 330,000km (205,000 miles) from Earth.

Switch trouble

The oxygen tank – a vital part of the spaceship's fuel system – had exploded when a heating switch malfunctioned. The trouble this caused abruptly doubled, when another oxygen tank linked to it emptied out

Pre-flight, Swigert, Lovell and Haise (from left) meet the press.

into the vacuum of space.

The crew, and staff at Mission Control, Houston (where every aspect of the flight was being carefully monitored), were bewildered. Engineers had assumed that anything which knocked out two oxygen tanks would also annihilate the spaceship. One senior engineer summed up their strategy for such an event: "You can kiss those guys goodbye". But the crew were still very much alive.

Apollo crew

Apollo 13 carried three men. Commander Jim Lovell, 42, on his second trip to the Moon, was America's most experienced

Mission Control at Houston, during the *Apollo 13* mission. (Astronaut Fred Haise can be seen on the TV screen.) From here hundreds of technicians monitored every aspect of the flight, and were in constant radio contact with the crew.

astronaut. His good fortune was legendary – "If Jim fell in a creek," said a colleague, "he'd come up with a trout in his pocket." In the depths of this disaster, fate was still smiling on him. Although his fellow crewmen were new to space, they both had other experience which would now be invaluable. Command module pilot Jack Swigert, 38, was an expert on *Apollo* emergency procedures. Lunar module pilot Fred Haise, 36, had spent 14 months in the factory that built his spacecraft. He knew it inside out.

Space breakdown

At first the crew did not realize just how seriously *Apollo 13* had been damaged. But 14 minutes after the explosion, Lovell noticed a cloud of white gas drifting past a window. This was oxygen – an essential part of *Apollo 13*'s fuel supply. So much had been lost that it now enveloped the ship like a cloak. An icy fear settled in the pit of his stomach as he realized *Apollo 13* could become his tomb, locked in a perpetual orbit between Earth and Moon.

Instruments indicating power and oxygen supplies were now all heading determinedly to zero. The command module was close to breaking down and would only keep the crew alive for a couple of hours. To survive they needed to move into the craft which was to have landed them on the Moon – the lunar module. This part of *Apollo 13* had so far remained unused. Now hundreds of switches had to be operated to bring the

*NASA – America's space agency the National Aeronautics and Space Administration.

Apollo 13 – 3,000 tons of technology

The *Apollo* spacecraft could take three astronauts to the Moon. It was an unwieldy looking machine made up of three connecting sections, and was blasted into space on top of a huge *Saturn 5* rocket.

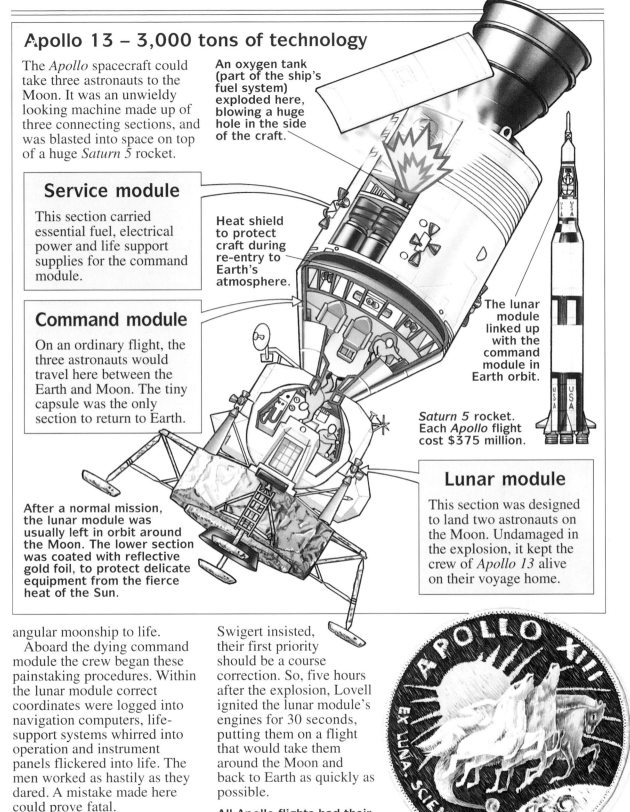

An oxygen tank (part of the ship's fuel system) exploded here, blowing a huge hole in the side of the craft.

Service module

This section carried essential fuel, electrical power and life support supplies for the command module.

Heat shield to protect craft during re-entry to Earth's atmosphere.

Command module

On an ordinary flight, the three astronauts would travel here between the Earth and Moon. The tiny capsule was the only section to return to Earth.

The lunar module linked up with the command module in Earth orbit.

Saturn 5 rocket. Each *Apollo* flight cost $375 million.

After a normal mission, the lunar module was usually left in orbit around the Moon. The lower section was coated with reflective gold foil, to protect delicate equipment from the fierce heat of the Sun.

Lunar module

This section was designed to land two astronauts on the Moon. Undamaged in the explosion, it kept the crew of *Apollo 13* alive on their voyage home.

angular moonship to life.

Aboard the dying command module the crew began these painstaking procedures. Within the lunar module correct coordinates were logged into navigation computers, life-support systems whirred into operation and instrument panels flickered into life. The men worked as hastily as they dared. A mistake made here could prove fatal.

Shifting to the lunar module solved the immediate problem of keeping them alive. Now,

Swigert insisted, their first priority should be a course correction. So, five hours after the explosion, Lovell ignited the lunar module's engines for 30 seconds, putting them on a flight that would take them around the Moon and back to Earth as quickly as possible.

All Apollo flights had their own emblem. The Latin motto *Ex Luna Scientia* means "knowledge from the Moon".

Lunar lifeboat

The crew then set about assessing their situation. The lunar module had been designed to keep two men alive on the Moon for two days. Now it would have to sustain three men for the four-day return journey. The supply situation looked like this...
• Power (electricity and fuel). Bad. This was where the explosion had done the most serious damage.
• Food. Bad. Most was freeze-dried. It required hot water, which was no longer available, to make it edible.
• Air. Good. There was enough to last until *Apollo 13* returned to Earth.
• Water. Bad. All of the craft's electronic systems generated heat. Without water to cool them, they would overheat and fail.

Bare essentials•

The simple truth was that the most durable items on *Apollo 13* were the three astronauts. They would be able to keep going on little or no heat or fuel for longer than any of the ship's equipment. In practical terms, this meant severe hardship for the crew. There was barely enough power to supply their essential equipment, so heating the craft became an expendable and unaffordable luxury.

As the cabin temperature dropped to half its normal level, the astronauts began to suffer. They were ill-equipped for such conditions. Their clothing and sleeping bags were intended for a warm environment, and made of thin, light materials. Improvising as best they could, the men wore two sets of underwear under their jumpsuits and Moon boots on their freezing feet.

The gnawing cold chilled the moisture in their breath and a clammy dampness settled on the spacecraft's interior. They began to feel, said Lovell, "as cold as frogs in a frozen pool."

No comfort for crew

Balanced on a knife edge between survival and an icy, suffocating death, there was little to comfort the crew. Hot food was unavailable, and the cold and worry prevented any of them from sleeping for more than two or three hours at a time. The shortage of drinking water was less of a trial, as space voyagers do not feel thirsty, although their bodies still need water. To conserve as much as possible, the men drank virtually no water at all for the rest of the flight and became dangerously dehydrated.

On the night of April 14, as *Apollo 13* swung around the Moon, the crew prepared to make a second course correction. As Lovell ran through the complex procedures needed to ignite the engines, he was astonished to notice Swigert and Haise busy photographing the Moon's surface. "If we don't make this next move correctly," snapped Lovell, "you won't get your pictures developed." Swigert and Haise were unrepentant. "You've been here before," they said, "and we haven't."

Lethal atmosphere

But once around the Moon, another deadly problem confronted them. As well as supplying its crew with air to breathe, a spacecraft also needs to remove the poisonous carbon dioxide which they exhale with every breath. In an enclosed area this can soon build up to fatal levels. Carbon dioxide filters aboard the lunar module could not cope with the amount the three men were producing.

Back on Earth, NASA technicians had been working on a solution and came up with an ingenious idea. There were several carbon dioxide filters in the now empty command module. These could be removed, placed in an airtight box, and used to filter the air aboard the lunar module.

Poisoning averted

As there were no airtight boxes aboard *Apollo 13,* the astronauts would have to improvise with storage bags, tape, air hoses and the covers of *Apollo 13*'s flight manuals. Instructions were radioed up to the beleaguered spacecraft, the contraption was built and the danger of carbon dioxide poisoning was averted.

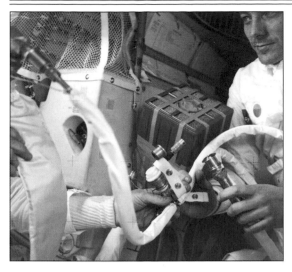

Jack Swigert assembles the makeshift carbon dioxide filter.

Final hurdle

After four days, *Apollo 13* was well on the way home, "whistling in like a high-speed train," said Swigert. One final, formidable hurdle remained – re-entry into Earth's atmosphere.

Even today, re-entry remains one of the most dangerous parts of a space mission. If *Apollo 13* approached on too steep a flight path, then it would burn up like a meteor as it hit the Earth's atmosphere. If the flight path was too shallow, it would bounce off into space, like a spinning pebble skimming across a lake. The margin for error was just a degree and a half wide.

This was not the crew's only problem. *Apollo 13* was to land in the Pacific Ocean (all American spaceships landed at sea in the 1970s) and rescue vessels had to be close at hand. To land in the right place, they would have to find a single spot above the Earth's atmosphere, called the "entry corridor", that was only 16km (10 miles) wide. Re-entry would be particularly difficult for *Apollo 13*. As with all *Apollo* spacecraft, the only section that was designed to come back to Earth was the command module, so the crew had to leave the relative safety of the lunar module and return to the crippled craft, left unused for the last four days. The command module was now as cold as a refrigerator. Water droplets had formed on every surface, from seat harnesses to instrument panels. Lovell wondered if the electronics behind the panels were just as waterlogged. They were so low on power that their equipment, if it worked at all, would have to work first time.

New instructions

Usually the command module engines would place the ship in the right position for re-entry. This time the lunar module engine would have to do it – a task it had never been designed for. At Mission Control, technicians prepared a new set of re-entry calculations and position shifts, and these were radioed up to the crew. NASA would usually take three months to prepare such a schedule, this one they put together in two days.

Flight to disaster

1. Lift off from Cape Kennedy, Florida, USA. April 11, 1970.

2. Leave Earth orbit. April 11.

3. Oxygen tank explodes 330,000km (205,000 miles) from Earth. April 13.

4. Mission abandoned. Lunar module engines steer *Apollo 13* around Moon, and set course to Earth. April 14.

5. Crew leave lunar module and prepare for re-entry. April 17.

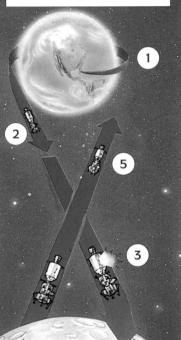

Apollo 13's return to Earth involved the most dangerous re-entry ever undertaken.

1. *Apollo 13* moves into re-entry flight path, using lunar module engines.

2. Service module released.

Re-entry

Aboard *Apollo 13* the crew struggled to understand these new instructions. In 1970 the fax machine was still too primitive to be worth installing in a spacecraft, and Swigert took two hours to write all the hundreds of procedures down in full. He was not sure that he would understand abbreviations in the tense moments to come.

As re-entry drew closer, the damaged service module was finally uncoupled. Looking out at the silver cylinder as it slowly floated away from them, the crew saw for the first time how much damage had been caused. At the site of the explosion a tangle of wires dangled from a ruptured metal cavity. Lovell told Mission Control that one whole side of the craft was missing.

Now, having placed them firmly in the correct re-entry position, only the lunar module remained to be cast off. As the astronauts watched it drift away, they felt a strong surge of affection for the craft which had saved their lives. Then they prepared themselves for the most dangerous 20 minutes of their lives.

Broken communication

Re-entry is always a time when communications between ground control and spacecraft are broken. The turbulence of the air around the blazing hot craft makes radio transmission impossible. At Mission Control, technicians waited anxiously by their consoles. Three minutes passed – the usual gap in re-entry communication – and nothing was heard. Then, a minute later, Swigert's voice, muttering a terse "OK," came over the radio. The men had survived. Bizarrely, it had rained within the capsule, as the upheaval of re-entry had loosened the water droplets within the craft.

Parachute landing

One final uncertainty lay between survival and catastrophe. Hurtling toward the Pacific Ocean, the astronauts lay strapped to their seats, wondering if there was enough power left to operate the parachutes which would slow their craft to a safe landing speed.

Four minutes later a nearby rescue helicopter relayed live video pictures to Houston, confirming that the chutes had opened. *Apollo 13* astonished the world by landing only 5.5 km (3.5 miles) away from its rescue ship – the nearest to date of any *Apollo* flight.

Below. Safely back on Earth, the *Apollo 13* crew squeeze out of their floating craft onto a life raft dropped by a circling helicopter.

3. Lunar module released.

4. Re-entry. When the command module hit Earth's atmosphere the heatshield had to withstand temperatures of 5,000°F (2,750°C).

Heatshield

5. Parachutes open at 7,000m (23,000ft) to slow Apollo to a safe landing speed.

6. Splashdown. *Apollo 13* floats in the Pacific Ocean. Crew await rescue by ship and helicopter.

Simpson's icy tomb

Joe Simpson woke soon after dawn, in a snow hole near the summit of Siula Grande, in the Peruvian Andes. He and climbing partner Simon Yates had burrowed this shelter when night overtook them on the return journey to their base camp, 16km (10 miles) away in the valley below. The climb up the mountain had been difficult. Disaster had trailed them like a stalking predator, and a fierce storm on the summit had almost claimed their lives. Perhaps today would be easier.

Joe Simpson

Simpson broke a small hole in the thin wall of ice above his head, and bright sunlight streamed in to bathe his face. He breathed in lungfuls of crisp, chilly air, which quickly dispelled the warm, sleepy atmosphere of the burrow.

Framed in his icy window, stretching as far as the horizon, were the peaks of South America's most formidable mountains. Dark shadows shaded their folds and fissures. Snowdrifts and glaciers gleamed blue-white in the sharp light of early morning.

Search for solid ground

As they left their snow hole shelters to set off down the mountain, they could see the descent was lined with hazardous drifts and crevasses. Wearily, they searched for solid ground, both feeling they had bitten off more than they could chew.

They hammered in toe-holds down the ice cliff that led from the summit. Progress was slow. Simpson gingerly picked a route down, clinging to the wall with ice axe and crampons*. Then, without warning, the ice cracked and he lurched into space.

Shattering agony

Simpson was linked to Yates with a climbing rope, so he did not fall far, but he crashed hard into the rock face below. His right knee shattered in fiery, explosive agony, and the intense pain made him scream out loud. Nausea swept through his body.

Yates clambered down to his injured companion as quickly as he could. One look at Simpson's misshapen, swollen knee told him his friend was as good as dead. On such a dangerous mountain, the two of them faced one of a climber's worst nightmares: Simpson was too badly injured to get back to base unassisted, Yates could easily kill himself if he helped. There was no chance of rescue.

Abseil down

Despite the extreme risk, Yates could not abandon his companion, so he worked out a technique to lower him off the mountain. For 900m (3,000ft) they abseiled down the steep slope. Yates fashioned a hollow in the snow, and sitting in it, gradually let out rope as Simpson slid down. Then, when the rope was paid out, Simpson anchored himself to the slope, and dug another hollow for Yates. Sliding down like this was incredibly painful, and the agony Simpson felt in his knee was made worse by nausea and light-headedness.

Ice axe

Yates too was suffering. His hands were black with frost bite, and the strain of lowering Simpson down the mountain was wearing him out. But after nine hours the two had made progress and had almost cleared the steepest section of the mountain. Simpson began to feel he might get out of this alive. But this dawning optimism was shattered by a catastrophe even worse than his initial fall.

As Yates let out the rope on another agonizing slide down, Simpson saw a sharp drop loom before him. He tried desperately to stop, but the ground disappeared beneath him and he plunged over an overhanging cliff face.

The situation was horrific. Yates, wedged in a snow hollow above the cliff face, did not have the strength to pull his friend back out. Simpson

*Metal frames with spikes, that can be strapped to climbing boots.

dangled 4.5m (15ft) down, 3m (10ft) away from sheer ice walls. The drop below receded 30m (100ft) into icy shadow, and the gaping mouth of a large crevasse.

Crevasses

On mountains such as Siula Grande, ice and snow drifts off immense slopes and forms into gigantic frozen rivers called glaciers. Very deep cracks called crevasses form in these glaciers. They are often hidden by fresh snowfalls.

As Simpson dangled, the cold ate into his bones, and he became sluggish and light-headed. The struggle to get off the mountain had failed, and he waited for death to take him.

Yates too was slowly dying of cold. Soon he would be too weak to maintain his grip and, unless he cut the rope, both of them would die. Hope faded with the falling dusk. With grim determination Yates took out his knife and sliced through the rope. Dangling in space for over an hour, Simpson

had been lost in an almost pleasant semi-consciousness. Above him he could see stars in the night sky twinkling like precious stones. But then the stars went out and he plunged into the dark chasm below.

Simpson waited for the impact of his landing to crush the life out of him. But instead he just felt an intense pain in his leg, and realized that he must still be alive. He had not plummeted to the bottom of the crevasse, but had fallen 18m (60ft) down it onto a ledge.

Ice prison

Shining a flashlight around his new surroundings, Simpson could see a huge cavern of snow and ice – as still and silent as a deserted cathedral. The walls of his prison were 15m (50ft) apart, blue, silver and green, and stretched 18m (60ft) above his head to a tiny hole to the outside world, where he had fallen through. Below the ledge the steep walls were swallowed by a forbidding darkness.

Joe Simpson was expecting to die, but he had hoped to have his life dashed out of him in a brief, violent flurry. He never expected to be stranded in a crevasse, with a mangled leg, left to gradually fade away in a delirious twilight of thirst, hunger and pain.

Severed strands

He tugged the rope, and it fell down on him. Simpson could tell from the cleanly severed strands that Yates had cut the rope, but he knew that his friend had had no choice.

The night dragged on and Simpson cried to

himself. When morning finally arrived with a bright beam of sunlight fanning into the roof of his icy cage, he shouted desperately for help.

But Simon Yates had gone. After he cut the rope, he burrowed into the snow to sleep, and then set off for base camp at dawn. He knew that cutting the rope was the only thing he could have done, and he had assumed that the fall down the crevasse had killed his wounded companion.

Simpson realized he was stuck there alone. He could not climb up, and he did not want to fade away slowly on the ledge. The only option left was to go down. The severed rope was at least 46m (150ft) long. He anchored it to the ledge with an ice piton (screw) and lowered himself into the gloom. He did not even look down to see what was below. If he came to the end of the rope without reaching ground, he would just let himself fall into oblivion.

Snow floor

But luck was with him. When Simpson did look down he saw a snow-covered floor. It ran the whole length of the crevasse and sloped up away from him to a sunlit crack at the top. Here was a route out!

Then he noticed black holes in the snow, and realized that this was not a floor he was hanging above – it was a drift of snow across the divide!

He had no other choice but to lower himself gingerly into the snow. He tried to put as little pressure as possible on his mangled leg, and gently, gently, he dropped onto the crisp white carpet. As the rope went slack, he found that the drift would take his weight,

Simpson attached his severed rope to an ice piton.

and he sat totally still for five minutes, hardly daring to move. Then, spread-eagled on his stomach, he began to wriggle slowly toward the distant sunlight.

Muffled thumps below jarred every nerve in his body. This noise was snow beneath him, dislodged by his movements, falling into the depths of the crevasse.

He pressed on, hoping the snow would not crumble. The slope stretched 45° up to the ceiling for maybe 40m (130ft). The final 6m (20ft) looked even steeper – maybe 65°. If he had been fit, the climb would have taken 10 minutes, but with his damaged leg it took five hours. Digging his ice axe into the snow, and inching up the slope, his sobs and curses echoed around this strange, unearthly world.

Outside world

Finally he reached the top, unhooked the rope and emerged to slump exhausted into the outside world. The bright blue sky, hot sun, and awesome ridges and folds of the surrounding mountains overwhelmed his senses, and he lay dazed in a shattered stupor.

Simpson had beaten the crevasse, but was he any better off than he had been inside it? He had no food or water, he was dying of exhaustion, his leg was useless and now frostbite had begun to disable his fingers.

Enter the voice

But Simpson was not going to give up now. An extraordinary change came over him. He began

to hear a voice in his head telling him clearly what he must do.

The voice told him to go to the glacier below. Dragging his shattered limb behind him, he crawled off, tumbling down snowy slopes, and crying out in agony every time he snagged

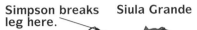

Simpson breaks leg here.   **Siula Grande**

Crevasse

Base camp

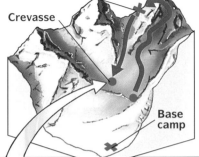

Crevasse dungeon

Simpson's fall into the crevasse, and his escape route.

5

1

4

2

3

1. Simpson falls through snow roof of crevasse.

2. Fall broken by ice ledge.

3. Using severed rope, Simpson lowers himself down to snow floor.

4. Route to surface.

5. Exit hole.

Crevasse beneath snow floor.

Snow floor

his leg. All day he continued, convinced that as long as he obeyed the voice he would be alright.

He passed an uncomfortable night in a snow hole, and pressed on. By early afternoon on the next day the snow thinned out, and he had reached the lower rocky slopes of Siula Grande.

Here he would have to hobble instead of crawl. Using his sleeping mat, he made a crude bandage and strapped it to his injured leg. After a couple of attempts he managed to hobble forward, using his axe as a walking stick.

The trip through the rocks was even more agonizing than the crawl through the snow. The day dragged on, but eventually the shadows grew long and cold, and it was night once again.

Too weary to stand

Next morning the voice forced him to his feet. It told him that if he did not return to camp that day he would die. Although he was totally exhausted he struggled on, muttering deliriously, his strength completely gone.

Day slowly turned to night and rain began to fall. Then, he saw flashing lights. Conversation drifted up to him, from far away. Was this a hallucination? He called out desperately, and they shouted back. A bobbing light flashed before him, as Simon Yates ran up to him with a flashlight.

Simpson could not speak. Retching, sobbing, giggling, tears streaming down his face, he had dragged himself from the very jaws of death, and now he was safe.

Death or glory for "Last Gladiator"

With his blue alligator hide shoes, white leather suit, and gold-topped cane, motorcycle stunt rider Robert "Evel" Knievel (pronounced Kuh-nee-val) was the stuff legends are made of. Over 300 jumps across snake pits, lion cages, fountains and trucks, before hordes of paying customers, had brought Evel a Rolls Royce and an income of $500,000 a year.

Of course, there were some disadvantages to the job. In five years of stunt riding, 11 serious crashes had left him with one leg slightly shorter than the other and over one hundred broken bones, held together with steel joints and screws. Evel was philosophical. Quizzed by a perplexed reporter he swaggered "I'm a competitor. I face the greatest competition any man can face, and that, my friend, is death."

Final challenge

But Knievel was becoming weary of his death or glory life on the road. Wife Linda and three children were tempting him to hang up his crash helmet before he made one jump too many.

Still, there was one final challenge the great competitor had yet to face. For years he

Stunt rider "Evel" Knievel meets the press prior to his Snake River jump, September, 1974. The former safecracker and jailbird told reporters "If it doesn't work, I'll spit the canyon wall in the eye just before I hit."

had wanted to hurtle up a ramp at full throttle, launch himself into the blue sky and power his bike from one side of a canyon to another. A scheme like that would sell enough tickets to pay for a very comfortable retirement.

Navaho veto

The Arizona Grand Canyon was the ideal choice. A national landmark, and the greatest chasm on the face of the Earth.

But the Navaho Indians, who owned the land, considered it sacred and would have nothing to do with a gaudy showbiz prankster like Knievel. Even $40,000 wouldn't make them change their minds.

The Snake River canyon in Idaho would do instead. It was 1.6km (1 mile) across and its dark jagged walls, and even darker river, made a suitably sinister spot for Knievel's last stand. Land was leased, and former NASA rocket engineer John Truax was commissioned to design a vehicle to cross it.

Million dollar rocket

Truax presented Knievel with the *Sky Cycle*. It may have been called a cycle, after Knievel's usual mode of stunt transportation, but it was in fact one million dollars' worth of steam-powered rocket. The plan was simple. Knievel would sit in this projectile, and be fired up a ramp and over the gaping mouth of the canyon. Once across, a parachute would slow the *Sky Cycle*'s descent to a safe landing speed. The whole escapade would take about three minutes.

Knievel played up the danger of his stunt for all it was worth. He told reporters he would make it... "if the heater doesn't

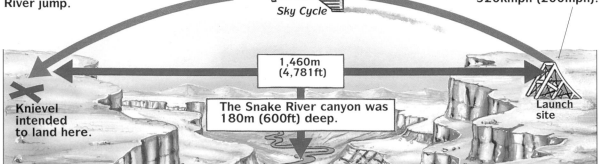

Proposed route of *Sky Cycle* rocket for Snake River jump.

Sky Cycle

The *Sky Cycle* would leave the launch ramp at 320kmph (200mph).

1,460m (4,781ft)

The Snake River canyon was 180m (600ft) deep.

Knievel intended to land here.

Launch site

blow up and scald me to death, if the *Sky Cycle* goes straight up and doesn't flip over backward, if I reach 3,000ft, if the parachute opens and if I don't hit the canyon wall at 300mph."

The date was set – September 8, 1974. Word went out and within weeks the audacious stunt had captured the imagination of newspaper editors throughout the world. Fifteen different businesses invested in it. There would be toys, T-shirts, records, even statuettes ($450 in bronze, $20,000 in silver, $140,000 in gold).

As the date drew near, 50,000 spectators gathered at the Snake River site, paying $25 a ticket. Most lucrative of all was the plan to broadcast the action to several million paying customers in theatres throughout the world.

Hero or zero?

Opinion on Knievel was sharply divided. To his thousands of fans he was "the last gladiator", shaking a defiant fist at the fiery holocaust or watery grave that awaited. Many believed he was actually going to die. According to his publicity men, his escapade would most likely "leave behind the richest widow in America".

But to others the stunt was a con, and the danger had been exaggerated beyond all reason. A bright teenager, they said, could have calculated the rocket's flight path and concluded that Knievel would land perfectly safely. One

cynic, regarding the surly mob of desperado bikers who made up most of the Snake River spectators, speculated that the crowd was more dangerous than the *Sky Cycle*.

Even the man himself was unsure. "I don't know if I'm an athlete, a daredevil, a promoter, a hoax, or just a nut".

So it was, on the afternoon of September 8, 1974, that Evel Knievel mounted his

Knievel doll, complete with gold-topped cane. Publicity from the Snake River jump led to sales of millions of toys such as this.

Festooned with sponsors' logos, the million dollar *Sky Cycle* is prepared for liftoff. Two previous, unmanned flights ended in disaster.

Sky Cycle, and launched himself into the air. But his flight was to be less than glorious. As the rocket sped from the 58° ramp, a parachute accidentally opened right in the way of its steam-powered thruster.

The flight of the *Sky Cycle* was now fatally flawed and it lurched into the canyon,

parachute billowing behind. Knievel struggled to escape his tiny cockpit, but could not free himself in time to make his own parachute jump to safety. The *Sky Cycle* grazed the craggy wall of the canyon, and then deposited the hapless stunt man in the Snake River.

Knievel, swiftly rescued by boat and helicopter, appeared shaken but uninjured. His stunt had turned out to be hair-raisingly dangerous after all. However, disappointed by his unspectacular performance, sections of the crowd promptly rioted. They attempted to storm the press enclosure and were beaten off by policemen.

But injured pride was a small price to pay. With a guaranteed minimum fee of $5,500,000, or 60 per cent of all takings, Knievel's final performance had blossomed into an awesome retirement pay off.

Marooned in a polar wilderness

Sir Ernest Shackleton was a professional adventurer. When not exploring, he made a living writing books and giving lectures about his expeditions.

With a screeching and groaning that would have done justice to a dying mammoth, the *Endurance* finally began to break up. Crushed for months by massive sheets of pack ice, the ship was slowly sinking. Even her hardened hull (made from greenheart, a wood heavier than iron) could not withstand such tremendous pressure.

The Trans-Antarctic Expedition

Watching in numb resignation were the 29 men of Ernest Shackleton's Trans-Antarctic Expedition. This hand-picked mixture of seamen, scientists and craftsmen was accompanied by 70 dogs, a cat and a stowaway – 18-year-old Canadian Percy Blackboro. When discovered, Shackleton had told him "If anyone has to be eaten, you'll be the first."

They had intended to spend 1914-15 attempting the first crossing of the Antarctic. Now, in November, 1915, they were stranded, 1,900km (1,200 miles) from the nearest human beings, in one of the most hostile places on Earth.

***Endurance*, trapped in ice. In other boats, caught in similar conditions, crews had gone mad or squabbled violently. Shackleton ensured his men were well occupied as they waited for the ice to melt.**

The *Endurance* had sailed from London. When they reached Antarctic waters, icebergs soon surrounded the ship. As they passed gingerly through, Shackleton described their unearthly environment as

Most of Antarctica (see shaded area) was unexplored at the time of Shackleton's expedition.

"a gigantic and interminable jigsaw". But shortly after crossing the Antarctic Circle the ice closed in and packed itself tightly around them. Soon they could move neither forward nor backward, and there they stayed for nine months, waiting for the ice to clear.

The expedition coped with the waiting, the cold and the interminable darkness of an Antarctic winter with remarkable cheerfulness. Shackleton, called "the Boss" by the crew, kept them busy organizing dog training, soccer and hockey matches, party games and lectures. The men even carved blocks of ice into elaborate, beautiful dog kennels. In anticipation of such delays, the *Endurance* had also been equipped with an ample library.

Ocean Camp

But now the ship had sunk, and the men made a camp on the ice. Surrounded by an untidy mixture of three lifeboats, salvaged equipment and supplies,

they christened their new home "Ocean Camp". Here Shackleton gathered his companions around him. They were too far from civilization to be rescued, he told them. If they were to survive, drastic measures were called for.

Their only option, he said, was to haul the lifeboats through the ice to the open sea, and then sail 1,300km (800 miles) back to South Georgia – the nearest inhabited island. Each man could only bring 1kg (2lbs) of personal possessions, and would have to leave most of his belongings behind.

To emphasize this point, Shackleton threw to the ground his watch and chain, and a pocketful of gold coins. Then, to everyone's amazement, a Bible the Queen of England had given him at the start of the voyage was also discarded.

Shackleton's men discarded anything that was not essential for their trip back home.

Banjo sing-along

Men were allowed to keep their diaries. Leonard Hussey, the expedition meteorologist, was told to keep his banjo – a sing-along was always good for morale. A sleeping bag, metal cup, knife, spoon and the heavy clothes they stood in, were the only other possessions they were allowed to take.

Food supplies were so limited that there would not be enough for both the members of the expedition and their animals. Some of the dogs, and the ship's cat, were reluctantly shot. It was kinder than letting them starve to death.

By the time they were ready to set off on their trek, it was almost Christmas and well into the Antarctic summer. (In the northern and southern

***Endurance* sinks into the ice, November, 1915.**

hemispheres, seasons occur at opposite times of the year.) Shackleton, impatient to depart, designated December 22, the day before their leaving, to be Christmas Day.

Christmas feast

Despite the shortages, this was celebrated with a feast of ham, sausage, stewed hare, pickle and peaches. The men, fortified and in good spirits, loaded the boats

and sleighs and began towing toward the sea.

Hauling their loads was hot, exhausting work, so they stumbled on in the below-zero cool of the night. In the first five days they managed only 14km (9 miles) and morale slumped alarmingly. Illness swept through the party. More dogs had to be shot. Arguments broke out and Shackleton had to remind mutinous men that their pay, which they would receive in a lump sum at the end of the expedition, could be stopped.

Three-month drift

Shackleton decided their best hope was to make another camp, and drift north on the shifting ice. This they did for three months, and food and fuel supplies dwindled alarmingly.

Then, one morning, a huge leopard seal poked its head out of a crack in the ice and stared at Seaman Thomas McLeod. Both eyed the other as a potential meal, but McLeod was shrewder.

He began flapping his arms like a penguin – the seal's main prey – and, as the beast

Hauling one of the lifeboats, (the *James Caird**) to the sea. December, 1915.

lumbered out of the ice and after him, it was briskly shot. A catch as substantial as this provided the expedition with enough seal meat to allay fears of starvation and plenty of blubber to burn in their stoves.

The open ocean

At last, in early April, 1916, they reached open ocean and the three lifeboats were put to sea. Elephant Island was the nearest land, and it was here they headed. The boats were small, crammed with men and supplies, and open to the terrible weather. At night, if they slept in the boats, schools of killer whales would surround them. If they stopped to make camp on an ice floe, sleeping men would plunge through cracks into the freezing sea and have to scramble out before the ice closed above them.

Elephant Island

Seven days of unrelenting misery and constant bailing passed before the snow covered peaks of Elephant Island loomed before them. The expedition was still 1,100km (700 miles) away from the nearest inhabited land, but the men were deliriously happy to have survived such an appalling journey. It was their first time on solid ground for nearly one and a half years.

This narrow, 37km (23 miles) long island was bare rock. There were no trees, but there were plenty of birds and elephant seals to eat. As they lacked any other shelter, the two smaller boats were turned upside down and made into huts.

Recruiting a crew

This was Shackleton's third trip to the Antarctic. Although explorers had reached the South Pole, no one had yet crossed the continent, and that was the intention of this expedition. Once his plans became known, 5,000 letters of application flooded into Shackleton's central London headquarters in Burlington Street. He had already decided on some of the key members, but the rest of the crew he picked on instinct, often taking only seconds to hire complete strangers.

Good teeth and temper

Expedition scientist Reginald James was asked if his teeth were good, if he had a good temper and if he could sing. When he looked shocked at this question, Shackleton explained he wanted someone who could "shout a bit with the boys". On a trip such as this, getting along with other people was just as important as scientific expertise.

Strange dream

Endurance's captain Frank Worsley joined the team after a strange dream. "One night I dreamed that Burlington Street was full of ice blocks and that I was navigating a ship along it." Next morning he went to Burlington Street where a sign reading "Imperial Trans-Antarctic Expedition" caught his eye. Worsley recalled "Shackleton was there, and the moment I set eyes on him I knew he was a man with whom I would be proud to work."

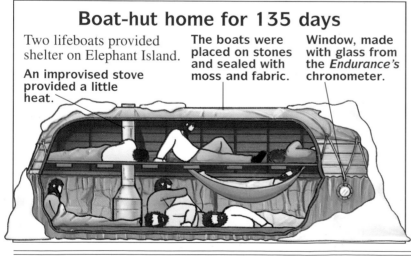

Boat-hut home for 135 days

Two lifeboats provided shelter on Elephant Island.

An improvised stove provided a little heat.

The boats were placed on stones and sealed with moss and fabric.

Window, made with glass from the *Endurance's* chronometer.

*Shackleton tactfully named *Endurance*'s lifeboats after his expedition's most generous supporters.

Back to sea

No one would find them on Elephant Island, it was too remote, but Shackleton was wary of putting his vulnerable fleet to sea again. He decided to take the biggest boat, the *James Caird*, and a small crew, and return to sea. The rest of his expedition would wait on the island for rescue.

One of Shackleton's greatest talents as a leader was his ability to pick the right people for a job, and for this perilous trip he chose a mixture of the most able and most troublesome men. The latter he took to save the patience of those who would have to endure a depressingly long wait on Elephant Island.

To South Georgia

The *James Caird* and its crew of six set out to travel 1,125km (700 miles) to South Georgia, where there were several whaling stations. Once again they had to battle through blizzards and gales. Constantly soaked and freezing, they suffered from raging thirst as salt water had contaminated their water supply.

After 17 days at sea they reached South Georgia. Just off the coast a terrible gale ripped away their rudder and they were washed up on the opposite side of the island to the whaling stations.

South Georgia was long and narrow, like Elephant Island, but it was also mountainous. As the boat was no longer fit to sail, and the walk around the coast was over 240km (150 miles), they would have to risk their lives again to cross these uncharted mountains.

Into the unknown

On May 19, 1916, taking only 15m (50ft) of rope and a carpenter's axe, Shackleton, *Endurance's* captain Frank Worsley and officer Thomas Crean began their climb into the unknown. Two men too weak to go on were left behind, with a third to look after them.

Shackleton and his two companions pressed on, up and down for two days, one time tobogganing down a steep ice slope on their coiled-up rope, another time climbing down a waterfall. Once, when they stopped to rest, Shackleton let

the other two sleep for five minutes, and then woke them, telling them half an hour had passed by.

Stromness

On May 20, at 7:00am, the men heard a factory whistle at Stromness whaling station. For the first time since December 1914, here was evidence that other human beings were close by.

Dreaming of vegetables

Although the expedition never did run out of food, everyone became desperately weary of their diet of meat. During the day they would huddle around a blubber stove and fantasize aloud about puddings and pastries. At night they dreamed of salads and omelettes.

Adelie penguins were their staple diet. They were easy to catch, but too small to provide much nourishment.

Occasionally a leopard seal was caught. Although its meat was unappetizing, a seal provided enough blubber (fat) for two weeks' cooking fuel. The one that chased Thomas McLeod had 50 undigested fish in its stomach, which made a welcome change from seal and penguin meat.

As they walked toward the factory, two boys, terrified by these ragged apparitions, ran away screaming. Shackleton asked to be taken to the home of factory manager Thoralf Sørlle, whom he knew well. When he opened the door, Sørlle gawped at them in astonishment and said "Who the hell are you?" Like everyone at Grytviken, he had assumed that the *Endurance* had been lost with all aboard. When Shackleton told him, Sørlle was moved to tears.

A hot bath and a hearty meal was all Shackleton's party needed before they set out to rescue their stranded companions. The men on the other side of South Georgia were picked up the next day, but Elephant Island was more difficult to reach. It was 14 frustrating weeks before the Trans-Antarctic Expedition was finally reunited. Severe ice, fog and violent storms thwarted several rescue attempts.

Shackleton sailed out on a relief ship on May 23, but ice blocked his route. A second attempt to reach the island was thwarted by fog. On the third attempt, rough weather forced them to turn back.

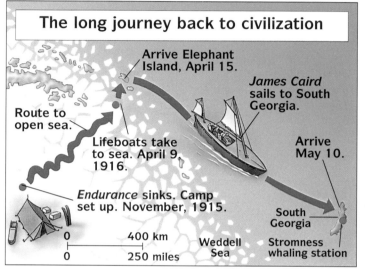

The long journey back to civilization

Arrive Elephant Island, April 15.

James Caird sails to South Georgia.

Route to open sea.

Lifeboats take to sea. April 9, 1916.

Arrive May 10.

Endurance sinks. Camp set up. November, 1915.

South Georgia

Weddell Sea

Stromness whaling station

0 400 km
0 250 miles

The stranded expedition fought their way to Elephant Island. From here Shackleton and five others reached South Georgia. The rest of the men were rescued in August, 1916 (below).

Rescue at last

Shackleton and his relief ship finally reached Elephant Island on August 30, 1916. A small boat was dispatched toward the shore and Shackleton, standing on its bow, anxiously counted the 22 men he had left behind.

They were all there. The four-month wait had been a tedious ordeal, best summed up in a diary entry by one of *Endurance*'s officers, Lionel Greenstreet: "So passes another goddam rotten day." Although the men had suffered from infections and boils, the only real casualty of the two-year adventure had been the ship's stowaway, Percy Blackboro. He had lost the toes of his left foot to frostbite. Shackleton had managed, through good judgment and great leadership, to bring his entire expedition back to civilization alive.

Film crew in lava inferno

Few things in nature match the forbidding power of a smoking volcano, threatening to unleash massive destruction with a terrifying roar and rumble. Its sinister might has become a potent symbol for movie makers. During the filming of *Sliver* in 1992, director Phillip Noyce dispatched Hollywood film cameramen Michael Benson, 42, and Chris Duddy, 31, to Pu'u O'o (pronounced POO oo OH oo) in Hawaii's Volcanoes National Park, to capture a steaming volcano in action.

Madame Pele

Benson, a veteran of films such as *Patriot Games* and *Terminator II*, was a seasoned professional. He was also superstitious. Local folklore told of a fearsome goddess, named Madame Pele, who lurked within the volcano's fiery cone. She was reputed to be very fond of gin, so, as a gesture of goodwill, the crew brought a bottle with them to throw into the crater, hoping to ensure their safety and good weather for filming.

Hawaiian carving of Madame Pele.

On the morning of Saturday, November 21, they hired pilot Craig Hosking, 34, and his Bell Jet Ranger helicopter, and flew from Hilo Bay airfield to Pu'u O'o. The weather was damp and foggy, and showed little sign of clearing as they approached the ash-strewn summit. Below, a steaming, bubbling cauldron lurked within a jagged, disfigured peak. Corrosive, choking gases, venting from the glowing lava pits inside the massive crater, cast thick clouds over the volcano, making it almost impossible to see.

Even in the relative comfort and safety of the helicopter, the fumes caught in the men's throats. As they made their first pass over the rim, Benson lobbed the gin bottle into the crater.

Engine trouble

Gaps in the clouds came and went, allowing Benson and Duddy to shoot some film. But as they prepared to make a final flight over before returning home, the helicopter engine began to splutter.

Hosking, wide-eyed with alarm, wrestled with the controls, desperate to avoid having to make a landing inside the steaming crater.

But he was fighting a losing battle and the craft was heading straight over the rim. Narrowly missing a deep pool of glowing lava in the middle of the crater, he tried to direct the stricken helicopter to a flat rock ledge.

Crash landing

As they pitched and rolled, the rotor hit the ground and shattered. The craft dropped with a sickening thud and broke in half. Benson, Duddy and Hosking scrambled out, battered but uninjured, and found themselves in a hellish environment.

Although they were fortunate enough to have landed on a thin crust of solid rock, the heat of the molten lava beneath penetrated through their boots. An intense and constant roar filled their ears as pools of lava bubbled and boiled, and steam hissed and spluttered from cracks in the ground. Clouds of acrid gas drifted by and the men could barely see their hands in front of their faces.

No chance of rescue

Within the shattered cockpit, the radio was dead. There was no chance of immediate rescue – they were not expected back for another hour. The obvious option was to head for the rim, 50m (150ft) above. The rocky surroundings they scrambled through regularly gave way to deep ash and crumbling stone, and they sank knee-deep in hot black soot.

The camera crew threw a bottle of gin into the volcano as a goodwill offering.

After about 15 minutes the three had climbed halfway up the slope to the top, but could go no higher. The rock ahead rose to 45°, then jutted into an overhanging rim that looked almost impassable.

Radio repair

It seemed impossible to get out without assistance, but all three knew no one would see them in the crater. Hosking had one reckless idea – he would go back to the helicopter and try to repair the radio.

Benson tried to persuade him not to return, since the craft was enveloped in poisonous, choking fumes. But Hosking knew he had no option. Wrapping his shirt around his face to keep out the worst of the acrid air, he returned to the helicopter.

Help on the way

Hosking could only work at the radio for short bursts, emerging occasionally to climb to a clearer spot and breathe some fresher air. But he managed to take a film camera battery and hook it to the radio, and after a grim hour he was able to fix it. An SOS call soon caught the attention of colleagues back at his base. Within an hour, pilot Don Shearer, who had often worked on rescue missions in the Hawaii area, was flying over the volcano. Shearer, in radio contact with Hosking, reported that he could see nothing in the smoking crater. Hosking would have to guide him in.

Peering blindly into the swirling smoke, Hosking could now faintly hear the dull thrubbing of rotor blades, and was able to bring Sheerer down close by. As the craft hovered a couple of feet above the ground, Hosking leaped inside,

Pu'u O'o

The helicopter crashed when its engine failed on a final flight over the smoking volcano. Rescue teams on the rim could not reach the trapped men.

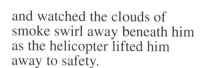

Bell Jet Ranger helicopter.

The overhanging rim was 50m (150ft) above the film crew.

Helicopter crashed here.

The crater was 300m (1,000ft) across.

Lava pool

and watched the clouds of smoke swirl away beneath him as the helicopter lifted him away to safety.

One out

One man at least had escaped the clutches of Madame Pele, but Benson and Duddy were still awaiting rescue, crouching on a ledge, halfway up the crater. They had noticed the helicopter's arrival and were distressed to hear its engines recede into the distance.

But above them, help had arrived from another quarter. Hosking's radio SOS had also been picked up by the local National Park rangers. Two rangers had climbed to the tip of the rim, and were trying to spot the survivors. So deadly was the atmosphere around the volcano summit that the rangers had to wear gas masks, and acidic fumes corroded their climbing ropes.

Benson and Duddy could hear faint shouts from their would-be rescuers above the roar of the lava pits. Waving frantically, they shouted themselves hoarse. But the cloudy fumes were too thick, and their muffled voices echoed around the rim, making it impossible for them to be located.

The rangers threw down ropes in the vague hope that one would land near the trapped men, but this was unsuccessful. Darkness fell, and the rescuers gave up, intending to return the next morning.

Night brought torrential rain and the next day the weather was even rougher. Don Shearer was no longer able to help because his helicopter had been damaged by corrosive fumes when he rescued Hosking and it was now unsafe to fly. On the rim of the crater, the rangers could hardly see 3m (10ft) in front of them.

The day wore on and Benson

and Duddy faced another night in the crater, to be baked by glowing lava, and frozen by lashing rain. Choked by fumes, their eyes streaming, the two had only their shirts to wrap around their faces to protect them from the poisonous surroundings.

Desperate move

By mid-afternoon on the second day in the crater, Duddy could take no more. Maybe there was another way out? Whatever happened, trying to escape was better than sitting there suffocating. Benson, who was older, and not so confident of his climbing ability, decided to stay where he was.

Duddy's gamble paid off. After an exhausting climb through crumbling rock and sooty gravel, he eventually made it to the top, and was rescued by Park rangers. He shouted down to Benson, but his voice was lost in the huge, hollow cauldron.

Night supplies

Night was now falling and, for want of any better plan of action, the rangers tossed food and water packets into the rim, hoping that Benson might stumble on one.

But the well-meaning gesture only brought him more misery. Seeing one of the packages fall through the mist, he thought it was Duddy falling to his death, and was overwhelmed by guilt for bringing his crew here at all.

Again, it rained for most of the night and Benson, who had not found any of the packets tossed to him, was weakening fast. Breathing was now a painful effort. His mouth was so dry he could no longer call for help, and the fumes were causing him to hallucinate.

He battled with a raging thirst, catching rain in the face of his camera light meter, and drinking a mouthful at a time.

But help was on its way from yet another quarter. Overnight, Benson's colleagues had managed to contact helicopter pilot Tom Hauptman, famed for his daring rescues. Soon after first light Hauptman flew over the crater rim, and for the first time, through a temporary gap in the clouds, he managed to spot Benson, who waved frantically back.

Net rescue

Hauptman's helicopter was equipped with a large net, and this was dangled down. It was like fishing in a muddy pool, for Hauptman could only guess where Benson was, as the clouds obscured his view. Twice the net went down, and twice it came out empty. But on the third attempt it landed right in front of the ailing cameraman. He saw his chance and lunged into it. Intense relief flooded through him as the helicopter pulled away from the crater – he was safe at last.

Benson drank the rainwater that collected in a light meter, to quench his thirst.

World record

The helicopter landed nearby, and Benson was bundled into an ambulance and rushed to Hawaii's Hilo hospital. The cameraman had been exposed to the volcano's poisonous fumes for over 48 hours. He had serious damage to his lungs, but was able to make a full recovery. Duddy and Hosking were lucky enough to escape with fairly minor injuries.

Benson might have taken some comfort from the fact that the rangers who rescued him were convinced that he had set a world record for the length of time anyone had managed to survive inside an active volcano.

Michael Benson, surrounded by medical personnel, after his dramatic rescue from Pu'u O'o.

Plenty of fish in sea, says scientist

The Fonvieille quayside was packed that bright May afternoon in 1952. The crowd's attention focused on two men busily preparing an inflatable dinghy, *L'Hérétique,* for an extraordinary journey. A young French doctor, Alain Bombard, and his English navigator, Jack Palmer, planned to take their rubber boat on a trial run through the Mediterranean and then sail across the Atlantic.

To take this tiny boat on such a voyage was foolhardy enough, but Bombard and Palmer intended to live entirely on what they caught on the journey. They had supplies of food and drink, but these were sealed, and only intended for a life-or-death emergency. Bombard had an untried theory which he was burning to prove: that all the water and food a castaway needed to survive was in the sea around him.

Doctor Bombard. His concern for castaways prompted a daring solo Atlantic crossing.

Shipwreck concern

Doctor Bombard's concern for castaways began when he worked in a hospital near the coast and was called out to attend to shipwreck victims. He discovered that over 200,000 people died in shipwrecks every year. Of that number, 50,000 made it to lifeboats, but 90 per cent of these survivors died within three days.

Most, it was supposed, died of exhaustion and despair.

Bombard felt that if castaways knew how to live off the resources of the sea, then their chances of survival would be increased dramatically.

He decided to study this idea in detail, and was provided with facilities and support at the Museum of Oceanography in Monaco. Here he studied case histories of previous successful castaways (including the *Bounty* survivors, see p. 13-17), and made detailed research into human nutritional needs and the type of nutrition provided by the sea.

Saltwater drink

Bombard's findings showed that there would be enough nutriment in the sea to sustain a castaway. His most controversial theory was that it was possible to drink sea water. He knew it caused serious damage to the kidneys, but argued that if a castaway only drank one litre (1.5 pints) a day, for no longer than five days, his health would not suffer. It was most important to drink sea water immediately, however, rather than wait until the body became dehydrated. Within five days, suggested Bombard, the castaway would then be able to find water from other sources such as rain and fish.

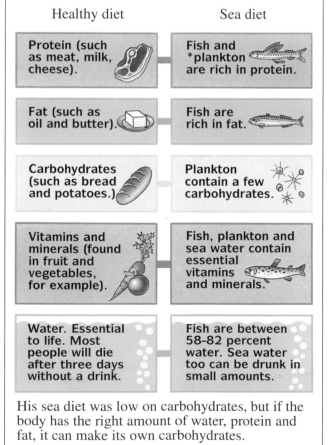

Bombard's sea diet

A healthy diet needs a mixture of particular kinds of food. Bombard believed that the sea could provide almost all of them.

Healthy diet	Sea diet
Protein (such as meat, milk, cheese).	**Fish and *plankton are rich in protein.**
Fat (such as oil and butter).	**Fish are rich in fat.**
Carbohydrates (such as bread and potatoes.)	**Plankton contain a few carbohydrates.**
Vitamins and minerals (found in fruit and vegetables, for example).	**Fish, plankton and sea water contain essential vitamins and minerals.**
Water. Essential to life. Most people will die after three days without a drink.	**Fish are between 58-82 percent water. Sea water too can be drunk in small amounts.**

His sea diet was low on carbohydrates, but if the body has the right amount of water, protein and fat, it can make its own carbohydrates.

*Plankton are minute animals and plants which live in the sea.

The voyage begins

So, on May 26, 1952, Doctor Bombard and his English companion set off to prove to the world that his theories were correct. Although he had many eminent supporters, the Press were quick to dismiss him as an eccentric and poured scorn on the voyage.

However, the trial run across the Mediterranean was encouraging. They drank salt water and lived. They caught enough fish to ward off starvation. The boat was subjected to some frightening storms, but did not sink.

After 14 days, *L'Hérétique* landed at Minorca, the first island on their route. They had proved it was possible to survive perfectly well. Anxious not to waste any more time and effort before the real test of the Atlantic Ocean, they packed their equipment and headed for Tangiers by ocean liner.

Before they faced the Atlantic, Bombard decided he needed a new boat and flew to Paris to arrange this. Rubber dinghies wear out and it was best to make the ocean crossing with a new one. He returned with an identical model, which he christened with the same name.

Delays were inevitable and Jack Palmer began to lose heart. Bombard, sensing his reluctance, and afraid they no longer had a common purpose, decided he would have to make the voyage on his own.

Atlantic odyssey

On August 14, Bombard sailed into the Atlantic Ocean alone. He realized at once that this voyage would be different from the trial run. Here, time was measured in weeks not days, and distances by thousands rather than tens of miles.

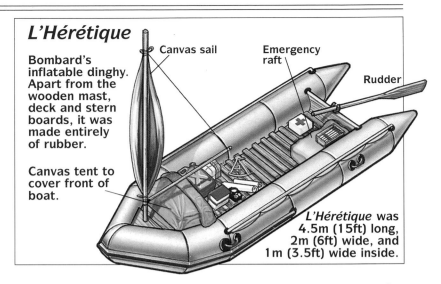

L'Hérétique

Bombard's inflatable dinghy. Apart from the wooden mast, deck and stern boards, it was made entirely of rubber.

Canvas tent to cover front of boat.

Canvas sail

Emergency raft

Rudder

L'Hérétique was 4.5m (15ft) long, 2m (6ft) wide, and 1m (3.5ft) wide inside.

Going alone was an act of extraordinary courage. Palmer was an expert navigator and Bombard now had to acquire his ex-partner's skills. He had packed navigation books and charts for the voyage, and these he pored over, learning as quickly as he could.

Following a brief stopover in Casablanca, after a week at sea, he set out for the Canary Islands. Again, food was no problem, the coastal waters of the Atlantic were rich in fish, but his log betrayed his real problems.

Fish techniques

Fish are an essential ingredient in the castaway's diet so it is vital to be able to catch them. A simple line and hook, or harpoon, are all a castaway needs. Bombard also offered these suggestions.
• Night time is the best time to catch fish and plankton. Both come closer to the surface after dark and are easier to catch.
• A straining cloth, folded into a net, and attached to a 20m (60ft) line, can be used to catch plankton.

"Sunday, August 24 ...Use of sextant becoming more complicated, having doubts about this longitude business." "Thursday, August 28... Horribly alone. Nothing in sight. Complete novice as navigator. Do not know where I am, but only suppose I do."

Canary stopover

By September 3, Bombard reached the Canary Islands, 11 days after leaving Casablanca. Here he found out that his wife Ginette had given birth to a baby girl, Natalie, so he flew back to Paris to see her.

Although the Press were quick to ridicule his efforts, and even Jack Palmer was now describing the final and longest leg of the journey as "suicidal madness", Bombard returned to the Canaries with his wife's blessing, determined to complete his voyage.

Before he set off again, he installed a radio receiver in *L'Hérétique*. He had missed Palmer very much and badly needed some human company, even if it was only a voice on the radio.

His voyage resumed on October 19. Heading west, the nearest land was now the islands of the Caribbean.

This was 6,000km (3,750 miles) away, and Bombard hoped to get there in 40 days. If anything went wrong he had no way of calling for help.

The monotony of the voyage was broken by violent storms, when Bombard had to bail constantly to stop his boat from becoming swamped. In a storm he had one clear philosophy which ensured his survival. "Be more obstinate than the sea, and you will win."

Five days out from the Canaries, disaster struck. His sail was torn in half by the wind and Bombard spent a day carefully sewing it back together. For the rest of the voyage he worried constantly that it would rip again.

Failure and success

As the voyage progressed, his morale dropped. Soaked, shivering, encrusted with salt, Bombard spent long nights waiting wearily for the sun to rise and offer him a little comfort. Although he did not know it, he began to make serious errors of navigation.

But he also had some successes. Trying to use as much makeshift equipment as

Fishing, repairing the boat and keeping a detailed log took up most of Bombard's day. To relax he read books or music scores.

he could (he reasoned that a castaway would not have proper fishing equipment) Bombard made a useful harpoon with a knife and oar. When he caught a dorado fish, he fashioned a hook from a bone found behind its gills. He caught plenty of fish with this crude equipment.

His greatest trials came from

the sheer, unrelenting hostility of his environment. Bombard tried to make his circumstances as close to those of a real castaway as possible. He wore only everyday clothes (again reasoning that a castaway would not have protective clothing) and his body soon began to suffer the effects of prolonged exposure to constant

Bombard's busy day

Despair is quick to settle on a castaway because his unchanging existence is so soul-destroying. Bombard strove to bring a clear, disciplined structure to his day. His philosophy was that castaways should remain masters of events, rather than just react to them. He rose with the dawn and slept at dusk, and took careful records of his health and diet.

Morning
• **Wake at dawn. Clear flying fish which have landed on *L'Hérétique* overnight. Eat two largest for breakfast.**
• **Fish for one hour. Divide haul into lunch and supper.**
• **Inspect boat for one hour. Ensure nothing is scraping on rubber skin. Run fingers over entire surface, feeling for leaks. Make repairs.**
• **Exercise for half an hour.**
• **Catch two spoonfuls of plankton. This is rich in vitamin C, vital for keeping scurvy* at bay.**
• **12:00 noon. Take position with sextant.**

Afternoon
• **Eat lunch.**
• **Write log.**
• **2:00pm. Medical check up. Record details of temperature, blood pressure, condition of skin, hair and nails, morale, memory, reflexes.**
• **Relax. Read books and music scores.**

Evening
• **Evening medical.**
• **Write log.**
• **Eat supper.**

Dusk
• **Listen to radio.**
• **Go to sleep.**

20

*Scurvy – a disease which harms skin, teeth and blood.

damp, cold and salt water. Bombard's diet kept hunger and thirst at bay. He found he could drink enough water by cutting slits in the flanks of fish and sucking the juice. But the diet was not enough to keep him healthy. He lost weight, and his body became covered in red sores and rashes. Sitting and lying down became uncomfortable. Fingernails and toenails dropped off. He began to crave the food his body needed – fruit and vegetables – and he longed for a huge glass of ice-cold beer.

Shark shock

One warm night he discovered he could attract shoals of fish by shining a flashlight into the sea. As he amused himself moving the beam and watching the fish dart after it, a huge shark, ferocious teeth flashing, lunged out of the water. Thrashing around the boat, it soaked him to the skin and butted the rubber keel with its sandpapery snout. Bombard sat stock-still, almost too terrified to breathe, until the monster lost interest and left.

Although he was attacked by several other sharks, and a swordfish, he usually took comfort from the sea creatures he encountered. One dolphin shoal stayed with him for days. When his boat slowed down in a low wind, they would smack the floats with their tails, as if to hurry him along.

Lost at sea

After 11 days at sea, Bombard was convinced he had completed a quarter of the journey. But he had covered far less than that and was still well to the north of the Cape Verde Islands. Bombard became

increasingly baffled by his sextant sightings, and even began to think his compass was playing tricks on him. He did not seem to be where he thought he was at all.

His sense of isolation deepened as the batteries of his radio faded. Continuous storms and rain tormented him, and his log entries show a man in deep depression. The low, grey sky, he recalled, "seemed about to crush me." When the weather turned, and the sky, cleared he was baked rather than frozen.

The night offered no refuge from his despair. Fear of shark or swordfish attack, or of being swamped by a huge wave, kept him wide awake. On November 27, after 40 days at sea, his log reads "I have had enough". By December 6 his health had deteriorated so much that he wrote his will. An upset stomach, and the dehydration this caused, had exhausted him.

The flapping sail irritated him unbearably and he began to feel persecuted by the objects on the boat. When writing his log, he would feel that his pencil had deliberately hidden itself when he wanted to use it.

Arakaka arrives

But on December 9, he spotted a large cargo ship heading straight for him. He grabbed his heliograph*, and began to flash at the bridge, and soon he

was being helped on board the British vessel *Arakaka*. The news that he was 960km (600 miles) farther east than he thought came as a bitter blow, and Bombard almost gave up then and there. But he wanted to convince his critics, especially the Press, that his theories were correct. Only a complete voyage across the Atlantic would satisfy them.

A freshwater shower, a small meal, new batteries for his radio and a new set of books to navigate by, were all provided by the helpful crew. Greatly encouraged, and reassured that his wife would know he was safe, Bombard continued on his journey.

Nearly there

For 12 more days he battled against the Atlantic. Aside from the usual problems, his boat had now started to deteriorate. Water was seeping in through the bottom and Bombard spent much of the rest of the voyage bailing.

The flashes of a lighthouse indicated that the end was near, and by dawn the next day the coast of Barbados was in sight. Local fishermen helped him ashore, but were eager to grab as much of his supplies and equipment as they could lay their hands on.

For a few horrible moments Bombard thought they would seize his sealed food and water supplies, destroying the sole proof that he had survived only on what the sea had provided. Fortunately, a policeman arrived to restore order. He took Bombard to the local police station, and gave him tea and bread and butter. It seemed a strange way to celebrate after a total of 65 continuous days at sea.

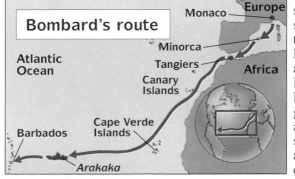

Bombard's route

Monaco — Europe
Minorca
Tangiers
Atlantic Ocean
Canary Islands
Africa
Cape Verde Islands
Barbados
Arakaka

Terror in the skies

Griffiths' iron grip

On a crisp December morning in 1942, a Boston bomber took off from Wayzata airfield, Minnesota, USA. Climbing into a cloudless sky were American test pilot Sid Gerow, 29, and Canadian test observer Harry Griffiths, 20. Their job was to give the factory-fresh aircraft a thorough checking before it flew the Atlantic to serve in World War Two.

When the plane reached 2,100m (7,000ft) Gerow began to test the controls and engines, while Griffiths monitored the instrument panel. There were no problems and all that remained to be inspected was the bombsight* in the forward section. Griffiths climbed inside the perspex nose of the plane and lay on his stomach.

Bottom falls out of world

As he peered into the sight, which was set at the very tip of the nose, Griffiths felt the floor beneath give way. The forward entry hatch, which he had been lying on, had fallen off.

Instinctively he gripped the bombsight with both hands, but an immense gust of freezing air sucked him out of the aircraft. With the wind roaring in his ears, he found himself halfway out of the plane, legs and lower body pressed against the fuselage.

Griffiths' fingers quickly lost their grip on the polished metal instrument. As his head slipped out of the plane, he clutched desperately at the wooden fitting beneath the sight. The surrounding temperature was -25°C (-13°F) and fierce cold gnawed at his battered body.

Harry Griffiths was small, but he was immensely strong.

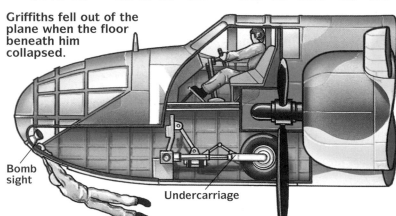

Griffiths fell out of the plane when the floor beneath him collapsed.

Bomb sight

Undercarriage

He wrapped his fingers around the wooden fitting and held on with a vice-like grip. Buffeted mercilessly by the plane's turbulent slipstream, few other men could have clung to such a precarious niche.

But cling he did, for he had no other option. He called feebly for help, but his cries were snatched away by the fierce wind. Very soon, his grip would weaken, and he would fall to his death.

Help at hand?

In the cockpit above the open hatch, Sid Gerow was all too aware of what had happened. Cold air had billowed into the plane, and a fierce wind howled around his boots. Griffiths had not answered his urgent enquiries, but Gerow imagined he could hear his comrade's faint shouts for help.

But, if Griffiths was still alive, there was precious little the pilot could do for him. He could not leave the controls, for without him the plane would plummet to the ground. He could not land – if he lowered the undercarriage, the front wheel would dislodge his dangling companion. Gerow wracked his brains, desperate for something, anything, to

save Griffiths' life. As he flew on, the sun caught in the frozen waters of Lake St. Louis 2,100m (7,000ft) below, momentarily dazzling him. Inspiration struck. Gerow quickly dived, approaching the lake as low and as slowly as he dared. Anyone falling from a speeding plane onto earth or water would surely die. But ice... maybe that would be different?

Ice crash landing

Beneath the plane Griffiths understood at once what he needed to do. As the ice raced beneath him at over 160kmph (100mph) he released his grip. For a brief moment he glided above the surface, then hit the ice with a sickening thud, shooting along the frozen surface for 1km (half a mile).

Circling above, Gerow watched his partner slowly drift to a halt. He lay quite still, but then, miraculously, hauled himself to his feet and walked toward the shore.

Harry Griffiths was rushed to hospital and the next eight days of his life were a total blank. But apart from severe bruising, and mild frostbite, he had survived his extraordinary ordeal without serious injury.

Captain Lancaster's window exit

Captain Lancaster

It was a routine trip for Captain Timothy Lancaster and copilot Alastair Atchison, flying a British Airways BAC 1-11 from Birmingham, England, to Malaga, Spain, on June 8, 1990. But as the plane reached 7,000m (23,000ft), a front window panel, which had just been refitted, blew off.

Air inside the cabin was sucked out with tremendous force, taking stray papers, flight routes, jackets and cups with it. Lancaster too was hauled from his seat into the gaping hole. As he shot out, his leg struck the flight controls, and the plane banked alarmingly, terrifying the passengers. At that very moment, steward Nigel Ogden had been serving hot drinks to the crew, and made a frantic grab for the pilot's legs. Steward John Heward also rushed to the cabin and, strapping himself into Lancaster's seat, he held on to both Ogden and the pilot.

Lancaster, pinned to the top of the plane by an 800kmph (500mph) slipstream, struggled desperately for breath. His shirt had been ripped off and the temperature outside was -25°C (-13°F). He tried to shout for help, but soon drifted in and out of consciousness.

For the next 15 minutes, cabin crew struggled unsuccessfully to pull Lancaster back inside the plane and to comfort passengers who believed they were in mortal danger. Copilot Atchison knew he had to lose height at once, before Lancaster suffocated in the thin air. He was almost certain that the pilot was already dead since his body was now covered in a thin film of frost. He looked so contorted as he flapped around the cabin window, that the crew thought he must have broken his back.

The nearest airport was Southampton and permission for an emergency landing was quickly secured. As two crew members clung desperately to Lancaster's legs, Atchinson executed a perfect landing.

The plane was swiftly surrounded by airport firecrew, who were amazed to see Lancaster lift his head and ask what had happened. The pilot they all thought was dead had suffered only a touch of frostbite and minor fractures to his arms.

Vulovic's record breaking fall

Yugoslavian stewardess Vesna Vulovic busied herself in the rear galley of the plane, tidying meal trays for her handful of passengers, in the early evening of January 27, 1972.

It had been a quiet flight. The DC-9, flying from Stockholm to Belgrade, was only a quarter full. The crew had heard that Yugoslav Prime Minister Dzemal Bijedic would be on the plane, but he had not boarded.

As they flew 10,000m (33,000ft) above the East German-Czechoslovakian border, Vulovic stared nonchalantly out of a window, hoping to catch a glimpse of the moonlit Erzgebirge mountains. But as she did so, a bomb planted by Croatian terrorists intending to assassinate Bijedic, detonated.

In the tail of the plane, Vulovic watched in horror as a terrible explosion ripped through the aircraft. The tail section broke away and began to plummet inexorably to the ground. As she spun around the freezing night sky she knew her life was over and awaited the hideous blow that would end it. But instead of a thud, there was a huge splash. The tail had landed in a deep pond at Serbska Kamenice, in Czechoslovakia.

Vulovic remembered very little after that, except regaining consciousness and talking to a doctor who had rushed to the disaster. She was gravely injured, but unlike everyone else on the flight, she had survived. To this day, no one else has fallen from a greater height and lived.

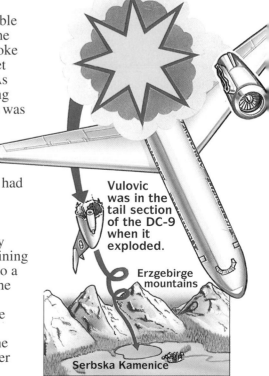

Vulovic was in the tail section of the DC-9 when it exploded.

Erzgebirge mountains

Serbska Kamenice

Wolff to the rescue

The news that filtered back to London in the summer of 1843 was disturbing. Two British army officers, named Conolly and Stoddard, were being held prisoner in the city of Bukhara, in central Asia.

Their captor was Emir* Nasrullah Khan. He was known to be extremely hostile to foreigners and his reputation for wanton cruelty had reached even Britain, 8,000km (5,000 miles) away.

The two officers had been tortured and thrown into a pit full of deadly snakes and insects. Whether they were still alive was unclear.

Joseph Wolff. Born in Bavaria, he settled in England after 20 years of travel as a missionary.

Marauding gangs

Bukhara nestled on the edge of inhospitable desert terrain, where marauding bandit gangs plagued any visitor unfortunate enough to cross their path. In the 1840s only a handful of intrepid Europeans had ever dared to go there.

Many people in London felt that if Conolly and Stoddard were still alive, then someone ought try to rescue them. But the British Government was not prepared to send anyone on such a hazardous mission.

Bavarian Wolff

The plight of the two soldiers soon reached the ears of a country parson who was visiting friends in London. He was 52, Bavarian, magnificently overweight and, some thought, quite mad. His name was Joseph Wolff.

Apart from Conolly and Stoddard, Wolff was the only man in England who had been to Bukhara. He had visited as a missionary, 10 years before. He spoke the language and

Nasrullah Khan, Emir of Bukhara. Despite his cruel reputation he was a shrewd and incorruptible ruler.

was familiar with local custom.

Over the years, the British Army had rescued him from certain death several times and he felt he owed them a great debt. A rescue mission to Bukhara would be one way of repaying it.

So he placed a letter in the *Morning Herald* newspaper seeking money for an expedition. This brought in sufficient funds and an offer from the P & O shipping line of free travel as far as Turkey.

Before he settled into his life as a country parson, Wolff had spent two decades working as a missionary in Asia and Africa, where he had acquired a reputation as a born survivor. Attacked and robbed from Bukhara to Timbuktu, he had endured a succession of extraordinary misfortunes. On one occasion he was tied to a horse's tail by slave traders and dragged across the desert. On another, bandits stole all his clothes, leaving him to cross the snowy Hindu Kush mountains stark naked. After that, the dysentery, cholera, earthquakes and shipwrecks he endured were minor irritations.

It was not just physical resilience that kept him alive; he also had personal qualities that were indispensable. Unlike some European visitors, he had a healthy respect for the cultures he visited and an uncanny ability to make influential friends.

Grand Dervish

Wolff's plan to rescue Conolly and Stoddard was simple, and typical of his tremendous daring. He would march into Bukhara with as much pomp and ceremony as he could muster and ask the notorious Emir to release the two officers. Supposing that the more important he looked and sounded, the more reluctant the Emir would be to harm him, Wolff packed his finest clerical clothing and invented a title for himself: "Grand Dervish* of

*An Emir is a Muslim ruler.

*Dervish is an Arabic word for holy man.

England, Scotland and Ireland, and the whole of Europe and America". He also took 24 Bibles, a collection of maps, 36 silver watches and 36 copies of *Robinson Crusoe*, translated into Arabic. Wolff knew the value of a good bribe in a tight situation. Silver watches were always a source of great interest and *Robinson Crusoe*, he was sure was the sort of book anyone would be eager to read.

Bukhara bound

So, with no official support or authority from the British Government, Wolff set sail from Southampton for Constantinople (now Istanbul) in October, 1843.

During an idle moment, Wolff glanced through the ship's visitors' book, where distinguished passengers recorded their names. A shiver of foreboding ran through him as he came across the signature of Arthur Conolly, who had taken the very same boat on his way to Bukhara, several years previously.

At Constantinople, Wolff persuaded the Sultan* and the highest ranking Islamic officials to provide him with letters of introduction. These

The trip from Southampton to Bukhara – by steamship, horse and foot – took 28 weeks.

might convince the chieftains and governors he met on his travels that he was well connected, and maybe they would be more likely to help rather than harm him.

Trip to Tehran

Wolff recruited guides and servants in Constantinople and, making his way on foot and horseback, he pressed on to Tehran, the capital of Persia (now called Iran).

Here, British Ambassador Justin Sheil tried to persuade Wolff to abandon his mission. Sheil was certain Conolly and Stoddard had been executed, and believed anyone sent to investigate their deaths would be killed too.

Wolff had come to the same conclusion, but felt obliged to continue. He wrote that if he returned home without going to Bukhara, then everyone would say that his expedition "had been a piece of humbug and was the work of a braggart."

While he was in Tehran, Sheil introduced Wolff to the Shah (King) of Persia. The Shah took a liking to the portly Bavarian and wrote to the Emir asking him to treat Wolff as a respected visitor.

Desert escort

Between Tehran and Bukhara lay 1,000km (600 miles) of harsh desert terrain, populated

by slave traders and bandits. Fortunately, in Meshed, near the Persian border, Wolff acquired another useful ally – the local governor. He warned Wolff of the dangers ahead, and provided him with nine armed guards.

But as the rock and rubble of the desert gradually changed to the green pastures of Bukhara, his escort grew fearful, and one by one they began to slip away. Wolff marched on at the head of his dwindling party, reading aloud from the Bible, as if to ward off the evil he felt closing in on him.

The sight of a huge fat man, resplendent in his scarlet silk hood and fine clerical uniform soon attracted much attention. By the time Wolff arrived at the city gates on April 27, huge crowds had turned out to see him.

Grand arrival

A visitor arriving in such a flamboyant style as this could not fail to secure an audience with the Emir. Besides, Wolff also had letters from sultans, shahs and ambassadors, beseeching Nasrullah Khan to see him. He was brought to a grand palace and ushered through cool marble corridors into a crowded court room. At one end, surrounded by fawning advisors, sat the Emir. Clothed in plain cottons, distant and withdrawn, he was as still and

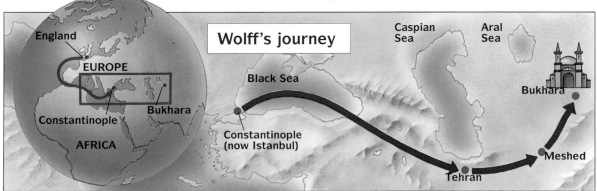

Wolff arrived in Bukhara with letters of introduction from eminent Islamic rulers.

silent as a statue. On top of his head perched a neat silk turban, and much of his face was covered by a black, bushy beard. His dark eyes were the only part of him that moved, and they turned a venomous gaze on the strange man who approached him.

Maximum manners

Wolff was well versed in the correct way to behave at such meetings. He knew it was necessary to show an almost religious reverence to the ruler. He stood before the inscrutable Emir and recited the customary greeting of his court, "Refuge of the World, Peace to the King," which any visitor was required to say three times, while stroking his own beard (another mark of respect).

Keen to show

maximum deference, Wolff repeated the greeting 30 times before the ghost of a smile flickered across Nasrullah's face. Then the Emir burst out laughing. He looked upon Wolff as if he were some strange exhibit. "Thou eccentric man," he mused. "So thou art Joseph Wolff!"

Clashing cultures

Wolff immediately asked what had happened to Conolly and Stoddard, and was abruptly told they had been executed. Conolly, explained the Emir, "had a long nose" (meaning he was arrogant), and Stoddard "had not paid him the proper respect".

It soon became clear that there was more to it than that. Aside from the two officers' haughty European superiority, the Emir was sure that both men had been involved in a plot to overthrow him.

The society Wolff found

Contemporary engraving of Bukhara. This is the house of Abdul Samut Khan, one of the Emir's principal advisors, and Wolff's greatest enemy.

himself in was one of curious contradictions. The Emir was undoubtedly cruel and tyrannous, and had the most extraordinary temper, but even the poorest of his subjects were permitted to approach him for advice or judgment. He was honest, and could not be bribed. He seemed genuinely astonished that Wolff had come all this way just to inquire about the fate of two British officers, and seemed concerned that the situation had caused ill feeling in Britain.

Wolff was given an apartment in the palace and for a few weeks he remained as the Emir's guest. Nasrullah Khan was eager to learn about his visitor and the far away country he represented. He was fascinated to hear about steamships and locomotives, and curious to know whether there was witchcraft in Britain, and why Queen Victoria did not execute more of her subjects.

Terror and treachery

But the longer Wolff stayed in this exotic and unfamiliar court, the more uncomfortable he became, especially when he was taken to Conolly and Stoddard's place of execution and shown their heads.

Soon after he arrived in Bukhara he was befriended by one of the Emir's principal advisers, Abdul Samut Khan, known as the Naib. This man told him how hard he had worked to save the lives of the two British officers. He seemed like a useful ally, but the price of his friendship was money. When Wolff's funds ran out, four weeks into his stay, the Naib turned against him, and boasted that it was he, after all, who had persuaded the Emir to kill Conolly and Stoddard.

Lost gamble

Although Wolff's requests to leave were always granted, whenever the date of departure arrived he was forbidden to go. The Emir and Naib amused themselves with his increasing discomfort, and began to taunt him openly. When Wolff requested the remains of Conolly and Stoddard to take home, the Emir told him that the only bones that would be returning to England would be his own.

Wolff realized that patience was not going to win him this particular battle, and attempted to escape. He failed, and was placed under house arrest.

His fate looked grim. The Emir departed to a distant province on a campaign to subdue a rebellion against him and while he was away, the Naib began to suggest openly to court advisors that Wolff be executed.

Wolff tried hard not to be seen to be intimidated. Confined indoors throughout the steamy summer, he attempted to cheer himself up by singing German romantic songs at the top of his voice.

Court intrigue

Although he was a prisoner, and constantly watched, he was still allowed to have visitors. He had made friends among the small Jewish community in Bukhara, and they called on him regularly. They conversed in Hebrew, a language Wolff's guards did not understand and, pretending to read aloud to each other from the Bible, they were able to speak freely of the latest talk concerning his fate.

But one morning, an Islamic holy man visited and demanded that Wolff renounce his Christianity and become a Muslim. Enraged, Wolff drove him from the room with an angry bellow. He began to fear that death was only days away.

His next visitor was the Bukharan executioner who had put to death Conolly and Stoddard. The man explained he had come to inspect him, so he could best judge how to kill him. Wolff was overcome. Despite his audacity he was not a brave man and faced his fate with icy dread.

Final message

He prayed fervently and wrote a last message in his Bible to his loved ones.
"My dearest Georgiana and Henry, I have loved both of you unto death, Your affectionate husband and father, J.Wolff." And then he waited, left alone with his fear. The thought of the executioners blade slitting his poor throat filled him with a livid terror.

The hours dragged by, then footsteps approached. The door flew open and Wolff was dragged from his room.

Behind the scenes

But it was to the Emir's palace, rather than the execution ground that he was taken. Behind the scenes Wolff's strategy of enlisting the support of anyone who might prove useful had paid off. The Shah of Persia, hearing of his plight, had sent an ambassador, Abbas Kouli Khan, to plead for his release. Fortunately for Wolff, Nasrullah's campaign to subdue his rebellious province had gone badly. He returned to Bukhara feeling vulnerable, and certainly not strong enough to antagonize the Shah, who was the most powerful ruler in the area. Executing Wolff was not worth the trouble it would cause. The Emir summoned the Persian ambassador and told him "I make a present to you of Joseph Wolff."

Showered with gifts

Wolff was brought before Nasrullah Khan and showered with money and gifts. The Emir asked that Wolff return home with a Bukharan ambassador, and stated that he wished to be on good terms with England. Dazed by his good fortune, Wolff prepared to depart. His life, which had hung by a very slender thread, was now spared.

On August 3, 1844, the people of Bukhara once again turned out in their thousands to see Joseph Wolff. He had arrived almost alone, reading from his Bible. He left in a splendid, noisy procession of ambassadors, merchants, holy men and 2,000 camels.

Wolff was given a horse, a shawl and 90 tillahs (Bukharan gold coins) as compensation for his imprisonment.

Ted cheats death on sinking Hood

In the chilly waters of the North Atlantic, just below the perpetual ice field of the Arctic Ocean, a grey May dawn broke before 2:00am. Pitching through a rolling grey sea, scything wind and flurries of snow, a great grey battleship headed relentlessly toward its prey. The year was 1941.

The ship was *HMS Hood* – the most celebrated vessel in the British Navy. The 1,421 men on board had been ready for battle throughout the night. Most were finding it was impossible to sleep, for they were about to engage in a life or death struggle with two of Germany's mightiest warships – *Bismarck* and *Prinz Eugen*.

Platform perch

High above the deck, in the dimly lit compass platform, sat Vice-Admiral Lancelot Holland. Surrounded by his chief lieutenants – the ship's captain, and navigation, signal and gunnery officers – Holland scoured the horizon, his fingers tapping anxiously on his binoculars.

Signalman Ted Briggs in 1941.

Waiting on the *Hood*'s masters in this lofty perch was 18-year-old signalman Ted Briggs, whose task it was to carry messages to other parts of the ship. Briggs had first set eyes on the *Hood* on a trip to the Yorkshire coast in 1935, when he was 12. It was love at first sight, and he had decided then and there to join the Navy to sail on her. Now, six years later, here he was, watching the calm deliberations of her senior officers with a mixture of fear and fascination.

Compass platform

The *Bismarck*. The striped camouflage was intended to make the ship look smaller.

The ship's emblem was the crest of statesman Count von Bismarck.

The *Hood* in 1937. The 262m (860ft) long vessel was said to be the most beautiful in the British Navy. Her destruction stunned the British public, as she was believed by many to be unsinkable.

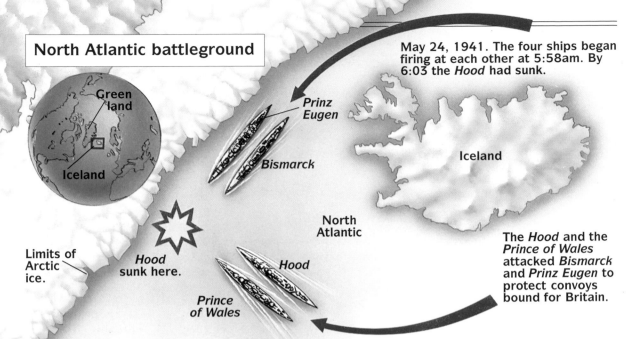

North Atlantic battleground

May 24, 1941. The four ships began firing at each other at 5:58am. By 6:03 the *Hood* had sunk.

Greenland

Iceland

Prinz Eugen

Bismarck

Iceland

North Atlantic

The *Hood* and the *Prince of Wales* attacked *Bismarck* and *Prinz Eugen* to protect convoys bound for Britain.

Hood

Prince of Wales

Limits of Arctic ice.

Hood sunk here.

Fighting novice

The *Hood* had never before had to fight another ship.

Briggs knew it would be a bloody business, but he was confident that his beloved *Hood*, and the battleship *Prince of Wales*, which was sailing alongside her, would soon dispatch any ship that crossed their path.

But Briggs was mistaken. *Bismarck* was an opponent no one would have wished for. Heavily armed and well protected, the aggressive angles and sweep of the ship made a striking contrast with the stately elegance of the *Hood*.

Like the *Hood*, she was over 0.25km (1/6 mile) long, but she was also 20 years younger and the very model of modern naval technology. Compared to the *Bismarck*, the *Hood* looked positively antiquated.

Battle begins

The two German ships were sighted at 5:35am. Ominous black dots 27km (17 miles) away, they would soon be within range of the *Hood*'s huge guns.

At 20km (13 miles) the *Hood* opened fire, her shells hurling toward *Bismarck* and *Prinz Eugen* at over twice the speed of sound. Nearly half a minute passed before huge plumes of water, as high as tower blocks, rose around the two approaching ships. The *Hood* had missed.

Terrified anticipation

Up on the compass platform, Briggs watched the *Bismarck*'s retort. Gold flashes with red cores winked from the distant ship. A low whine built to a howling crescendo as the shells made a 20-second journey between the two ships.

The *Hood*'s emblem – a crow holding an anchor. This symbol was found on everything from engine room controls to the ship's stationery.

Briggs' terrified anticipation ended when four huge columns of foam erupted to the right of the ship. Then an explosion knocked him off his feet.

The *Hood* had been hit at the base of its mainmast and fire spread rapidly. On deck, anti-aircraft shells exploded like firecrackers. On the platform, the screams of wounded men trickled from the voice-pipes* that kept the ship's commanders in touch with their vessel.

---

* Hollow tubes which could be used to relay messages.

Fatal blow

As the *Hood* turned to give its gunners a better view of the approaching enemy, another huge explosion rocked the ship, and Briggs was again thrown off his feet. A shell from *Bismarck* had penetrated deep within the hull and detonated her main ammunition supplies.

Aboard the *Prince of Wales* men saw an eerily silent explosion – like a huge red tongue – shoot four times the height of the ship. Pieces of the mainmast, a huge crane and part of a gun turret flew through the air.

When Briggs got up he felt in mortal fear for his life and knew instinctively that his ship had been fatally damaged. The *Hood* listed slowly to the right and the helmsman shouted through the voice-pipe that the ship's steering had failed.

To Briggs' relief the *Hood* rolled slowly back to level, but this relief was short-lived. The

The *Hood* from *Prince of Wales*. Moments after this photograph was taken a huge explosion four times the height of the mainmast would sink the ship.

ship lurched to the left and began to roll over. There was no order to abandon ship. As the floor became steeper and steeper the crew on the compass platform headed unprompted to the exit ladder. An officer stood aside to let Briggs go first. Slumped in his chair, Vice-Admiral

Lancelot Holland sat stunned and defeated.

The Hood sinks

Briggs climbed down a ladder to a lower deck on the tilting ship, but the sea was already gushing around his legs. With desperate haste he began to discard any clothing that would weigh him down, managing to lose his steel helmet and gas mask before being sucked into the icy water.

Dragged deep beneath the ship he felt an intense pressure in his ears and thought he was going to die. Unable to reach the surface and desperate to breathe he gulped down mouthfuls of water. As he was drowning, panic subsided. A childlike, blissful security swept over him, and Briggs thought of his mother tucking him into bed. But his peaceful resignation was interrupted. A great surge of water suddenly shot him to the surface.

The sinking of the Hood

Ted Briggs, Bill Dundas and Bob Tilburn were the only survivors when the *Hood* sank. A direct hit caused her magazines (stores of shells) to explode and broke the ship in half. She sank in under three minutes.

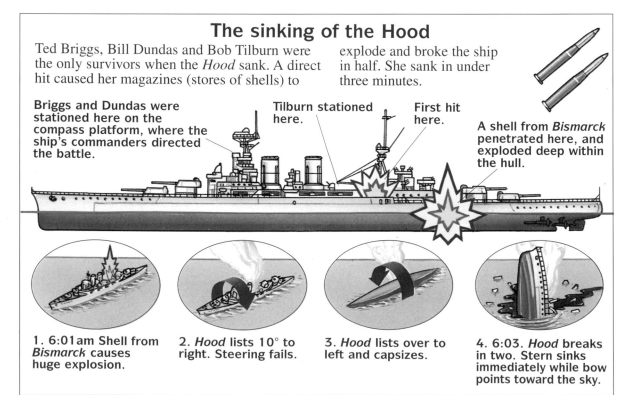

Briggs and Dundas were stationed here on the compass platform, where the ship's commanders directed the battle.

Tilburn stationed here.

First hit here.

A shell from *Bismarck* penetrated here, and exploded deep within the hull.

1. 6:01am Shell from *Bismarck* causes huge explosion.

2. *Hood* lists 10° to right. Steering fails.

3. *Hood* lists over to left and capsizes.

4. 6:03. *Hood* breaks in two. Stern sinks immediately while bow points toward the sky.

Choking and spluttering, Briggs gasped down great lungfuls of air, and took in a scene of unimaginable horror. All around were blazing pools of oil. What remained of the *Hood* was 45m (150ft) away. Her bows were vertical in the sea, the dislocated guns in her forward turrets were disappearing fast into the water. She was making a horrific hissing sound as white-hot metal and bubbling, blistering paint and wood made contact with the icy water. The *Prince of Wales* sailed close by, nearly colliding with the wreckage. The bow of the Hood towered over her like a nightmarish spire.

When the ship's radio wiring came down on him, Bob Tilburn had to cut himself free.

Briggs escapes

Realizing he was close enough to be sucked down again by the whirlpool currents the huge sinking ship was making, Briggs swam away through the oily sea as hard as he could. All around were dozens of small wooden rafts which had floated away when the *Hood* capsized, and he hauled himself onto one.

Looking back, nothing remained of the ship except a small patch of blazing oil where the bow had disappeared. It was a mere three minutes since the *Bismarck*'s guns had found their target.

Briggs was still in terrible danger. Shells from *Bismarck* and *Prinz Eugen* were falling around the *Prince of Wales*, only yards away, and the oil that surrounded him could ignite at any moment.

Other survivors

As he paddled away from the oil, he looked for other survivors. Two were close by. All three paddled toward one another and held their rafts together by linking arms.

On one raft was Midshipman (junior officer) Bill Dundas, who had been on the compass platform with Briggs. When the *Hood* capsized he kicked his way out of a window and swam away from the ship.

The other man was Able Seaman Bob Tilburn, who had been manning a gun position at the side of the ship. His had been the luckiest escape. He had survived exploding ammunition lockers and had been showered with falling debris and the bodies of men from the decks above. When the *Hood* capsized, he jumped into the water only to have the ship come down on top of him. Radio wiring had wrapped itself around his seaboots and he had cut himself free with a knife.

The three men were now in danger of freezing to death. To stop them from falling asleep and dying of exposure Dundas made them sing *Roll out the barrel* – a wartime pop song.

Fortunately they did not have to wait too long for help to arrive. The British destroyer *Electra* had spotted the three men and was heading toward them.

Ted Briggs was too cold to haul himself up to the ship and had to be lifted aboard. In *Electra*'s sick bay, frozen clothes were cut from his body and he was given rum to warm him up.

The *Electra* and three other ships had been sent to look for survivors. There was so little sign of life when they arrived at the scene of the sinking that they thought they must have gone off course. Briggs, Dundas and Tilburn, and a few wooden rafts, were all that was left. The *Hood* had taken the rest of her 1,421 crew – Vice-Admiral to engine room stoker – to the bottom of the North Atlantic.

Ted Briggs with his mother and sister, a week after the *Hood* went down. Mrs Briggs received a telegram telling her he was safe only an hour after radio reports announced that the *Hood* had sunk with little chance of survivors.

Surviving for yourself

Many survival skills can be easily learned. Following a disaster, the techniques shown here could make the difference between life and death.

Help signals

One of the most vital skills a survivor can have is knowing how to signal for help. Making three fires, or three columns of smoke, for example, are help signals which are recognized throughout the world.

Smoke from a signal fire can be made to contrast with the surrounding environment.

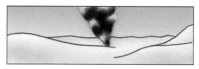

In deserts, rubber can be burned to create thick, black smoke.

In jungles, green leaves can be used to create white smoke.

Six blasts or flashes from a whistle, mirror or flashlight, at one minute intervals, is also a way of calling for help. If you do not have a mirror, use a belt buckle, polished cup or anything else that reflects the Sun's rays. These flashes can be seen up to 100km (60 miles) away. In deserts, flashes have been seen at distances of up to 160km (100 miles).

Morse code

Morse code is a signal system where each letter of the alphabet is represented by a sequence of dots (short signals) and dashes (longer signals). Mirrors, flashlights or whistles are three ways in which you can transmit it.

The emergency help signal in Morse code is SOS. Many people think this stands for "Save Our Souls", but these letters were chosen because S and O are the two easiest letters to remember in Morse. S is three dots . . . O is three

dashes - - - . To do this signal with a flashlight you would need to make three quick flashes, followed by three longer flashes, then another three quick flashes.

Other signals

The letters SOS can also be written on the ground. The best place for this is on high ground, or in a clearing. You can use stones or branches. Make the letters as big as possible, so they can be seen from the air. This works especially well if the letters are large enough to make shadows, which makes them stand out even better.

Extreme heat

In very hot conditions you may suffer from heatstroke. This causes fever, and can lead to convulsions and coma. It may even be fatal. Survivors stranded in hot surroundings can take these precautions:
• Drink as much water as you can. In high temperatures your body may need four times as much water as usual.
• If your supply of water is low, only use it to moisten your mouth. You can also suck a small pebble

Cardboard mask

as this stimulates saliva glands in your mouth and relieves thirst. Chewing on grass will also provide a little moisture.
• Shelter from the Sun during the day. Travel only at night.
• Keep clothes on – this helps prevent sunburn and water loss, as sweat evaporates more slowly from your skin.
• Keep your head covered at all times. If you do not have a hat, wrap a loose-fitting cloth around your head.
• You can make a simple mask to cut down on glare from bright sunlight. Use available materials, such as cardboard and elastic bands.

Making fire

To start a fire, you need three basic materials, called tinder, kindling and fuel. If you do not have matches to light your fire, you could use a glass lens to focus the Sun's rays, or chip a flint stone against steel, to make sparks.

Tinder
This is quite easy to ignite and will set fire to kindling.

Straw *Wood shavings*

Kindling
This increases the temperature enough to set fire to fuel.

Twigs *Paper*

Fuel
This generates heat for warmth and cooking, and smoke for signals.

Wood

Extreme cold

One of the survivor's greatest enemies is cold – even deserts are cold at night. If your body temperature drops more than a couple of degrees you may suffer from hypothermia. This causes drowsiness and disorientation, and can be fatal. Extreme cold may also freeze your flesh, causing a condition known as frostbite. Follow these steps to prevent frostbite and hypothermia:
• Keep dry. When you are wet, you become even colder as water evaporates from clothes.
• If you have been out in snow, brush it off when returning to shelter. Otherwise it will melt and soak your clothing.
• Wrinkle your face, and wriggle your fingers and toes at regular intervals. This keeps blood circulating in the extremities of your body.
• Do not wear tight clothing. This restricts circulation. With looser clothes, an insulating layer of air keeps out cold.
• Wear as many clothes as possible. A layer of dry leaves or moss stuffed between two pairs of socks will also help insulate your feet. (Be careful not to stuff them too tight.)

Snow shelter

A shelter is essential in cold conditions. The diagram on the right shows how survivors trapped in a snowy forest can make themselves a snow shelter using a large blanket.

Fill blanket with leaves and sticks, to make a semicircular structure. Shape snow over blanket and allow to harden.

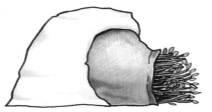

Pull out contents of sack. Door can be made with small bag filled with sticks. Insulate floor with leaves and twigs.

Air hole
Door

Thirst

Without food, you could live for a month. Without water you may die after three days. If you are stranded with little water, take these precautions:
• In high temperatures, take shelter or wear protective clothing. You can sweat as much as 4 litres (7 pints) of water in an hour.
• In cold conditions, always breathe through your nose rather than your mouth. This warms air entering your lungs. You lose water in your breath, especially if the air you inhale is cold.
• Eat as little as possible. When you digest food your body uses a lot of water.
• Do as little exercise as you can, as this makes you sweat.
• Do not drink sea water. This has a high salt content and will make you even more thirsty*.

Finding water

At sea, collect as much rain as possible. In a desert, plants and animals indicate that water is nearby. An area with some vegetation will be a good place to build a solar still – a device for extracting water from the air and soil.

A still like the one below will also collect water from the dew that falls at dawn.

Sun heats interior and water within sand evaporates. Droplets form on sheet and run into container.

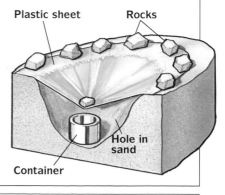

Plastic sheet *Rocks*

Hole in sand

Container

*This is disputed. See p. 46.

After the ordeal

Apollo 13

(Space catastrophe for unlucky 13 p.28-32)

One American newspaper remarked of *Apollo 13*'s close escape "Never in recorded history has a journey of such peril been watched and waited-out by almost the entire human race." The three astronauts arrived back at their home town of Houston, Texas, to find US president Richard Nixon waiting to greet them. None returned to space again.

James Lovell retired from NASA in 1973 to work for the Centel Corporation in Chicago. **Fred Haise** was at the controls of the first Space Shuttle *Enterprise* when it made its maiden Earth flight in 1977. **Jack Swigert** took up a career in politics. He was elected to public office in Colorado in November, 1982, but died a month later of bone cancer.

William Bligh

("Breadfruit" Bligh's boatload of trouble p.13-17)

Bligh returned to his family in England to discover that he was the father of twin girls and to write a best selling account of the *Bounty* mutiny. In the summer of 1790, he faced a court-martial for the loss of his ship, but was acquitted.

The following year he was given a new ship, *HMS Providence*, returned to Tahiti, and successfully transported breadfruit plants to the West Indies, where they still grow to this day.

In 1808, he was appointed Governor of New South Wales, Australia. His attempts to restrict the import of alcohol to the territory led to an army mutiny against him, and he was imprisoned by his own troops for 26 months. This did not harm his Navy career. By the time he retired he had reached the rank of rear admiral. He died at 63, in 1817.

Fletcher Christian, who led the *Bounty* mutiny, fled with nine other mutineers and 18 Tahitians to remote and uninhabited Pitcairn Island, in the South Pacific. Here, Christian and most of his companions met violent deaths, squabbling among themselves or with the Tahitians.

Today, the island is inhabited by 18 families. Between them they have only four surnames, three of which – Christian, Young and Brown – belong to the original mutineers.

This 1808 engraving depicts Bligh attempting to evade mutinous troops in Australia.

Alain Bombard

(Plenty of fish in sea, says scientist p.46-49)

Alain Bombard returned to France to write an account of his voyage across the Atlantic – *The Bombard Story**. He also founded a marine research laboratory at St. Malo, France. His boat *L'Hérétique* found a home in the French Navy Museum in Paris. Today, he is a familiar face on French television, where he is well known as an environmental campaigner.

Ted Briggs

(Ted cheats death on sinking Hood, p.56-59)

Ted Briggs survived the war. Serving for 35 years in the British Royal Navy, he rose to the rank of lieutenant, and was awarded the MBE (Member of the British Empire) by the British Government. He now lives in Hampshire, England, and is a prominent member of the Hood Association – an organization set up to preserve the memory of his former ship.

The Hindenburg

(Hindenburg's hydrogen hell p.9-12)

In Germany, the ruling Nazi regime saw the *Hindenburg* as a symbol of their power and prestige. They were quick to blame the disaster on sabotage, but could produce no serious evidence to back this up. Hugo Eckener, chairman of the Zeppelin Reederei, described the fire as "the hopeless end of a great dream". The notion of huge airships carrying passengers across the oceans died in the flames at Lakehurst. To this day, airships remain an airborne gimmick, suitable mainly for advertising slogans.

Evel Knievel

(Death or glory for "Last Gladiator" p.36-37)

The Snake River jump was such a financially successful "retirement", Knievel could not resist the lure of further stunts, including a motorbike leap over 13 buses at Wembley Stadium, London, in 1976. These earned him an alleged $65 million (£43 million)

 *See Further reading p. 64.

fortune, and an entry in the *Guinness Book of Records* for the greatest number of broken bones (433 in total).

Following a baseball bat attack on a journalist who had written an uncomplimentary biography, he spent five months in prison. Currently claiming to be broke ("I don't own so much as a block of wood now," he was reported as saying in 1994), he makes a living selling his own paintings and managing his stunt rider son Robbie.

Pu'u O'o

(Film crew in lava inferno p.43-45)

The film *Sliver* was completed without any shots of smoking volcanoes. One leading character in the film does confess, however, to a great fascination in volcanoes, and admits he has fantasies about flying into one. **Don Shearer** and **Tom Hauptman**, who flew rescue helicopters into Pu'u O'o, are both thanked in the film's credits.

Susie Rijnhart

(Susie Rijnhart's Tibetan trek p.18-21)

After reaching safe territory in China, Rijnhart made her way back to Canada. Several years later she remarried and returned to Tibet with her husband, intent on further missionary work. She died in childbirth three weeks after crossing into Tibet from China.

Saint-Exupéry

(Mirage misery for Saint-Exupéry p.22-25)

Following his desert rescue, Saint-Ex spent the remainder of his life continuing to enhance his reputation as both a writer

and a pioneer aviator. His experiences in the Sahara are recounted in his book *Terre des hommes** (*Wind, Sand and Stars*) published in 1939. His most famous book, the fable *Le Petit Prince* (*The Little Prince*) was published in 1943.

During World War Two he served in the French Air Force, and fled to New York when France surrendered. Returning to serve with the Free French Forces in North Africa, he was shot down and killed during a reconnaissance flight over Corsica. He was 44. After his death the French government awarded him the Commandeur de la Légion d'Honneur medal.

Ernest Shackleton

(Marooned in a polar wilderness p.38-42)

The survivors of Shackleton's Antarctic expedition returned to a Europe ensnared in World War One. Almost all volunteered for the armed services and two, a junior officer and a seaman, were killed in action. Shackleton, his deputy **Frank Wild** and *Endurance*'s captain **Frank Worsley** were sent to the North Russian front, where their knowledge of polar conditions would be useful. Many of *Endurance*'s crew served in minesweepers.

In 1921, Shackleton returned to the Antarctic with many of his *Endurance* shipmates, intent on further exploration. He died of a heart attack at Grytviken, South Georgia, in January, 1922, and is buried on the island.

Joe Simpson

(Simpson's icy tomb p.33-35)

Following his reunion with Simon Yates, Simpson endured a six day wait before receiving

medical attention for his injured leg. Back home in Britain, Doctors warned him he would never climb again. Defying medical opinion he made an extraordinary recovery and now climbs all over the world. In 1992, he returned to Peru and climbed six mountains in three weeks. He now divides his time between mountaineering, writing and working as a guide for a trekking company. His account of his mishap on Siula Grande, *Touching The Void**, has sold 500,000 copies and been translated into 14 languages.

Squalus

(Dive to disaster p.4-8)

Squalus was salvaged six months after its disastrous crash-dive. Renamed *Sailfish* (navies traditionally rename all salvaged ships), she fought in World War Two. On December 4, 1943, she sank the Japanese aircraft carrier *Chuyo*. By an extraordinary coincidence, among the survivors were members of the submarine *Sculpin*, which had assisted in the rescue of the *Squalus*. They had been taken prisoner when their submarine was sunk and *Chuyo* had been ferrying them into captivity.

Joseph Wolff

(Wolff to the rescue p.52-55)

It took Wolff nine months to travel from Bukhara back to England. He finally arrived home in April, 1845.

Promising his family he would never travel abroad again, he spent the rest of his days as vicar of the quiet country parish of Ile Brewers in Somerset, where his eccentric manner continued to bemuse all those who knew him. He died in 1862, aged 67.

Further reading

If you would like to know more about some of these stories, the following books contain useful information.

Apollo Expeditions to the Moon edited by Edgar Cortright (NASA, 1980). Contains James Lovell's account of the *Apollo 13* disaster: *"Houston, We've had a Problem"*.
The Bombard Story by Alain Bombard (André Deutsch, 1953)
Captain Bligh and Mr. Christian by Richard Hough (Cassell Ltd, 1979)
Endurance – Shackleton's Incredible Voyage by Alfred Lansing (Hodder and Stoughton, 1959)
Few Survived – A Comprehensive Survey of Submarine Accidents and Disasters by Edwyn Gray (Leo Cooper, 1986)
Flagship Hood by Alan Coles and Ted Briggs (Robert Hale Ltd, 1985)
The Giant Airships by Douglas Botting (Time-Life Books, 1981)
Improve Your Survival Skills by Lucy Smith (Usborne Publishing, 1987)
A Mission to Bokhara by Joseph Wolff (Routledge and Kegan Paul, 1969 – Facsimile of original 1852 edition)
Touching the Void by Joe Simpson (Jonathan Cape, Ltd, 1988)
Wind, Sand and Stars by Antoine de Saint-Exupéry (William Heinemann, 1939)
With the Tibetans in Tent and Temple by Susie Carson Rijnhart (Oliphant, Anderson & Ferrier, 1901)

Acknowledgements and photo credits

The Publishers would like to thank the following for their help and advice:

John Barry, Llanrwst. Ted Briggs, Fareham. Clive Bunyan, Science Museum, London. Dr. David Killingray, Reader in History, Goldsmiths College, University of London. Iain MacKenzie, Maritime Information Centre, National Maritime Museum, London. Doug Millard, Associate Curator for Space Technology, Science Museum, London. Raja Rahawani Raja Mamat and Norhashimi Saad, Coventry. Joe Simpson, Sheffield.

The publishers would also like to thank the following for permission to reproduce their photographs in this book: Associated Press, London (45); Bilderdienst Süddeutscher Verlag, Munich (10 bottom right); Ted Briggs, Fareham, UK (3, 56 top, 59); Ray Delany/Perpetual Unit Trust, UK (33); e.t. archive/National Maritime Museum, London (13 bottom); Hulton-Deutsch, London (38 bottom, 52); Imperial War Museum, London (58); NASA, Houston, USA (28, 31, 32); National Archives, Washington, USA (4, 5, 6, 8); Popperfoto, Overstone, UK (10-11, 56 bottom); Press Association, London (51); Roger-Viollet, Paris (46); Roger-Viollet © Collection Viollet (22, 25); Royal Geographical Society, London (38 top, 39); Frank Spooner Pictures, London/ Gamma/David Burdett (36, 37); Topham Picture Source, Edenbridge, UK (11 right, 42); Ullstein Bilderdienst, Berlin (9, 10 bottom left, 12).

Picture Researcher: Diana Morris.

USBORNE READER'S LIBRARY

TALES OF REAL
ESCAPE

Paul Dowswell

Designed by Mary Cartwright
and Nigel Reece

Illustrated by Peter Ross and Tony Jackson

Additional illustrations by Janos Marffy
and Sean Wilkinson

Editorial assistance by Lisa Miles

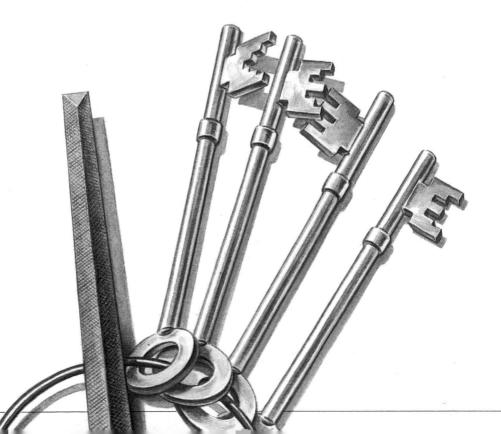

Contents

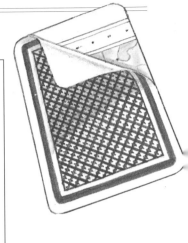

Escapers at work

These stories are about prisoners who tried to escape. Spies and slaves, soldiers and civilians, politicians and criminals, all held against their will by guards, locks and chains, barbed wire or sheer stone walls.

There are many thousands of ways of escaping, almost all of them are dangerous. Digging a tunnel, climbing a barbed wire fence or throwing a rope from a roof, could all result in death or serious injury. Going through checkpoints with a forged pass, or impersonating a prison official, requires extraordinary cunning and an iron nerve. Escape plans like these need a great deal of time to prepare, but this is something most prisoners have more than enough of.

Special equipment

In wartime, those most likely to be captured (aircrews, spies, commandos) are issued with equipment and clothing to help them escape if they fall into enemy hands. This might include flying boots that can be turned into civilian shoes, a water bottle with a compass in the stopper, or laces which conceal a small hacksaw, ideal for sawing through bars.

Many of the escapers in these stories, though, had no such aids to help them.

The essential ingredient

In every escape one thing counts more than anything else. No matter how carefully planned or ruthlessly pursued, without luck, an escape will fail. An escaper who is in the wrong place when a guard turns around, or who is picked out of a crowd by a wary policeman, is always worse off than one who passes through a checkpoint when the guards are tired, or who has a shortsighted policeman examine his forged pass. These stories are about luck, but they are also about courage, and the perils people put themselves through to gain their liberty.

Snakes and sharks guide jungle prison

Herded off the steamship *Martinière* at gunpoint, around 600 shaven-headed convicts lined up on the quay of St. Laurent, deep in the jungle of French Guiana. A random collection of thieves, swindlers, thugs and murderers, all had been sentenced by French courts to exile or imprisonment in this remote and inhospitable South American colony.

The *Martinière* sailed twice a year from France and those on board endured a diabolic 18 day journey. Packed 90 a time in cages and fed from buckets, they were hosed down with seawater every morning. Not everyone survived the voyage.

Exhaustion and disease

Nothing these men had seen in Paris, Marseilles, or a hundred other provincial towns had prepared them for St. Laurent. The hot, sticky air carried a forewarning of exhaustion and disease. Emerald vegetation beyond the town and river banks concealed a dense, dark world, infested by insect legions and poisonous snakes. From time to time strange birds broke cover, shimmering by in a blaze of reds, greens and blues.

A ragbag crowd

Everybody in St. Laurent stood staring by the quay. The ship's arrival was the main event of the year. Chinese shopkeepers, Guianan bushmen, the wives and children of the guards, and prison officials in spotless white suits, all gazed with curiosity as the *Martinière* disgorged its bedraggled human cargo.

Most convicts boarding the *Martinière* (top) never saw France again. Their journey, sketched above by a fellow convict, was a harrowing one.

Two French Guianan convicts, 1938. Their tattoos are typical of the prison colony population.

Creatures such as this poisonous coral snake inhabited the jungle around the prison camps.

Painful memories

Scattered among the crowd were a handful of pitiful, dead-eyed men, whose ragged clothes hung loose on ravaged, tattooed bodies. The *Martinière* stirred up painful memories for them. They too had arrived in this way, perhaps decades before. A life of hellish brutality, disease and degradation lay behind them. Now they waited for death to release them. Any new arrival who saw these embittered figures would have shuddered. If they survived, this would be their future. Many convicts faced a life sentence, but even those with limited time to serve would probably spend the rest of their life there. The law required them to remain as residents for a period equal to their original sentence.

A veteran of 20 years of prison colony life. 1930s.

The penal colony of French Guiana

French Guiana
South America

The prison camps of French Guiana were known as the *bange*. Some were located deep in the jungle, but the largest were attached to local towns, or on the Iles du Salut. These were the main ones.

Ile du Diable

Ile Royale

Ile St. Joseph

Sandbanks

Atlantic Ocean

Dangerous currents

Shark infested water

Maroni River

Dense jungle

The Iles du Salut

These three islands (called the "Isles of Salvation") were 8km (5 miles) off the coast.

Ile Royale

Home for 700 of the most dangerous convicts in the colony. The island had one poorly supplied hospital.

Ile St. Joseph

Recaptured prisoners were sent here for solitary confinement. (There were 450 cells.) Talking was forbidden and the only noises on the island were the cries of those driven insane by their seclusion.

Ile du Diable

Political prisoners were sent here. This former leper colony was the smallest of the three islands and known throughout the world as "Devil's Island". Around 30 prisoners lived here, at any one time.

St. Laurent

The population of around 5,000 included 3,000 convicts. Work gangs kept the streets, houses and gardens immaculately neat. The prison camp had 16 concrete barracks and a hospital. Convicts could come and go during the day, but had to be back in the camp at night.

Cayenne

The best camp in the colony. Discipline was light and many convicts worked in the town. Up to 1,300 stayed here in three stone buildings.

A dreadful warning

Near the quay stood the prison gates, where the unnerved arrivals were greeted by the prison director. He made the same speech to all newcomers.

"You are all worthless criminals, sent here to pay for your crimes. If you behave yourselves you'll find life is not too unbearable. If you don't behave, you'll find yourself in more trouble than you can begin to imagine.

Most of you here are already thinking about your escape – forget it! You will have plenty of freedom in your camps and in town. You'll find that the real guards here are the jungle and the sea."

But life was unbearable. Men spent exhausting days toiling in jungle work gangs, tormented by insects, and supervised by guards who had the power of life or death over them.

Worse than villains

These guards were often more corrupt than their prisoners. The French Emperor Napoleon III set up the prison camps in 1854, to rid France of its worst criminals and help revive an ailing, underdeveloped overseas colony. He was asked by an aide:

"Who, Sire, will you find to guard these villains?"

He replied:

"People more villainous than they are."

Napoleon III was as good as his word. Tales of torture, sudden execution, and burial alive, perpetrated by guards such as "Tiger" Bonini, or "The Scourge" Alari, filtered back to civilization.

These guards reported their victims as having "died from the effects of a fit" and convicts would do anything to avoid falling into their clutches. Members of a work gang supervised by Bonini were said to have hanged themselves with jungle creepers, rather than spend another day working for him. Others deliberately infected themselves with tuberculosis or leprosy, risking death or disfigurement to avoid the jungle work parties.

17,508 hours alone. Solitary confinement on St. Joseph

The guillotine was the most severe punishment a convict in French Guiana could expect. Almost as bad were the solitary confinement cells on the island of St. Joseph. Here men could be sent to spend up to five years alone, and four out of five went insane or died.

Solitary confinement cell

Iron bars

Hinged plank bed

Chamber pot

Iron door

Hatch

The cells were stark, and inmates were given barely enough food to keep them alive. In the cell blocks all was silent. Prisoners were forbidden to talk. The guards even wore slippers to cut down on noise.

Papillon

Some did survive though. One famous description of these cells comes from the book *Papillon* by Henri Charrière. He was sentenced to French Guiana in 1931 for murder – a crime he claimed he did not commit. Many people believe this book about his life as a convict is only partly true, but its account of solitary confinement is thought to be realistic.

Cigarettes and coconuts

Charrière, who spent two years in solitary confinement following an unsuccessful escape attempt, stayed healthy for most of the time.

Feeding time in the cells, depicted by a convict artist.

Friends arranged for five cigarettes and a coconut to be smuggled to him every day. The coconut supplemented his poor diet and the cigarettes enabled him to break the monotony of his day.

Chasing centipedes

He kept sane by passing secret messages to other prisoners and chasing centipedes. Most of the time he led a rich fantasy life, dreaming about girls, countries

Night-time feuds

Night offered no relief. Convicts were locked into huge prison camp dormitories – the scene of interminable fighting between feuding gangs. Here men were terrorized into giving up their last meagre possessions or silently murdered in the stale, stinking dark.

50,000 escapes

Despite the prison director's warning, most convicts did try to leave the colony. Life was so bad that the punishment for escaping, two or more years of solitary confinement, was not a sufficient deterrent. 70,000 men were sent here between 1854 and 1937, and over

he had visited, and his childhood.

One year and nine months into his sentence, his daily supply of coconuts and cigarettes was discovered and stopped. Without his extra rations and the distraction of cigarettes, his health and sanity declined rapidly. Fortunately, he had only three more months to go. After 17,508 hours of isolation he was released, and sent back into the penal colony.

Henri Charrière, during his trial in 1931.

50,000 escape attempts were recorded.

It was not difficult to slip away from the camps or work gangs, and roll calls were only held twice a day. Getting out of the jungle was the hard part.

An uncertain fate

Only one in six escapers avoided recapture, and it is impossible to say how many of these actually got away. Many nearby countries returned convicts to their captors, so those who fled kept quiet about their past.

Most men probably paid for an escape with their lives. The director's warning about the jungle and the sea was not a bluff. Rough seas and strong currents overturned flimsy boats, leaving their occupants to drown.

Men escaping by land fell victim to poisonous snakes. Others found themselves hopelessly lost in the dense jungle, and died starving and alone. Insects ate their bodies, leaving no trace.

Safety in numbers?

Convicts almost always escaped in groups, as the perils they faced were too great to cope with alone. However, ruthless men, hardened by years of captivity, do not always make the best travelling companions.

The Longuevilles

In one incident in the 1920s, brothers Marcel and Dedé Longueville escaped with four other convicts. The Longuevilles, huge, tattooed thugs, were two of the most terrifying convicts in the colony. Three of the other escapers contributed money towards the cost of a boat. The fourth did not. He claimed to be an experienced sailor and his skill paid for his place on the trip.

The six men left St. Laurent one December night, planning to sail their well-equipped boat down the Maroni River and on to Cuba. A strong current carried them under the noses of the guards and out to sea.

But here their troubles began. The estuary where the Maroni meets the Atlantic Ocean has sandbanks which stretch for miles along the coast.

No sooner had they taken to sea than the boat became stuck on such a sandbank. Dedé Longueville, overcome by a towering rage, stabbed the sailor to death.

Stranded

The remaining five waded ashore. A large wave washed away their supplies so they had to look for food in the jungle. There were only small crabs to eat, and after a few days they were starving. Two of the party, a tough Parisian villain named Pascal and his young companion, were sent into the jungle to search for food.

The next morning Pascal returned alone, and told them he had lost his friend. Although the Longuevilles would kill a man who let them down, they would not desert a fellow convict. They took Pascal back into the jungle to look for his companion.

A terrible discovery

Inland, they made a terrible discovery. Pascal had killed his friend and eaten parts of his body. The Longuevilles were filled with disgust and killed him on the spot. However, later that night their hunger overcame their scruples. Pascal himself was eaten and the grisly evidence was discreetly buried.

A few days later the men were recaptured by the local police. They returned to French Guiana to spend two years in solitary confinement.

The Guianese assassin

A few years earlier, other runaways had also faced an unpleasant fate. Some local colonists could be bribed to help convicts escape, but others, such as fisherman Victor Bixier des Ages, would take a bribe and then kill a man for the rest of his money.

Bixier des Ages agreed to take parties of five or six to Brazil on his boat. A day into the voyage he would sail through sandbanks and ask passengers to step out, so the boat could float over the shallow water. As they stood up to their knees in the muddy bank, he would reach for his gun and shoot them dead.

Cold-blooded murder

No one knows how many died this way, but eventually Bixier des Ages grew careless. On one occasion, as he dispatched a party of five escapers, he ran out of ammunition. One man managed to wade to the shore and evade his executioner in dense jungle.

This man survived to be recaptured, and told the prison authorities his tale. The fisherman was arrested and sentenced to 20 years on Ile Royale, where all native French Guianese were sent. Even here he continued to bring grief to the convicts of the colony. He became a turnkey, a trusted prisoner whose job it was to track down escapers.

A trip to Brazil

Some convicts did survive to reach other countries. Eugene Dieudonné made three attempts before he succeeded. One time he fled with two others, on a raft made from ladders lashed to barrels. They spent two days surrounded by sharks, their legs dangling between the ladder rungs. Although they were not attacked, their nerve gave out and they returned to captivity, and a spell in the solitary confinement cells on Ile St. Joseph.

Drowned in mud

Dieudonné finally escaped from the colony in 1927, this time with five others. They bribed a fisherman to take them in his boat, but were soon stranded on coastal mudbanks. Although the boat was refloated it sank in heavy seas a day later. The escape party managed to swim to the shore, but one, a young

Police photograph of Eugene Dieudonné. 1912.

man named Venet, sank up to his shoulders in the muddy slime of the seashore. His companions attempted to reach him with branches torn from trees, but Venet drowned when the tide returned.

Jungle hideaway

The party split into two groups, with Dieudonné pairing up with a Breton named Jean-Marie. The other couple were soon recaptured but Dieudonné and the Breton hid in the forest for a month, paying two old convicts to supply them with food. These convicts also put them in touch with a reputable sailor, known as "Strong Devil", who agreed to take them to Brazil.

They sailed with three other fugitives in an open fishing boat which had to be constantly bailed out. The voyage drained the strength from the already exhausted escapers, but "Strong Devil" lived up to his name. He navigated the boat through heavy seas and they reached the Brazilian coast after seven days. Slipping past the local police they headed inland to the town of Belem, where they hoped to find work.

Carnival tramps

With great good fortune the escapers arrived during the annual carnival, and revellers assumed they were dressed for the occasion as carnival tramps. Dieudonné and Jean-Marie set about making a fresh start. They gave themselves new identities, found a room to rent, and lived a quiet respectable life. Dieudonné worked as a cabinet maker and Jean-Marie assisted him. But the past caught up with them. After four months the two were betrayed, and arrested by the local police.

Famous convicts

However, Dieudonné was a famous man. He had been part of a notorious terrorist gang in France. After the gang was arrested, four of them were guillotined, but Dieudonné, who was only a minor member of the gang, was sent to French Guiana. At the time, many people felt his sentence was too harsh. The Brazilians decided they were not going to send a possibly innocent man back to the horrors of French Guiana.

Jean-Marie had no such luck. His past was not so interesting and he was sent back to the penal colony, but Dieudonné became the focus of an international press campaign, and the French government was persuaded to pardon him. Not only had he escaped from the penal colony, but he was able to return to France as a free man.

Endless terror

Others returned to France too, but as escaped, unforgiven criminals. They led shadowy lives, forever in fear of an unexpected knock on their door. They could be arrested at any time, and have to go through the awful voyage on board the *Martinière*, two years of solitary confinement, and more endless years in the jungle of French Guiana. More often than not they were betrayed by an acquaintance, or even a member of their own family.

A French journalist known to be sympathetic to the plight of these fugitives, once received a letter from such a man, whose wife and child knew nothing of his former life as a convict.

Sometimes I start to shake when someone stops too long at my stairwell, or each time there are voices from the other side of my door.

When he wrote the words above he had been on the run for 22 years.

Where they went – escape destinations

Vessels used by escapers.

Canoe

Barrels and ladders

Fishing boat

The most practical way out of French Guiana was by sea. Convicts escaped in a variety of vessels, from cobbled together ladders and barrels, to dug-out canoes and small fishing boats.

For those who survived their journey out of the colony there were plenty of destinations to head for, although wherever a convict went, he faced an uncertain future.

British Guiana

Escapers were not welcome here, nor in any other British territory. Most convicts were permitted to head for other countries, rather than returned to French Guiana.

Martinique and Guadaloupe

French territory. Both islands returned convicts to the prison colony immediately.

Venezuela

Convicts were accepted here and work was available. However, in 1935 the army hired a French convict to assassinate president Juan Vincente Gomez. He failed. In the reprisals that followed, all former French convicts were rounded up and returned to the prison colony.

Trinidad

Trinidad declared in 1933 that it would help escapers. It became too popular a destination, so began to send runaways on to other countries.

Dutch Surinam

Until 1924, this was the best place to go. All but the worst convicts were allowed to stay here, and work was easy to find. However, in 1924, a drunken escaper burned down a shop when he was refused service, killing the owner and his family. After this, all convicts were sent straight back to French Guiana.

Brazil

Escapers were usually sent back, but Brazil is so big many of them were able to hide from the authorities.

Argentina

It was difficult to reach from French Guiana, but there was plenty of work for seasoned criminals in Buenos Aires – the crime capital of South America.

Churchill's track to fame and freedom

Winston Churchill in 1899.

Winston Churchill, journalist for the London *Morning Post*, crouched low outside the high wall of a Pretoria school where he had been held captive. He had leapt over, as a guard beneath turned to light his pipe. Now he had been waiting 15 minutes for two other prisoners to follow him. People were passing by. The guard stood a breath away.

The school had been turned into a prisoner of war camp during the Boer War. The Boers (descendants of Dutch settlers) had rebelled against British rule in South Africa in 1899, and set up their own territory.

Churchill had been captured by Boers when they ambushed his train. He had put up such a fight that they refused to believe he was a journalist and held him prisoner with British troops. Now, hidden only by a small bush, he was in terrible trouble. His fellow escapers were obviously not going

to join him, but his journey to British territory depended on them. They had money, maps and a compass, and one spoke Dutch – a language understood by his captors. He could not go back, because the wall outside the school was too high to climb.

Bold gamble

Churchill had no choice but to escape alone. As he wore civilian clothes he decided he might not be noticed. He stood up slowly and walked straight past a sentry by the main gate of the school. He walked down the town's main street toward the station, nervously whistling to himself. A railway line ran between Pretoria and the

port of Lourenço Marques (now named Maputo) which was in neutral territory, so he decided to hide on a train.

Railway getaway

Churchill lay in wait outside Pretoria Station. With great risk to his life he boarded a train by climbing up onto the couplings between two wagons. The train he had chosen was full of

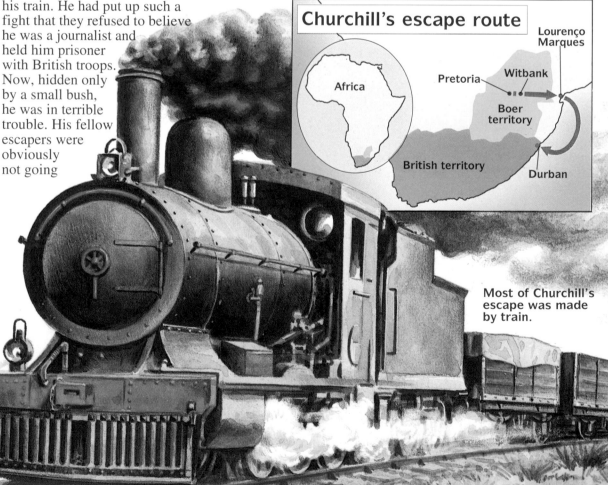

Churchill's escape route

Africa

Pretoria · Witbank · Lourenço Marques

Boer territory

British territory

Durban

Most of Churchill's escape was made by train.

empty coal bags, and it trundled slowly through the night to Witbank, a small mining town 95km (60 miles) east of Pretoria.

As dawn broke, Churchill feared he would be seen. Leaping from the train he hid in a forest, intending to board another train that evening. In the undergrowth he lay so still that a vulture, thinking he was dying, kept him company. By dusk Churchill was beginning to feel very hungry, so he made his way to some nearby lights, which turned out to be a town.

Held at gunpoint

Knocking on the door of a house, he was greeted by a man who pointed a pistol at him. Churchill told him he was "Doctor Bentinck" and that he had fallen off a train and lost his way. This unlikely story was unconvincing, so Churchill told him the truth.

Fortunately his captor, John Howard, was English. Howard told him that this was the only house in 30km (20 miles) where he would not have been arrested.

Dead or alive

By now Churchill's escape had been featured in the British newspapers and the Boers were anxious to find him. They were offering a £25 reward for the Englishman "dead or alive", so Howard decided to hide his fugitive in the town mine.

Churchill spent three dark days in a pit pony stable infested with rats, who soon ate his supply of candles. In such grim surroundings he became ill, and was taken to the surface and hidden in a store room.

Howard had a friend, Charles Burnham, who came to their

While Churchill hid in a mine, rats ate his candles.

rescue. He hid Churchill in a delivery of wool he was sending by train to the coast. The journey passed without incident, but at the border Churchill had to endure an 18 hour wait. The train was searched, but he was too well concealed to be discovered.

Hero's welcome

When the train arrived at Lourenço Marques, Churchill immediately boarded a boat to the British territory in South Africa. At the port of Durban he was greeted by an excited crowd. Already quite well known as a journalist, his escape had turned him into a national hero.

On his return, Churchill joined the British forces in South Africa to fight his former captors. He also continued to work as a journalist, and his fame enabled him to become the highest paid war correspondent of his day.

These pictures of Churchill's escape appeared in a London magazine.

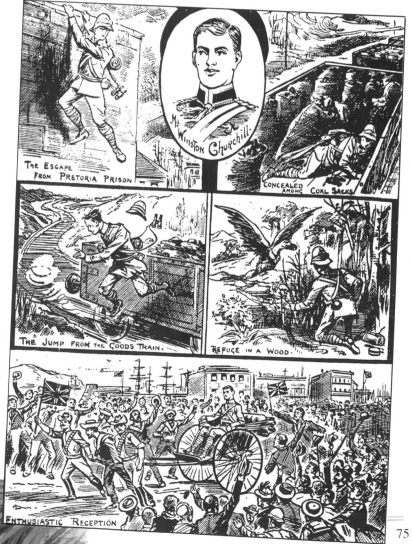

THE ESCAPE FROM PRETORIA PRISON

Mr. Winston Churchill.

CONCEALED AMONG COAL SACKS.

THE JUMP FROM THE GOODS TRAIN.

REFUGE IN A WOOD.

ENTHUSIASTIC RECEPTION.

Alcatraz accordionists break out of the Rock

The long corridors of cellblock B were buzzing. Behind steel bar doors, convicts called out chess moves to nearby opponents. Others swapped jibes and threats, or washed and undressed for the night. Activity ceased abruptly at half past nine, when the lights were switched off.

Frank Morris, bank robber and burglar, stared at the ceiling, alone in his cell. His world measured three paces by five. Day one of his ten year sentence on "the Rock" – Alcatraz Top Security Island Penitentiary – was over. All around him were men regarded as the most hardened, desperate criminals in the entire USA. The Rock was their ultimate escape-proof punishment.

Escape organizer Frank Morris.

Alcatraz island lay 2.5km (1.5 miles) out from San Francisco.

San Francisco Bay

Angel Island

Golden Gate Bridge

Pacific Ocean

San Francisco

San Francisco

United States of America

0 —— 10 Km
0 —— 6 Miles

Foghorns and footsteps

The stillness beyond was broken only by the distant boom of a foghorn and the footsteps of a patrolling guard. In the cavernous steel and concrete block the sound of each step took a second to settle. Morris noted the time it took the guard to walk the length of a corridor before he turned around. Already he was planning his escape.

260 closely packed men

In the dead of night all that remained to remind Morris of his fellow inmates was the dark, brooding smell of 260 closely packed men and a high, sharp whiff of disinfectant. It unsettled him at first, but after a few days there he would no longer notice.

Outside, the winter wind stirred. Howling across San Francisco Bay, it tugged at the jagged island fortress, and lashed the cold, dark sea. The wind rose and fell, seeping through windows and doors, penetrating the cell blocks, stairwells and galleries of the prison.

Razor sharp

Morris's pleasant face and amiable manner hid a ruthless determination and razor sharp mind. Escaping was in his blood. His mother Clara escaped from home aged 11, a school for wayward girls at 14, and a reformatory at 17. Morris was born, and abandoned, shortly after.

A childhood of foster parents and children's homes followed, and a career in burglary. A series of prison sentences, escapes and recaptures, led him to Alcatraz.

Rock routine

As the days went by he became accustomed to the routine of the Rock: the daily workshop visit to earn money making brushes or gloves; the journey back to the cells through a metal detector; random body searches and half-hourly head counts; two afternoon hours' recreation in the yard; three meals in the prison canteen, with its ominous riot precautions – rifle slits in the wall and silver tear gas bombs nestling in the ceiling.

After the evening meal the men were locked in their cells. They had four hours to themselves before the lights went out, to paint, read, or play a musical instrument. Then they settled down to a long dreary night which dissolved into the harsh wake-up blast of the 6:00am horn.

Alcatraz – the island of pelicans

In 1775 Spanish explorers named the island *Isla de Alcatraces* – "the Isle of Pelicans", after the birds that nested on it. In 1850 a fort and lighthouse were built there. The army used the island as a disciplinary barracks, and between 1906-1911 they built the prison that still stands today.

Alcatraz became notorious when many of the infamous gangsters of the 1930s were sent there. "Creepy" Karpis, "Machine Gun" Kelly and Al Capone were all residents. Its reputation for impregnability and harshness was deliberately encouraged by an American government intent on discouraging lawbreakers.

Al Capone, top gangster and Alcatraz resident.

Cellblocks for 336 men in individual cells. The escapers were held in B block.

Prison workshops. Work was a privilege at Alcatraz. Convicts were paid a small wage.

Homes for guards and their families. The children of Alcatraz were not allowed toy guns or knives, in case convicts stole them, and used them in an escape attempt.

Light House. At night the beacon flashed every five seconds.

Exercise yard. Ballgames were permitted during exercise periods.

Jetty. The *Warden Johnson* ferry made a 12 minute trip to the mainland 22 times a day, from 5:00am to 2:00am.

Warden's House. The last warden, Olin D. Blackwell, said "It's hard to find a prisoner to work in the house because if they can be trusted to do that, they don't belong on the island."

Cell blocks of Alcatraz

Each block had three rows of cells placed one on top of the other. By 1962 A and D Block were no longer in use.

Guard room and armoury

Library

D Block

C Block

C Block

Dining Hall

B Block

B Block

Warden's office

A Block

Kitchen

Fellow felons

Morris soon got to know his fellow felons. In the cell next door was Allen West, an accordion-playing New York car thief. Unlike the quiet Morris, West was full of boundless conversation.

In the canteen Morris met the Anglin brothers, John and Clarence – burly Florida farm hands, bank robbers and hardened prison veterans. Their cells were on the same level, farther down the corridor.

A way out ?

In conversation with another prisoner, Morris learned that three years before, a large fan motor was removed from a rooftop ventilator shaft above his block. It was never replaced. His sharp mind instantly envisaged a daring night-time getaway through the shaft. There was a way out of impregnable Alcatraz, just 9m (30ft) above his head.

Bank robber brothers John (left) and Clarence Anglin.

Inspiration strikes

Morris began to plot. It seemed impossible to reach the shaft from a locked cell, but one day inspiration struck.

A small air vent sat just below his sink. Beyond it lay a narrow utility corridor carrying water, electricity and sewer pipes. If Morris could take out the vent and make a hole big enough to crawl through, he could climb up to the rooftop ventilator shaft and out onto the roof. He picked at the

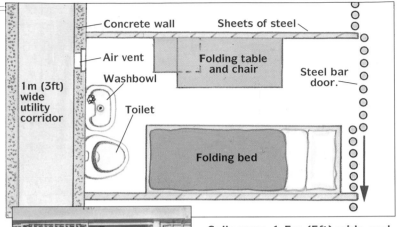

Concrete wall • Sheets of steel • Air vent • Folding table and chair • Steel bar door. • 1m (3ft) wide utility corridor • Washbowl • Toilet • Folding bed

concrete around the vent with nail clippers. Tiny flakes fell at his feet.

Hiding the hole would be difficult, but not impossible. An accordion like West's would be big enough to cover the early excavations. He ordered one, paying with money earned in the glove workshop.

A fake wall

Then he hit on the idea of making a false section of wall, complete with painted air vent. A dummy head could be made too, from papier-mâché, to place in his bed while he was away from the cell. The more he plotted, the more he realized this plan would work better with others to escape with him.

Escape committee

West and the Anglin brothers were recruited. Their close proximity in the cell block would be useful. The four became an escape committee. Their first move was to all take

Cells were 1.5m (5ft) wide and 2.5m (8ft) long. The bar doors were made of cable embedded in alloy steel.

up painting as a hobby. This gave them an excuse to order brushes, paints and drawing boards to make their dummy heads and false walls.

First steps

While West watched for patrolling guards from his adjoining cell, Morris began to dig away at the air vent with a nail clipper. After a slow hour he had collected a small pile of fragments.

Work stopped before lights-out, debris was cleaned away and the accordion placed over the evening's work. Morris's fingers ached. The nail clipper would take months to dig through the concrete.

A new tool

The team met next morning at breakfast. The Anglins had been digging too, and had found it tough going. A more solid tool was needed. Their breakfast spoons were good and heavy – perhaps they could be put to use?

Morris slipped his into a pocket, and that night he prepared his cell for some ingenious improvised metalwork. He broke the handle off the stolen spoon and removed the blade from his nail clippers. With this, he shaved slivers of silver from a dime. Then, he tied fifty or so matches into a tight bundle.

Morris intended to melt the silver to solder the blade to the spoon handle. The blade and handle were held in place above the matches with piles of books, and silver scraps were sprinkled between them. The matches were lit and a fierce heat welded silver, blade and handle together.

The new tool made digging less tiring, but even so, it was still not strong enough to hack through 20cm (8in) of concrete. Even greater ingenuity was needed.

West to the rescue

Making use of his job as a prison cleaner, West managed to steal a vacuum cleaner motor, and with parts pilfered from the prison workshop, he was able to turn it into a makeshift drill.

It was extremely noisy, and could only be used during the prison music hour, when inmates were allowed to play their instruments. So great was the risk of discovery that the escapers only used the drill to make the initial holes in their walls, and continued to chip away at the walls at night with their digging tools.

Drawing board wall

Work also began on the false walls, which would be made from drawing boards. They were painted the same shade as the cell wall, and an air vent was added.

When completed they were placed over the holes in the real walls which were chipped away to the same size. In bright light the fake walls would not survive a second glance, but in the dim recess of a cell they blended in well enough. Taking turns keeping watch, the escapers drilled and chipped at

their walls day after day. Eventually they made holes large enough to squeeze through.

Dummy heads

Next, pages from magazines were torn up, and soaked in the cell sinks. The soggy paper was mashed up into a pulp to make papier-mâché, and fashioned into the shape of four dummy heads. A few nights later the heads were dry enough to paint.

Clarence Anglin, who worked as a prison barber, added an authentic touch. He supplied his fellow escapers with plenty of hair, which was glued onto the scalps and eyebrows of the dummies. These they intended to leave poking out of their bedclothes while they were absent from their cells.

Trip to the top

When the heads were finished, Morris took a trip to the roof. He placed his dummy head in the bed and squeezed through into the utility corridor. It was dark and damp and smelled of the seawater that flowed through the sewage pipes. He climbed up a pipe through the tangle of conduits, mesh, wiring and catwalks, and reached the roof ventilator shaft. It hung down 1.5m (5ft) from the ceiling and took a sharp right angle 30cm (1ft) inside.

A spoon, nail clipper, matches and a silver dime were used to make digging tools.

Vacuum cleaner drill

Here is how a vacuum cleaner motor was used to drill holes in the cell walls.

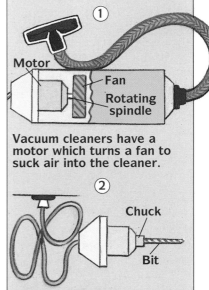

Vacuum cleaners have a motor which turns a fan to suck air into the cleaner.

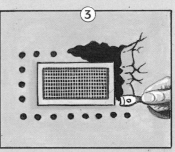

The motor from the cleaner, and a drill chuck and bit stolen from the prison workshop were attached to the spindle. (Motor was plugged into light socket in cell.)

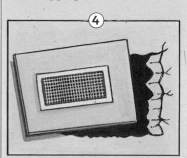

Holes drilled around air vent and concrete scooped out with digging tool.

False wall made from art class drawing board placed over hole.

Morris would need someone to help lift him inside. He also noted that there was ample space near the shaft to store material for the swim to the mainland, 2.5m (1.5 miles) away. The escapers planned to make water wings, or even a raft, from plastic raincoat sleeves. Filled with air, these would provide buoyancy in the numbing waters of the bay.

Stealing plastic raincoats was easy. A large pile was freely available near the basement workshop. John Anglin wore a new one every day on the way back to his cell.

Escape route blocked

Morris made another trip to the roof. Clarence Anglin came too, to help him into the shaft. What he saw inside filled him with misery. Although the fan blade and motor were no longer there, the top of the vent was still blocked by two bars,

An accordion was large enough to conceal a hole in the wall.

a grille and a rain hood. All were firmly anchored in position by solid steel rivets.

A new plan

Over the next few days Morris mulled over this setback. The two bars could be bent back with a length of pipe left in the utility corridor, but the rivet-held grille and hood were far more of a problem. The vacuum cleaner drill would have been handy, but the noise it would make in the still of the night made it impossible to use.

Carborundum string, a thin cord, coated in abrasive powder, was suggested. It was used to saw through metal in intricate repair work in the prison workshops. It would mean many more evenings of extra work, but this was the only way to remove the rivets. The cord was duly stolen.

By mid-summer of 1962, six months after the first digging began, the rivets were finally detached. The escapers replaced them with rivet-shaped balls of soap, which they painted black. They did not want a guard to peer into the shaft and notice the rivets were missing.

Time to go

Now nothing stood in their way. All they needed was to agree on a date. The Anglins pressed to go at once. Morris, ever cautious, wanted to research tides and currents in the treacherous water of the bay, so they agreed to wait for ten days.

The ventilator shaft rivets were removed with cord coated with abrasive powder.

But their anxiety was growing. Up in the ceiling a pile of sleeves and sleeveless raincoats awaited discovery.

Cell search

That week cells were being searched at random. Both Anglin brothers returned from meals to find subtle changes – a towel moved here, a book moved there. West was yet to be visited, but he worried incessantly about his fake wall, which kept slipping. There was a bag of cement in the tunnel, so he decided to patch up the fake wall until the night of the escape.

Premature departure

Seven days before the agreed date, the Anglins could wait no longer. Around nine o' clock on the evening of June 11, Morris heard a voice behind his fake wall. John Anglin was telling him they were going NOW. Before Morris could argue, Anglin was off up the corridor. Next door, West was panic-stricken. Unprepared, he began chipping at the hardened cement seal around his fake wall, choking with anger and frustration.

West deserted

Morris kept watch for West. For now, the clamour of the cell block's evening activities muffled West's frantic digging. But soon the lights would go out, and silence would fall on the block. Morris could wait no longer. He left the desperate West and climbed the pipe to the roof where the

Anglins were waiting. All agreed on the need for silence – whispers only, no banging. Noise travels further at night.

A dangerous mistake?

Squeezing into the shaft, Morris removed the soap rivet heads, his face starkly lit by the recurrent flash of the lighthouse beacon. The grille was gently eased from its moorings and handed down. But as the rain hood was lifted away, a gust of wind seized it, and it clattered noisily to the roof. Morris felt his muscles tense to near paralysis.

Below, the noise was noted by a patrolling guard. He consulted an officer. They were not too concerned. It could be a bucket, or an empty can of paint. There was plenty of loose junk to blow around in the wind.

Out on the roof

Five minutes passed before Morris emerged onto the roof, blinking at the dazzling beacon. The Anglins followed.

The route from rooftop to island shore passed by brightly floodlit areas, overlooked by gun towers. They could wait for a sea fog to settle on the island, or move immediately and risk being spotted. They moved onward.

Hugging the shadows, they crawled to the edge of the roof. Below was a 15m (50ft) drop. Morris lowered himself over the rim and onto the pipe with infinite slowness, lest a sudden movement catch the eye of a guard, and slid down the floodlit wall with the same deliberation. Reaching the bottom of the pipe without being seen, he crawled over to the safety of the shadows at the other end of the block. The others followed.

Into the ocean

They made their way over a succession of small barriers – a cyclone fence here, a barbed wire fence there – and down a shallow cliff to the seashore.

The mainland beckoned. Crouching in damp sand, the three inflated their raincoat water wings, then waded through a sharp wind into the dark, freezing waters of San Francisco Bay.

Empty beds

At daybreak guards sent to wake the missing men found only dummy heads in their empty beds. Other prison officers recalled the noise that roused their suspicions the night before. They estimated the escapers must have entered the water around 10:00pm, when the bay was calm, and the currents advantageous. If they survived the cold they had every chance of reaching the mainland.

Boats, planes, soldiers and dogs were sent out to find them. Two days later a plastic bag was recovered from the bay. Inside were sixty family-album photographs, addresses and a receipt belonging to Clarence Anglin.

After that, nothing. No bodies. No clothing. No sightings. No trace. The three could have been washed out to sea and drowned. But it was equally likely that they escaped. Whether they are still alive, or met an early death in the criminal underworld they no doubt returned to, no one knows.

As for West, he finally chipped away his false wall after midnight. He shinned up to the roof but Morris and the Anglins were long gone. Poking his head through the ventilator, he disturbed a flock of seagulls. They made such a screeching cacophony that he panicked, and fled back to his cell.

He spent the rest of his sentence wondering what would have happened if the Anglins had given fair warning of the escape. Maybe he'd be in a quiet backwater bar, with a long cool drink and a beautiful girl. Maybe he'd be lying at the bottom of the Pacific Ocean, his bleached bones picked clean by crabs.

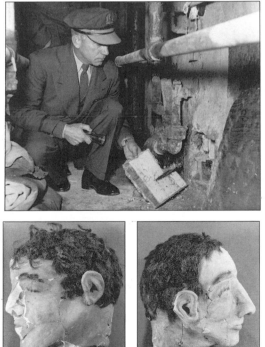

Right. A day after the breakout a guard inspects the hole and fake wall in the utility corridor behind the escapers' cells.

Below. The dummy heads used by Morris and the Anglin brothers in this escape can still be seen on display at the National Maritime Museum in San Francisco.

Ivan Bagerov – Royal Bulgarian Navy

Lieutenant Ivan Bagerov of the Royal Bulgarian Navy would present a benign, if slightly puzzling figure, to the minor officials he would encounter on his travels around northern Germany. He spoke almost no German, and carried a collection of Bulgarian documents that would be quite incomprehensible to the average policeman, guard, or railway ticket inspector.

At least that was what Bagerov hoped. He was really Lieutenant David James, of the British Royal Navy, and he was about to escape from the German prisoner of war camp of Marlag und Milag Nord, near Bremen. The year was 1943.

Ingenious outfit

His disguise, and the props that accompanied it, were ingenious. As a foreigner who spoke almost no German, he thought he would be most convincing posing as another foreigner. He decided he would be a naval officer, because his own uniform was a naval one.

Bulgaria was one of Germany's allies during the Second World War. James thought few people would know what their naval uniform looked like, especially as the Bulgarian navy was very small.

British Navy brass buttons.

Bulgarian Navy shoulder insignia.

To add credibility to this disguise, he sewed a gold and blue insignia to the shoulder of his uniform. On this, in the letters of the Bulgarian alphabet, were the initials KBVMF, which stood for Royal Bulgarian Navy.

A flimsy cover

Bulgaria was also a monarchy, like Britain, so this would explain the crowns on the brass buttons on James's naval uniform. James was gambling on the fact that no one he met would see though this flimsy disguise and recognize his British naval uniform.

The forged Bulgarian identity papers he carried were another asset. Every day, policemen and soldiers checked the papers of German civilians, or Dutch or French workers. They would probably have never seen a Bulgarian document before, and would be less likely to spot a forgery.

Pure fiction

The identity card was pure fiction. No one in his prisoner of war camp had any idea what this should look like. James had no photograph of himself, so a magazine picture of a German naval captain was used. The face was obscured by a fake Bulgarian stamp.

Once he reached friendly territory he would need to prove he really was David James. Rather than carry his real identity papers in his case, where they could be found by a curious soldier or policeman, he sewed them into the lining of his uniform. James made sure that everything in his suitcase looked Bulgarian. He even scraped the brand name

James's fictitious Bulgarian Navy identity card used a photograph taken from a magazine.

off his soap, and replaced it with a Bulgarian letter. Labels for his clothes were more difficult to change. Two Greek officers gave him their tailors' labels. The Greek lettering was nothing like the Bulgarian alphabet, but at least it was different from the British words on James's labels.

Love letters from a ballerina

Also in the case were several love letters, written in a Russian hand (which uses the same alphabet as Bulgaria), and a photograph of glamorous English ballet dancer Margot Fonteyn. James intended to tell anyone searching his luggage that Fonteyn was his Bulgarian fiancée. The picture would, he hoped, divert their attention.

A bogus letter of introduction to show to any suspicious official was also concocted by a friend in the camp. This was vague enough to explain his presence at any port he might be able to reach, and also excused his poor knowledge of German.

Almost everything in James's case was faked, or modified to make it look Bulgarian.

The letter read: "Lieutenant Bagerov is engaged in liaison duties of a technical nature which involve him in much travel. Since he speaks very little German, the usual benevolent assistance of all German officials is confidently solicited on his behalf."

Major setback

James planned to travel to the nearby city of Bremen were he could take a train to the coast. Unfortunately, just as he was about to begin his escape, a group of British naval prisoners from the camp were taken to Bremen for medical treatment. This meant that local people would know for certain what British naval uniforms looked like, and James's thin disguise would be even more risky.

Danish disguise

This problem was solved by modifying his uniform yet again. He would travel to Bremen dressed as a Danish workman, and take on his Bulgarian disguise at the station. James set about inventing a character for himself. He would become Christof Lindholm, a Danish electrician who was spending a few days in the countryside.

The brass buttons on his jacket were covered with black silk, and a cloth cap was made out of a pocket lining. A check scarf and grey flannel trousers completed the outfit.

Grave doubts

On the day of the escape, December 8, 1943, he began to have grave doubts. It was a horrible cold morning, there was a nice warm fire in his room, and besides, he was acutely nervous. But as so many fellow prisoners had helped him prepare for the escape, he felt he could not let them down.

The escape begins

Getting out of the prison camp was easy. James climbed out of a shower room window in a building right on the perimeter. Walking away in his disguise, he could have been any local workman.

Half way up the road away from the camp, James faced his first test. He was stopped and questioned by the local policeman. This man was suspicious and looked in his case. Fortunately James had had the foresight to hide his Bulgarian documents. They were strapped to his leg with sticking plaster. All the policeman could see were clothes, but still he was uncertain.

Roadside interrogation

The questioning began. Where was he staying? Who was he staying with? The first thought that came into James's head was that the local priest was looking after him. He did not know his name, and told the policeman he just referred to him as "Father". Thinking desperately, he tried to flesh out his story. He was staying in a church. The priest was an older man with grey hair. These rather obvious details were still not enough to convince his interrogator.

A fortunate forgery

However, James had another trick up his sleeve – a forged letter from the local hospital, telling him to report there that afternoon. This finally convinced the policeman, who sent the escaper on his way, and he reached Bremen station without further incident. Once there, he went into the station lavatory and changed into his Bulgarian naval officer's uniform, stuffing cap and trousers behind a water pipe. As a final touch he darkened his light hair and moustache with theatrical make-up, to try and make himself look convincingly eastern European.

Beer and tickets

Back on the platform he was stopped by a guard. James handed over his letter of introduction and was presently provided with an assistant. This man bought him a ticket to the port of Lübeck, found out which train he should take, and then took him to the waiting room and ordered him a beer.

The train arrived and James headed for the coast. Wherever he presented the fake Bulgarian pass, it was accepted without question, even though the only intelligible thing on it was a photo of someone else, and a serial number.

Changing trains at Hamburg, James went to the station restaurant to eat. Here he was eyed suspiciously by a German soldier sitting at his table. Fearful that the man could recognize his British uniform, James stared back defiantly, and embarrassed the soldier enough to make him turn away.

That night he spent an uncomfortable few hours in a waiting room in Bad Kleinen. He had covered almost 320km (200 miles) in a single day.

Noisy Nazis

Next day he continued on to the Baltic port of Stettin, sharing a compartment with several noisy Nazi soldiers. Here he got off and searched the town's docks for a Swedish ship. Sweden was a neutral country, and if the ship's crew could be persuaded to take him out of Germany, he could travel back to England from Sweden. But there were no Swedish ships in Stettin, so James consoled himself by visiting several of the town's bars, where he kept his ears open for any Swedish voices.

Lucky Lübeck?

He took the train to the port of Lübeck, breaking his journey overnight at Neu-Brandenburg to sleep at the *Wehrmachtsunterkunft* (a military rest camp similar to the YMCA). Again James felt extremely anxious that his uniform would be recognized.

James's escape route

James made his escape by rail, with tickets bought by helpful German officials.

84

He spent a very uncomfortable, uneasy night sleeping at a table opposite a German naval officer and several German sailors. But they must have been even more tired than he was, for they failed to recognize his uniform. Arriving at Lübeck he went first to a barber shop and asked for a shave. Two days of stubble on his chin was beginning to undermine his smart military appearance. This was a near fatal mistake. The

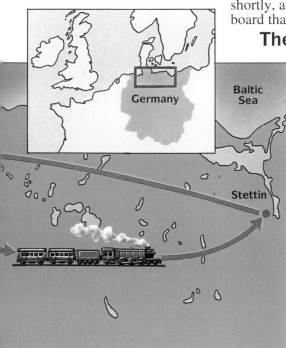

barber looked astonished, and as far as James could understand, said that soap was rationed, and that he had not been offering shaves to his customers for two years. James fled, attracting many a curious glance.

Swedish ships

Feeling flustered, James booked into a hotel, left his suitcase, and headed for the docks. Almost immediately he came upon a couple of Swedish ships. The dock gates were guarded, but James sneaked in by walking behind a goods van that passed between him and the sentry. James walked up the gangplank

of one of the ships, which was loading coal. He knocked on a cabin door and explained who he was, and asked if the crew could take him to Sweden.

The Swedish sailor he spoke to immediately recognized his uniform. He was friendly, but explained that the ship could not take him. They needed to refuel and several German dock hands would be coming aboard. He said that the other Swedish ship was leaving very shortly, and James should board that one.

The tide turns

James begged the Swedish sailor to let him stay. In the three days he had been on the run this was the first time he had felt safe, and now his nerve was going. Even the short walk between these two ships seemed like a huge, unreachable distance. But the Swede was adamant. If James stayed aboard he would be discovered by German dock hands.

As James reluctantly left the ship he saw to his dismay that the one he was heading for was casting off its ropes and leaving the quayside. He debated whether or not to run for the boat and jump onto the deck, but he knew someone would spot him and the boat would be stopped before it left German waters.

Dockyard detention

His luck had run out, and now things really started to go wrong. James was spotted leaving the docks and a guard insisted on taking him to the police station to have his papers thoroughly checked.

At the station a policeman examined the Bulgarian pass with a magnifying glass. The man looked up at him and said "Where did you escape from?". James had been caught.

Cordial captors

The conversation that followed was surprisingly cordial. While one policeman mocked his forged pass, another congratulated James on doing so well with the very limited resources available in a prison camp. He even told James he should have put *Polizei Präsident* instead of *Polizei Kommissar* on one document.

By now James had a small audience, and the local police were quite amused by his tale. The man who escorted him back to the local military jail said he was sorry he had had such bad luck.

Second time lucky

James was sent back to Marlag und Milag Nord, and spent ten days in a punishment cell. But this did not deter him. He escaped five weeks later, this time disguised as a merchant seaman. Taking the same route, he successfully boarded a ship to Sweden. Once in this neutral country he was able to return safely to England.

Knitting needle escape for Soviet master spy

Soviet spy George Blake

Soviet spy George Blake's escape from prison on October 22, 1966, began with a discussion about wrestling on television. Blake, an inmate of Wormwood Scrubs in West London, asked a guard whether he thought the fights were faked. The guard suspected nothing of the well-behaved prisoner, who was now four years into a 42 year sentence.

But this was no idle chat. The guard became so absorbed in the conversation that he failed to notice another inmate, who was a friend of Blake's, remove two panes of glass from a window above his head.

Outside assistance

Outside the prison, in an alley that separated it from Hammersmith Hospital, another friend of Blake's, Sean Bourke, waited nervously in a car. He carried a large pot of yellow chrysanthemums, and every so often he spoke into them. They concealed a walkie-talkie radio. Blake too had one of these radios, smuggled in by Bourke on a recent visit.

Celebration meal

Bourke had made friends with Blake in prison, and had recently been released. He had been planning this escape for a year and had confidently prepared a meal of steak, and strawberries and cream, to celebrate Blake's release.

When Bourke first arrived at the alley a prison official had frightened him off. But now he was back and waiting impatiently for Blake to let him know when to throw a ladder over the prison wall.

Wormwood Scrubs was a huge, drafty, understaffed, Victorian building. Many of its prisoners were small-time criminals, serving short sentences. Blake was an obvious exception, and his removal to a more high-security prison had been requested four times since he arrived there.

Unfortunately there were no suitable prisons for him in London. But the British secret service needed to interview him from time to time, and it was convenient for them to have him in the capital.

Popular prisoner

Despite public outrage caused by his spying, Blake was a popular man in Wormwood Scrubs. He taught illiterate prisoners to read and write and many inmates felt some sympathy for him. A few shared his communist beliefs, while others felt his 42 year sentence was too harsh. He had made several good friends in prison, and now they were prepared to help him escape.

George Blake's patchwork past

Blake came from a mixed background, and his loyalty lay with his belief in communism, rather than with any one country.

He was born in Holland, his mother was Dutch and his father was Egyptian. He fled to Britain during the Second World War, after fighting against the Nazis with the Dutch Resistance.

He became a British citizen and joined the navy, and then MI6, the British secret service.

It was here that he began to work for the communist Soviet Union (now Russia), passing on information about British spies working there and in eastern Europe.

Blake's spying caused outrage in Britain when newspapers reported he had betrayed 40 British spies.

No. 18,993

DAILY EXPRESS

TUESDAY JUNE 20 1961

9 a.m. forecast: Sunny

Price 3d.

40 AGENTS BETRAYED
AND ALL BY THIS MAN

New shock over spy Blake

By CHAPMAN PINCHER

GEORGE BLAKE, the Secret S...

Torchlight police hunt for nature boy Tony

TREATING THIS AS A CRIME

2 am: Miners in 'grave danger'

Escape recipe

Bourke was Blake's most important ally, and had planned this escape well. He began by contacting Blake's family to raise funds for the scheme. Blake's sister even flew in

Sean Bourke

from Bangkok, where she now lived, to discuss this.

The cost of the escape, Bourke calculated, would be around £700. He worked out exactly what was required to get Blake out of the country, and needed funds to cover the following items:

• One home-made rope ladder to throw over the prison wall – three clothes lines and 30 size 13 knitting needles to make rungs for the ladder.
• Two walkie-talkie radios to communicate between the prison and outside world.
• One pot of chysanthemums to hide the walkie-talkie.
• One set of civilian clothes. (Blake wore a prison uniform.)
• One getaway car – a Humber Hawk.
• One hideaway. (This would need a month's rent paid in advance, plus weekly rent until it was no longer needed.)
• Two boat/plane tickets to Europe.
• Two false passports.

Bourke soon squabbled with the family however, as they wanted him to account for every penny he spent. They were naturally suspicious of a man who had been to prison, and could not be sure that he was a genuine friend of Blake's. They also felt that his plan was too simple to work.

Damning evidence

Bourke, on the other hand, felt it was unreasonable of them to expect him to keep receipts for forged documents, and did not want to store up evidence against himself if the police became suspicious. He turned instead to friends who were sympathetic to Blake, and they provided the money he needed.

Faking a passport

This is how Sean Bourke prepared a fake passport for himself. Due to changes in British passport design this technique is now no longer possible.

1
Remove photograph from stolen passport by holding over steam, taking care not to damage the stamp on it.

2
Mix up quantity of plaster of Paris. Press part of photo with stamp on down hard in plaster of Paris. Leave to set, then remove photo.

3
Place new passport photo on indent in plaster of Paris. Scribble hard over back with pencil.

4
Stamp will be transferred to new photo.

5
Place new photo in position on old passport, taking care to match the transferred stamp with the stamp on the passport.

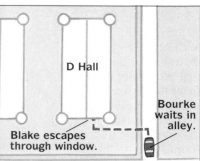

Wormwood Scrubs prison in West London. When Blake leapt from the top of the wall into this alley, he broke his wrist.

Escape route blocked

By the autumn of 1966 the escape plan was finalized, but this was nearly ruined by another breakout, which took place in D Hall where Blake himself was held.

Four men broke out of a large window at the end of the hall, which Blake intended to use, and climbed over the prison wall. Plans were immediately made to place wire mesh over all large windows in the prison.

Blake breaks out

The window at D Hall was only a week away from being strengthened when George Blake made his escape. He and Bourke had planned it for a Saturday, between six and seven o'clock. At this time the hall was quiet, with few guards in attendance. Most guards and prisoners were at a weekly film show in the prison theatre.

As soon as Blake was alone he contacted Bourke on his walkie-talkie to make sure he was ready, and headed for the window where a hole had just been made for him. He squeezed through, leapt down to a porch roof, and onto a flat waste container.

From here, he leapt to the ground and his next hurdle was the outer prison wall. This was where Bourke would prove most useful. Using his walkie-talkie, Blake told him he had escaped out of the window and was now by the wall. Bourke was busy trying to get rid of a car containing a courting couple, and did not reply for several minutes.

Blake crouched in the dark expecting to be spotted at any second by a patrolling guard. Eventually Bourke hurled the rope ladder over the 6m (20ft) wall, and Blake climbed up it.

A painful fall

The wait for Bourke had unnerved Blake. He knew that if he was caught he would probably never have another chance. In his desperation to escape he jumped down from the top of the high wall and landed badly, breaking his wrist and cutting his face.

Bundled away

Bourke bundled him into the back of his car, leaving the ladder and chrysanthemums behind. In their haste to get away they nearly ran over two hospital visitors, and bumped into the back of another car. Flustered and near panic, Bourke drove off to merge into the early evening London traffic. He had succeeded in freeing Blake, now he had to keep him hidden.

Bourke had prepared a house near the prison as a hideaway for them both. They would lie low for a month or so, and then try to leave the country. When they arrived there Blake's face was streaming with blood and his left hand hung limp on his wrist. A doctor was clearly going to be needed.

Bourke went off to dump the car, which he was sure the police would soon be looking for. He returned to the house with whiskey and brandy to celebrate their success.

They spent the evening watching television, where news of the escape was interrupting the evening schedule. The next day a sympathetic doctor was found. He fixed Blake's broken wrist, but it was a terribly painful business.

Chrysanthemum calling card

For the next few days the newspapers continued to be full of stories about the escape, many of them quite fantastic. Some newspapers assumed the pot of chrysanthemums Bourke had left at the scene of the escape was a mysterious calling card.

One national radio station even reported a theory that Blake had never been in prison at all. A substitute had been sent in his place and allowed to escape, while Blake had returned to Moscow as a double-agent.

With so much interest in Blake's escape, his liberators began to worry about keeping his location secret. He and Bourke were taken to another house, but had to move shortly after. (The wife of the couple who were sheltering them had told her psychiatrist that they were hiding two men from the police.)

By now Bourke's getaway car, which he had carelessly used his own name to buy, had been found. The police were making intense efforts to locate him, and his name was given to radio, television and newspapers.

Berlin getaway

By early November, the two men were hiding in the home of Bourke's friend Pat Pottle, who had provided some of the funds to finance the escape. Blake was exhausted by his ordeal and anxious to leave the country as soon as possible. It was decided that the safest course of action would be to hide him in a car and drive to communist East Germany*.

Camper van hideaway

Bourke offered to drive, but this idea was quickly rejected. If he was recognized he would be arrested and his car would be searched at once. So another friend, Michael Randle, volunteered. He would take his family and pretend to be going on holiday to East Germany. Money left in the escape fund was used to buy a camper van, and its blanket compartment was enlarged so that Blake could be concealed within it.

Carsick spy

Randle set off on Saturday December 17, reaching East Germany without a hitch. A stiff and slightly carsick Blake was dropped off a short distance outside East Berlin and left to make contact with the local authorities. The East German soldiers he introduced himself to did not believe who he was.

Blake had to argue forcibly to persuade them to contact the Soviet intelligence service in East Berlin. When this was finally done an officer who knew Blake was sent to identify him.

When this man walked in and hugged Blake, shouting "It's him! It's him!", the renegade spy knew his troubles were over. Several days later he was flown to Moscow, the capital of the Soviet Union.

Bourke escapes

Bourke slipped out of the country on a false passport, flying from London to Berlin, and from there to Moscow. He intended to stay in Moscow for a while and then return to his native Ireland when the fuss had died down. The KGB (Soviet secret police) had different ideas.

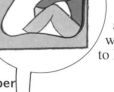

Michael Randle's Volkswagen camper van. Blake spent most of the 36 hour journey hiding in the blanket box.

They wanted him to stay in the Soviet Union for at least five years more.

Moscow betrayal

Blake and Bourke were naturally delighted to see each other, and several celebration meals followed. They got on so well that Blake suggested that he and Bourke live together. But the two soon quarrelled. Blake had been cordial and charming in Wormwood Scrubs, but now he was arrogant and ill-mannered. He turned on the man who had set him free, and even hinted to the KGB that Bourke should be eliminated. Bourke spent two years trying to persuade the KGB to let him return to Ireland.

Betrayed by his friend and uncomfortable in the Soviet Union, this was a poor reward for someone who had risked everything to assist Blake in his escape. He was finally allowed to go home to Ireland in October, 1968.

Moscow

United Kingdom

Berlin

London

Randle drove Blake to communist East Berlin. From there he was flown to Moscow.

* At the time, the eastern part of Germany was controlled by the Soviet Union.

Plüschow's dockland disguise

For Kapitänleutnant Gunter Plüschow of the German Naval Air Service, the summer of 1915 was the most tedious he had spent in his life. Held captive at Donington Hall prisoner of war camp, England, he was aching to escape and return to fight for his country in the First World War.

The camp itself was not too unpleasant. He received parcels and letters from home, and poured his frustrations into playing endless games of hockey. But Plüschow, a lively, energetic man, found the constraints of captivity difficult to bear.

Chinese dragon

He began the war in one of its more remote battlefields – China. Here he had acquired a Chinese dragon tattoo, an unusual adornment for an officer. The war here had gone badly for Germany, and Plüschow had just managed to escape with his life from a besieged city. He succeeded in boarding a steamship to San Francisco, USA, and made his way to New York, where he took a boat to Italy. (At this stage of the war the USA and Italy were both neutral countries.)

Unfortunately for him, the boat stopped at the British port of Gibraltar where he was arrested as a prisoner of war, and sent on to Donington Hall stately home, near Derby in England.

Oberleutnant Trefftz

At Donington he met with Oberleutnant Trefftz, who spoke English, and knew England well. Plüschow decided they would make a good team, and suggested they escape together. Trefftz agreed, and the two set about plotting their getaway.

Kapitänleutnant Gunter Plüschow of the German Naval Air Service.

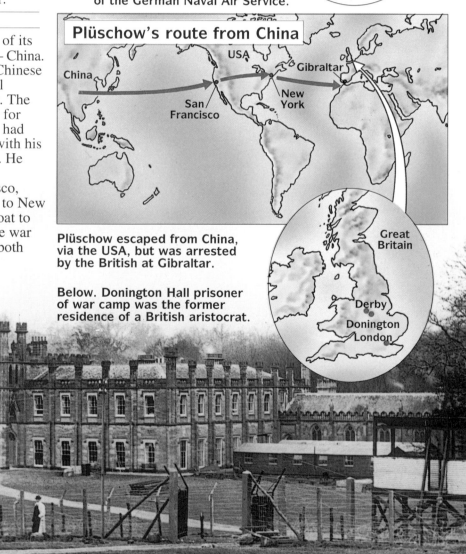

Plüschow's route from China

China · San Francisco · USA · New York · Gibraltar

Plüschow escaped from China, via the USA, but was arrested by the British at Gibraltar.

Below. Donington Hall prisoner of war camp was the former residence of a British aristocrat.

Great Britain · Derby · Donington · London

Plüschow's plan

Plüschow knew from camp gossip that the town of Derby, with its rail link to London, lay a few miles to the north. Once in London he and Trefitz could stow away on a boat heading for a neutral country, such as Holland, and then return to their homeland.

They began by making a detailed study of the guards' routine and camp security. There were two main areas, a day and a night boundary. The day boundary took in the grounds of Donington Hall, which were encircled by a large barbed wire fence. At night, all prisoners retired to the night boundary, which surrounded the camp huts.

Hostile territory

Both men knew breaking out of the camp would be relatively easy. The real difficulty would be crossing hundreds of miles of hostile territory. Plüschow and Trefitz told their fellow officers about their plans, and enlisted their help to keep their getaway hidden from the camp guards.

Sick list

The escape began on July 4, 1915, when both men claimed to be ill. Their names were placed on the camp sick list, and they were given permission to stay in bed while the other prisoners attended roll call.

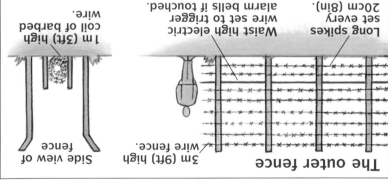

The outer fence

Long spikes set every 20cm (8in).

Waist high electric wire set to trigger alarm bells if touched.

3m (9ft) high wire fence.

Side view of fence.

1m (3ft) high coil of barbed wire.

After a day of rest, they got up around 4:00pm. Plüschow put on a suit he had bought with him from China, a blue sweater, and a smart grey overcoat. The prisoners wore their own military uniforms around the camp so both men wore officers' caps and coats over their escape outfits. After they had dressed they ate as many buttered rolls as they could bear, for they knew they were unlikely to find food on their journey.

Garden hiding place

Outside, it was perfect escape weather. Torrential rain fell in sheets. The camp guards stood frozen and miserable in their sentry boxes, in no mood to keep a sharp eye out for escapers. The two men wandered into the park within the day boundary of the camp. A few footsteps away from the barbed wire perimeter there was a large pile of garden chairs. They looked around to make sure no one was watching them, and then crouched down and hid among the chairs.

An hour passed. The camp clock struck six – the cue for the evening roll call. This was the time when help from their fellow prisoners would be most useful. The two escapers were reported sick, and as soon as the roll call was over, two German officers ran back to Plüschow and Trefitz's beds. The camp guard sent to check on them saw two sleeping figures, and marked them present.

After the roll call the day boundary became forbidden territory for the prisoners, and the sentries withdrew to the night boundary. This left the two escapers outside the guarded area of the camp.

Final hurdle

There was one final hurdle to overcome. Just before bedtime a guard checked on all prisoners by going from hut to hut. Plüschow and Trefitz's comrades knew this routine well. They made sure the two escapers' beds were occupied when the guard entered their rooms.

Footsteps from freedom

Crouching in the dark, the two men listened for any sign that their escape had been discovered. An hour passed. Silently they crept from their hiding place and began an uncomfortable climb over the three barbed wire fences that made up the outer perimeter. They crossed without serious mishap, although Plüschow did tear a large hole in his trousers.

London bound

Once beyond the wire the men discarded their army clothing. As they walked briskly away an English soldier loomed out of the dark. They had already agreed what to do if this occurred. As the man approached the escapers embraced like two lovers and the soldier walked away, tutting with embarrassment. Shortly afterwards they came to a sign post. It was so dark Treffitz had to climb up it to feel the letters with his fingers. It said "Derby" – they were on the right track.

Roadside wash and brush-up

They walked throughout the night, arriving at the outskirts of Derby as dawn broke. Here they stopped to tidy themselves up. Plüschow repaired his trousers with the needle and thread he always carried with him, and both men shaved, using spit as shaving soap. They headed for the railway station and then separated, agreeing to meet on the steps of St. Paul's Cathedral in London, at seven that evening.

Plüschow's journey passed without incident but that night Treffitz did not appear at St. Paul's. A weary Plüschow made his way to Hyde Park in central London intending to find a quiet place to sleep.

Hedge seat for a concert

The park was closed so he crept into the garden of a nearby house and hid under a thick hedge. After an hour several people came out to enjoy the cool night air. Plüschow, fearing he would be discovered at any moment, lay rigid with fright. As they wandered around, a beautiful soprano voice accompanied by a piano floated out across the garden.

Lulled by the singing, Plüschow drifted off to sleep.

The sound of a policeman's boots tramping along the road woke him early next morning. Fearing he would be spotted, he made his way to Hyde Park, which opened at dawn, and slept on a bench until 9:00am.

Wanted!

His sleep refreshed him, but his spirits sank when he went into a station. A huge poster announced news of his escape. It stated that Treffitz had been captured, and the police were looking for Plüschow. A newspaper he bought gave a very accurate description of his appearance and tattoo. It went on to say:

"He is particularly smart and dapper in appearance, has very good teeth, which he shows somewhat prominently when talking or smiling, is very English in manner and knows this country well."

Knowing he might be recognized at any time made Plüschow very nervous. He needed to change his appearance at once, starting with his stylish overcoat. This he decided to leave in a cloakroom at Blackfriars Station. When handing it over, the attendant asked his name. Plüschow's anxiety boiled over. He replied in German:

"Meinen?" (Mine?)

"Oh I see" said the attendant. "Mr. Mine, M.i.n.e." and handed over a receipt. Two policemen stood nearby watching inquisitively, no doubt wondering why Plüschow looked so terrified. He needed a quiet spot to hide away and calm down.

On the run in London

Plüschow arrived in London to find his escape and description featured prominently in the papers. He headed for Tilbury Docks, where he hoped to stow away aboard a boat to Europe.

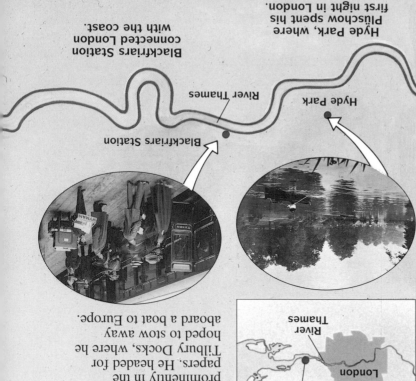

River Thames

Tilbury Docks

London

Blackfriars Station connected London with the coast.

Hyde Park, where Plüschow spent his first night in London.

River Thames

Blackfriars Station

Hyde Park

Hat, collar and tie were thrown into the River Thames. He rubbed Vaseline, boot-black and coal dust into his scalp, to make his blond hair black and greasy. He dirtied his clothes, and found a flat cap to wear.

Dockworker disguise

Smart and dapper Gunter Plüschow was gone. In his place stood George Mine, dock worker. Plüschow even altered his posture, slouching about with hands in pockets, and spitting casually, as he imagined dock workers did.

Next day, on top of a bus he overheard two businessmen talking. They said a Dutch steamer arrived at Tilbury Docks every afternoon, leaving early next morning for Holland. Plüschow caught a train to Tilbury at once.

The Mecklenburg

Arriving at the docks an hour later he went down to the riverside and sure enough, a Dutch steamer, the *Mecklenburg*, arrived. Plüschow decided he would swim out to her under cover of darkness, hide on board, and then jump ship at Holland. But getting aboard was to be more difficult than he imagined.

Slimy, stinking mud

Standing on the river bank Plüschow sank to his hips in stinking, slimy mud. Making a desperate grab for a plank, he

Plüschow as George Mine. Boot polish and Vaseline transformed the dapper German officer.

Tilbury Docks was London's main port for neutral Holland.

Tilbury Docks

saved himself from a horrible drowning death.

The next night he stole a small dinghy, and began to row towards the *Mecklenburg*. But the boat filled with water and ran aground. Plüschow waded wearily through the mud back to dry land.

Finally he succeeded in reaching the steamer with another stolen boat. Climbing the ship's anchor cable and hauling himself on board, he hid under the canvas cover of a lifeboat. In this safe haven he collapsed, and sank into an exhausted sleep.

Across the channel

Plüschow was awakened by the ship's shrill siren several hours later, and peeped from under the canvas cover to see that the *Mecklenburg* was docking in Holland. He was now in a neutral country, and free to travel home. Pulling out his knife, he sliced open the canvas and with a dramatic flourish stood up, revealing himself to all. He expected to be arrested at once by the ship's crew, but much to his surprise, he was ignored completely. The crew were too busy landing the boat, the passengers were preoccupied with their luggage.

Exit forbidden

Ambling off the boat with the passengers, Plüschow sneaked through a door marked "Exit forbidden". He was eager to avoid having to explain himself to customs officials, and once through, he was free.

That night he booked into a hotel, had a long bath, and ate enough for three. The following day, July 13, 1915, he took the train for Germany. Pacing about his compartment, too excited to sit down, he was at last heading for home.

Harry Houdini – escaping for a living

The packed theatre crowd simmered with excitement. Harry Houdini had just performed a series of escapes that had left them perplexed and astonished.

He had wrestled out of a straitjacket, and then changed places, in the blink of an eye, with an assistant locked within a rope-bound box. Now he was to perform an escape so dangerous he could drown attempting it.

Underwater terror

An iron can, large enough to hold a man, was placed in the middle of the stage and filled with water. Houdini appeared in a bathing suit and announced he was to be placed inside, and padlocked in.

He told the crowd he would demonstrate how long he could remain underwater, and invited the healthiest among them to hold their own breath as he submerged. Then he stepped into the can and vanished. After one or two minutes the audience were gasping for breath, but Houdini himself emerged three minutes later.

Locked in

Houdini was then handcuffed and taking a final deep breath, he disappeared under the water. A lid was placed on top and secured with locks. A small curtain was placed just in front of the can. A single spotlight shone on the curtain as the theatre band played a tune called *Many Brave Hearts Lie Asleep in the Deep*.

Two minutes went by, then three. The crowd grew anxious. Three and a half minutes passed. Then, a dripping wet Houdini emerged from behind the curtain, breathless but triumphant. The theatre erupted into thunderous applause.

HOUDINI'S DEATH-DEFYING MYSTERY
ESCAPE FROM A GALVANIZED IRON CAN FILLED WITH WATER AND SECURED BY MASSIVE LOCKS.

FAILURE MEANS A DROWNING DEATH

Poster and publicity photograph for the water can trick. Houdini often escaped wearing a swimsuit, to prove to his audience there were no tools or keys hidden in his clothing.

One row of rivets on the can was false. Once the stage curtain was drawn, Houdini pushed up the top of the churn and escaped.

World famous

When Houdini took this act around North America and Europe in 1908, he was the world's most famous escape artist. Many of his audience thought he had magical powers. They said he could vanish into thin air, or slip through a keyhole.

Unique ability

Many of Houdini's tricks relied on deceptions and illusions familiar to most magicians, but he also had two exceptional abilities which made his act unique.

The first sprang from a fascination with locks. There was not a lock in the world he could not pick. He worked this skill into his act by escaping from handcuffs and padlocked manacles. He invited audiences to bring their own locks or cuffs, to prove that the ones he opened up were not fake.

Houdini's other great asset was his body. He was very muscular, fit and agile. His fingers were strong enough to untie knots or buckles through a canvas bag or straitjacket. His feet were almost as nimble as his hands, and he could also unfasten knots and buckles with his teeth. He trained himself to hold his breath (to allow him to stay underwater) for over four minutes.

New tricks

When he first became famous his act was based mainly around his lock picking abilities. But he realized this would not interest people forever. Part of Houdini's success lay in knowing when to move on. He was constantly striving to offer his audience a new and exciting escape.

Upside-down straitjacket

Escaping from a straitjacket had long been part of his act. It was not a trick – Houdini relied on his own brute strength and agility to wrestle out of this canvas and leather restraint. He kept audiences interested in the stunt by performing it in public, suspended upside down from a construction crane, or dangling from the top of a tall building.

Even more exhausting was the wet sheet escape. Here Houdini was wrapped in two linen sheets, and tied with bandages to a metal frame bed. The sheets were then soaked in warm water, which tightened them around his body. With intense effort, Houdini then proceeded to wriggle out. The trick held a curious fascination for him, and he continued to perform it even though most audiences found it unexciting.

Lock picking

Locks can be opened with a special metal strip or wire (called a pick) instead of a key. A key works in a lock by lifting a series of levers and a skilled lock picker can lift these levers with a pick. This is very difficult and requires a detailed knowledge of the structure of the lock being picked.

Straitjacket escape, Broadway, New York, USA. Stunts such as this generated excellent free publicity for Houdini's stage performances.

Any escape stunt that was suggested by his audience always attracted far more interest than one Houdini concocted himself. He began to accept challenges to escape from boxes or cases that anyone, whether manufacturers or members of the public, could provide. These would be displayed in a theatre foyer, and could be examined by whoever wanted to see them.

A trusted assistant would break into the theatre at night and alter these containers. He would replace long nails with short ones, or file through screws or bolts. He was careful to make sure his tamperings were not discovered, and there was nothing to arouse the suspicions of the audience who watched Houdini emerge, as if by magic, from these containers.

Chinese torture

Another trick, called the Chinese water torture cell, was similar to the water churn escape. Houdini had his ankles placed into wooden stocks and was lowered headfirst into a tank full of water (see poster below). This escape was very popular. Even today, only a handful of people know how he did it.

Bridge jumps

Houdini was also an expert at generating his own publicity. He would publicize theatre appearances by leaping off bridges into rivers, tied by chains, or weighed down with an iron ball.

A chained Houdini about to jump into the Charles River, Boston, USA. His wife Bess stands behind him.

One bridge jump in Pittsburg attracted an audience of over 40,000 people. The danger was all too obvious. In the dark water no stage hand could save him if anything went wrong.

When stunts such as this became too familiar to attract much attention, he made them even more daring. In New York in the summer of 1912, a manacled Houdini was nailed into a weighted box, which was then bound with rope and steel cables, and lowered into the East River. As thousands watched, he cheated death before their eyes, emerging from the water moments later.

Near fatal mistakes

The need for constant variety had a price. In a variation of the water can escape, the container was filled with beer.

Houdini was overcome with alcohol fumes, and had to be rescued. On another occasion he was chained up inside the body of a giant squid. Fumes from the chemicals used to preserve the animal nearly killed him. But Houdini was not deterred. Even in his late 40s he continued to think up more daring escapes and stunts. He even planned on escaping from a block of ice, or being buried alive, but both of these were too dangerous to perform.

Houdini and water

Crowds became more excited the longer Houdini stayed underwater, so he trained himself to submerge for as long as possible in his bathtub at home. Iceblocks were also placed in the tub, to get his body prepared for winter bridge jumps.

An untimely death

After a lifetime of genuine danger, his death was the result of an unfortunate incident. In Montreal, a student named J. Gordon Whitehead asked if it was true he could be punched in the stomach without feeling pain. This was so, said Houdini, but first he had to brace himself – that is, tense his muscles. On hearing this Whitehead attacked in a frenzy, lashing out before he was ready.

12 hours to live

Houdini insisted he had not been badly hurt, but he collapsed in Detroit a few days later and was rushed to hospital with a ruptured appendix. Doctors gave him 12 hours to live, but Houdini refused to die. Fighting for his life he told visitors he would soon be back on his feet. But his body was fatally poisoned. He struggled for seven days and died on Halloween – October 31, 1926.

Harry Houdini – A lifetime escaping

1874 Erich Weiss, known as Houdini, is born on March 3, in Budapest, Hungary to Rabbi Samuel and Cecilia Weiss. He is one of six children.

1878 The family move to USA.

1888 Takes job as tie-cutter in New York factory.

1891 Becomes professional magician and escaper. Takes stage name Houdini, after his hero, French magician Robert-Houdon. Spends seven years performing to indifferent audiences, earning $25 a week.

1894 Meets fellow performer Bess Rahmer – one of The Floral Sisters (billed as "Neat Song and Dance Artists"). They marry within a fortnight. Bess becomes his stage assistant. (Houdini is a devoted husband, and writes daily love letters, even though he and his wife are hardly ever apart.)

1899 Hits on the idea of a public "Challenge", where audience is invited to provide their own locks and chains. His wages pick up.

Success in Europe

1900 Travels to Europe. Agent arranges visit to London Police Headquarters. Houdini handcuffed to a pillar by police who say they will return in an hour to free him. Houdini escapes before they have even left the room.

1901 Great success in Germany. Krupps steelworks in Essen make manacles especially for him. Riot at the theatre when thousands turn up to watch him escape.

German police, worried that he is encouraging criminals, accuse him of cheating. Houdini sues. He escapes from locks and cuffs in front of a judge and jury and wins the case.

Challenge to the World

1903 Issues "Challenge to the World". Offers $1,000 to anyone who can better him.

His act is the most popular in Europe. He now earns up to $2,000 a week.

1905 Returns to America where he is equally acclaimed. In one successful publicity stunt he escapes from the

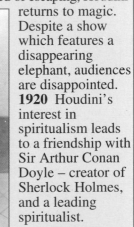

Houdini's films featured dramatic stunts and escapes.

former prison cell of Charles J. Guiteau (assassin of President Garfield in 1881). Further escapes from giant footballs, iron boilers and sealed glass boxes ensure packed out performances.

1906 Begins to publicize shows by jumping off bridges, tied by locks and chains.

1910 Buys aircraft, a Voisin bi-plane, and becomes obsessed with flying. During a trip to Australia, becomes the first person to fly there. Flying takes up so much of his time and energy, his performances suffer, so he gives it up.

1913 Becomes interested in spiritualism (communicating with the souls of the dead) following the death of his mother whom he loved intensely. Although he longs to believe in it, his experience as a magician convinces him that the spirit appearances and voices he witnesses at spiritualist gatherings are fake.

Returns to magic

1918 Tired of escaping, Houdini returns to magic. Despite a show which features a disappearing elephant, audiences are disappointed.

1920 Houdini's interest in spiritualism leads to a friendship with Sir Arthur Conan Doyle – creator of Sherlock Holmes, and a leading spiritualist.

Film failure

1921 Sets up film company to make films featuring escapes. Houdini is a poor actor, and finds love scenes deeply embarrasing. After initial success, company goes bankrupt.

1924 Publishes a book, *A Magician Among the Spirits,* which describes spiritualism as a fraud. Doyle is deeply offended, and his friendship with Houdini ends.

1926 Following a violent assault in Montreal, Houdini collapses in Detroit. He dies of a burst appendix, on October 31, and is buried next to his mother in New York.

Colditz Castle – escape-proof ?

Towering over the town of Colditz, in east Germany, is a grey granite, high-walled castle. During the Second World War it was used as a high-security prison for persistent escapers from German prisoner of war camps. Nazi Reichsmarschall Hermann Goering visited and declared it escape-proof.

International escapers

The castle could hold 800 prisoners – men from all over the world who had fought against Nazi Germany. There were over 800 guards. Every day of the year, four times a day, a parade was held where every man was counted. Sometimes the men were even called out in the dead of night, and stood shivering for hours, until their captors were satisfied that every one of the prisoners was present.

Soldiers with guard dogs stalked the courtyards and catwalks which covered the high walls and battlements. Machine gun posts were set up on roofs and watchtowers. At night searchlights probed every shadow. Sound detectors listened for digging noises, or any other clues of escapers at work.

Over, under, or disguise

Despite these fierce restrictions hundreds of escape attempts were made between 1939 and 1945. As with any prison there were basically two ways out. One was to perfect a convincing disguise and walk out of the castle gates under the noses of the guards. This required great courage, but worked for some. The other was to find a way over or under the castle walls with the minimum risk of death or detection.

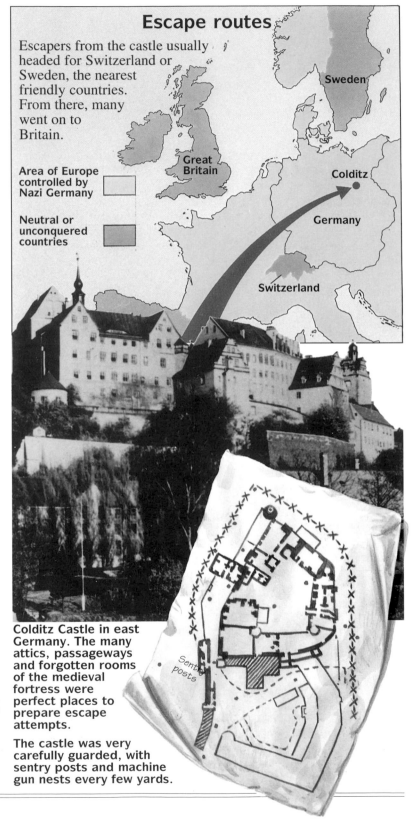

Escape routes

Escapers from the castle usually headed for Switzerland or Sweden, the nearest friendly countries. From there, many went on to Britain.

Area of Europe controlled by Nazi Germany

Neutral or unconquered countries

Sweden

Great Britain

Colditz

Germany

Switzerland

Senby posts

Colditz Castle in east Germany. The many attics, passageways and forgotten rooms of the medieval fortress were perfect places to prepare escape attempts.

The castle was very carefully guarded, with sentry posts and machine gun nests every few yards.

Sheet rope escape

Some escapers tried the most obvious routes out of the castle. In May 1941, two Polish officers, Lieutenants Surmanowicz and Chmiel, made a rope of knotted bed sheets.

Attic breakout

They broke into an attic which had a window overlooking the castle wall, and began to climb carefully down the 37m (120ft) drop. Unfortunately Chmiel's heavy boots made a loud scraping sound as they passed by the guardroom window. The two were spotted at once by a suspicious officer and guns were swiftly pointed at the helpless escapers.

The Polish prisoners' sheet rope. Such obvious escape plans were usually unsuccessful.

Doomed escapes

The authorities at Colditz used several strategies to demoralize escapers. Sometimes, when an escape plan was discovered, the camp guards let the prisoners continue with their efforts. They felt it was better to have inmates working on a project they knew about, than on one they did not.

They also felt that stopping an escape at the last moment, after so much painstaking planning, would be more disheartening, and discourage prisoners from plotting further escapes.

Wasted – eight months of digging for their lives

Most escapes involved months of preparation. In 1941, 21 French officers spent eight months digging a tunnel which began underneath the castle clock tower. The entrance was reached by climbing 33m (110ft) down the inside of the tower on a rope ladder. After several weeks of digging, the guards realized a tunnel was being built. They noticed a ceiling beam in the French quarters had begun to crack. A search of the attic above revealed huge heaps of earth and rock.

Top to bottom search

The tunnel entrance was so cleverly hidden however, that a top to bottom search of the castle failed to find it. In the middle of the night the French could even be heard digging away, but still their tunnel could not be found.

Eventually their luck ran out.

A German officer remembered that the clock tower had only been given the briefest of inspections in the initial search. The floorboards at the top of the tower were removed, and a small guard was lowered into the dark shaft. At once he heard the French digging away. Soldiers were immediately sent to the tower basement where the entrance was discovered. By now the tunnel reached beyond the castle walls and eight months' work had been wasted, only days before an escape could have been made.

The entrance to the tunnel was hidden in a disused wine cellar underneath the castle clock tower.

The tunnel reached under the castle walls before it was discovered. It ran through hardened timbers, solid rock, and heaps of earth.

Electricity was diverted from the prison chapel to light the tunnel. If guards approached, the lights could be flashed on and off as a warning.

Bed boards were used as props, to prevent the tunnel from collapsing.

Dummy Moritz dupes guards while two escape down drain

There were other, more cunning attempts to break out of the castle. A group of Dutch prisoners discovered a manhole in a park next to the castle, where men were taken to exercise. It would be a perfect place to leave a couple of escapers behind.

Cloak camouflage

The first to try out the manhole were Lieutenants Larive and Steinmetz. For the plan to work they needed the help of their fellow prisoners. On the day of the escape they were smuggled into the park by a group of Dutch inmates, hidden beneath the cloaks of the two tallest men. The escapers had not been counted by the guards on the way to the park, so they would not be missed on the way back.

Once in the park the group gathered and pretended to hold a Bible class, huddling close around the manhole. Larive and Steinmetz, hidden by the crowd, eased off the cover with a makeshift lever and climbed inside.

To conceal their absence at the next parade two dummies, dubbed Max and Moritz, had been created. A Polish officer who was an amateur sculptor, made two heads with plaster. This was obtained by bribing a local builder who frequently visited the castle. Paint stolen from prison art classes added realistic features. The heads were placed on long army coats, and carried like ventriloquist dummies. In the middle of a rank of men they went unnoticed.

An escape success

That night, the two Dutchmen emerged from the manhole to begin a successful escape to Switzerland. Over the next few weeks four more men escaped in this way (although two were later recaptured). The scheme eventually fell apart when guards noticed another two men being smuggled into the manhole. The dummies were not found until several months later, and were used to cover roll call absences for other escapers.

Dutch officers with Moritz the dummy.

Escape equipment

In order to escape across hostile territory, the right clothes, fake passes, maps, and a compass, were all invaluable. Here are some of the ingenious items manufactured in Colditz to help escapers on their way.

Compass in walnut shell.

Playing cards. The backs peeled off. Put together in the right order they would make a map.

Forged travel document. A typewriter was built to imitate typefaces on official German documents. Each letter was carved from wood.

Fake document stamps cut from linoleum.

Rooftop flight

The most daring escape plan of all involved the use of a glider, which was designed and built by a team of British airmen led by Flight Lieutenants Jack Best and Bill Goldfinch. It had a 10m (33ft) wingspan and was large enough to carry two men.

Secret workshop

The glider was built over ten months at one end of a long attic and hidden from view by a false wall made of wood and hessian fabric. This was camouflaged with plaster and mud to match the shade of the surrounding walls. Jack Best, who had been a farmer in Kenya, had learned how to make African mud huts, so he supervised its construction.

Cigarette bribe

The false wall was discovered by a German guard. Luckily for the British he used this information to bargain with the glider builders, rather than report it to his officers. He agreed to keep quiet about the wall in exchange for 500 cigarettes. This guard later died from natural causes, but a story went around that

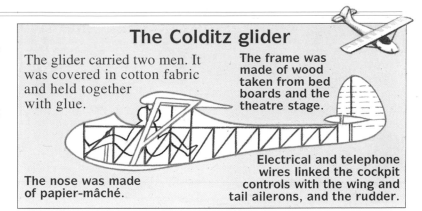

The Colditz glider

The glider carried two men. It was covered in cotton fabric and held together with glue.

The frame was made of wood taken from bed boards and the theatre stage.

The nose was made of papier-mâché.

Electrical and telephone wires linked the cockpit controls with the wing and tail ailerons, and the rudder.

his demise was caused by smoking too many cigarettes.

Bathtub launching

The airmen intended to launch the glider by carrying it out to a flat roof next to their attic workshop. They would place it on a trolley, which would be attached to a long rope tied to a bathtub full of concrete.

They calculated that if the tub was pushed off the roof it would fall with sufficient speed to pull the glider fast enough to launch it into the air, when it went off the edge of the roof. The rope would be released and the craft would glide silently onto the meadows outside the castle. Here its crew could make good their escape.

This dangerous plan could easily have resulted in the death of the escapers, and fortunately it was never tried out. By the time the glider was completed, in January 1945, the prisoners knew from their secret radio sets that the war was drawing to an end and would soon be over.

One in ten

During the war there were over 300 escape attempts from Colditz Castle. Most ended in immediate recapture or even death. Despite this, 130 men succeeded in getting away from the "escape-proof" castle. Although many were arrested trying to reach friendly territory, 30 managed to get home safely.

Coathanger and cotton spool with compartments that could conceal a map or small compass.

Map, compass, and sweets concealed in a bar of soap.

Electricians, officers and German housewives

Not every escape attempt from Colditz involved such intense physical effort or danger. It was possible for a prisoner to walk out of the castle right under the gaze of the guards, if he was wearing a convincing enough disguise.

The electrician's double

André Perodeau (left), attempts to impersonate electrician Willy Pöhnert (right).

One French officer, Lieutenant André Perodeau had noticed a close resemblance between himself and the castle electrician, a local tradesman named Willy Pöhnert. Not only did they look alike, but they were almost the same age, height and weight. They even wore similar glasses. Perodeau hoped a good impersonation might enable him to escape.

Perodeau had tried a similar scheme before. He had been sent to Colditz following an escape from his previous prisoner of war camp, where he had disguised himself as a refuse collector. He had got out of the camp, but was recaptured only hours later.

He began to observe Pöhnert closely, and tried to copy his walk and posture. Clothes were found to match the electrician's, and when no suitable match existed, they were made from bed clothes, blankets and sheets, and dyed the correct shade. A forged pass with Pöhnert's name on it was also prepared for him.

The escape was planned for a December evening. An impostor would be harder to spot in the dark. There was a good chance too that the guards may be toasting the coming Christmas with a few drinks, and be less vigilant than usual.

A well-timed arrival

The French sabotaged the electricity in their living quarters, so that Pöhnert would be summoned to the castle. They timed it so the electrician would arrive just before the guard changed. Perodeau did not want to walk past the same sentries who had let Pöhnert in.

After checking that Pöhnert had in fact arrived, Perodeau put on his disguise and walked toward the first of four checkpoints. His pass was glanced at, and the gate was unlocked. As he walked through, the sentry asked him a question. Perodeau spoke almost no German but he was prepared for this, and had practiced his reply. *"Ich habe etwas vergessen."* (I have forgotten something.)

He walked on to the next checkpoint, but this time his pass was examined carefully. It contained a number of glaring mistakes. The guard became suspicious, and kept looking up from the pass and asking questions. Not understanding

him Perodeau could only stand and stare. The escape had failed.

A hat and wig

The problem of getting past the prison checkpoints could be avoided by taking on a disguise outside the castle. Frenchman Lieutenant Boulé was one escaper who tried to do this.

He and his fellow officers marched to the local park every day to exercise. Boulé had noticed that at one point on the journey they turned a corner and were briefly out of sight of the guards. This was where he would change his appearance.

So one day he wore women's clothing under his long army coat, and when he turned this particular corner he took off the coat, popped a hat and wig onto his head, and began to walk the other way. This worked perfectly until he dropped his watch. A British soldier, who did not know what Boulé was doing, picked it up and gave it to a guard, pointing at "the lady" who had dropped it. The guard shouted after him, and Boulé, assuming he had been spotted, gave himself up.

Lieutenant Boulé disguised as a German woman.

Failure photographed

The photographs here were taken by the Germans as evidence of unsuccessful escape attempts. The shots were shown to new guards to warn them what to expect from the prisoners.

The Nazi officers

The British and Dutch worked together on the most daring disguise of all – that of a German officer. Uniforms were tailored and dyed to resemble officers' overcoats, and suitable rank badges were carved from wood, and painted gold and silver.

A passageway leading to the German quarters of the castle had been discovered. Two escapers dressed as Germans could make their way down it, and then walk out of the castle. Englishman Airey Neave and Dutchman Toni Luteyn (who spoke perfect German) were chosen to try this out.

A swaggering air

On a freezing January evening, the two men walked out of the German quarters of the castle with a slowness to match the dignity of their rank. They swaggered along as sentries opened gates and doors, snapping to attention as they passed by.

However, on their way out of the castle one soldier began to stare at them suspiciously. Luteyn, feeling that their bluff was about to be called, shouted angrily in German "Why do you not salute?". The soldier promptly complied, and the two impostors walked on.

They scrambled over an oak fence, and then had to climb a high stone wall. By now, both were numb with cold and it was difficult to grip the icy surface of the wall. Luteyn's fingers failed him, and Neave had to haul him over. But the two men were out of Colditz, and three days later they had managed to steal through Germany to the safety of neutral Switzerland.

Making a fake uniform

Neave and Luteyn adapted their own uniforms to look like German uniforms, dyed them to match, and added buttons and insignia made from materials available in the camp.

Buttons made from melted lead pipe and poured into wooden cast.

Gold piping (trimming) for hat, made from plaited electrical wiring.

Pistol carved from wooden floorboard.

Belt cut from linoleum (fabric floor covering), and painted. Buckle added from another belt.

Badge cut from cardboard and painted.

Harriet "Moses" Tubman leads slaves to freedom

One August afternoon in 1844, on a farm in Maryland, USA, a black slave named Harriet Tubman was chopping wood under a hot sun. The work was hard, but she dare not stop to rest, for fear of being beaten.

As she worked a shadow fell over her, and she looked up to see a white woman watching her. The woman smiled sympathetically and began to talk in a friendly way. She asked about the welts that covered Tubman's neck, and the huge scar that ran across the top of her head. Tubman explained that the welts were the consequence of several childhood whippings.

When she was seven she had been sent to work in the home of her owner. She had to clean and polish and look after her mistress's children. This was exhausting work for such a young child, but if she ever fell asleep she was callously whipped.

The scar was a more recent injury, caused by a badly aimed iron weight, thrown at another slave by a brutal overseer.

The white woman looked around to make sure that they were alone. She drew closer and quietly explained that she lived on a farm nearby, and that if Tubman was ever in trouble she was prepared to help her.

Harriet Tubman was nicknamed "Moses" after the biblical character who led his tribe from slavery to freedom.

Secret association

This was Harriet Tubman's first contact with "the underground railroad" – a secret organization which helped thousands of black slaves to escape from the farms and plantations of the southern USA.

Slave master dies

Shortly after this meeting, Tubman's slave master died. Although she had no love for him this was a great blow. Tubman lived with her husband and family on his farm, and his death would probably mean that all his slaves would be sold to other farms and plantations. The owners did not care if this meant that families would be broken up.

Naturally Tubman did not want her family to be separated, so she tried to persuade them to all run away together. Her family was too afraid to go, however, as runaway slaves were whipped if they were recaptured. But Tubman had suffered enough. She decided to escape alone.

In this poster of 1853 a trader offers $1,200 or more for negro slaves. Harriet Tubman's rescue missions cost slave owners so much money that they offered $40,000 for her recapture.

This painting by W.A. Walker shows slaves working on a cotton plantation in the south of the USA, before the civil war.

Slavery in the USA

Two hundred years ago slavery was legal in the USA. Slaves were shipped from Africa to work in plantations in the southern states. They produced cotton and tobacco and other goods.

The whip was the most common punishment for escapers.

United States

This whip has a leather thong attached to an iron chain.

Slave states in the USA

States where slavery was not permitted.

Pronged neck ring. A slave who wore such a device could not even lie down to sleep.

Slaves were regarded as property, and could be sold, like a piece of furniture, or a house. Slaves who ran away and were recaptured faced cruel punishments, some of which are shown here. Slavery was abolished in the USA in 1865 following the American Civil War between northern and southern states. Around 4 million slaves were freed.

These hooks were designed to catch in brambles and branches and prevent slaves from escaping.

Slave auction in New Orleans.

This headpiece was hung with bells, which would make a furtive escape almost impossible.

Most slave houses were simple wooden shacks, with few comforts.

Slaves were sometimes branded with the initials of their owner, like farm animals are today.

Led by a star

Tubman slipped away one day, carrying only a small bag of food. She hurried over to the house of the woman she had met while chopping wood.

The woman recognized her at once and explained three essential rules for escape. She must head for the north of the United States, where slavery was not permitted, she should travel by night, and she should always follow the North Star.

Stations and tickets

Tubman also discovered more about the "underground railroad". This organization used the language of the railroad to describe the work they did. Slaves were "passengers". A friendly house was a "station". A letter telling a fugitive how to find such a house was a "ticket". Anyone accompanying a runaway slave from one station to another was a "conductor".

The woman gave Tubman some money, and a description of a farm house that she was to head for. She told the slave to hurry before her owner sent dogs to trail her scent.

Tubman ran off and eventually found this house. A white woman came to the door and hurried Tubman inside. She gave her new clothes, and burned the old ones, explaining that this would stop the dogs from following her scent.

The night horse and cart

When night fell, a man arrived with a horse and cart. He told Tubman to lie on the floor of the cart and covered her with straw. They drove all night, and the next morning she was told to spend the day hiding in a wood and continue her journey north that evening.

The man gave her a ticket to the next house, and so she continued, for nearly 160km (100 miles).

Free at last

Once out of Maryland she headed through New Jersey to New York, where slavery had been abolished since 1799. Here she found a job in a hotel, working as a cook.

Although she was delighted to be free, Tubman was alone

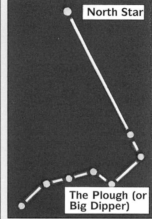

How to find the North Star

North Star

The Plough (or Big Dipper)

The North Star, known to astronomers as Polaris, is directly above the North Pole, so it shows which direction is north. If you live in the northern part of the world you can find it by looking for a group of stars called the Plough (also known as the Big Dipper). A line through the end of the Plough points to the North Star.

in this huge city. She decided to return to Maryland and bring out the rest of her family.

She took a terrible risk returning to the village where she used to live. It was likely that she would be recognized, and there was a reward for her recapture. To hide her identity Tubman disguised herself as an old lady, and wore a big old sun-bonnet to cover the scar on her head. The first couple of trips were successful, and she managed to bring back a sister and a brother. Then she returned for a third time to rescue her husband, John Tubman.

Tubman's heartbreak

But John Tubman had thought his wife was dead, and when she found him he was living with another woman. Although Harriet Tubman was upset, it

did not discourage her. Determined not to waste a journey, she returned to the north with another group of runaway slaves. They were so grateful to be free that Tubman decided to help whoever she could, and not just her own family.

Using the money earned as a cook, Tubman turned herself into a one woman escape organization, returning time and time again to the farms and plantations of the south.

$40,000 reward

But slave owners began to fight back. The underground railroad was becoming too successful. Tubman's fame spread with every rescue, and a $40,000 reward was offered for her capture.

In 1850 the government was persuaded by slave owners to introduce the Fugitive Slave Law. This made the work of the underground railroad much more difficult. Slaves who had escaped to the north could be recaptured, and anyone who helped them escape could be fined or imprisoned.

A hostile stranger

On one expedition soon after this, Tubman went to a house which served as one of the stations on her route. A stranger answered the door and told her angrily that the occupiers had been arrested for helping slaves escape.

Tubman and her group of runaways were in great danger. She knew the stranger would alert the local police and so hid her group on a grassy island on a nearby river. It was midwinter and rain fell unceasingly. The group spent a miserable day shivering in the grass, too frightened to talk to each other.

That evening they saw a man walking along the river bank, dressed as a preacher and carrying a Bible. As he walked he read aloud, as if from the book. Tubman knew the Bible well, but she did not recognize these words. He was saying that there was a wagon in the farmyard across the road, and a horse in the stable. The preacher walked on, calling out his message as he went along.

When it got dark, Tubman and her group went over to the farm. There was a wagon, and a horse, just as the preacher had said. Food and blankets had also been left for the fugitives.

They drove throughout the night to the next station on the route. Here their helpers had not been arrested, and the escape party were able to carry on until they reached Canada. Due to the Fugitive Slave Law this was now the safest place to head for.

Go on or die!

Tubman had one rule for escapers. Once they agreed to go there was no turning back. She carried a pistol, and if anyone dropped down exhausted and refused to go on she would point the gun at their head and say "Dead men tell no tales. Go on or die". She never did shoot anybody, and no one was recaptured and tortured into betraying the secrets of the underground railroad.

Slavery abolished

Between 1860 and 1865 a bitter civil war took place in the United States between the northern and southern states. During the conflict Tubman worked for the North as a scout, spy and nurse.

The war ended with victory for the North. Slavery was abolished and Tubman's work ended. Altogether she had made an extraordinary 19 trips on the underground railroad, and rescued between 300 and 400 slaves.

Midnight welcome at Levi's refuge

Most of the stations on the underground railroad were the houses of freed slaves, but many white Americans also provided shelter. Many were Christians with a deep hatred of slavery, and who suffered fines and imprisonment, and even branding, for their trouble. Despite the threat of such punishments the underground carried between 75,000 and 100,000 passengers before slavery was abolished. One famous station was operated by a Quaker named Levi Coffin, who appears in the painting above. He wrote about his experiences in his book *Reminiscences*. Coffin lived at Newport, Wayne County, Indiana, near Cincinnati, where he was a successful businessman.

His wealth and influence in his community protected him from harassment or arrest. His house became a station from the mid 1820s. Three routes, from Cincinnati, Madison and Jeffersonville all converged on

his house. When it became known in that area that he helped slaves, he lost many customers, but his business was strong enough to survive. He was prosperous enough to be able to keep a wagon and horses in constant readiness for passengers. Coffin says in his book that rarely a week went by without a knock at the door in the dead of the night.

He was a generous man, and because of his wealth he could afford to look after slaves whose health had suffered during their escape.

His account tells of the condition of his visitors when they arrived. "Sometimes fugitives come to our house in rags, and almost wild, having been out for several months, hiding in thickets during the day, being lost and making little headway at night, particulary in cloudy weather, when the north star could not be seen, sometimes almost perishing for want of food, and afraid of every white person they saw..."

Escape or death for Devigny

André Devigny, shackled and alone in Montluc Military Prison in Lyon, was awaiting a death sentence. This French Resistance fighter had been imprisoned here by the Gestapo* in April 1943. He had been brutally beaten, and now he was to face a firing squad.

Montluc Military Prison, in Lyon, France, held captured French Resistance members.

Impossible escape

Escape seemed almost impossible. He was on an upper floor of the prison, and a solid oak door blocked his way. If he succeeded in breaking through the door he would have to clamber up to a skylight leading to the roof, creep across a courtyard, climb on top of another block, and then sneak over the outer wall of the prison. At any stage, he could be shot on sight. But he was to be executed, so there was nothing to lose.

A pin for a pick

Shortly after Devigny arrived at Montluc, a fellow prisoner offered him a glimmer of hope by giving him a pin to pick the lock on his handcuffs. The cuffs were very basic and could be opened by pushing down a spring inside the lock. He was told how to do this by a prisoner in the next cell who tapped messages to him. (The code was simple – a tap for each letter of the alphabet: A was one tap, followed by a pause, B was two taps, and so on.) It took time, but prisoners have more than enough time on their hands.

His door was also not as formidable as it looked.

A prison spoon was turned into a chisel.

Devigny's handcuffs were quite basic. They could be opened by pushing down a spring inside the lock.

It was made of oak but the beams that held it to its frame were made of softer wood. A sharp tool could lever them off.

Devigny did not have such a sharp tool, but he had been given an iron spoon. He took off his handcuffs when he felt sure he would not be disturbed and scraped the spoon on his cell door making a sharp edge.

He also began to make a rope. Using a razor blade slipped to him by another prisoner, he cut bedding and clothing into thin strips. These he plaited together, strengthening the strands with wire from his mattress. At the end of the rope he attached iron prongs pilfered from a light shade. These would serve as a grappling hook, anchoring the rope to any object it was thrown over.

New arrival

Just before he planned to go, the Gestapo placed another prisoner in his cell, a teenager called Gimenez. This was very awkward. If Devigny escaped and Gimenez did not raise the alarm, he would be shot. Devigny would have to take Gimenez with him.

Shortly before midnight one moonless August evening, Devigny removed a section of the cell door with his sharpened spoon. He and Gimenez squeezed out and headed for the skylight.

* Nazi secret police

Devigny's rope was plaited from twisted cloth, shredded by a razor blade.

Devigny stood on his cellmate's shoulders. After several attempts he managed to wriggle out. Four months in prison had weakened him, and already he felt exhausted.

Gimenez followed, and the two stood on the roof, panting for breath under a clear night sky. Now they were outside, any sound they made could alert the guards. Fortunately a railway line passed by the prison, so they moved only when a train thundered by.

Cigarettes and bayonets

Trains came every ten minutes and gradually the two crept a little further along their route to the outer wall. They reached the roof parapet and looked down on the courtyard below. Straining into the gloom, they could pick out the shapes of the guards, where a glowing cigarette end, or a glimmer of light on a bayonet or buckle gave their positions away. Unfortunately, one sentry stood directly in their path.

The prison clock chimed midnight, and signalled the changing of the guard. Devigny watched the new sentry for an hour, studying his routine. As another train passed, he and Gimenez lowered their rope into the dark.

As the clock struck one, Devigny climbed over, not even knowing if the rope was long enough to reach the ground. He slid down so quickly he tore his hands, then ran across the courtyard and hid behind a wall. The sentry stood before him.

A grim choice

Devigny came to a harrowing decision. The only way to get past this sentry was to kill him. As the man turned, Devigny sprang from the shadows, grabbed him by the throat, and strangled him.

When he was dead, Devigny whistled up to Gimenez to join him. Now they had to scale a wall and a roof. Devigny was too weak to climb the wall so Gimenez scrambled up and passed down the rope. From here they climbed over a sloping roof that took them to the edge of the prison. They had a good view of the wire around the prison perimeter. 5m (18ft) separated them from freedom. A single guard cycled by every three minutes.

Despair and relief

A voice drifted up to them. Two other guards must be hidden in the dark. This would make an escape almost impossible. The men were filled with despair, but then realized the voice they heard was the cyclist talking to himself.

They would have to choose their moment carefully, but the urge to hurry was intense. An open cell door and a dead sentry were both waiting to be discovered.

The clock struck three. Devigny waited for the sentry to cycle by, and then threw the rope over the outer wall. The grapple gripped and they pulled the rope tight, and tied it to the roof.

A final risk

The guard came around again, cycling beneath the rope. Dawn was breaking. Time was running out. Both men feared that their rope would snap as they crossed over, leaving them injured in the perimeter, or stranded on the roof. So near to success, neither believed that their luck would hold.

The sky grew lighter still. The circling guard even stopped beneath them to rest for a while, but he never did look up. Eventually, after a fiercely whispered argument about who should go first, Devigny scrambled across, and Gimenez followed.

Early morning shift

Once over the perimeter, the two men crawled along the top of the wall to a section where it was low enough to jump down. Both were dressed in civilian clothes, as the prison had no uniform, and once outside they walked down the street, mingling with a crowd of workmen on their way to start the early morning shift at a local factory. By the time the guards at Montluc had discovered their open cell door and the dead body of the sentry, Devigny and Gimenez had vanished into the countryside.

Breakout at Pretoria Prison

By December 1979 Tim Jenkin, Stephen Lee and Alex Moumbaris were finally ready to tackle the ten locked doors that lay between them and the streets outside Pretoria Prison, South Africa.

Jenkin and Lee, who had been friends since university, had been plotting this escape since their arrival here in June 1978. Neither was prepared to sit out the 12 and eight year sentences imposed on them for being active members of the African National Congress (ANC), a political party that had been banned in South Africa.

Hatching a plot

They soon discovered that most of their fellow prisoners had reconciled themselves to long sentences and abandoned any hope of escape from this top security prison. But not Alex Moumbaris, a fellow ANC member, who had been given

Tim Jenkin (left), Alex Moumbaris (middle) and Stephen Lee (right).

Pretoria top security prison, South Africa. The cells overlooked a courtyard watched over by a fierce dog and armed guards.

a 12 year sentence in 1973. When Jenkin mentioned that they were planning a breakout, Moumbaris replied that if any escape plans were being hatched then "he would definitely like to be one of the chickens".

Political prisoners

Pretoria Prison, built in the 1960s, was an L-shaped, three floor building containing 52 cells. Those convicted of illegal political activity, such as Jenkin, Lee and Moumbaris, were kept separately in one corridor on the first floor. The rest of the cells were occupied by men awaiting trial.

The cell windows overlooked a large yard, containing a garden and tennis court, encircled by a 6m (20ft) high fence. Above the yard was a glass-covered catwalk, which held an armed guard. At night the yard was lit by dazzling searchlights, and occupied by a savage dog, trained to rip any escaper to pieces. It seemed to be formidable, but if Pretoria Prison had any weak spots, then Jenkin, Lee and Moumbaris were determined to exploit them.

Jail routine

Like any prisoners they soon became wearily familiar with the jail's routines. But this could be a tremendous advantage to a would-be escaper. The three were soon able to predict almost exactly what their guards were doing at any time of the day. This enabled them to judge when they were least likely to be disturbed, for example, during the guards' meal times. They also discovered that at night, when everyone was locked in their cell, there was only one warder on duty.

Good manners

Moumbaris was usually hostile and insolent to his jailors, and refused to keep his cell tidy. But Jenkin and Lee realized that aggressive prisoners were watched more closely. They managed to persuade him to be more pleasant to his captors, and as a result he was left alone much more. This intimate knowledge of

Locks, tumblers and counterfeit keys

In Pretoria Prison ten locked doors lay between a cell and the streets outside. In order to escape, Jenkin, Lee and Moumbaris had to learn how locks worked, and how to make wooden or metal keys that would open them.

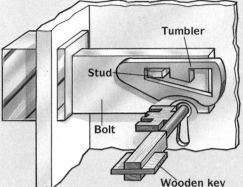

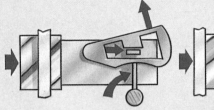

1. Inside a lock several levers, called tumblers, hold a bolt in place against a stud, and prevent it from moving.

2. When a key is turned, it lifts the tumblers over the stud.

3. As the key turns it also draws back the bolt, allowing the door to be opened.

The escapers made separate components for the keys in the prison workshop. They were then put together and filed into shape in the privacy of their cells. Their wooden keys looked like the one shown on the right.

Making a key

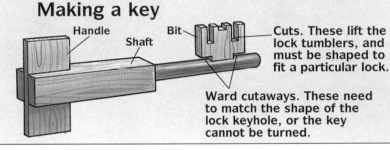

Cuts. These lift the lock tumblers, and must be shaped to fit a particular lock.

Ward cutaways. These need to match the shape of the lock keyhole, or the key cannot be turned.

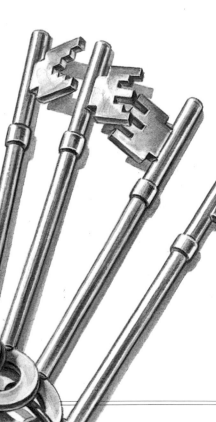

the prison's routine, and a more relaxed relationship with the guards enabled the three to concentrate on their main objective of getting out.

4:30 lockup

Part of the prison routine was that prisoners were locked in their cells at 4:30 each afternoon.

Before then, they were allowed access to certain areas of the prison and exercise yard. This gave them ample opportunity to study escape routes. The simplest route was to break into the yard and attempt to climb over the outer wall, but this also carried the greatest risk of death or serious injury.

Jenkin and Moumbaris began to test out the first hurdle on this route – the yard dog – which they hoped to divert with scraps of food. Several dogs were used

on a weekly rota, and although some were prepared to take food off the men, they were highly unpredictable.

After several weeks of deliberating, the three men decided that the safest route out was the way they had come in – through ten locked doors. This would involve making forged keys for each of these doors and developing lock picking skills which none of them possessed. It would take a huge amount of time, but that was one thing they had more than enough of.

Only one chance

They knew there would only be one chance to escape. If they were caught in their attempt, they would be marked down as troublesome prisoners. Several years could be added to their sentences. Supervision would be considerably tighter, and they could even be sent to a much tougher prison.

Jangling taunts

The keys for the locks they needed were all around them. The guards carried them on their waists, in big jangling bunches. Jenkin thought they enjoyed waving them around, demonstrating the power they had over their prisoners. But, extraordinarily enough, there were some keys that were left in locks, in areas that prisoners had access to during the day.

Stealing these would be too obvious. It would alert the guards to a possible escape, and the cells would all be searched from top to bottom in the hunt for the missing keys. Any key they needed would have to be copied.

Material and tools to do this could be stolen from the prison workshop, where inmates spent some of their day making furniture. Here they were watched over by a guard so sleepy and sluggish that Jenkin told the others that his brain only flickered into life when he sucked on his pipe.

First steps

Jenkin began on a lock he had constant access to – the one on his cell door. He measured the size of the keyhole with a stolen ruler, and worked out the rough position of the levers within the lock by placing a strip of paper within, and making impressions on it with a thin knife.

Whenever a warder locked or unlocked his cell door Jenkin made a mental note of the shape of the key, and by a process of trial and error, managed to file down his own wooden key to the correct shape. All the cell doors worked on the same key, so Jenkin was able to copy it for his fellow escapers.

Broom crank

The next lock to overcome was the steel outer door of the cell. This was far more difficult as it could only be unlocked from outside. But there was a way around the problem. Each cell had a window overlooking the corridor and the escapers managed to get to the lock by employing an ingenious cranking device, made out of a broom handle and parts made in the workshop. Another wooden key was shaped in the same painstaking way as the first, but it took four long months of trial and error to get it right.

Moumbaris kept the device in several pieces in his cell, where he assembled it when needed.

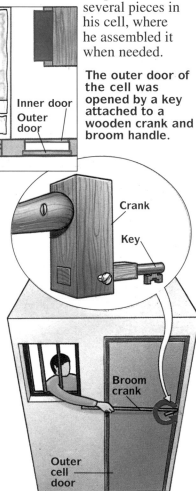

The outer door of the cell was opened by a key attached to a wooden crank and broom handle.

Inner door
Outer door

Crank

Key

Broom crank

Outer cell door

The broom handle was kept, naturally enough, attached to a broom, and the key crank was disguised as a coat hook. The key itself, the only part of the mechanism which could arouse suspicion, was hidden away.

After solving the problem of the first two locks, the escapers then set out to make keys for every other door they needed to open, or cupboard they may need to gain access to.

Impressions in soap

Some of the keys they needed were ones which were left in locks during the day. While a guard was looking the other way these could be whisked out of their locks and pressed hard into a bar of soap – leaving an impression that could then be copied at leisure.

Other locks in less obvious places could even be temporarily removed and taken apart to work out the size and shape of the key needed to open it.

Key collection

As their key collection grew they began to realize that some were very similar to ones they had made already, and would only require minor adjustments to make them work in other locks. Even better was the fact that some keys they had already copied would unlock at least one other door on the way out.

But one of the doors they had to open had no key. It was electrically operated from the main office where the night warder sat. They would have to make sure that the guard was elsewhere when this door was to be opened.

Damning evidence

After several months, so much incriminating material had been collected by Jenkin, Lee and Moumbaris that they were

Imprints of keys were made in soap.

becoming anxious that it would be discovered.

Clothes were a distinct worry. Obviously the three could not escape in their prison uniforms, so had set about collecting any civilian clothing they could find. Surprisingly, this had been quite easy. T-shirts were ordered for "sportswear", and bundles of rags for washing the floor included perfectly wearable jeans and shirts.

Jenkin's escape outfit was salvaged from rags used to clean the prison.

Shower storeroom

They were soon presented with a golden opportunity to hide their hoard. One day workmen came to repair a faulty shower heater, housed in a cupboard behind the shower room, and carelessly left this cupboard door open.

The escapers unscrewed the lock on this door, studied it to make a key, and replaced it before any guard noticed it was missing. They were then able to keep their escape equipment in this cupboard. This was especially convenient because if it was discovered, then the guards would not be able to tell who it belonged to.

Time runs out

The pressure on them to escape shortly was growing. Jenkin had managed to smuggle in enough money to pay for the initial journey away from the prison. But South Africa's currency was changing, and this money would soon be out of date.

Also, another prisoner, John Matthews, was due for release very soon. The three felt sure that if they broke out after his release, the South African authorities would try and implicate him in the escape, and possibly return him to prison. They had to go before he was set free.

Lastly, the escape clothes they had gathered together were only suitable for the summer, which was fast coming to an end. Clearly, an escape had to be mounted soon, but there were still some final details which needed to be sorted out.

Mystery locks

In their thorough preparations, almost all the forged keys had been tested in the locks they were intended for. But two keys remained untried. One was for a door in the corridor on the way to the exit, the other was for the final outer door to the prison. These would have to be tried on the night of their getaway. If they did not work, the escapers would have to resort to chisels, files and screwdrivers.

They also needed to make sure the right man was on duty on the night that they chose to go. The right man in this case was Sergeant Vermeulen – he was the most lackadaisical, inefficient guard they could think of.

Fragrant getaway

So on December 11, 1979, the final preparations for the escape were made. That afternoon, as

Hiding keys

Keys for the escape were concealed in several hiding places around a cell, for example in a box of soap powder, or jar of sugar. Some were placed in plastic bags and buried in the garden in the yard, underneath a particular plant, to help the escapers remember where they had left it.

they daydreamed about food they would soon be able to eat, and friends they would shortly be seeing again, the three tidied their cells, intending to leave no clues. If they did get out of Pretoria Prison, dogs would be sent to trail them, so they washed the clothes they had worn that day, sprayed the cell beds with deodorant, and sprinkled pepper over their prison shoes.

Plans flushed away

All secret letters and plans were flushed down the lavatory. Jenkin felt a strong sense of regret as he did this, and was surprised to realize that he was destroying items that had come to possess great sentimental value for him. Spare keys were given to a trusted cell mate to bury in the garden for any future escape. Jenkin even dyed his footwear – bright yellow running shoes – a less conspicuous shade of blue. Dummies made of prison overalls stuffed with towels, clothes and books, were placed in their cell beds. Shoes were positioned at the bottom of the beds, to look like feet.

Ready to go

Despite the preparations the day passed slowly. The escapers tried to remain as calm as possible, and the guards gave no indication that they suspected an escape was imminent. Perhaps they too were bluffing, and waiting to pounce.

At shower time the heater cupboard was opened up, and civilian clothes were placed in order for speedy dressing. A set of workshop tools was prepared – a screwdriver and chisel for stubborn locks, and a file to adjust any faulty keys.

At supper, to fortify themselves for the ordeal ahead, the three ate as much of the almost inedible prison soup as they could, and returned to their cells.

They then set out to see if the plan they had so painstakingly prepared would actually succeed. The diagram below shows what happened next.

Door C

③

Door B

Door A

②

①

Shower room

Moumbaris's cell

Jenkin's cell

Lee's cell

①

①

①

④ ⑤

①
At 4:40pm Jenkin, Lee and Moumbaris unlock their inner cell grilles (door A) with forged keys. Moumbaris opens his outer cell door (B) with the broom crank, and then opens the outer doors of Jenkin and Lee's cells.

②
Escape equipment (clothing, keys and door-breaking tools) is collected from the shower room cupboard.

③
Jenkin unlocks corridor door (C) with a forged key. A fuse box on the landing wall next to this door is forced open and sabotaged, which causes all the lights to go out on the first floor.

④
Locking door C behind them, the three escapers go down the stairs to the ground floor and hide in a storage cupboard in the stairwell.

⑤
Alerted by noise from protesting prisoners, night warder Vermeulen unlocks the ground floor corridor door (D) and goes upstairs to investigate the "power failure".

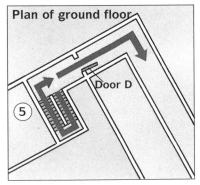

Plan of ground floor

Door D

⑤

After Vermeulen has passed them and is safely up in the first floor corridor attempting to settle complaining inmates, the three emerge from the cupboard and hurry through open door D.

A fake gun – handy or hazardous?

During the planning of the escape there was a fierce debate about whether or not to carry a gun. It would be useful to threaten any warder who got in the way, but on the other hand, the police might be more inclined to shoot armed escapers on sight, rather than try to arrest them. A stolen gun would soon be missed, so the escapers made a fake one. In the *Reader's Digest* (available in the prison library) there were several photographs of a Beretta pistol. Jenkin used these to make an accurate blueprint of this gun, and a wooden duplicate was created in the prison workshop. Shading with a soft pencil gave it a realistic metallic hue.

In the event the gun was never used, as the final escape plan avoided any contact with the prison warders.

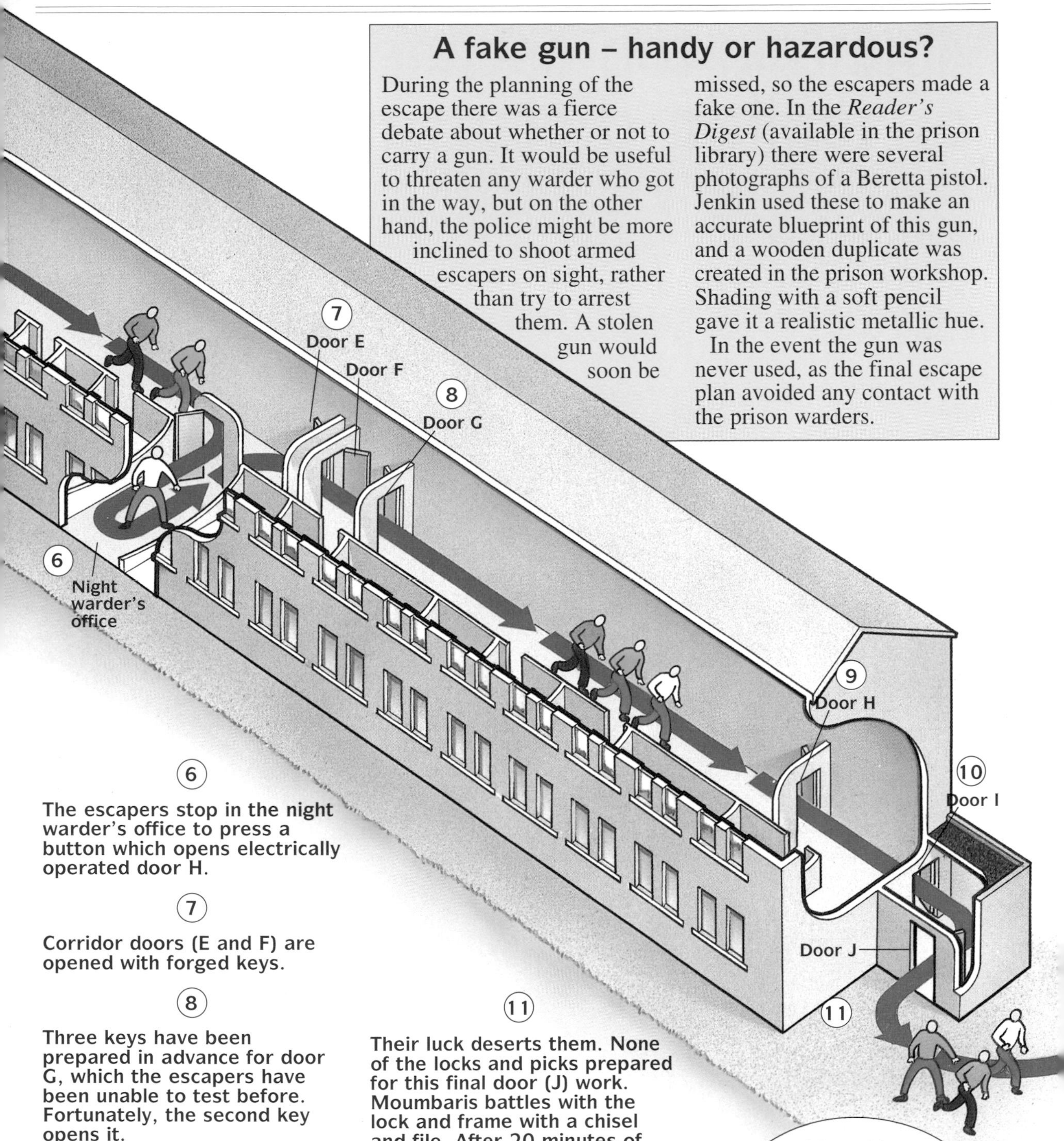

(7)
Door E
Door F
(8)
Door G

(6)
Night warder's office

(9)
Door H

(10)
Door I

Door J

(11)

(6)

The escapers stop in the night warder's office to press a button which opens electrically operated door H.

(7)

Corridor doors (E and F) are opened with forged keys.

(8)

Three keys have been prepared in advance for door G, which the escapers have been unable to test before. Fortunately, the second key opens it.

(9)

Escapers pass through electrically operated door H already opened at stage 6.

(10)

Outer hall door (I) opened with no problems, with key already forged for visitors waiting room.

(11)

Their luck deserts them. None of the locks and picks prepared for this final door (J) work. Moumbaris battles with the lock and frame with a chisel and file. After 20 minutes of banging and cursing the door is finally wrenched open.

By some miracle the noise goes unnoticed and the three men walk past the unguarded outer yard and out through the open prison gates. They wave down a taxi. A few days later they have been smuggled out of South Africa to Maputo in Mozambique.

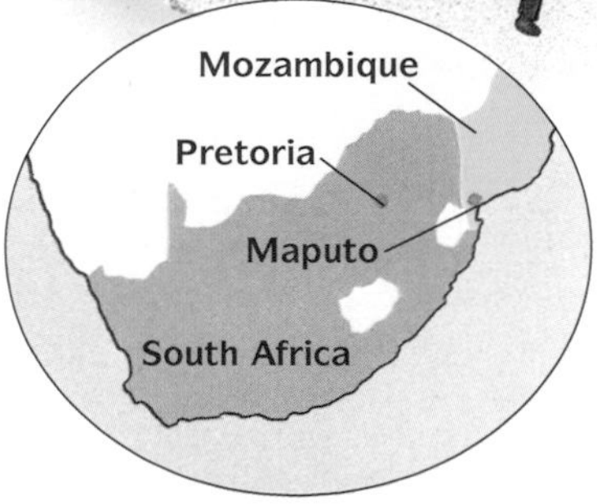

Mozambique

Pretoria

Maputo

South Africa

Mountain-top escape for Italian dictator

On a July morning in 1943, commando captain Otto Skorzeny stood nervously in an outer office of "the wolf's lair", Adolf Hitler's secret headquarters in east Prussia. He had seen the German dictator before, as a distant, revered figure at huge military parades, but never met him face to face.

Benito Mussolini (right). His decision to join Germany in World War Two led to his overthrow. The Italian Government tried to stop German troops from rescuing the fallen dictator by hiding him in different locations (below).

Hiding Mussolini

Corsica

③ September. Flown by seaplane to hotel in Apennine mountains.

Sardinia

② August. Taken from Ponza by cruiser to Italian naval base at La Maddalena.

Rome

Albergo-Rifugio.

① July. Arrested in Rome. Taken in ambulance to Ponza.

Italy

Hitler's friend

With great formality he was ushered into his leader's presence and promptly told some extraordinary news. Benito Mussolini, Italy's fascist leader and Hitler's friend, had been arrested by his own countrymen. Italy, Germany's closest partner in the Second World War, was on the brink of surrender. Hitler told

Otto Skorzeny

Skorzeny he expected him to fly to Italy and rescue Mussolini. No risk was too great. Once he was free, the Germans, (who had troops all over Italy) would return him to power. Germany and Italy could then continue to fight their enemies* together.

The most hated man in Italy

Mussolini, who had ruled Italy for 20 years, had been taken prisoner on July 25, after a meeting with the Italian King. The King told him the war seemed lost, and that he, Mussolini, was now "the most

hated man in Italy". Soldiers bundled him into an ambulance and drove off to a secret location. The Italians knew the Germans would want to rescue Mussolini, and would stop at nothing to find him.

Message intercepted

So the hunt for Mussolini began. Over the summer he was taken to three different hiding places (see map), and it took several weeks for the Germans to track him down. Skorzeny knew Mussolini was being held by the Italian soldier General Gueli, and when a coded message from Gueli was intercepted, giving away his hiding place, the Germans prepared to attack.

A mountain prison

The Italians had hidden Mussolini and 250 guards at the hotel Albergo-Rifugio, near to Gran Sasso, the highest

peak of the Apennine mountains. It was a good hiding place. Only a mountain cable car connected it to the outside world.

It was impossible to attack the hotel from below, but too dangerous to send in parachute troops. Skorzeny decided the only way to seize it would be to take his men there in troop-carrying gliders.

A shaky start

September 12 was chosen as the day for the attack. An Italian officer, General Soleti, agreed to accompany the rescue team. His job was to order the hotel guards not to open fire.

From an airport in Rome, gliders packed with Skorzeny's commandos were towed into the air. But things immediately began to go wrong. The glider that was to guide the attack crashed on take-off, so Skorzeny himself would have to lead the way. As he was wedged into his seat by the equipment he was carrying, he had to hack a hole in the side of the glider to see where it was going.

After an hour, they were over the mountains, and the hotel came into view. The nearer they got to their landing spot, the more dangerous it looked. It was very small, sloped steeply and was covered with boulders.

Reckless landing

Recalling Hitler's orders to rescue Mussolini at all costs, Skorzeny pressed home his attack. His glider hit the ground, and cleaved its way through a rock-strewn meadow. It came to a halt only 18m (60ft) from the hotel. Five more gliders followed, although one was smashed to pieces on the mountainside.

Hurtling out of their craft, the commandos stormed into the main hotel entrance, with Soleti shouting at the astonished Italian troops, telling them not to fire. Skorzeny, pausing only to kick over an Italian radio transmitter, dashed up the main staircase. Mussolini was in the first room he entered and two stunned officers guarding him were overpowered.

Skorzeny called on the Italians to surrender. After a short pause the Italian commanding officer accepted defeat. As a white sheet was hung from a hotel window an Italian colonel presented Skorzeny with a goblet of red wine.

The Storch which rescued Mussolini. The two-man plane could land and take off in less than 180m (600ft).

Over a ravine

Mussolini still had to be whisked away from his mountain-top prison, before the alarm was raised and more Italian troops arrived to stop them. Overhead circled a tiny two-man Storch reconnaissance plane, which landed next to the hotel. Mussolini helped his rescuers clear away boulders to make a safer runway, and then he and Skorzeny squeezed into the tiny plane and it attempted a take-off.

But the Storch was perilously overloaded. Before they were in the air they lurched over the edge of a ravine, and plummeted toward the valley floor. The ground loomed up alarmingly, but luck was with them. The pilot expertly eased his craft out of its near-fatal dive, and headed for a German airfield in Rome. Skorzeny spent a bumpy flight straining to hear the dictator as he raged against his former captors.

Wolf's lair reunion

At Rome they were transferred to a larger plane and flown to Hitler's headquarters in east Prussia. Hitler himself was waiting to greet them at the airport, overjoyed to see his old ally, and impatient to seek vengeance on the soldiers and politicians who had betrayed them both.

Mussolini (above) leaves the hotel Albergo-Rifugio, surrounded by German and Italian troops. His former jailer, General Gueli, carries his raincoat.

This pencil sketch of the rescue (left) was featured in *Signal*, a Nazi magazine sent out to all troops fighting alongside Germany.

Signal

Una información especial

La liberación de Mussolini

Berlin – the prison city

Wolfgang Fuchs' fourth tunnel was his most ambitious yet. Excavated over six months in 1964, it was over 130m (140yd) long. Thirty seven people helped with the backbreaking work, risking their lives in the hot, stale air, burrowing through mud, concrete and grime.

The tunnel could collapse or flood. If it was discovered, grenades or gas bombs could be thrown into it, killing any occupant without warning. Some of the team working on it could be double-agents who would betray their fellow workers, or even kill them.

Like most secret tunnels, it passed under a guarded wall. But this wall was not a prison boundary, it separated an entire city.

Divided lives

The Berlin Wall was one of the most infamous barricades in history. From 1961 to 1989 it separated the east and west of the city.

East Berlin was controlled by a strict communist regime, while in the west, people were freer to live as they chose. Crossing from east to west was forbidden but for many, the risks were worth taking – the hope of a better life lay on the other side.

Password Tokyo

Fuchs' escape plan worked like this.

Right. An escaper scurries through Wolfgang Fuchs' tunnel, to West Berlin.
Below. A five year old boy is lowered into the tunnel by one of its builders.

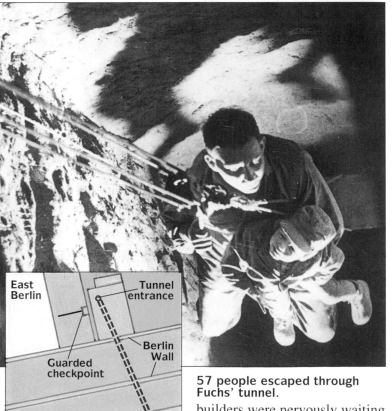

East Berlin — Tunnel entrance — Berlin Wall — Guarded checkpoint — West Berlin — Tunnel exit

57 people escaped through Fuchs' tunnel.

On the nights of October 4 and 5, escapers arrived at 55 Strelitzer Strasse, where the tunnel entrance was located, and gave the password "Tokyo" (the host city of the Olympic Games that year). On the first night 28 people escaped – crawling for 20 minutes along the damp, airless passage to West Berlin. On the second night 29 passed through. Then things began to go wrong. Four of the tunnel builders were nervously waiting on the eastern side for more escapers, when two men arrived. They did not know the password but seemed very frightened, so the tunnellers assumed they were genuine escapers.

After a moment, the men left, saying they had to collect a friend who had lost his nerve. But they were secret policemen and returned with a soldier, announcing that all the tunnel builders were under arrest. A warning shot was fired but this turned into a full-scale gunfight, and in the crossfire the soldier was killed. The tunnellers fled back to West Berlin, but those who should have followed lost their chance of freedom.

Why was the Wall built?

When World War II ended in 1945, Germany was defeated and divided into four areas by the victors: USA, Soviet Union, Britain and France. Although the former capital, Berlin, was in the Soviet area, (East Germany) it was also divided among the four victors. However, relations between the Soviet Union and its former allies soon became very hostile.

The Soviet Union was a communist country, where the government controlled every aspect of industry, business and people's lives. The Soviets made East Germany communist too.

The other countries were democracies. Here the government has less control over industry, business and daily life, so people had more freedom.

Many people in East Germany felt they could live more exciting and rewarding lives if they moved to the

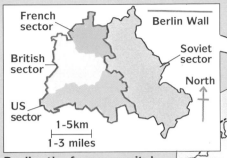

Berlin, the former capital of Germany, was deep in Soviet controlled territory.

west. Between 1949 and 1961 nearly a sixth of East Germany's population (2½ million people) left, mainly through Berlin.

Blockade set up

By August 1961 around 2,000 people were leaving every day. The government worried that it was losing its most able citizens, so it decided to stop them leaving.

A blockade between East and West Berlin was set up by 40,000 troops on the night of August 12-13, 1961, and the

Wall was built behind it. At first, barbed wire barricades blocked the roads, and a concrete wall was built behind them. Underground and railway train stations were padlocked shut. Barbed wire fences were also placed beneath the canals and rivers that passed between the east and west of the city. Even the sewers had heavy iron bars fitted across them.

Building the Wall

To begin with, the Berlin Wall was just barbed wire and concrete blocks, but over the next 28 years four different versions were built. Each was more efficient than the last, and so escape became more difficult. The final version was built in 1986. This diagram shows the Wall at its most complex. There were sections which were simpler.

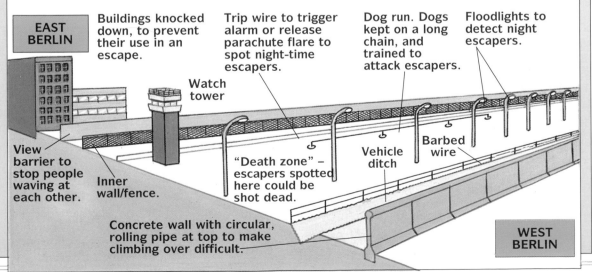

EAST BERLIN

Buildings knocked down, to prevent their use in an escape.

Trip wire to trigger alarm or release parachute flare to spot night-time escapers.

Dog run. Dogs kept on a long chain, and trained to attack escapers.

Floodlights to detect night escapers.

Watch tower

View barrier to stop people waving at each other.

Inner wall/fence.

"Death zone" – escapers spotted here could be shot dead.

Vehicle ditch

Barbed wire

Concrete wall with circular, rolling pipe at top to make climbing over difficult.

WEST BERLIN

Fourth floor leaps and cold-blooded murder

At first, the Wall was quite easy to cross. Some houses and apartment blocks in the east overlooked the west, and people crossed by climbing out of windows in these homes. As workmen were sent to board them up, many people tried to make a hasty leap for freedom.

This led to awful scenes where escapers were pulled to and fro between East Berlin soldiers and West Berliners on the other side. As the lower floor windows were boarded up, people jumped from greater heights into blankets held by the West Berlin fire service. The first death caused by the Wall occurred in this way when 47 year old Rudolf Urban fell to his death when jumping from his apartment, a week after the Wall went up.

18 year old shot dead

In the first year over 30 people were shot dead or fatally injured trying to cross the Wall. Most of these incidents happened at night, and were usually not witnessed. However, on August 17, 1962 an 18 year old East Berliner named Peter Fechter was shot dead in broad daylight as he tried to escape. He ran toward the Wall with a friend who managed to pick his way successfully over the barbed wire. Peter was not so lucky. He was caught by a bullet as he scaled the concrete blockade. As he lay dying, West Berlin policemen could see him but were powerless to help. East German soldiers waited an hour before they fetched his body.

East German soldiers carry away the body of Peter Fechter.

West Berliners were so angered by this cold-blooded murder that they threw stones at Soviet soldiers visiting West Berlin, and demonstrations against the shooting turned into riots.

A boy leaps from a fourth floor window overlooking the Wall.

Hail of bullets halts runaway bus

Some tried to break though checkpoints in the Wall by ramming them with buses or cars. This was highly dangerous. In one desperate incident on May 12, 1963, a bus containing 12 East Berlin escapers was driven through a hail of bullets at one such checkpoint.

The driver pressed on for 100m (110yd) as his passengers threw themselves onto the floor of the vehicle. Eventually he was hit and the bus slewed into a road barrier. Most of his passengers were also injured.

Over the Wall with a luminous hammer

Many escapes would have been impossible without the help of West Berliners. East Berliner Heinz Holzapfel cooperating with friends in the west, was able to escape with his family in this way.

Holzapfel was a maintenance worker in a government building right next to the Wall, known as the "Ministeries House". Every day he went to the roof to check equipment, and up here he could peer over into the West. The idea of escape soon became irresistable.

After making careful plans he smuggled his wife and nine year old son into the building and hid them in a lavatory. When everyone had gone home they made their way up to the roof.

That night, at an agreed time, friends on the western side sabotaged the power to local Wall lights. Concealed by the dark, Holzapfel threw over a hammer which had been coated in luminous paint. Attached to it was a strong nylon rope. His friends tied a steel cable to the rope, which was then hauled up

to the roof. The cable was pulled taut and secured, and Holzapfel and his family took it in turns to slide down on chair harnesses which they had made for themselves.

Frontier guards assumed that an electrical fault had caused the lights to go out, and the escape was only discovered the next morning, when the steel cable was found draped over the Wall.

Two other people escaped in a similar way when they used a bow and arrow to shoot over a line to friends in the west.

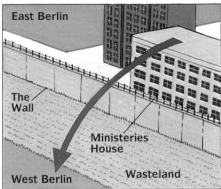

East Berlin
The Wall
Ministeries House
West Berlin
Wasteland

The route over the Wall.

Heinz Holzapfel demonstrates the harness his son used in the escape.

The luminous hammer could be seen clearly in the dark.

"Impossible" hiding place helps nine to freedom

Cars were a common hiding place to smuggle refugees through Wall checkpoints. At first these were in quite obvious places, such as under seats, but tighter controls were introduced and the border guards had to check each vehicle. So the hiding places became more ingenious.

In one case, an Isetta bubble car had its petrol tank removed and replaced with a smaller one, allowing just enough room for an escaper. This car was so small it was thought to be

impossible to hide anyone in it and it was exempt from the border checks. There were nine successful escapes, but on the tenth trip the Isetta's passenger shifted her position, and guards noticed the car wobbling for no apparent reason. Both driver and escaper were arrested.

The cramped journey was mercifully brief.

Isetta bubble car. The door was at the front of the vehicle.

Professional assistance – making money from the Wall

People in the west were prepared to pay professional "escape assistants" to have a family member or partner brought over from the east. These escapes were made possible by the fact that West Germans were allowed to enter East Berlin and East Germany.

Many professional escape organizations were thorough and efficient, but a few of them were callous exploiters who took their customers' money and provided little or nothing in return.

The cable reel carried four escapers.

Safe escapes (almost)

Among the best professionals were Albert Schutz, Karl-Heinz Bley, and Dietrich Jensch. One of their methods involved hiding escapers in a hollow cable reel. This was carried on the back of a lorry driven over from West Berlin, pretending to be making a delivery in the east. Four people could be carried at a time. It worked perfectly on two occasions.

Unfortunately it had to be abandoned after East German

The cow had a hatch in its side.

security police blackmailed one of the escapers. They told her they would punish the family she had left behind in the east if she did not return and tell them how she had escaped.

Bley also thought up a most unlikely escape technique involving a stuffed cow bought from a theatrical shop. He fitted a reinforced compartment in the belly, just big enough to conceal one small person.

The cow was placed on the back of a truck and driven from west to east. East German frontier guards were told it was being taken to a theatre performance. The driver then picked up an escaper at an agreed location, and drove back to the west. This worked well for the first three trips, but eventually checkpoint guards became suspicious. When an East German girl named Monika Schubert was being smuggled out, the cow was examined. Schubert was discovered, and both she and the driver were arrested.

Russian disguise fools saluting guards

A few escapers succeeded by impersonating Soviet soldiers, who were allowed to travel into West Berlin. This was first tried in 1963 by a young East Berliner who made Soviet officers' uniforms for her boyfriend and two other friends. The men hid her in their car, drove to a checkpoint, and were waved through by frontier guards, who saluted respectfully.

Once news of the escape reached East Berlin, soldiers passing between east and west were inspected more carefully.

The four escapers model their fake uniforms for West German news photographers.

The guardians of the Wall

Most of the Wall guards were young East Germans on compulsory military service. Many of them did not wish to be there. Their orders were clear. Any determined escaper should pay with their life:

"If suspicious persons are in the vicinity of the border, order them to stop. If they proceed further in the direction of the demarcation line (the Wall), fire two warning shots into the air. If this step fails, shoot low to wound. If this fails, shoot to kill."

These orders gave shooting to kill as a last resort, but many escapers were killed with little or no warning. In the heat of the moment, a guard often had only one brief opportunity to shoot.

Defending the guards

Dieter Jentzen, one East German guard who escaped to the west, issued a statement defending his ex-comrades. He said that most guards were simply carrying out orders and could have killed or captured at least ten times

more escapers if they had really wanted to.

He explained that guards who made suggestions for improving Wall security, or who made many arrests were rewarded with promotion, and extra pay and leave.

An East German checkpoint guard makes a successful escape in 1961.

Soldiers who were thought to have deliberately aimed to miss an escaper were punished severely.

Jentzen begged those in the west not to taunt or despise the

guards. They were in a situation over which they had no control, and were anxious for their fellow countrymen to understand this.

1,300 soldiers escape

The East German authorities knew all too well that many of their own troops were unhappy. In the two years after the Wall was built 1,300 soldiers escaped from Berlin or over the East German border. As a precaution the Wall guards were made to patrol in twos or threes, to keep watch on each other.

Pairs of guards were changed regularly to prevent friendships forming. The atmosphere between troops was suspicious. If a soldier confided to another that he wanted to escape, he could be reported and sent to prison.

Some soldiers did overcome the atmosphere of suspicion between them. Once, two young conscripts locked another soldier they did not trust in a watchtower. With him out of the way, they were free to make a successful escape.

The Wall comes down

In 1989 the communist system collapsed in the Soviet Union and Eastern Europe. Thousands of East Germans fled from their country via Poland, Hungary and Czechoslovakia, which now had open borders with Western Europe.

In Berlin angry crowds demonstrated against the Wall, attacking it with pickaxes, and taunting patrolling guards.

The East German government decided there was no further point in preventing its citizens from escaping to the west, and the Wall checkpoints were thrown open on November 9, 1989. By the time East and West Germany

were reunited a year later, the Wall had been almost entirely demolished.

Despite the difficulties, around 5,000 East Germans succeeded in crossing the Wall before it was opened up in 1989. However, at least 172 people are known to have been killed trying to cross, and over 60,000 East Germans were sent to prison for attempting to escape.

The German magazine *Der Spiegel* records the events of November, 1989, on its front cover.

DER SPIEGEL

Q 7997 C
Nr. 46
43. Jahrgang · DM 4,50
13. November 1989

DDR
DAS VOLK SIEGT
Offene Grenzen
Freie Wahlen

Escape films – fact or fantasy?

Around half of the stories in this book have featured in films which you can still see from time to time on television. While many take the true story as the basis for a more exciting, but quite fanciful adventure, others attempt to portray events as they really happened.

Hollywood's Houdini

Houdini, as a professional entertainer, made several of his own adventure films (see page 97), including *The Grim Game* (1919), *Terror Island* (1920) and *The Man From Beyond* (1921). He was tired of repeatedly performing his famous escapes and saw films as a means of reaching a large audience without having to tour.

He was also the subject of two film biographies. The first, *Houdini*, made in 1953,

Tony Curtis and Janet Leigh in *Houdini*.

Below. A scene from *Houdini*, **showing a packing case escape from a frozen river**.

was a glossy Hollywood romance. The scene shown at the bottom of the page is typical of the film's unrealistic approach. Here Houdini is chained up inside a well-secured packing case and lowered through a hole in the ice of a frozen river. Although Houdini did perform river escapes during the winter, he never attempted a trick like this under ice.

Death scene

The film ends with him dying during a performance of his Chinese Water Torture Cell trick. His actual death, from a burst appendix following an accident, was thought too unglamorous for the film. A more faithful version of his life story, *The Great Houdinis*, starring Paul Michael Glaser, was made for television in 1976.

Eastwood's Alcatraz

Clint Eastwood, as Frank Morris, makes a dummy head in *Escape from Alcatraz*.

Frank Morris's story (see pages 76-81) is portrayed in *Escape from Alcatraz*, made in 1979. It was filmed mainly on location at the island, and $500,000 was spent reconnecting electricity and decorating the prison, which had been closed for 16 years.

The director Don Siegel knew that only the actor Clint Eastwood could make the restrained character of Frank Morris interesting to an audience, and some critics rate Eastwood's depiction of the Alcatraz convict as his best ever performance.

Close to the facts

The plot sticks closely to the known facts, although many of the film's minor characters are fictitious. Most of the actors in the film became ill working in the musty environs of the prison, which gave their performances a realistic convict lethargy.

Alcatraz has been the subject of several other films, including *The Birdman of Alcatraz*, which was made in 1962 and starred Burt Lancaster.

Churchill's double

Winston Churchill's escape from the Boers in South Africa (see pages 74-75) and his subsequent adventures in the Boer War are featured in the 1972 film, *Young Winston*.

Simon Ward, whose resemblance to the young Churchill is striking, plays the intrepid journalist.

Devigny helps out

André Devigny's breakout from Montluc Prison (see pages 108-109) is depicted in *A Man Escaped*. To make it as accurate as possible, director Robert Bresson shot the film at Montluc and hired Devigny himself as an advisor.

The actors in *A Man Escaped* used the actual rope that Devigny made for his escape.

The lure of Devil's Island

The seediness and cruelty of the penal colony in French Guiana (see pages 68-73) captured the imagination of many film makers, and several films have been made about ficticious escapes. The most controversial was *Devil's Island*, made by Warner Brothers in 1939 and starring Boris Karloff.

Film offends

The film's harsh portrayal of life in French Guiana greatly offended the French government (who were very sensitive to criticism of the penal colony), and they retaliated by banning all Warner Brothers films from France. This cost the film company a great deal in lost ticket sales so they withdrew the film, and re-edited it to satisfy the French government.

Henri Charrière's book *Papillon*, was turned into a successful film of the same name in 1973, starring Steve McQueen and Dustin Hoffman. Although the conditions it portrays are realistic ($13 million was spent recreating the prison camps on the nearby island of Jamaica), the story, like the book, has little basis in real events.

Above. Steve McQueen plays Henri Charrière in *Papillon*. Here, while in solitary confinement, he sticks his head out of his cell to be shaved.

Below. In *Devil's Island*, Boris Karloff plays a wrongfully convicted French surgeon, who faces execution by the guillotine. In this scene he is reprieved seconds from death.

After the escape

Alcatraz Prison

(Alcatraz accordionists break out of the Rock, p.76-81)

The escape of **Frank Morris** and **John** and **Clarence Anglin** in 1962 embarrassed the Alcatraz Prison authorities. Warder Olin Blackwell had to tell newspapers that the concrete structure of the prison was crumbling away, and this had enabled the escapers to break out of their cells.

Also, by 1962 many people felt that Alcatraz had outlived its usefulness. It had been set up in the turbulent 1930s to strike fear into the hearts of American gangsters, and was now no longer necessary. So in 1963 all the inmates were shipped off the island and dispersed throughout the American penal system. Alcatraz remains open though, as a popular tourist spot, which still attracts hundreds of thousands of visitors every year.

$1 million reward

In 1993 Red & White Fleet, Inc., which ferries tourists to Alcatraz, offered a $1 million reward for the capture of the three escapers. It stated "Frank Morris, John Anglin and Clarence Anglin are excluded from this offer and are ineligible to claim the reward".

Frank Heaney, a former guard and leading authority on Alcatraz, has spoken to relatives of the Anglins, who claim to have received South American postcards from the two brothers. Frank Morris, however, has vanished without trace. Allen West, who was thwarted in his plan to escape, never regained his freedom. He died in a Florida prison in 1978.

Clarence Anglin

John William Anglin

Frank Lee Morris

These computer generated images were produced by the Fox Broadcasting Company, for the television documentary *America's Most Wanted*. They show what Morris and the Anglins could look like if they are still alive today.

Berlin Wall

(Berlin – the prison city, p.118-123)

Since the opening of the border between East and West Germany in 1989, the Wall has been slowly demolished. Whole sections have been ground down to produce gravel for building work.

Souvenir hunters or small time traders, dubbed *Mauerspechte* (Wall Woodpeckers) by the Germans, broke up parts of the Wall with hammers and chisels, and sold them on street stalls all over Europe. Now only a few sections of the Wall remain as historic landmarks.

George Blake

(Knitting needle escape for Soviet master spy, p.86-89)

Blake fled to the Soviet Union, where he was handsomely looked after by the Soviet government. He married and found work in a Moscow institute, researching politics and economics.

Sean Bourke, who helped him escape, returned to Ireland, where he wrote *The Springing of George Blake,* an account of his time with Blake. The book sold well and this encouraged him to become a full-time writer. However, this career was not a success and he died in poverty in Kilkee, County Clare, Ireland, in 1982.

Winston Churchill

(Churchill's track to fame and freedom, p.74-75)

Churchill returned to Britain to a hero's welcome, following his South African escape. He was courted by the country's leading political parties and became a Conservative Member of Parliament in 1900. He had a lifelong career in politics, becoming First Lord of the Admiralty during the First World War, and Prime Minister during the Second World War. He died in 1965.

Colditz Castle

(Colditz Castle – escape proof?, p.98-103)

Englishman **Airey Neave**, who escaped disguised as a German officer, spent 26 years as a Conservative Member of Parliament. His career ended tragically in 1979, when he was assassinated by terrorists.

His partner in the escape, Dutchman **Toni Luteyn**, remained a professional soldier in the Royal Netherlands Indies Army.

Frenchman **André Perodeau** became friends with **Willy Pöhnert**, the German electrician he had tried to impersonate. After the war Pöhnert visited Perodeau's home in Paris.

André Devigny

(Escape or death for Devigny, p.108-109)

Following his breakout from Montluc Prison, Devigny successfully escaped from France. His companion, **Gimenez**, was not so lucky. He was recaptured and his fate is unknown.

Devigny parachuted back into occupied France and carried out further undercover work with the French Resistance and the French army, during 1944 and 1945. His bravery won him many medals, including *Commandeur de la Légion d'Honneur*, and the *Croix de Guerre*. After the war he had a successful career as a soldier, and became director of physical education and sport for the French army.

French Guiana

(Snakes and sharks guard jungle prison, p.68-73)

Prisoners in the French penal colony suffered terribly during the Second World War (1939-1945), when food supplies from France virtually ceased. After the war, the French Government voted to abolish the penal settlements and bring all the remaining prisoners back to France.

Henri Charrière (Papillon) found fame and wealth when his books about life in the French penal colony, *Papillon*

and *Banco,* became best sellers. Royalties from the film *Papillon* added to his fortune. He settled in Spain, but died in 1973, only five years after *Papillon* was published. (See film section, p.124-125, and *Further Reading*, p.128).

Eugene Dieudonné returned to Paris, following his official pardon in 1929. He remarried his wife (they divorced when he was deported), and returned to his former trade as a cabinet-maker.

Harry Houdini

(Harry Houdini – escaping for a living, p.94-97)

Both Houdini and his wife **Beth** were fascinated with the supernatural and spirit world. Before his untimely death in 1926, Houdini had promised Beth that if he died before her, he would do everything he could to contact her from beyond the grave.

For the next ten years Beth held a seance (a ceremony where people try to make contact with the dead) on the anniversary of his death, but no message came, and she gave up trying to reach him.

David James

(Ivan Bagerov – Royal Bulgarian Navy, p.82-85)

After the war David James became an Antarctic explorer, and was a Conservative Member of Parliament between 1959-64 and 1970-79.

Benito Mussolini

(Mountain-top escape for Italian dictator, p.116-117)

Following his escape from the Apennine mountains, Mussolini became leader of a fascist republic in northern Italy, which fought alongside Germany. He was captured by

Italian guerrillas in April 1945, and executed.

German commando **Otto Skorzeny**, who rescued him from the Gran Sasso, survived the war and was tried as a war criminal, but charges against him were dismissed. He moved to Spain, where he became involved in the ODESSA organization, smuggling former Nazis to South America, where they would not be prosecuted for their war crimes.

Gunter Plüschow

(Plüschow's dockland disguise, p.90-93)

Plüschow's successful escape won him an Iron Cross medal, personally presented by Kaiser Wilhelm II. He survived the First World War to write about his adventure in the book *My Escape from Donington Hall*. (See *Further Reading*, p.128.)

Pretoria Prison

(Breakout at Pretoria Prison, p.110-115)

Tim Jenkin returned to South Africa in 1991 and now lives in Johannesburg, where he works as a press officer for the African National Congress. **Stephen Lee** lives in London where he works as an electrician for a national newspaper. **Alex Moumbaris** lives in Paris where he works in the computer industry.

Harriet Tubman

(Harriet "Moses" Tubman leads slaves to freedom, p.104-107)

Harriet Tubman spent the years following the abolition of slavery looking after her parents in a small house she had built in Auburn in New York State. She was buried there when she died, aged 93. Her tombstone states "She never ran her train off the track and never lost a passenger".

Further Reading

Berlin then and now by Tony Le Tissier (Battle of Britain Prints International Ltd, 1992)

Camera in Colditz by Ron Baybutt (Hodder and Stoughton, 1982)

Devil's Island – Colony of the Damned by Alexander Miles (Ten Speed Press, 1988)

Escape from Alcatraz by J. Campbell Bruce (Futura Publications Ltd, 1979)

Escape from Montluc by André Devigny (Dennis Dobson, 1957)

Escape from Pretoria by Tim Jenkin (Kliptown Books Ltd, 1987)

Escaper's Progress by David James (Corgi Books, 1978)

Inside the Walls of Alcatraz by Frank Heaney and Gay Machado (1987)

My Escape from Donington Hall by Gunter Plüschow (John Lane, The Bodley Head Ltd, 1922)

Papillon by Henri Charrière (Granada Publishing Ltd, 1980)

The Life and Many Deaths of Harry Houdini by Ruth Brandon (Secker & Warburg, 1993)

Acknowledgements and photo credits

The publishers would like to thank the following for their help and advice: Hans-Juergen Dyck, Haus am Checkpoint Charlie, Berlin. Frank Heaney, Red and White Fleet, Inc., San Francisco. Tim Jenkin, Johannesburg. Dr. David Killingray, Goldsmiths College, University of London. Micheline and Gérard Laruelle, La Châtre. Sidney H. Radner, Houdini Historical Center, Wisconsin. Mark Seaman, Imperial War Museum, London. Marina Tchejina, St. Petersburg.

The publishers would also like to thank the following for permission to reproduce their photographs in this book: Associated Press, London (68, bottom; 77, top right; 120, top right); Centre d' Historie de la Résistance et de la Déportation, Lyon (108); Cincinnati Art Museum, Subscription Purchase/Charles T. Webber (107); Daily Express, London (86, bottom); Der Spiegel/Spiegel-Verlag, Hamburg (123, bottom); Fox Broadcasting Company (126); Golden Gate National Recreation Area, San Francisco, USA (78 middle; D. Denevi, 76, top; 78 left; Richard Frear, 81, bottom; Charles R. McKinnon, 81 middle); Haus am Checkpoint Charlie, Berlin (118; 120, top left; 121; 122; 123, top); Hulton Deutsch, London (69, top right, bottom left; 74; 86, top; 87; 88; 92, right; 93, right; 96, middle; 116, top; 117; 125, top left); Hulton Deutsch/ Bettman Archive (95); Imperial War Museum, London (98; 99; 100; 102); Peter Jenkin © Tim Jenkin (113); The Kobal Collection, London (124; 125); Leicestershire Museums, Arts and Records Service, Leicester, UK (90; 93, middle); Mary Evans Picture Library (92, middle); Pacific Aerial Surveys, Oakland, USA (77, middle); Peter Newark's Western Americana, Bath (104, top and bottom; 105, middle); Courtesy of the Sidney H. Radner Collection, Houdini Historical Center, Appleton, WI, USA (94, bottom right; 96, bottom left; 97); Robert Hunt Library (116, middle); H. Roger-Viollet © Collection Viollet, Paris (67; 68, top right, middle; 70; 71; 72); H. Roger-Viollet © Harlingue-Viollet, Paris (69, bottom right); Eli Weinberg © Tim Jenkin (110, top).

The trade name Vaseline is used with permission of Chesebrough-Ponds. Illustrations on page 93 are used with permission of Unilever History Archive (Vaseline jar) and Sarah Lee H & PC (Kiwi polish). The illustration on page 109 is used with permission of Thiers-Issard.

The publishers would also like to acknowledge the following for the use of the film stills on pages 124-125: Columbia/Open Road/Hugh French (Carl Foreman); Papillon Partnership/Corona/General Production Co./Robert Dortmann; Paramount (George Pal); Paramount/Malpaso (Don Siegel); Warner (Brian Foy).

Every effort has been made to trace the copyright holders of material in this book. If any rights have been omitted, the publishers offer to rectify this in any subsequent editions following notification.

USBORNE READER'S LIBRARY

TALES OF REAL
HEROISM

Paul Dowswell

Designed by
Nigel Reece, Karen Tomlins
and Helen Westwood

Illustrated by Ian Jackson

and

Aziz Khan, Janos Marffy,

Guy Smith and Sean Wilkinson

Contents

Whose hero?

Everyone has their heroes. Some, such as Yuri Gagarin and Bob Geldof, are familiar to millions. Others, such as the ill-fated Chernobyl firemen, are known only to a few. Heroes are usually people who inspire intense adoration, but not everyone in this book is universally admired. While organizing the Live Aid concerts of 1985 Bob Geldof was constantly faced with malicious accusations that he was an opportunist out to further his own career. To unrepentant Nazis, Claus von Stauffenberg was a traitor who deserved to die. Geronimo's surviving relatives still receive hate mail or provoke barroom brawls because their grandfather is seen by many as a barbaric murderer.

Fashion victims

Heroes go in and out of fashion. Alexei Stakhanov's heroism was invented by a dictator. Now he is regarded with scorn. Nurse Mary Seacole was forgotten by history for 150 years. Today she is a popular subject for school and university projects.

Lives on the line

Most of the people in this book, whether in one blinding moment of bravery, or years of suffering and struggle, took huge risks, or placed their lives on the line for others. Some achieved phenomenal results under massive pressure, while the whole world watched. You can find out about these extraordinary men and women in the following pages of Tales of Real Heroism.

Boomtown Bob's global jukebox

Bob Geldof in 1985. The Dublin singer had made many friends in the music business, and was well placed to organize the Band Aid and Live Aid projects.

In October, 1984, BBC News reporter Michael Buerk and a small camera crew wandered around a dusty plain in Ethiopia. Packed around them, as far as the eye could see, were an unfathomable number of emaciated refugees. They had gathered here to be fed by a European charity.

Reporting for the evening news, Buerk patiently described the combination of civil war and drought that had led so many starving people to congregate in this hellish place. The camera closed in on a young aid-worker whose job it was to select from the waiting thousands a few hundred to be fed. Those chosen were ushered into a small compound and given a simple meal.

Ethiopia was already extremely poor before the civil war and famine of the 1980s.

Africa

Ethiopia

It was barely enough, even for them, but it would keep them alive for another day. Those who had not been selected waited outside the compound, condemned to watch others eat, while they starved to death.

Boomtown Bob

Watching this report at his London home was pop star Bob Geldof, singer with Dublin's Boomtown Rats. The group had had great success in the late 1970s and early 1980s, but now no one was buying their records. Geldof had spent a dispiriting day trying to promote their latest single to a disinterested media, but what he was seeing on TV made his own problems seem insignificant. To Geldof, the people he watched looked like beings from another planet. Their limbs were skeleton-thin, and from their shrunken heads huge vacant eyes stared out at him.

That night Geldof lay awake haunted by the images he had seen, and felt a mounting

Refugees were fed a mixture of oats, powdered milk and sugar.

As famine swept through Ethiopia and Sudan thousands of refugees gathered at feeding stations such as this.

indignation that such a catastrophe had been allowed to happen.

He wondered what he could do. Perhaps he could record a song with other pop musicians, and give the profits to Ethiopia. A sociable and charismatic character, Geldof had made many friends in the music business, so the next day he began phoning as many as he dared.

Eager to help

Many of those contacted had seen Michael Buerk's report and were eager to help. In one afternoon Geldof had roped in an impressive handful of famous British pop musicians. Now all he needed was a song.

He had the germ of a tune, and the words came to him in the back of a taxi. He scribbled them down in his diary, and when he played the song to a positive reception, Geldof knew he had something that would work.

Everything for free

The idea picked up an unstoppable momentum. His record company pledged their support, and before the song was even completed he had persuaded everybody involved to donate their services for free.

Usually, the retailer made the greatest profit. In the United Kingdom almost all records were sold in one of six chain stores. Geldof rang each in turn, telling them they were the last on his list and that their five competitors had agreed not to take a share of the profits. Naturally, all agreed, not wanting to be singled out as the one company who had put profit before charity.

Spending day after day

Record costs

In 1984 most pop music was sold on vinyl discs. A single record cost £1.30. The money would be shared out as shown below.

Geldof persuaded all those involved in the project to donate both time and material for free. At first the British government was unwilling to waive their tax, but eventually relented.

seemingly glued to a telephone, Geldof persuaded ICI, the huge British chemical company, to contribute the vinyl material to make the record, and ZTT studio to donate free recording time. Eventually the entire cost of the record was covered by companies and individuals giving their time and material for free.

Sunday November 25 was chosen as the recording day, and aided by his friend and fellow musician Midge Ure, Geldof rushed to complete his song. It was called *Do they know it's Christmas?* and the musicians recording it would be called Band Aid.

Band Aid day

At the recording the most famous stars took turns to sing a couple of lines from each verse, while the rest played or sang along in the catchy football-crowd-like chorus. The publicity that surrounded such a gathering, and the concern in the country for the Ethiopian famine, made success inevitable, but its scale was surprising.

Unflagging crusade

Geldof pushed the song unflaggingly on TV and radio, and his crusade to make as much money as possible took on an abrasive edge.

"The price of a life this year is a piece of plastic with a hole in the middle," he told radio listeners. "How many more children will you let die in your living room before you act... Even if you hate the song, buy it and throw it away."

It became the United Kingdom's biggest selling

Geldof persuaded renowned British artist Peter Blake to create a cover for *Do they know it's Christmas?*. Blake's most famous work was the cover of The Beatles' *Sergeant Pepper* album.

single ever. Over 3.6 million copies were sold in the UK (8.1 million were sold internationally). Some people even bought the record by the box, and sent them as Christmas cards.

Direct aid

By January, the record had raised over £5 million. Wondering how best to spend it, Geldof spoke to several well-known charities, but all said they would have to take a substantial part of the money to cover administration costs. But Geldof had promised the public that every penny they spent on his record would go directly to feed starving people. He also began to feel that, as the money had come from all over the world, then no single country should have access to it. It became apparent that the best thing to do would be to go to Ethiopia himself, to see how best to spend it.

He could not afford to pay for the trip, so he persuaded a TV station and tabloid newspaper to pay for a flight to the Ethiopian capital Addis Ababa, and a hotel. The press followed him out. Millions had contributed to Band Aid, and the newspapers knew these people were desperate to know what Geldof was doing with their money.

Blunt talk

Once in Addis Ababa Geldof was characteristically blunt about what he thought needed to be done. He was beginning to realize Band Aid had a unique opportunity to do something special. Unlike a government, he was offering aid without expecting anything in return. Unlike a charity, he did not have to worry about keeping up long-term good relations with local politicians.

The next day Geldof and a horde of British newspaper men were taken to a feeding station at Lalibela to witness the famine first hand. Geldof was determined not to give the newspapers the photograph they all wanted – "Saint Bob" (as the press had jokingly begun to call him) comforting a starving child. Not everyone respected his wishes, but most photographers were too shocked to take pictures, sensing these children deserved more than to be the subject of

Geldof with Ethiopian families during his trip in January, 1985.

a sentimental photograph. The trip was useful. Geldof was able to speak face to face with aid workers and make direct contact with the people he intended to help.

From Ethiopia he also visited Sudan, where a crisis as serious as that in Ethiopia was now brewing.

World concert

Geldof returned to Britain with a burning anger, and the solid awareness that Band Aid needed an appropriate organization to administer the money it had made. He recruited a collection of well-respected government and media figures as a board of directors, and an office was set up, where, in the spirit of Band Aid, all equipment was donated.

Bad news soon poured into the office. In early 1985 there were 22 million people starving to death. The £8 million raised so far would be enough to keep them alive for two weeks. But Geldof had another more audacious idea to bring money to both Ethiopia and Sudan. The Band Aid concept had been taken up all over the world, with many countries recording their own famine relief song. A global concert could be the next step.

Geldof envisaged a concert in Britain, at the same time as a concert in the United States, broadcast around the world, with acts alternating on either stage. Between sets there would be constant appeals for money, and people could phone in with credit card donations, or promises to send money via their bank accounts. It would be the biggest concert in history, and hopefully it would raise a massive amount of money. The idea was to become known as Live Aid.

The Boomtown Rats were touring in early 1985. The day after the tour ended Geldof rang Wembley stadium in London, and booked it for Saturday July 13. He had 20 weeks to organize the event.

As with the record, Geldof had no problem recruiting acts to perform. The most renowned names in pop volunteered their services, and famous groups which had split up offered to get back together for the day. Before the week was out Geldof was contemplating an event featuring about fifty acts, each one performing their most popular songs for 15-20 minutes. It would be like a "global jukebox" he explained. In that way no one watching would get bored and switch off. The more who watched, the more who could be persuaded to donate money.

Goldsmith and Graham

Although the idea was fraught with potential catastrophe Geldof had two huge aces up his sleeve. Britain's foremost pop promoter Harvey Goldsmith had offered his services. He was well respected and a brilliant organizer. In the United States, Bill Graham, an equally prestigious pop promoter, was also recruited. With fourteen weeks to go, the involvement of both men reassured would-be performers that the event was unlikely to be a shambles.

But problems were mounting. The owners of Wembley stadium were demanding £150,000 for its use. Geldof wanted the venue for free. American singer Bruce Springsteen was playing there the day before. Although he was uncertain about whether to perform, he had already agreed to let Live Aid use his stage and

amplification equipment. This, despite the cost, was one good reason to use Wembley. The owners were bartered down to £100,000, and the venue was confirmed.

TV headache

Persuading TV stations to broadcast the concert was not as easy as Geldof hoped. As well as making money from the viewers he also intended to charge the TV stations for taking the concert. However, it would last about 17 hours, and most companies thought this was too long. Rearranging their schedules would also cost any TV company a substantial amount in cancellation fees. Eight weeks before the concert there was still no TV coverage lined up. Without it the concerts would be a waste of time.

But in late May, the BBC agreed to broadcast. Shortly afterwards Ireland agreed to broadcast Live Aid in its entirety, and the European TV

Transporting food from the UK to Africa was vastly expensive. So instead of paying the cost of hiring ships to transport goods to Ethiopia, Band Aid leased several boats long-term to take both their goods, and the supplies of other charities.

The Band Aid Logo (background) of a round map of the world like a plate with a knife and fork, was Geldof's idea.

companies came on board. But in the USA, there was still no agreement.

Further problems were coming from Wembley. The catering company there was refusing to donate their profits. With everyone else working for free to help starving people, it seemed obscene that a food company should be the only one making a profit. Geldof threatened to ask everyone to bring their own food. "I don't think you can do that" said the company. "I can do what I like, pal" Geldof bristled, and sure enough, that was what he did.

But there were triumphs too. The London police agreed to attend the event for free, saving the organizers many thousands of pounds. Throughout the UK, companies with large switchboards volunteered to operate them during the concert, so people could phone in pledges.

With only a few weeks before the concert, there was still no US venue, so Geldof flew to the States to straighten

BAND AID I
HAMBURG

things out. The city of Philadelphia offered its John F. Kennedy stadium. The Live Aid organizers would have preferred a more well-known and easily accessible venue, but at least this one was free.

The press conference to announce the event was held the day after Philadelphia was confirmed as the location for the US concert. Geldof was now exhausted. Weeks of cajoling and blustering his way through phone calls and meetings, and the round of nonstop journeys had drained him. But whenever his will to go on wavered, the images he had seen on TV would return to haunt him.

Almost every famous pop star from the previous 25 years was on the Live Aid bill. Geldof was also able to tell the press what his organization had been doing. Two Band Aid ships loaded with food and medicine were sailing for Ethiopia. Food was already being flown there. Band Aid was also negotiating to buy a fleet of their own trucks as African trucking companies usually charged extortionate prices to transport food to trouble spots.

Cash from chaos

Tickets for Wembley sold out in three days, but problems still loomed with television coverage. Many European stations seemed to be treating the event as a pop concert, rather than a money-raising exercise. Geldof threatened to withdraw their right to broadcast unless they organized appropriate money-collecting facilities.

In the United States, things were still chaotic. With three weeks to go, Geldof and Harvey Goldsmith flew out to see what was going on.

Although the venue had been decided, there were no tickets on sale. There was no final bill of artists. Even the stage plans (vital to ensure a quick turn around of the large number of acts) had been lost.

They also discovered that, apart from the performers, almost everyone else expected to be paid. The stage sound, lighting, and television technicians, stadium security staff and others would cost $3.5 million. (Wembley, by comparison, would only cost $250,000.) However, the Pepsi-Cola company, and others, had agreed to sponsor the Philadelphia show, and their money covered the stadium's huge costs.

Pulled apart

As the date grew nearer, the pressure on Geldof increased. Sponsors and television companies wrangled for special privileges or made unreasonable demands in

Geldof, glued to a telephone, in the final run up to the concert.

return for their services. The American network ABC for example demanded that all the biggest stars should perform during one three-hour slot, when they estimated that most people would be watching.

Geldof felt that he was being pulled apart. Massively overworked, he could not even sleep, as phone calls from Australia and California (where there is a nine to ten hour time difference) came in throughout the night.

He was plagued by a fear of failure. At night he lay awake bathed in cold sweat. If he did sleep, he would wake at six, his stomach in a knot. There were no contracts with the performers. If pop stars began to suspect things were going wrong, they would pull out. The concert would collapse, and Geldof would look like the world's biggest charlatan.

Moving mountains

But there were promising signals. Performers were moving mountains to be there. The Prince and Princess of Wales had agreed to attend. The BBC had found 500 telephone lines around the UK that could be used to take donations.

The night before the concert Geldof went to bed early with an aching back. At 2:00am the phone rang. It was an American manager threatening to pull out unless his group was given more time to perform. "******* pull out then," snapped Geldof, "I'm going to bed."

Live Aid day

Backpain kept him awake half the night, but Geldof woke the next day to a beautiful sunny morning. Driving through the streets of London en route to Wembley, passers-by shouted their good wishes, and he could sense that history was being made. If all went according to plan 85 percent of the world's television sets would be tuned into the concert.

At Wembley, he was relieved to see that the acts who had agreed to perform were actually turning up. Until then, the only group Geldof knew for certain would play was his own, and, as he put it, "17 hours of the Boomtown Rats would be too much for anybody."

Blur

The day passed in a blur – the Prince and Princess of Wales, the band of Guardsmen starting the concert with the national anthem, his own performance where he told the 80,000 Wembley crowd "This is the best day of my life", his TV interview afterward where he swore at British viewers for not sending enough money (donations soared shortly afterward), the Arab oil sheikh who donated £1 million.

Finale

Such was the improvised nature of the day that although the schedule proclaimed "Finale" at the end of the concert, nothing had actually been rehearsed. Geldof, now in considerable pain with a trapped nerve in his back, gathered as many performers as he could to rehearse *Do they know it's Christmas?* at the back of the stage.

As they ran through the song with an unamplified electric guitar the power failed and they carried on in the dark.

At 10:00pm the concert finished with a ragged but glorious version of the song. Geldof, who had fallen asleep from sheer exhaustion moments before, was hoisted onto the shoulders of rock's greatest performers, and the Wembley crowd shouted out the chorus of "Feed the World" to a global audience of one and a half billion people.

Rocking all over the world

The Wembley crowd erupted as Geldof walked on stage. "The noise was just incredible," he recalled in 1995. "The band had just started but I couldn't hear a note."

Right. Backstage pass for Wembley stadium.

Below. Eric Clapton performs for the Philadelphia crowd.

Below. Live Aid performers sing *"Do they know it's Christmas?"* as the British leg of the concert draws to an end. Pictured with Geldof, alongside other performers, are George Michael, former Beatle Paul McCartney, Elton John and Sting.

BAND AID presents
LIVE AID
SAT 13th JULY 1985
WEMBLEY STADIUM
ALL DAY
ARTIST

Punching a hole in the sky

In the summer of 1947 a huge silver B-29 bomber soared off the windswept runway at Muroc Airbase, California. As it climbed into a cloudless August sky, the sun gleamed brightly on a strange bullet-shaped aircraft slung under its belly. This was the Bell X-1 rocket, a machine designed to fly beyond the known frontiers of aviation science.

The X-1's pilot, a 24-year-old US Air Force captain named Chuck Yeager, knew he was gambling with death every time he took to the sky. But before the year was out, Yeager was determined to fly this rocket beyond the speed of sound – faster than any man had ever flown before.

In 1947 supersonic* flight was dark, forbidding territory. Yeager joked that it might make his ears fall off, but some aircraft attempting to break the sound barrier had literally disintegrated – shaken apart by invisible forces no one understood. Most aviation engineers believed no aircraft could fly faster than sound. They believed there was a "sound barrier" – an invisible wall of turbulence that would tear apart any plane that tried to break through it.

Dangerous missions such as these were rarely flown by military pilots. A highly paid civilian test pilot named "Slick" Goodlin had begun the project. As the X-1 tests approached the speed of sound, he demanded a $150,000 bonus for an actual attempt on the sound barrier. The United States military could no longer afford him, and decided to recruit a pilot from within their own ranks.

Despite the obvious dangers, Yeager volunteered. Flying filled him with an indescribable joy. The chance to pilot a beautiful aircraft like the X-1 was heaven sent. Besides, in the competitive world of the test pilot, the opportunity to become the first man to travel faster than sound was too good to miss. He took the job on his standard captain's pay of $283 a month.

Oddball

With his slow West Virginian country drawl, Yeager was something of an oddball in the high-powered world of experimental flying, but his exceptional skill and quick thinking coolness under pressure made him the best test pilot at Muroc.

Now, on this breezy August

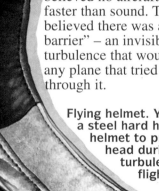

Flying helmet. Yeager wore a steel hard hat over his helmet to protect his head during the turbulent X-1 flights.

Speed of sound

Supersonic speed is measured in Mach numbers, after the Austrian physicist Ernst Mach who first measured it. The speed of sound is known as Mach 1. Mach .5 is half the speed of sound.

*Faster than sound.

day Yeager was about to pilot the X-1 on his first powered flight. He had flown the plane before, but only on glide flights. This time it was brimming with liquid oxygen and alcohol fuel.

At the flick of a rocket ignition switch his craft could shoot straight to the top of the sky, or it could explode into a thousand flaming pieces. He was nervous, but told himself fear was the pilot's friend. It sharpened the senses and kept the mind focused on the job he had to do.

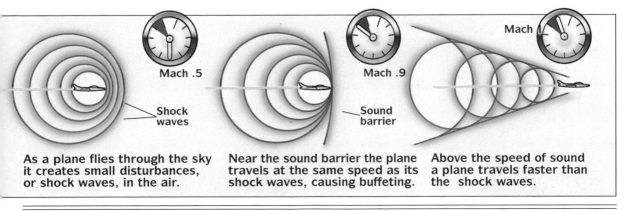

The X-1 was launched in the air from a B-29 bomber to save fuel on takeoff.

Small stages

Attempting to break through the sound barrier was so dangerous it would only be attempted in small stages. The X-1 would be dropped from the bomb bay at 8,000m (25,000ft) and then Yeager would ignite the rockets, and fly off into the horizon. Being unleashed from the B-29, rather than taking off in the usual way, saved weight on fuel. The less weight the X-1 carried, the faster it was going to fly.

Awkward entry

Yeager didn't sit in the X-1 at takeoff in case it accidentally dropped from the B-29 before they reached a safe height for the rocket to fly. Near the drop zone he left the B-29's cockpit

and squeezed through a narrow corridor to the bomb bay. Here he could see right down to the surface of the Earth.

Yeager had to climb down a ladder to a small metal platform and squeeze feet first through the hatch into his craft. At such a height it was viciously cold, and the wind threatened to tear his frozen fingers from the ladder's metal rungs.

Once he was inside, the door to the hatch was lowered down by his flight engineer and good friend Jack Ridley. He stood on the ladder and held it in place as it was locked from the inside. Yeager trusted Ridley with his life. Only 29, he had already established a reputation as a brilliant scientist.

"Let's go to work"

Some people said the X-1 was the most beautiful aircraft ever built. Yeager knew it was certainly the coldest. It was so chilly under the darkened bomb bay that he had to bang his gloved hands together to keep them from becoming numb. The X-1 cockpit had no heating and directly behind the seat sat several hundred gallons of freezing liquid oxygen fuel, which had coated the belly of the craft in a thin film of ice.

But now was no time to worry about the cold. "All set," radioed in Ridley, back inside the B-29's more comfortable interior. "You bet," said Yeager. "Let's go to work."

Roaring flame

The X-1 dropped like a stone. Yeager was blinded by bright sunlight and wrestled to get his

As a plane flies through the sky it creates small disturbances, or shock waves, in the air.

Near the sound barrier the plane travels at the same speed as its shock waves, causing buffeting.

Above the speed of sound a plane travels faster than the shock waves.

The Bell X-1 – bullet across the sky

The X-1 was designed to investigate the problems of flying at supersonic speed. With all four rocket chambers firing there was enough fuel for two and a half minutes' powered flight. X stood for "experimental" and only three were built.

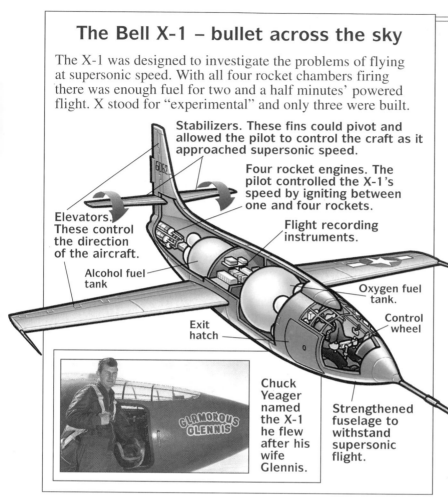

Stabilizers. These fins could pivot and allowed the pilot to control the craft as it approached supersonic speed.

Four rocket engines. The pilot controlled the X-1's speed by igniting between one and four rockets.

Elevators. These control the direction of the aircraft.

Flight recording instruments.

Alcohol fuel tank

Oxygen fuel tank.

Control wheel

Exit hatch

Chuck Yeager named the X-1 he flew after his wife Glennis.

Strengthened fuselage to withstand supersonic flight.

rattled every roof, window and coffee cup in the base. The X-1 shot back into the sky so fast it reached 11,000m (35,000ft) in under a minute. The fuel cut out, and Yeager glided down to the main runway, so excited he could not speak.

Everybody from Jack Ridley to his commanding officer Colonel Boyd was furious, and Yeager was seriously reprimanded . The X-1 project was one of the most dangerous series of test flights ever attempted. There was no space for fooling around.

Wheel jam

Subsequent trips proved this to be true. On his sixth powered flight on October 5, the X-1 began to be buffeted violently as Yeager reached Mach .86.

Through the window he could see the rocket's wings shaking wildly.

The next flight was even worse. As Yeager pushed his jolting craft to Mach .94 he found the control wheel jammed. This was serious. At the speed of sound it was assumed that the aircraft nose would either point up or down – something which the pilot would have to correct. If he was unable to do this, the craft could spin out of control and crash.

End of the line?

Yeager returned to base sure that the X-1 project would be cancelled. Everyone agreed, apart from Jack Ridley, who quickly scribbled some calculations on a piece of scrap paper. The flight engineer explained that the reason the control wheel jammed was that at such high speed the pressure of air flowing over the rocket prevented the wing and tail elevators from moving. If this

craft under control. Once the X-1 was flying level he flicked the first rocket ignition switch on his instrument panel. A luminous jet of flame roared from the tail exhaust, and a huge surge of power slammed him back into his seat. It seemed as if he was heading for the very roof of the sky, to punch his way into space itself.

One by one all four engines were ignited and as Yeager reached 14,000m (45,000ft) the sky turned from bright blue to dark indigo. He was on the edge of space, flying at Mach .8.

Muroc shake-up

Down at Muroc the research engineers and airbase technicians not working on the X-1 showed little interest in the

project, which they thought was doomed to failure. Experienced test pilots had been warned off volunteering for the flights. Most people thought Goodlin got out just in time.

But up on the roof of the sky the X-1 was flying beautifully. Yeager had reached maximum speed for this flight and still had half his fuel left. He thought it was time to show the Muroc personnel what his plane could do.

He cut the engines and dived toward the airbase. Lining up the rocket with the main runway he took it down to 90m (300ft) and headed for the control tower. Then Yeager hit the rocket ignition switches.

The four engines burst into life with an enormous streak of flame, making a roar that was the case, he suggested, then perhaps the aircraft could be controlled by moving the stabilizers on the tail, where air pressure was not as intense. Yeager had not done this before because he was afraid the tail might rip off, plunging the plane into a uncontrollable spin which could only end in a fiery explosion.

There was only one way to test Ridley's theory. Yeager flew back up to Mach .94, a whisker away from the speed of sound, and sure enough Ridley was right. Moving the stabilizer controls was enough to keep the X-1 flying steady, and gave Yeager the confidence to know that he would be able to keep control of his aircraft.

On target

Yeager now felt sure that he could break the sound barrier in the X-1 and survive. The next flight was planned for the following Tuesday.

On Sunday evening Yeager took his wife Glennis out riding, but disaster struck when he was thrown from his horse and fractured two ribs. The pain was intense but Yeager refused to go to the hospital at Muroc. He knew they would stop him from flying, and he was determined to finish the job.

Jack Ridley (right). His able mind saved the X-1 project from cancellation.

On Monday morning Glennis drove him to a local doctor who patched him up and told him to rest. But rest was the last thing on his mind. Despite the fact that he could do very little with his right hand Yeager drove over to Muroc and confided in Jack Ridley. He was convinced he could still make Tuesday's flight. He knew the aircraft really well now, and most of the controls would be no problem to operate.

However, lifting the handle to lock the door required a degree of strength his painful right arm did not possess. In the cramped cockpit he could not reach it with his left hand. There was a solution. Ridley found a broom and sawed off 25cm (10in). Yeager could use his good left arm to push the handle up with it. Getting down the ladder would be difficult too. Yeager jokingly suggested that Ridley could carry him piggyback.

Testing time

The B-29 took off at 8:00am on Tuesday, October 14, 1947. Officially Yeager was only meant to go to Mach .97 but, he reasoned, the more flights there were, the more chance there would be of an accident. He could be killed and the project could be cancelled. He was going to go for bust.

Getting down the ladder with two broken ribs was very painful but the broomstick worked fine. As the X-1 dropped from the bomb bay, Yeager felt perfectly in control. He ignited the rocket engines in quick succession and streaked towards the top of the sky. At Mach.88 the buffeting started and Yeager cut two of his engines and tilted the tail stabilizers. They worked perfectly. He kicked in rocket engine three again and continued to climb. The faster he went, the smoother the ride. The needle in his Mach instrument began to flutter, and then wavered off the scale.

Yeager was elated and radioed Jack Ridley in the B-29. "Hey Ridley," he giggled, "that Machmeter is acting screwy. It just went off the scale on me." "Son, you're imagining things," Ridley responded. "Must be," said Yeager in his particular slow drawl. "I'm still wearing my ears and nothing else fell off, neither."

Sonic boom

Aircraft flying faster than sound create air turbulence which causes an explosive noise called a "sonic boom", and down at Muroc a sound like distant thunder rolled over the airfield.

Only his instruments told Yeager he had broken the sound barrier. The X-1 was streaking smoothly along, and as he was flying faster than sound he did not even hear the sonic boom.

Its fuel expended, the rocket coasted down to earth, landing seven minutes later. Yeager's ribs still ached terribly, but the desert sun felt wonderful. Not since Orville and Wilbur Wright made the first powered flight in 1903 had an aircraft made such an extraordinary journey.

Terror stalks Chernobyl

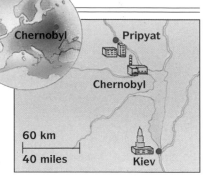

The towering red and white chimney of Chernobyl nuclear power station dominates the flat, swampy landscape of the Pripyat Marshes. Located 110km (70 miles) north of the Ukrainian capital of Kiev, the station had been built in the 1970s, when it was hailed as one of the Soviet Union's greatest scientific achievements.

Chief engineer Nikolai Fomin assured visitors that the chances of an explosion in this marvel of modern technology were about the same as being hit by a comet. But poor design and bad planning meant that Chernobyl was a disaster waiting to happen.

Fateful night

On the night of April 25-26, 1986, a team of engineers was carrying out tests on equipment at the number four reactor. In order to do this technicians had to slow the reactor down. Unfortunately they reduced the reactor's power so much that, like a fire about to go out, it began to shut down.

When this happens to this type of reactor it is dangerous to try to restart it. However, manager Anatoli Dyatlov, concerned that the power station would not be able to deliver enough power to nearby Kiev, ordered workers to

From control panels such as this, technicians tried to prevent the reactor from exploding.

The Chernobyl disaster spread pollution (red on inset globe) over much of Northern Europe.

restart the reactor.

Control room staff argued, but Dyatlov became enraged at their questioning his decision, and insisted they continue. In his clouded judgment he was just following procedures. An air of hysteria took hold of the control room as technicians began to grapple with tremendous forces they sensed were running out of control. They were right to feel afraid. As part of the tests the emergency water cooling system had also been cut off. The reactor began to overheat like a kettle boiling dry.

Earth shattering

In the control room technicians heard a series of ominous thumps, which made the ground tremble

Chernobyl's reactor

Nuclear power works by splitting the atoms of a metal called uranium. This creates energy in the form of heat, in a chamber known as a reactor.

At Chernobyl this process got out of hand when the reactor was slowed down and safety devices were switched off, during tests on equipment. A sudden increase in power caused the reactor to overheat and explode.

One of Chernobyl's four working reactors before the explosion.

beneath their feet. A worker rushed in with the horrific news that heavy steel covers on the reactor access points were jumping up and down in their sockets.

Then there was a huge thunderclap, the walls shook, and all the lights went out. Dust and smoke billowed in from the corridor, and the ceiling cracked open. A sharp, distinctive smell filled the air, like after a thunderstorm, only much, much stronger. It was 1:23am.

The reactor had disintegrated. It had exploded with such force that a 510 tonne (500 ton) concrete shield, which lay above it to protect power station workers from radiation, had been blown to one side. Other equipment, such as a massive fuel machine, had collapsed on top of it.

Catastrophe

In the control room foreman Valeri Perevozchenko's first thoughts were for his colleague Valera Khodemchuk, whom he had last seen in the reactor hall.

Glass and burning radioactive graphite was scattered over the reactor hall.

He dashed into the dark corridor, picking his way through clouds of dust and piles of blazing rubble, and made his way to the site of the explosion. The air seemed very thick, and he was also aware of another more sinister sensation. Deadly radiation released by the explosion was passing through him, and he could feel it burning his throat, lungs and eyes. His mouth tasted of sour apples.

Blind terror

His blood ran cold and Perevozchenko was seized by panic. He knew that his body was absorbing lethal doses of radiation, but instead of fleeing he steeled himself to stay and search for his colleague. Peering into the dark through a

After the disaster radiation levels were too high for instruments to record.

broken window that overlooked the reactor hall he could see only a mass of tangled wreckage.

By now he had absorbed so much radiation he felt as if his whole body was on fire. But then he remembered that there were several other men near to the explosion who might also be trapped.

Perevozchenko pressed on, running over floors that cracked with the sound of broken glass. He passed a colleague with a radiation

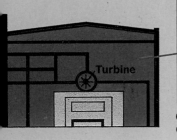

The reactor heated water into steam. The steam drove turbines which made electricity.

Turbine

Chernobyl's turbine hall narrowly escaped destruction in the fire that followed the explosion.

The number four reactor hall before and after the explosion.

monitoring tool, who told him one of his measuring instruments had already burned out, and the one in use was showing a reading that was completely off the scale.

Eerie shadows

Still Perevozchenko hurried on into the huge reactor hall. Looking far up to the ceiling he could dimly see that the roof had been blown off. Firemen summoned to tackle the blaze had already arrived, and their shouts rang around the huge hall. Small fires cast eerie shadows around the mangled mass of pipes and machinery. Streams of water gurgled and splattered from burst pipes. Oddest of all was the strange moaning sound of burning graphite, which was scattered around the floor. This material had come from the very heart of the reactor and was intensely radioactive.

Perevozchenko ran a flashlight over the scene and wondered what on earth he was doing in such a

The number four reactor after the explosion.

hellish place. Although he could not see it in the dark, the escaping radiation was rapidly turning his skin brown.

Still he stopped to listen, in case Khodemchuk was crying for help, then shouted desperately "Valera! Valera! I've come to rescue you." The echo of his voice died away, and all he could hear was the crackle of the flames.

Ahead lay a pile of rubble, and Perevozchenko tore his hands pulling aside concrete and graphite chunks trying to make his way forward, but neither Khodemchuk nor any other colleague could be found. Exhausted, he wandered back to the control room, passing the reactor itself on the way. He could see it had been completely destroyed in the explosion and was spewing out deadly radiation rays.

Bravery in vain

Perevozchenko knew that his comrades in the control room still believed the reactor was intact, and were struggling to open water vents to try to cool it down. He also realized that the best action to take was to get as many people as possible away from the radiation.

Back in the control room Perevozchenko struggled to remain conscious. He confronted shift foreman Alexander Akimov and begged him to evacuate the building. But

☢ Radiation ☢

When atoms split they give off invisible rays called radiation. If people are exposed to massive doses of radiation this can cause burns and cancer.

Akimov could not believe the reactor had been destroyed. Perevozchenko's bravery had been in vain. He had been unable to rescue his colleagues, nor warn others to escape before they too became fatally affected by radiation.

Heroic actions

But other workers who courageously endangered their lives had greater success. In the aftermath of the explosion power station staff in the turbine hall were able to drain highly inflammable fuels and gases from storage tanks near to the blazing wreckage. Four received lethal doses of radiation, and another four were hospitalized with painful injuries. Had they not succeeded then even greater disaster would have struck Chernobyl. There were another three working reactors at the station, and if the fire had spread, then they also could have been destroyed.

Others too had greater success rescuing colleagues. Laboratory chief Piotr Palamarchuk, in the control room at the time of the explosion, and Nikolai Gorbachenko, also set off through the rubble to search for their colleague Vladimir

Shashenok. He had been in a room next to the reactor.

They found him quickly enough, but Shashenok was trapped by a fallen girder and had been badly burned by radiation and scalding steam. They heaved the heavy girder from his body, and carried their injured comrade to the power station infirmary. Palamarchuk and Gorbachenko had exposed themselves to heavy doses of radiation, and they too remained at the infirmary.

Older heroes

Some of the older staff at the station deliberately chose to carry out the most dangerous tasks to spare their younger colleagues. Alexander Lelechenko, the head of the electrical workshop at Chernobyl, went three times into areas of lethal radiation to disconnect dangerous electrical equipment. Standing next to piles of radioactive rubble or knee deep in contaminated water he absorbed enough radiation to kill five people. He stopped briefly to be given first aid for radiation burns, but went immediately back to work for several more hours, and only stopped when he was too ill to continue.

Firefighters

Perhaps most of all it was the courage of the Chernobyl firemen that prevented the

Lieutenant Pravik (far left) and his team of firefighters prevented the fire from spreading out of control. All of the men pictured here died from radiation poisoning.

explosion from causing even worse damage. Lieutenant Vladimir Pravik and his crew dashed to the fire moments after the explosion. Within minutes they were on the roof of the reactor hall, pouring water down on the inferno.

Almost at once the firemen began to feel sick with radiation poisoning and felt unbearably hot both inside and outside their bodies. But they all carried on fighting the fire.

The roof could collapse at any moment. The tar that lined it was melting, releasing dense toxic smoke and sticking to the firefighters' boots. Radioactive dust fell on their uniforms. One by one they began to falter. For many, fainting and vomiting spells made it impossible to continue, but due to their heroic efforts the fires caused by the explosion did not spread to Chernobyl's other reactors, and had been extinguished by dawn. The firemen paid a heavy price. Later that day 17 were taken to a Moscow hospital for specialist treatment.

By now the greatest danger was over, but the tragedy still continued to run its course. The nearby town of Pripyat, where most of the Chernobyl workers lived, was completely evacuated. 21,000 people were taken away in convoys of buses, leaving their homes and possessions, never to return. (30,000 had already fled.)

Over the next days and months firefighters and construction workers continued to work at Chernobyl. Their main task was to prevent radiation pouring out of the ruptured

reactor. Helicopters flew over dropping sand on it, and eventually a huge casing was built around it.

The town of Pripyat remains abandoned to this day.

Over 100 people were taken into medical care after the first night of the disaster. Shashenok, Lelechenko, Perevozchenko and 28 others died over the next few weeks. Some lost their lives because they had tried to rescue injured colleagues. Others died because they had successfully prevented the fire spreading to the power station's other three reactors. Without their heroism Chernobyl would have faced a much greater catastrophe.

The Soviet Union gave this medal to those who fought the Chernobyl fire.

Owens' Olympic triumph

To American athlete Jesse Owens, fresh off the liner *Manhatten* en route to the 1936 Berlin Olympics, the streets of Germany were quite unlike anything he had ever seen before. Most striking of all were the swastika flags that hung from almost every window or shop front. The crooked black cross on a blood-red banner was the emblem of dictator Adolf Hitler and the Nazi Party. For three years they had ruled Germany with startling brutality.

Differing views

"The important thing at the Olympic Games is not to win, but to take part," the founding father of the modern Games Pierre de Coubertin said in his speech to the Berlin spectators, "just as the most important thing about life is not to conquer, but to struggle well."

The hosts of the Games weren't convinced. Germany's Nazi party saw the whole occasion as one big advertisement for their regime and its sinister beliefs.

The Nazis believed that the German people were the "Master Race", superior human beings whose destiny it was to rule the world. Their athletes – strong, lean and usually blond – were determined to prove their supremacy in the huge 110,000 capacity Berlin Olympic Stadium.

The Nazis had strong views about other races too, especially Jewish and black people. Nazi leaders were convinced that Jews were responsible for Germany's defeat in the First World War 18 years previously, and for the country's financial collapse in the 1920s. Jewish people in Germany were subjected to daily abuse and violence. The Nazi attitude to black people was less complicated. They simply saw them as subhuman.

Boycott or not

The Nazi regime provoked disgust throughout the world, and many people felt their countries should boycott the Olympics. Aware of this disapproval the regime had softened its racist policies in the months leading up to the Olympics – for example street graffiti, billboards and political newspaper articles denouncing Jews disappeared. In the end 52 nations had agreed to attend.

As an African-American Owens too had wondered whether he should go to Berlin. But at 22 he was one of America's most promising sportsmen – a phenomenal runner and long jumper – and the Olympic Games offered him an unmissable opportunity to compete against the world's greatest athletes.

Frosty or friendly?

Owens' coach had warned him to expect racist abuse from Nazi supporters among the German people and he had come to the Olympics determined not to allow this to affect his performance. In fact the Berlin crowds were fascinated by Owens, and no sooner had he arrived in the country than he was mobbed by sports fans who had already read about his record-breaking performances.

Owens made an ideal hero. Being tall and handsome obviously helped, but the athlete had a boyish charm and modesty that made him particularly likable. As he posed for photographs and signed endless autographs he talked to the crowd in a few words of German he had taken the trouble to learn. But his

Jesse Owens powers down the track during the 100m Olympic final.

popularity proved to be just as much a problem as the expected hostility. At night Owens was kept awake by fans who came to his bedroom window to take photographs or demand autographs.

10 vital seconds

The Games began on August 1 with a massive celebration which glorified the Nazi regime as much as it did the Olympics. Owens' first event, the 100m, was on the day after. This brief race is one of the most glamorous and exciting in athletics, and is always the cause of tremendous interest.

Interviewed for a TV documentary twenty years later Owens described the pressure he faced in the tense moments before a race he had trained for several years to win. "When I lined up for the final...I realized that five of the world's fastest humans wanted to beat me...I saw the finishing line, and knew that 10 seconds would climax the work of eight years."

On that cold, wet afternoon the crowd held its breath, the sound of the starting pistol reverberated around the stadium, and Owens shot from the starting line. He was ahead by the first 10m (30ft). Described by one journalist as having "the grace and poise of a deer" he had a natural style that made running look easy. Sweeping to a new Olympic record and an ecstatic reception from the stadium audience, he later described the moment he was presented with his first gold medal as the happiest of his career.

In his private stadium box Nazi

Owens won the 100m in 10.3 seconds. His victory put an end to Nazi hopes that German athletes would dominate the 1936 Games.

leader Adolf Hitler, a constant spectator of the Games, was not amused. When an aide suggested he invite Owens up to congratulate him (as he had with successful German athletes) Hitler was incensed. "Do you really think I will allow myself to be photographed shaking hands with a Negro?" he hissed.

Near disaster

The next day Owens competed in the long jump, but his three preliminary jumps nearly ended in disaster. Back home in America athletes were allowed

to make a trial run up to the long jump pit as a warm-up exercise. Here in Germany the rules were different. When Owens did this and ran into the sand the judges indicated that he had failed his first jump. Badly riled, he went on to fail his second jump too. As he prepared for his vital third jump, help came from an unexpected quarter. A fellow long jump competitor named Lutz Long, who was one of Germany's star athletes, whispered a few consoling words. Encouraged, Owens jumped successfully. The competition ended with Owens jumping to victory against Long in the final. The German could not match Owens' stupendous 8.06m (26ft 5 ¼in) leap.

Long and Owens left the stadium arena arm in arm, and

Hitler's view of the 110,000 capacity Berlin Olympic Stadium. The German dictator is second from the left.

Owens' winning jump. "I just decided I wasn't going to come down" he later told reporters. His record was only beaten in 1960.

that evening they met again at the Olympic Village and talked throughout the night. Long's blond, Germanic good looks and perfectly proportioned athlete's body were the epitome of the Nazi German racial ideal. But Long did not share his leader's racist notions. He and Owens found they had much in common. They were the same age, and from similar poor backgrounds, and both saw athletic success as a passport away from their humble origins. Long too was disturbed by the prejudice and violence he saw all around him in Germany.

More medals

There were more successes to come. On August 5 Owens took to the field to run in the 200m final. By now Nazi hopes that their athletes would sweep away all competition

had evaporated. The Nazi press had started to ridicule Owens, and German officials were heard complaining about "nonhumans" being allowed to take part in the Games.

Owens refused to be intimidated by this atmosphere of petty spite, and won the 200m in a record breaking 20.7 seconds. He had a particular technique for getting off to a good start. He noticed that the starting official would make some small gesture, a flexing of the legs, or tensing of the facial muscles, just before he fired the starting pistol. From the corner of his eye Owens would watch for these signs. Forewarned, he would shoot from the starting line the instant the gun fired.

The 200m was Owens' final event, and he settled back to enjoy the rest of the Games, unencumbered by the pressure of further competition. But the US coaches had other plans for him. He was in such top form they insisted he participate in the 4 x 100m relay. (Here four athletes run 100m each, passing a baton between them.) It was an unhappy decision, which caused much ill feeling, as the coaches dropped American Jewish athlete Marty Gluckman. Owens himself

protested. He'd won three gold medals already, he told the coach, and someone else should be given a chance. The coach was unmoved. "You'll do as you're told" he growled.

Another victory

So Owens once again took to the field. The American team was unbeatable. Starting the race, Owens was ahead by several paces when he passed the baton on to the second runner. Once again an Olympic record was set by the team, and Owens added a fourth medal to his collection.

It was a wonderful end to a wonderful performance, although Owens, with characteristic modesty, insisted another athlete occupy the top spot of the podium during the medals ceremony.

World famous

By now Owens was world famous, and he left Germany for a short tour of Europe, surrounded by press photographers and well-wishers.

But Hitler was deeply irritated by Owens' success. The 1936 Olympics were supposed to have been a great victory for the German Master Race. Now no one was going to forget the soft-spoken African-American who had quietly ridiculed Nazi assertions of German racial supremacy.

Owens on the winners' podium, following his long jump triumph. His friend and rival Lutz Long (right) gives the Nazi salute. Long was not a Nazi supporter, and was merely conforming with political demands.

12 seconds from death

An icy blast roared through the Skyvan transport plane as the rear door opened to the bright blue sky. On an April morning in 1991, above the flat fields of Cambridgeshire, England, three sky divers were about to make a parachute jump they would never forget.

Richard Maynard was making his first jump. He had paid £125 ($190) to plummet from 3,600m (12,000ft) strapped to Mike Smith, a skilled parachute instructor. Expecting this experience (known as a "tandem jump") to be the thrill of a lifetime, Maynard had also paid instructor Ronnie O'Brien to videotape him.

O'Brien leaped from the plane first to film Maynard and Smith's exit. The pair plunged down after him, accelerating to 290kmph (180mph) in the first 15 seconds. They soon overtook O'Brien, and Smith released a small drogue parachute to slow them down to a speed where it would be safe to open his main parachute. But here disaster struck. As the chute flew from its container the cord holding it became entangled around Smith's neck. It pulled tight, strangling him, and he lost consciousness.

Watching from 90m (300ft) above, O'Brien saw the two men spinning out of control, and when the drogue parachute failed to open he knew something had gone terribly wrong. Both men were just 45 seconds from instant obliteration.

O'Brien changed from the usual spread-eagled posture of a skydiver, and swooped down through the air toward the plummeting pair, with his legs pressed tightly together, and

Ronnie O'Brien

arms by his side. If he overshot he would have little chance of saving the two men, but this veteran of 4,000 jumps knew what he was doing.

Positioning himself in front of them he quickly realized what had happened, and tried to grab hold of Smith so he could release his main parachute. But diving at the same speed was difficult. O'Brien would be within arms length of the falling men, and then lurch out of reach. Then, suddenly, he fell way below.

Time was running out. The ground was a mere 20 seconds away, and O'Brien knew he had only one more chance. He spread his arms and legs out to slow his descent, and this time managed to connect with the pair. Whirling around and around, O'Brien searched frantically for Smith's parachute release handle.

With barely 12 seconds before they hit the ground, O'Brien found the handle and the large main chute billowed out above them. Slowed by the chute, Smith and Maynard shot away as O'Brien continued to plunge down. He released his own parachute when he was safely out of the way.

By the time the tandem pair had landed Smith had recovered consciousness, but collapsed almost immediately. Only then did Maynard realize something had gone wrong. Caught up in the excitement of the jump, with adrenaline coursing through his body and the wind roaring in his ears, he had had no idea that anything out of the ordinary had happened.

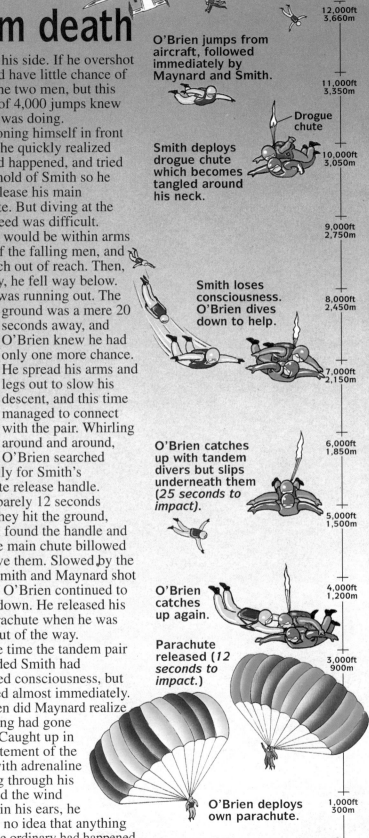

O'Brien jumps from aircraft, followed immediately by Maynard and Smith.

Smith deploys drogue chute which becomes tangled around his neck.

Drogue chute

Smith loses consciousness. O'Brien dives down to help.

O'Brien catches up with tandem divers but slips underneath them (*25 seconds to impact*).

O'Brien catches up again.

Parachute released (*12 seconds to impact.*)

O'Brien deploys own parachute.

12,000ft
3,660m

11,000ft
3,350m

10,000ft
3,050m

9,000ft
2,750m

8,000ft
2,450m

7,000ft
2,150m

6,000ft
1,850m

5,000ft
1,500m

4,000ft
1,200m

3,000ft
900m

1,000ft
300m

Geronimo's final stand

Geronimo in 1886. He fought so fiercely because he feared the arrival of Americans in Apache territory would lead to the demise of his people.

I n the foothills of the Sierra Madre mountains of northern Mexico, Apache warrior Geronimo had just discovered the bodies of his wife, mother and three children. Alongside were 20 other women and children of his tribe. The year was 1850.

All had been slaughtered by Mexican soldiers while Geronimo and an Apache trading party were separated from them, bartering goods with settlers in the nearby village of Janos. The Apaches had been at war with the Mexican army for the previous two centuries. The Mexican government intended to wipe out the tribe, and had offered a reward of $100 for every Apache warrior scalp*. (Women were worth $50 and children $25.)

A terrible rage welled up inside Geronimo, but his face gave nothing away. Apache custom frowned upon open expressions of emotion. For now there were too few Apaches to retaliate, but he did not doubt his time would come.

Shortly after the massacre Geronimo had a mystical

*Skin and hair from the top of the head, taken as a trophy from a dead enemy.

experience. Sitting alone grieving over the death of his family he heard a voice call his name. It said "No gun can ever kill you. I will take the bullets from the guns of the Mexicans... and I will guide your arrows." From that moment on Geronimo was utterly fearless in battle.

Direct attack

It was nine years before Geronimo was able to avenge the slaughter of his family. In 1859 he was part of a band of Apache braves (Indian warriors) led by Chief Mangus-Colorado. While skirmishing along the Mexican border at Arizpe, they came across Mexican soldiers whom Geronimo knew to be the ones who had massacred his family.

Geronimo's skill in battle was such that Mangus-Colorado gave him permission to direct an attack. Although outnumbered, Geronimo laid a careful ambush, hiding his men behind bushes in a hollow circle near to a river. As the Mexicans marched into the circle, the Indians charged.

For two terrifying hours they fought hand-to-hand. Eventually Geronimo and three other warriors stood alone on

the battlefield, surrounded by broken spears, arrows and the twisted bodies of fallen men.

New threat

As Mangus-Colorado and a small group of braves looked on from a distance, two Mexican soldiers armed with rifles dashed toward the four remaining Indians. Geronimo's three comrades fell to the Mexicans' bullets, leaving him to face his assailants alone. Grabbing a spear that had fallen nearby, he hurled it at one of them and felled the man. Picking up this soldier's sword he cut down the other Mexican. Although the Indians had won

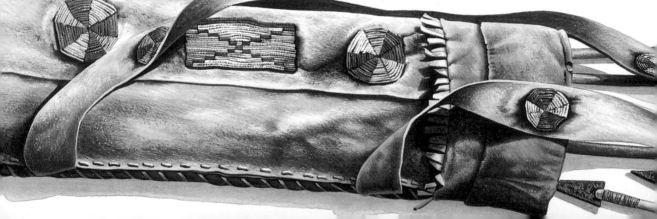

Apache lance. Weapons such as this were often made with blades taken from Mexican or American soldiers.

this battle, Geronimo was the only Apache to have fought who survived.

Commander shot

Geronimo fought scores of battles such as this, and his leadership and courage were to make him famous. On another occasion he crept up to the Mexican front line. At the exact moment their commander shouted the order for his men to charge, Geronimo shot him dead from close range. Although the ground around him was immediately peppered with gunfire, Geronimo ran for cover and escaped. Such bold actions gave great courage to his own soldiers and broke the spirit of his enemies.

The White Eyes

In the late 1850s North American settlers, dubbed "White Eyes" by the Indians, arrived in Apache territory. At first, the two cultures managed to live together, but in 1861 a series of misunderstandings sparked hostilities which would drag on for 25 years and have

devastating consequences for the Apache people.

In the 1870s the United States government attempted to solve their conflict with Indian tribes by placing all Indians on "reservations". These were specific areas where particular tribes were meant to live. The government was determined not to have bands of Indians marauding around territory where American settlers were setting up farms and towns.

Reservation life

The Apache people were nomads, used to roaming their land at will, and living in one particular spot was unknown to their culture. But threatened by the American army they settled on a reservation in southeast Arizona in 1872.

This was not too great a hardship because this land was part of their traditional territory. However, in 1876 the government decided the Apaches had too much freedom and should be moved north to San Carlos, where the US Army could keep a closer watch on them. Geronimo in particular, felt strongly that they should not go. It was a fly-blown, barren stretch of desert, with little food

and water to sustain his people.

A 24-year-old government agent named John Clum was appointed to carry out this resettlement. Clum had an arrogant, strutting manner, which the Apaches found irritating. They nicknamed him "Turkey Gobbler".

Although Clum managed to persuade some of the Apaches to go to San Carlos, many others looked to Geronimo to

The first Americans

Throughout the United States, from Lake Huron to Miami Beach, North Dakota to Wichita Falls, the country still bears the names of the first Americans. For three hundred years European newcomers and North American Indians waged war over possession of the land. Treaties were signed, arrangements were made, but no permanent settlement could be found. The wandering nomadic lifestyle of the Indians did not fit the European notion of towns and cities, farms and factories.

Some of the Indian chiefs believed the white man and his culture was too strong to resist, but others would not go without a struggle. The Navahos, the Cheyenne, the Sioux, the Apaches and many other tribes great and small, fought bitter battles with the American army and were massacred or imprisoned.

Apache arrow pouch and arrows. The bow was such an effective weapon that the Apaches continued to use it long after they acquired guns.

lead them away from reservation life. Over 700 joined him and fled to the hills. For three years they lived the nomadic life they were used to, gathering food where they could, and making sporadic raids in Mexico.

In 1877 Clum managed to persuade Geronimo to meet him to discuss settling in San Carlos reservation. The Indian leader and 100 Apache warriors turned up to negotiate at Warm Springs, a small town in New Mexico. But Clum had hidden 80 soldiers in the town. When Geronimo and his men arrived they were promptly surrounded. With no less than 20 rifles trained on him alone, Geronimo decided not to test his supposed invincibility to bullets, and ordered his braves to surrender.

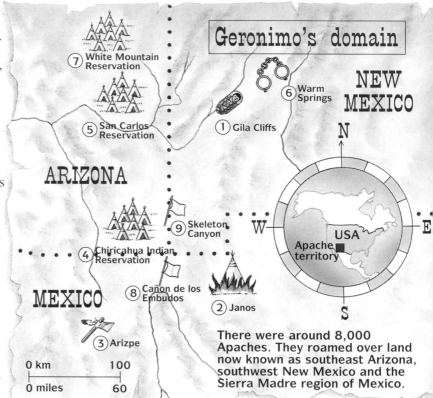

Geronimo's domain

There were around 8,000 Apaches. They roamed over land now known as southeast Arizona, southwest New Mexico and the Sierra Madre region of Mexico.

Clapped in irons

Geronimo had iron shackles placed around his ankles, and he and his warriors were taken to prison. For an Apache to be caged like a wild animal was a dreadful disgrace and Geronimo must have felt a keen sense of shame, especially as his capture was the result of a simple trick.

For two months Clum tried to get government permission to have Geronimo hanged. When this was refused, Clum resigned. His successor was more sympathetic, and released the Indian leader and his fellow braves from prison.

There followed a quieter period when Geronimo and his people tried to settle at San Carlos reservation. But some American newcomers were plundering Indian goods, or trying to provoke the Apaches into violent action so they could massacre them and take their land. On top of this many Apaches were homesick, and looked to Geronimo to lead them back to their hunting grounds. So in 1882 he and a band of warriors and their families turned their back on the listless life of the reservation to roam the territories of southeast America.

Grey Wolf

The Americans were not prepared to let them be. All other Indian tribes had been defeated, and their leaders were dead or in prison. General George Crook was given the job of tracking the Apaches down.

The Apaches respected Crook, whom they called "Grey Wolf". He met with them and eventually they agreed to return with him to live on a government reservation.

Geronimo was taken to the White Mountain reservation in Arizona, and made another

Geronimo (standing, right of horse) and Apaches who had fled with him from San Carlos. 1886.

attempt to settle down. The American government was trying to persuade the Apaches to become farmers, but some found this life impossible to get used to. There was too little to do, so they took to drinking beer, gambling, and loafing around. For a people used to living on the land and their wits, this was no life at all.

There were other problems too. Local newspapers were calling for Geronimo to be executed, and reports reached him that American soldiers were going to kill him. So in May 1885 he rounded up 145

of his tribe, and once again fled from a government reservation.

The Apaches were masters of their terrain. They vanished among a landscape of stony mountains, pine forests and empty deserts. In this barren wasteland they knew better than anyone where to find a spring, or how to survive on mesquite beans, juniper berries and piñon nuts.

For ten months Geronimo's braves roamed the American Southwest. Terrible tales of murder and mutilation appeared in American newspapers. How much was true it is difficult to say, but any atrocities committed by the Apaches were more than matched by those carried out against them by American soldiers.

Stiffened resolve

Crook's troops pursued them relentlessly but Apaches were skilled in leaving no trail and ran rings around their pursuers. Once, Geronimo even sneaked back to the White Mountain Reservation to collect his new wife and children, right under the noses of patrolling guards. By making his enemies look foolish Geronimo stiffened the resolve of his fellow braves.

But the stresses of being constantly trailed were beginning to tell. At 62 Geronimo was an old man. In March 1886 he agreed to see General Crook to discuss surrender terms. They met in Cañon de los Embudos, just south of the Mexican border.

Geronimo trusted Crook, who had great respect for the Apaches. He told him "Once I moved about like the wind. Now I surrender to you..."

Another escape

That night as the braves sat drinking whiskey, Geronimo heard again he might be hanged. Once more he fled into the Sierra Madre mountains with 34 of his followers. His escape was the final straw for General Crook. Exhausted by months of tracking such a cunning opponent, and dejected by the American Government's refusal to let him negotiate a fair settlement with his respected foes, Crook resigned.

He was replaced by General Nelson A. Miles who led an extraordinary campaign against the fugitive Apaches. Throughout Arizona and New Mexico signal teams were set up to flash Morse code messages across the country. One quarter of the entire US army (5,000 troops) were enlisted to fight 16 warriors, 12 women, and 6 children. Around 3,000 Mexican soldiers also joined the hunt. They searched in vain. Geronimo and his band had vanished into the wilderness.

Final surrender

Again, it was the strain of being constant fugitives that caused Geronimo and his group to give themselves up.

Geronimo (third from right on front row) with fellow Apache prisoners, on the way to Florida. 1886.

News also reached them that their tribe had been transported to Florida. This was a stunning blow. The Florida climate was completely unlike the arid desert terrain they were used to.

In August 1886 Geronimo met General Miles at Skeleton Canyon, Arizona, and offered his surrender. Miles's terms were reasonable. Geronimo was to be reunited with his family within five days. He would not be punished for his resistance. His tribe would once again be allowed to settle in a reservation in their Arizona homeland.

Punishment

But Miles's promises were lies. The American government had decided to punish the Apaches for their stubborn resistance. Geronimo escaped the hangman's noose by a whisker. Even American President Grover Cleveland, who had been following the Apache campaign in the newspapers, wanted Geronimo to hang.

But some justice still prevailed. The Apaches were sent to Florida, not as

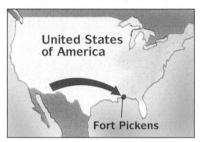

Geronimo and his Apache warriors were transported to Fort Pickens, Florida. During Geronimo's lifetime (1823-1909) the United States expanded from the green area shown here to the area it occupies today, and in many places the Indian peoples were wiped off the map.

criminals, but as prisoners of war. For 30 years they were kept from their homeland. Although the terms of their imprisonment were light, it was not until 1913 that they were allowed to return to the more familiar territory of Mescalero Reservation in New Mexico.

Last great leader

In 1898, Geronimo met General Miles once again and begged to be allowed to return home. "I have been away from Arizona now twelve years," he

said. "The acorn and piñon nut, the quail and wild turkey... they all miss me. They wonder where I've gone. They want me to come back." Miles was unmoved and Geronimo never saw his homeland again.

History remembers him as the last great Indian leader, and his capture marked the virtual end of Indian resistance against the American government. In defending his way of life against impossible odds Geronimo displayed a defiant heroism. He died in 1909, aged 85, and in his lifetime he had seen his tribe reduced to a quarter of their former number.

Geronimo in old age, in his garden. With him are his sixth wife and some of his children.

Brazil's rainforest hero

A soft light falls through the lush green canopy of giant trees and onto the dim forest floor. Here, a scurrying anteater rooting among the shadows is startled by a shrieking parrot, and bolts into thicker undergrowth. A butterfly, each shimmering blue wing the size of a man's hand, flutters from flower to flower.

The Brazilian rainforest in the Amazon basin is one of the most extraordinary and beautiful areas on Earth. There are so many plants and animals that scientists have only been able to identify a tiny fraction of them. Yet for much of the past twenty years this forest has been the scene of vast and ruthless devastation.

Alongside the Native American peoples who live here are some of the Amazon's more recent inhabitants – the rubber tappers. In the 1980s a tapper named Chico Mendes became a hero to millions in his struggle to save the forest from further destruction.

Remote region

Mendes was born in 1944 into a life of extreme poverty in the remote Acre (*Ak-ree*) region of the Amazon. Here there were no schools or hospitals, and only a few people could read and write. Like his father and grandfather he worked in the forest by making small cuts in rubber trees (known as tapping) to collect a fluid called latex, which is used to make rubber.

Chico Mendes in 1988.

The tappers were poorly paid by traders and landlords who treated them with great cruelty. On one occasion for example, a tapper who angered a landlord was wrapped in rubber and set on fire. Such actions went unpunished by the local police who considered the tappers to be little better than animals.

Inspiration

When he was nine, Mendes began to work as a tapper around Xapuri (*Sha-poo-rii*), a rickety riverside town deep in the Amazon forest. Residents remember him as an amiable but determined child. He was also very bright.

In his late teens he met Euclides Tavora, a local trader in his 50s with a keen interest in politics. Tavora taught Mendes to read and convinced him that the best thing the rubber tappers could do to improve their lives was to form a trade union.

During the 1960s Mendes tried unsuccessfully to do this. Most tappers were so afraid of their bosses that they accepted their grim lives with dejected apathy. But still, Mendes made many friends among his workmates, writing their letters and teaching them to read.

Changing world

The world Mendes grew up in was changing fast. When he was a child 90% of all Brazilians lived by the coast. The rest of the huge country was practically deserted. All this was to change.

In the 1950s the government decided to develop the interior of Brazil, which is mostly forest and rich in valuable minerals and metals. Over the next two decades roads were built, and businesses and landowners flocked to invest there.

Most of these landowners were ranchers raising cattle for Brazil's meat industry. Many were ruthless men who would kill anyone who stood in the way of a quick fortune.

Cattle need pasture to graze. Nearly 60% of Brazil was dense forest, and the ranchers began to tear it down to make grassland. The cheapest way to do this was to burn a huge area and then use aircraft to sow grass seeds. In this way forest could be turned into pasture in a few months, and ranchers could make quick profits.

But there was a dark side. Plants and animals were destroyed, and tappers and Native Americans who lived in the forest were driven away or murdered. As cattle fed on the land and rain washed away the soil, pasture created in this way became wasteland. After five years it was little more than desert.

Mendes addresses a meeting of Xapuri rubber tappers.

By then Chico Mendes had had some success organizing his workmates. He had joined forces with a tapper named Wilson Pinheiro who had set up the *Rural Workers Union*. They had come together to fight the rubber bosses for better pay, but now they were fighting against the ranchers for the very existence of the forest.

Peaceful protest

Mendes hated violence, and would not use force against his opponents. Instead, when word reached the Union that an area of forest was to be destroyed the tappers would turn up in large numbers and form a human chain to prevent ranch workers from carrying out their task. These protests did not always succeed, but large areas of Acre's forest were preserved in this way.

But Wilson Pinheiro was murdered for his resistance, and Mendes was severely beaten by hooded men in the pay of the ranchers. Death threats were a constant feature of his life, but this did not stop him becoming the president of the Xapuri branch of the *Rural Workers Union*. His warm personality brought many new recruits, and he was a talented organizer and

a persuasive spokesman.

Useful friends

The feud between ranchers and union continued into the early 1980s. During this time Mendes met a Brazilian academic named Mary Allegreti. She was greatly impressed by his decency and determination, and well aware that he could be murdered at any moment.

In October 1985 Allegreti organized a conference for rubber tappers in Brazil's capital, Brasilia. The conference was also attended by conservationists and journalists from Europe and the United States. By then many people were becoming concerned about the destruction of the forest. So many trees were being burned that scientists suggested this was contributing to global warming – heating up the world's climate and causing sea levels to rise.

As well as publicizing the tappers' plight, Allegreti hoped the conference would make Mendes famous. This would make it more difficult for the ranchers to kill him discreetly.

Suspicious government

The Brazilian government was suspicious of conservationists, whom they saw as standing in the way of progress. Mendes did not want to stop the development of the Amazon, but he felt there were better ways of using it than ranching. Long term, rubber tappers and small scale farmers and nut

The whole of the Amazon region is dense with forest.

Acre was one of the most remote areas of Brazil. It was not until the early 1970s that ranchers lured by cheap land began to arrive there. The forest's inhabitants were treated in the usual brutal way and there was so much violence it was said that the smell of gunpowder hung in the air.

Huge areas of forest were burned to make pasture.

gatherers could actually make more money for Brazil than ranchers, and also leave the forest intact for future generations. Mendes suggested that vast areas should be set aside for conservation.

Roads and Bankers

Following the conference Mendes turned his attention to another major problem. A road was being planned straight into the heart of Acre. It would only be useful to the ranchers and bring further destruction to the forest. Mendes decided to fight its construction by standing as a candidate in the government elections.

Local landowners were determined to thwart him, and bribed people to vote against him. Mendes was soundly defeated, but some good came of the campaign. His name became more widely known to Brazilian politicians and he was introduced to José Lutzenberger, a prominent Brazilian conservationist, who had close links with environmental groups in America. This was very useful. The road builders and ranchers were financed by money loaned by American banks. If American politicians and environmental groups could persuade the banks to stop lending money, this would stop further development.

Mendes decided to talk directly to them. In March 1987, wearing a suit taken from a batch of secondhand charity clothes, he visited another country for the first time in his life. Stepping into a sophisticated world of plush offices and sharp suits, Mendes was not intimidated. The businessmen and politicians he met were impressed with his keen intelligence and the reasonableness of his case. He persuaded bankers to withdraw funding for the new road until the Brazilian government took proper steps to protect the forest and its inhabitants.

Enemies within

In Acre the local ranchers were seething with rage. For years they had been able to get whatever they wanted. Now, without the new road, it would be even more difficult to expand their businesses and make more money.

One of the most ruthless Acre ranchers was Darli Alves da Silva. Darli was an unlikely looking villain – tall and thin with pipelike arms and legs, he had large glasses which perched uneasily on his bony face. Only a thin voice, which trickled out between clenched teeth, indicated that he was a dangerous man.

Determined to provoke a violent clash with Mendes and his union, Darli began to clear out tappers around the nearby town of Cachoeira (*Cash-ooo-eer-ah*), intending to turn the forest into pasture. Mendes responded with a campaign to have Cachoera declared a conservation area. Violent thugs sent by Darli interrupted protest meetings, and midnight telephone calls warned Mendes and his colleagues that they were going to be murdered.

But Mendes managed to persuade the Brazilian agricultural minister to turn Cachoeira into a conservation area – putting an end to any further destruction of the forest.

Darli was enraged with Mendes and sent his son Darci to kill him. On December 22, 1988, Mendes was shot dead as he walked into his back yard to take a shower.

"I want to live"

Shortly before he was killed Mendes said, "If a messenger came down from heaven and guaranteed that my death would strengthen our struggle, it would even be worth it." But he was doubtful. "Public rallies and big funerals won't save the Amazon," he said. "I want to live."

But he was wrong. His death caused an extraordinary outcry, catching the attention of international newspapers and TV stations. Support for his cause poured in from around the world.

His funeral was held on Christmas Day and thousands attended, including famous Brazilian politicians and

Mendes' funeral at Xapuri.

entertainers. The government sent 60 policemen to hunt down his killer. Darli and Darci were arrested, and sentenced to 19 years in prison.

Perhaps the best tribute to his life came from one of the people he fought so hard to defend – a poor Brazilian rubber tapper. "They thought they killed Chico Mendes," he told a British television crew. "They didn't. Because he's alive in each of us."

Animal heroes

Snowbound rescue

New Jersey winters are harsh, and February 1983 was no exception. Unable to travel to school because of a blizzard, Andrea Andersen and her sisters were spending the day at their seaside home. Bored, they went outside to play. Her sisters soon got cold and returned to the house, but Andrea remained outside. While she was on her own, a howling gale blew her into a snowdrift right on the edge of the icy North Atlantic. Numb with cold, Andrea found that she could not get out, and shouted frantically for help. But her cries were swallowed by the swirling wind.

Next door to the Andersens lived Dick and Lynda Veit, and their Newfoundland dog Villa. Dogs have very sensitive hearing, and Villa was able to recognize Andrea's desperate cries amid the howling wind. Immediately she left the house, leapt over a 1.5m (5ft) wall and set off in search of the girl.

Villa soon found Andrea and lowered her head into the drift.

Villa with Lynda Veit and Andrea Andersen.

The helpless schoolgirl grabbed hold of the dog, who dragged her out of the snow, and then led her back to her warm home.

Goose saves guardsman's bacon

In 1837 French Canadians were rebelling against British rule in Canada, and the Coldstream Guards (a regiment of the British army) was sent by the British government to help defend Quebec. One of them was guardsman John Kemp.

One day, while on sentry duty at a farm outside the city, Kemp noticed a handsome white goose searching for food. Close by and watching intently was a hungry fox. Sensing danger the goose looked up. Both animals stood frozen as if in a trance. Then the goose panicked, and ran shrieking between the guardsman's legs. Kemp reacted instinctively, and when the fox came hurtling along, he killed it with his bayonet.

Jacob and a British soldier. The brave goose was given a gold collar by grateful guardsmen.

The grateful goose rubbed his head against Kemp's legs. From that moment on the guardsman adopted him as a pet, and christened him Jacob. It was an alliance that would save his life.

Fowl play

Shortly afterwards, Kemp was standing guard outside the farm when he was attacked by a group of rebels. As he fought for his life Jacob came squawking to the rescue, wings flapping wildly, and pecking with his sharp beak. While the distracted intruders defended themselves, Kemp grabbed the rifle that had been knocked from his hand and fired. The shot alerted soldiers nearby who came to his rescue. Jacob had saved both Kemp and his comrades. They became so attached to their unusual pet that they took him with them when the Coldstream Guards returned to London.

Jan's best friend

Few people can have had such a loyal companion, nor owed so much to their dog as Jan Bozdech of Czechoslovakia.

Shortly before the Second World War Bozdech came across a starving German Shepherd puppy. He adopted the dog, named it Antis, and the two became inseparable.

Following the German take-over of his country in 1938, Bozdech fled to France, taking Antis with him. When war broke out he became a pilot in the French Air Force and flew several missions. When France also fell to the Germans, pilot and dog left for England, where Bozdech joined the British Air Force.

After the war they returned home. But Bozdech's troubles were far from over. Czechoslovakia was now controlled by the Soviet Union, and shortly after his return a strict communist system was set up, and citizens were forbidden to leave. Bozdech had spent the last ten years fighting such tyranny and was determined to escape. With Antis and two

friends he set off for Austria, the nearest non-communist country. His friends were not happy to travel with the dog, but Antis soon proved his worth, alerting them to the presence of police and border guard patrols.

During the journey the escapers had to cross a fast-flowing river under cover of darkness. Bozdech slipped, bashed his head on a boulder, and was carried away by the current. Antis bounded after him and, grabbing his master's jacket in his teeth, dragged him to the riverside. As he lay recovering, the German Shepherd trotted off to locate his two friends who had

vanished into the night.

Near the border the party stopped to rest in a quiet spot, leaving the dog to keep watch. After a while a border guard appeared and began to walk directly toward the sleeping men. Antis began to bark and leap around the guard, distracting him from his route, and saved the three escapers from almost certain arrest.

Once out of Czechoslovakia, Bozdech and Antis returned to England. The dog died in 1953 and Bozdech had him buried at Ilford Animal Cemetery in London. These words are written on his gravestone:
There is an old belief
That on some solemn shore
Beyond the sphere of grief
Dear friends shall meet
once more.

Heroic homing pigeons

Pigeons are able to return home over great distances. Soldiers have long made use of this ability by employing these birds to carry messages. Some pigeons give up easily in difficult circumstances, but others are determined to return home. Pigeons have completed their missions with bullet wounds, or after being mauled by hawks. One even walked back home with a broken wing.

During the First and Second World Wars pigeons were used in great numbers and many men owed their lives to the

birds. In Italy in 1943 one American carrier pigeon named G.I. Joe flew 32km (20 miles) in 20 minutes to warn a bomber squadron not to attack a village that had just been captured by American troops.

Another pigeon named Winkie was aboard a British bomber when it crashed in the North Sea. The crew survived but as no one at their base knew their position they were in danger of freezing to death. Winkie was covered in oil but

A metal tube on the pigeon's leg carries a message.

this did not prevent him flying 208km (129 miles) back home with a message reporting that the plane had crashed in the sea. A search was launched and the crew's lives were saved.

Odette's ordeal

On a May day in 1943, a bedraggled French woman sat before a military court at 84 Avenue Foch, the Parisian headquarters of the German Gestapo*. She had spent a month in prison, forbidden to bathe, exercise or change her clothes. Her feet were bandaged where she had been tortured, but she still managed to project a curiously detached dignity. Her name was Odette Sansom, housewife turned British agent, and she was on trial for her life.

Odette, who spoke no German, soon became bored, and her eyes wandered around the elegantly decorated room. But when a senior officer stood up and read a statement to her, she knew proceedings had come to an end.

She shrugged wearily and told the court she did not speak German. The officer frowned and explained in halting French that she had been sentenced to death on two counts. One as a British spy, the other as a member of the French Resistance.

Odette looked on these stiff, pompous men with derision and a giggle rose inside her. "Gentlemen," she said, " you must take your pick of the counts. I can die only once."

Childhood troubles

Odette was born in Amiens, France, in 1912. Her father was killed during the First World War, when she was four. At seven she caught polio and was blinded for a year, and then spent another year with partial paralysis. These disabilities forged a fiercely independent character.

At 19 she married Englishman Roy Sansom, and moved to London. The years before the Second World War were spent raising three daughters and living the life of an English housewife.

War broke out in 1939, and in less than two years Nazi Germany had conquered almost all of Europe. The fall of France in 1940 caused Odette much grief. Cut off from her family, she worried constantly about their safety.

In the spring of 1942 Odette heard a government radio broadcast appealing for holiday snapshots of French beaches. An invasion of France from Britain was being planned, and such photos would help decide which beaches were best for landing troops. Odette had spent her childhood by the sea, so wrote to offer her help.

Secret service summons

Shortly afterward she was summoned to London. The man who met her wasn't really interested in her photographs. Instead, he asked if she would like to go to France as an agent.

She declined, but over the next week Odette wrestled with her conscience. She was torn between a deep duty she felt to France, and responsibility for

British agent Odette Sansom.

her three children. Eventually she decided she would train as an agent, and found a convent boarding school for her daughters. Odette's work was so secret she could not even say what she was doing. She told them instead that she had joined the Army to work as a nurse.

So her training began. From the start the dangers were made transparently clear. "In many ways it's a beastly life" said her commanding officer Major Buckmaster. In wartime, the fate of a captured secret agent was almost always execution.

Physical fitness and self-protection training toughened her. She learned specialized skills too, such as which fields were best for aircraft to make secret landings, and how to tell the difference between German military uniforms.

Bound for France

Her final days in England were spent making her appear as French as possible. There was a new wardrobe of authentic French clothes, her English fillings were taken out and replaced with French ones, even her wedding ring was filed off and a new French one placed on her finger.

On Odette's last meeting with Buckmaster he supplied

Wartime France

Between 1940 and 1944 France was controlled by Nazi Germany.

Britain

London

Germany

Paris

France

Cannes

her with several different drugs – sickness pills, energy pills, sleeping pills, and most sinister of all, a brown, pea-shaped suicide pill. Buckmaster told her it would kill her in six seconds. "It's not a very pretty going-away present," he said, "so we've decided to give you another." He handed Odette a packet which contained a beautiful silver compact.

Home again

Odette was taken to France in November 1942, and began working in Cannes with a group of secret agents led by Peter Churchill, a British officer. She acted as a courier, delivering money to finance the work of the Resistance, and picking up stolen maps and documents to pass back to Britain. She found safe houses for other agents, and suitable locations for aircraft to land or drop weapons.

Churchill was impressed. His new agent was quick-thinking, and capable. She could also be very funny, and had an unstoppable determination.

Danger lurked at every turn. The Gestapo were constantly arresting Resistance workers, and anyone Odette met could be a double agent. Eventually the group was infiltrated by a traitor named Roger Bardet, who worked for the Abwehr – German Military Intelligence.

Betrayed

Churchill and Odette were seized on April 16, 1943. Even as they were bundled off at gunpoint, Odette had the presence of mind to conceal Churchill's wallet, containing radio

codes and names of other agents, and managed to stuff it down the side of a car seat en route to prison.

There was no denying they were both British agents, but Odette spun a complex tale for her captors, hoping at least to save her colleague's life. She said that they were married, and Peter Churchill was related to the British Prime Minister Winston Churchill. Her "husband" was merely an amateur dabbler, who had come to France on her insistence. It was she who had led the local resistance ring, and she who should be shot. This was a convincing story and the Germans paid much less attention to Peter Churchill.

Fresnes prison

A month after their arrest they were taken to Fresnes – a huge jail on the outskirts of Paris. Odette was placed in cell 108, and a campaign to break her spirit began. Outside her door a notice read "No books. No showers. No parcels. No exercise. No privileges."

Among many spying skills Odette learned to recognize particular German uniforms, and studied radio codes (seen here printed on a silk handkerchief that could be concealed in a wallet). Before she left for France her commanding officer gave her a silver powder compact and a suicide pill.

French Resistance

The Resistance were men and women who fought the Germans in France, after their country surrendered. The British secret services worked closely with them, organizing guerrilla fighters, assisting in sabotage operations, and sending back information to England.

It was here that Odette's interrogation by the Abwehr began in earnest. She also began her own campaign to survive. With a hairpin she carved a calendar on the wall and marked every day. A duct set high in the wall led to the cell below, and she was able to talk to a fellow prisoner named Michèle. This was an invaluable consolation as she was allowed no contact with other prisoners.

Gestapo summons

After two weeks the Abwehr realized their prisoner was not going to talk, and

Odette was taken to Gestapo headquarters at 84 Avenue Foch. On her first visit she was given a large meal, but despite a ravenous hunger she only ate a little. She knew it was intended to make her sleepy and dull-witted.

Her interviewer this time was a sophisticated young man, with Nordic good looks, who smelled of cold baths and eau de Cologne. He was polite, but Odette knew she was dealing with a trained torturer. His questions about Resistance activity were met with her stock response "I have nothing to say." The interview came to an end and Odette was returned to Fresnes for the night.

Torture and tea

The next day Odette knew would be more difficult. The suave young man had run out of patience. Her stomach tightened as a shadowy assistant slipped into the room and stood menacingly behind her. First this man applied a red-hot poker to the small of her back. Still Odette would not talk. Then he removed her toenails one by one.

Throughout this torture Odette gave no cry, although she several times expected to faint. As she was asked the same set of questions she replied with the same answer "I have nothing to say."

The young man offered her a cigarette and a cup of tea. Although she was in great pain, Odette felt elated. She had kept silent and won her own victory over these inhuman thugs.

Her questioner told her they were now going to start on her fingernails, and Odette's courage wavered. But before this was done, another Gestapo man came into the cell, and told them to stop wasting their time. This was one prisoner who was not going to crack.

Back at Fresnes Odette bound her feet in strips of wet cloth and lay on her bed, sick with fear at what the Gestapo would do next. Michèle called throughout the night but she was too weak to answer.

A few days later she was summoned to the Gestapo court at Avenue Foch, and sentenced to death.

Silent good night

Returning to her cell Odette felt curiously calm. She had not betrayed her fellow agents. Many were still free and working to overthrow the Nazi regime. She bid a silent good night to each of her three daughters and fell soundly asleep. But in the early hours she woke with a start. There was no date for her execution. From now on every footstep outside her door could herald the final summons to face a firing squad.

Despite this constant threat, Odette was determined not to give up hope. Her story about being related to Prime Minister Churchill was paying dividends. Many of the prison staff who guarded Odette were intelligent enough to realize that as the war was going badly it would pay to keep on the right side of one of his "relations".

As summer turned to autumn, Odette fell gravely ill and was moved to a warmer cell. Her health improved, and in May 1944 news came that she was to be transferred to a prison in Germany. As she left, Odette caught sight of one of her interrogators and waved at him gaily, shouting "Goodbye, Goodbye." She was determined to let him know he had not broken her spirit.

The bridge of ravens

Placed on a train with an armed guard she was taken east, and spent the next few weeks in several prisons. In July of 1944 Odette arrived at Ravensbrück, a Nazi concentration camp for women. Even the name – the bridge of ravens – sounded sinister.

Within the barbed wire enclave were row upon row of decrepit huts, where guards with whips and savage dogs terrorized their skeletal, shaven-headed prisoners. Smoke from the camp crematorium filled the sky, scattering a ghastly pall of dust and ashes over the stark grey interior. The Nazis sent their enemies here to be worked to death, and every morning those

who died in the night were carried away in crude wooden handcarts. As a young girl walking the cliffs of Normandy, Odette had sometimes wondered where she would die. As she entered Ravensbrück she felt she knew the answer.

Into the bunker

The commandant of the camp, Fritz Sühren, was eager to meet Odette. She noticed how clean and well fed he looked. Like most of her captors, Sühren was interested in her connection with Winston Churchill. He ordered her to be placed in "the bunker" – the camp's own solitary confinement cells.

Her cell was pitch black, and for three months she was kept in total darkness. But Odette had been blind for a year of her childhood. She was used to the dark. She passed the time thinking about her three daughters,

Commandant Fritz Sühren.

and how they had grown from babies into young girls. She decided to clothe them in her imagination, stitch by stitch, garment by garment. So completely did she fill her days deciding on the fabric, shade and style of these clothes that whenever she was visited by camp guards it seemed like an interruption, rather than the chance to make contact with other human beings.

In August southern France was invaded by French, British and American forces. This was where Odette had done most of her Resistance work. As a spiteful punishment the central heating in her cell was turned to maximum. Odette wrapped herself in a blanket soaked in cold water, but this did not stop her from becoming desperately ill. Near to death she was taken to the camp hospital. It was a strange way to treat someone who had been sentenced to execution. Perhaps the Nazis were still hoping they could break her, and she would tell them about her Resistance work.

Comfort in the dark

Away from the bunker she recovered and was returned to her cell. On the way back Odette found something that was to bring her great comfort. A single leaf had blown into the treeless camp and she scooped it into her clothing. In her dark world she would trace its spine and shape with her hands, and think about how the wind had blown a seed into the earth which had grown to a tree with leaves and branches that

A leaf Odette found in the dusty compound of Ravensbrück brought her great comfort in the darkened bunker where she was held prisoner.

rustled in the wind and basked in the sunlight.

Birthday trip

On April 27 Sühren visited her. He stood at the cell door then drew a finger across his throat. "You'll leave tomorrow morning at six o'clock" he said. Odette wondered if the end had come at last. On April 28 she would be 33. Was she to die on her birthday?

That morning she could hear that chaos had overtaken the camp. Sühren arrived and bundled her into a large black van with a few other inmates. Through the window she could see the guards fleeing from the camp.

On the shore of swampy Fürstenburg Lake, Ravensbrück was a dank living hell for its thousands of inmates.

Germany collapses – May 1945

During the war the Nazis had treated Russia with appalling brutality. When victorious Russian troops swept into east Germany in early 1945, German troops were fearful of reprisals. Many fled toward British and American forces who were overrunning their country to the west, preferring to surrender to them.

Ravensbrück

Russian forces

British and American forces

- Germany's wartime frontier
- Territory occupied by German troops at end of war

Free at last

The Americans offered her a place to sleep, but Odette wanted to spend her first night of freedom out in the open. She walked over to Sühren's abandoned car and sat in the front seat feeling neither triumph nor elation, just utter exhaustion. Nearby were a party of SS soldiers, who had been part of Sühren's escort. One came over and gave her his sheepskin coat to ward off the chill of the night.

To Odette, this act of kindness by a former enemy seemed part of a strange dream, and she expected to wake at any moment and find herself back in Ravensbrück. But the dream continued. She nestled into the coat, and stared up at the stars. The village clock chimed its quarter hours throughout the night, and it was so quiet she could hear her heart beating.

Odette returned to England. Looking back on her time in France she wrote "I am a very ordinary woman, to whom the chance has been given, to see human beings at their best and at their worst."

Odette, her three daughters and Peter Churchill in London, 1946. She has just been awarded the George Cross "for courage, endurance and self sacrifice of the highest possible order."

The van, together with an escort of SS* troops, drove west. It soon became clear that the war was all but over. For the next three days Sühren, his SS escort, and his small band of prisoners drove from one camp to another as Germany collapsed into anarchy.

Many prisoners, so near to freedom, but so close to death, were almost hysterical. Some whooped and screamed, making huge bonfires of anything they could find to burn. Others rushed at their guards only to be gunned down.

Sinister summons

It all seemed like a delirious nightmare. On the fourth day away from Ravensbrück a guard grabbed Odette and dragged her before Sühren. She was told not to bring her few belongings, and was certain she was to be shot. Bundled into Sühren's large staff car and with an escort of SS guards in two other cars, she sped away from the camp.

After two hours the three cars stopped by a deserted field and Sühren barked "get out". But this was not to be Odette's execution ground. Sühren offered Odette a sandwich and a glass of wine and told her he was handing her over to the Americans. At first she thought this was a cruel joke, but he seemed serious enough. Clearly he thought safely delivering Winston Churchill's relative would get him off to a good start with his captors.

At 10:00pm that night they drove into a village which had been occupied by American soldiers. Sühren marched up to an officer and said "This is Frau Churchill. She has been a prisoner. She is a relative of Winston Churchill." He handed Odette his revolver and surrendered.

Helicopter heroes save forty

The call that came into Royal Naval Air Station Culdrose, Cornwall, UK, was desperate. In October 1989, the Pakistani container ship *Murree* was caught in a severe storm off Start Bay, Dartmouth. Her cargo had shifted in the rough weather, and tons of water were flooding into the hold.

A lifeboat had been launched from nearby Brixham, but the turbulent sea made docking all but impossible.

Sea King helicopters were despatched to help in the rescue, and within minutes two Royal Navy divers, Petty Officers Steve Wright and Dave Wallace, had been lowered aboard the heaving deck of the *Murree*.

Wright and Wallace quickly discovered that there were 40 people on board the sinking vessel, including a number of women and children. As gale force winds lashed the sloping deck they supervised the terrified crew and passengers, strapping them two at a time into harnesses, so they could be lifted into waiting helicopters. But time was running out.

Just as the last two crew members were being winched off the deck, the *Murree* lurched alarmingly as the bow sank deep beneath the waves. Wright grabbed hold of a nearby deck railing to stop himself falling. Wallace was not so lucky and slithered down the tilting deck. Catching his legs in a coil of rope, he had to struggle frantically to break free.

The *Murree* was going down fast. On the stern of the ship the two divers grabbed at the harness from the helicopter overhead, but it slipped from their grip. There was only one thing to do. Leaping 27m (90ft) into the boiling sea they plunged deep underwater, and surfaced to see the stern towering over them.

Fearing they would be sucked under as the ship went down, the two swam for their lives. Battered by huge waves and debris from the wreckage they floundered in the sea until a Sea King helicopter plucked them from the water.

The *Murree*'s Captain Abdul Ajeeq, who was the last crew member to leave, said "These helicopter men are fantastic. They gave us our lives". A year later Wright and Wallace's courage was officially recognized when the British government presented them with the George Medal for bravery.

Moments before the *Murree* sinks a helicopter waits to rescue Wright and Wallace.

Wright (left) and Wallace (right), shortly after their ordeal.

Mother Seacole's Balaclava boys

In the winter of 1855, at the height of the Crimean War, the Russian town of Balaclava could have been anyone's idea of hell. It was here that wounded or diseased soldiers from the nearby siege of Sebastopol assembled to be taken by boat to hospitals a safe distance from the fighting.

Some sat uncomplaining on hillside or horseback, their dull eyes glazed in misery. Others, with bloody bandages covering disfiguring wounds, lay on stretchers writhing in agony. Amid the chaos dying men called desperately for attention.

Nurse Seacole

Along this grim procession strode an unlikely figure in a yellow dress and blue bonnet, dispensing medicine, food and encouragement. Many of the soldiers recognized this plump, middle-aged Jamaican woman. She was Mary Seacole, who ran a store and canteen close behind their front line. Some of the more delirious men took her to be their wife or mother, come to comfort them in their dying hour.

Seacole gave out medicines she had made herself, changed dressings, and gave sponge cake, broth and lemonade to the exhausted men. "They liked the cake better than anything else," she noted, "perhaps because it tasted of home." She knew that coarse army provisions were the last thing to tempt the appetite of an injured soldier.

Extraordinary life

Born in 1802 to a Jamaican hotelier and a Scottish army officer, Mary Seacole spent her childhood with British military men who she greatly admired. A brief marriage ended in her husband's death, but left her wealthy. She visited England, and Central America where she set up a string of hotels and prospected for gold.

She learned both western medicine and West Indian herbal remedies, was a skilled surgeon, and gained experience nursing cholera and yellow fever victims.

When newspaper reports of British troops suffering from cholera and typhus in the Crimea reached her in Jamaica, she was determined to help in any way she could.

The Crimean War

The Crimean War (1854-56) was fought between an alliance of Britain, France and Turkey against Russia. It focused on the Crimean peninsula and a siege of the Russian city and navy base of Sebastopol.

Crimea
Russia
Crimea
Sebastopol
Black Sea
Balaclava

Balaclava packed with ships carrying troops and supplies, 1855. The port is teeming with soldiers and traders, but no one stood still long enough to register on this early photograph.

Despite the valuable help she provided, Mary Seacole had not been welcome in the Crimea. Landing with a boat full of medicine and provisions she had been harangued by the port commander Admiral Boxer, who had recently met Florence Nightingale* and a group of British nurses. "Why are a parcel of women coming out to a place where they are not wanted?" he thundered. Boxer was only one of the hurdles Seacole had had to overcome before she could begin her work among the British troops.

Undeserved help

Although she had considerable nursing experience, her initial offer of help had been rejected by both the British War Office and Florence Nightingale's newly formed nursing organization. No explanation was given, but Seacole suspected her black skin was the reason.

Determined to help, Seacole had contacted a London relative, Thomas Day, and set up a trading company with him, intending to finance her nursing by running a store and canteen near to the battlefield. The firm of "Seacole & Day" was set up, provisions were purchased and the two had set sail for the Crimea, landing at Balaclava in early 1855.

The tribes of Balaclava

Balaclava was the main supply port for the war, and goods piled up on the quayside. There was a great deal of thieving and violence. The port was populated by Turkish, British and French soldiers, Maltese boatmen, and Greek and Italian traders – Seacole called them "the predatory tribes of Balaclava". They eyed each other suspiciously, and there

were occasional outbreaks of murderous violence. With only a small band of military police to keep the peace, it was a very dangerous place to be.

For the first six weeks Seacole sold supplies from the quayside. For her protection she carried a double-barrel pistol in the belt around her waist, but confessed "I couldn't have loaded it to save my life."

She looked after the wounded whenever she could, and at night slept aboard the supply ship *Medera*. This was loaded with gunpowder, and those on board were in constant danger of instant annihilation from a fire or stray shell.

The British Hotel

After a couple of months Seacole and Day managed to build themselves a small collection of huts close to Balaclava, which they named "The British Hotel". Built from rubble it included a general store, kitchen, canteen, officer's club, store and animal pen, and accommodation for Seacole, Day and their employees.

Seacole at the "British Hotel". In the 1850s governments provided their soldiers with very little, and armies going into battle were always accompanied by shopkeepers selling food and clothes to those who could afford them.

The store claimed to sell everything from "a needle to an anchor". It was a great success and Seacole soon became well known to many of the soldiers. Aside from the warm welcome and medical

Seacole's "British Hotel" was plagued by rats.

Busy day

Seacole led a hectic life throughout the war, and when it ended her health was badly affected. Her days were very much alike, except when fighting was heavy, and she was even busier. Sunday was her day of rest.

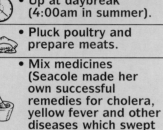

- Up at daybreak (4:00am in summer).
- Pluck poultry and prepare meats.
- Mix medicines (Seacole made her own successful remedies for cholera, yellow fever and other diseases which swept through the camps.)
- Sweep store and clean kitchen.
- 7:00-9:00am. Serve morning coffee and breakfast for troops.
- 9:30-12.00am. Attend to sick soldiers in field hospital.
- Afternoon. Run shop and canteen. (Unlike other establishments, no gambling was allowed, and only officers were permitted to drink alcohol.)
- 8:00pm. Close British Hotel.
- Evening meal and sleep.

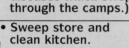

British and French soldiers pose uneasily for the camera during the Crimean War. These were the men Seacole nursed and cherished. They returned her affection, calling her "mother" or "auntie".

attention she provided, Seacole's cooking was unusually good.

Useful friends

Like many successful people Seacole had a knack for making useful friends. The Turkish leader Omar Pasha was a frequent visitor to her Hotel, and insisted she give him English lessons. He was able to learn no more than "Madame Seacole", "Good morning", and "More champagne", but he did give orders for his troops to protect Seacole's stores.

Life was still extraordinarily difficult. The Crimean winter was bitterly cold. Valuable supplies were swept away by a flash flood. On one December night 40 sheep froze to death, and thieving was a constant problem. On top of this, rats ate supplies and nibbled at sleeping hotel staff. But despite all her problems Seacole was not distracted from her work.

Front line

Seacole not only nursed soldiers at her hotel and the local field hospital, she also went out to the battlefield.

Brought up among soldiers, she loved the pageantry and glamour of military life, but she was very much aware of the horrors of war.

Nursing so near the fighting required an iron nerve. Enemy fire and exploding shells still fell where she worked, and all around looters would be stripping boots and uniforms

London's *Punch* magazine made Seacole a household name during the war, and openly condemned the prejudice she had faced in trying to get to the Crimea. This illustration shows her giving out the magazine to injured soldiers.

from the dead. After heavy fighting the ground would be thick with wounded men, often horribly mutilated. Some called urgently for her attention, others, crazed with pain, tugged desperately at her clothing as she passed.

Friend or foe

Anyone who needed attention, whether friend or foe, was given it. Russian troops, some of whom had never seen a black person before, often gawped at her in astonishment, but this did not stop her caring for them. One Russian officer she helped even gave her a ring from his finger to thank her. The London *Times* correspondent William Russell mentioned her several times in his dispatches from the war. He wrote "I have seen her go down, under fire, with her little store of creature comforts for our wounded men; and a more tender or skilled hand about a wound or broken limb could not be found among our best surgeons."

Bad news

Having come to know many of the soldiers well she was constantly having to cope with news of their death. "I used to think it was like having a large family of children ill with fever," she wrote, "and dreading to hear which one had passed away in the night."

Casualties from the fighting were far outnumbered by the many soldiers dying from terrible diseases. (3,754 British soldiers fell in battle, 15,830 died of disease.) No one was safe. When cholera broke out among the troops during the summer of 1855, it even claimed the life of the British commander-in-chief Lord Raglan.

Sebastopol falls

After eleven months, the besieged Russian troops began to lose heart, and following weeks of intense bombardment, Sebastopol finally fell in September 1855. Seacole had been taking bets with her soldiers that she would be the first woman to enter the city, and she was determined to win. Borrowing two mules she loaded them with food and medicine, and set off behind the first soldiers to enter the ruins.

Seacole had done many brave deeds in her time, but this was foolhardy. True, there were wounded men to comfort, but Sebastopol immediately after the Russians had fled more than matched the horrors of the battlefield. In blazing buildings fires raged unattended and out of control. Russian positions outside the city now turned their guns on their former territory and shells fell at random.

Soldiers guzzled down stocks of Russian wine, and were soon reeling through the streets, dangerously drunk. One party of men dressed in Russian frocks and bonnets were dancing and singing among the dead and wounded. Seacole too gathered her share of souvenirs, picking up a broken bell and cracked teapot.

Rough justice

In the chaos and smoke, she soon became separated from her own soldiers, and was waylaid by a group of drunken French troops who assumed she was a Russian spy. Seacole was outraged, and knocked the hat off one of them with her broken bell. They were in no mood to argue, and she was roughly seized and dragged away to be shot. But good fortune saved her. A French officer whom she had nursed in a previous battle recognized her and ordered her instant release.

With the fall of the city the war was almost over, and troops began to leave. Although she had succeeded in her aim of nursing the soldiers, Seacole's British Hotel had become a financial

Seacole gathered up flowers and pebbles from the graves of dead soldiers, to give to grieving relatives.

disaster. Despite its success, constant thieving and the large amount of unsold goods remaining at the end of the campaign left the Jamaican nurse deep in debt.

Bankrupt heroine

In the final few days before leaving she gathered flowers and pebbles from the graves of fallen soldiers who had been particularly close. These tokens she kept for herself, or passed on to the soldiers' relatives.

Seacole left the Crimea for London by steamboat, arriving bankrupt but a heroine, some months later. The very fact that she had made no profit from her hotel, when others with similar stores had made fortunes, made her even more appreciated by the British press and public. On the streets of London she was constantly stopped and thanked by soldiers who recognized her from the war. "Wherever I go" she wrote "I am sure to meet some smiling face." It was reward enough for this remarkable woman.

Stauffenberg's Secret Germany

On a spring morning in 1943 American fighter planes screamed over a Tunisian coastal road, pouring machine gun fire onto a column of German army vehicles. Fierce flames bellowed from blazing trucks and smeared the desert sky with oily black smoke. Amid the carnage lay Colonel Claus von Stauffenberg, one of Germany's most brilliant soldiers. Badly wounded, he was fighting for his life.

Best treatment

Stauffenberg was hastily transported to a Munich hospital, and given the best possible treatment. His left eye, right hand, and two fingers from his left hand had been lost in the attack. His legs were so badly damaged doctors

The *National Emblem* Nazi badge that all German soldiers were required to wear.

feared he would never be able to walk again.

Willing himself back from the brink of death, Stauffenberg was determined to overcome his disabilities. He refused all painkilling drugs, and learned to dress, bathe and write with his three remaining fingers. Before the summer was over he was demanding to be returned to active service.

Hospital staff were amazed by their patient's tenacity, but it was not to fight for Nazi leader Adolf Hitler that the colonel struggled so hard to recover. What Stauffenberg had in mind was Hitler's assassination.

Murder and disaster

He had supported the Nazis once, but their murderous racism, and Hitler's decision to plunge Europe into the Second World War sickened him.

Hitler was now directing the war with startling incompetence. After one disastrous campaign Stauffenberg asked a friend "Is there no officer in Hitler's headquarters capable

Stauffenberg before the air attack that left him seriously disabled.

of taking a pistol to the beast?" Lying in his hospital bed, Stauffenberg realized he was just the man for the job.

Invaluable asset

Blessed with a magnetic personality, Stauffenberg was a renowned commander. He also had a sensitive nature which invited fellow officers to confide in him. This was an invaluable asset for someone seeking allies to commit treason in the very heart of Nazi Germany.

When he recovered, Stauffenberg was appointed Chief of Staff to the Home Army. Here he became involved with General Friedrich Olbricht in a plot to dispose of Hitler and take over the German government.

Home Army hierarchy

The Home Army was a unit of the German Army made up of all soldiers stationed in Germany. It was also responsible for recruitment and training. These were its most senior commanders.

General Fromm
Commander in Chief

General Olbricht
Deputy Commander in Chief

Colonel Stauffenberg
Chief of Staff

Olbricht and Stauffenberg intended to use the Home Army to overthrow the Nazi regime. Their commander, Fromm, knew about the plot, but would neither join it, nor betray the conspirators.

Valkyrie

The Nazis had devised a plan called *Operation Valkyrie* to defend themselves against any rebellion within Germany. It worked like this: In the event of a revolt the Home Army had detailed instructions to seize control of all areas of government, and important radio and railway stations, so the revolt could be quickly put down, and prevented from spreading.

Rather than protect the Nazis, Stauffenberg and Olbricht proposed to use *Operation Valkyrie* to overthrow them. They intended to kill Hitler, and in the confusion that followed they would set *Operation Valkyrie* in motion, ordering their soldiers to arrest all Nazi leaders, and their chief supporters – the SS (regiments of fanatical Nazi soldiers) and Gestapo (secret police).

Two obstacles

There were two great obstacles to the plot. Killing Hitler would be difficult, as he was surrounded by bodyguards. Also, the head of the Home Army, General Friedrich Fromm, refused to join them. Like everyone in the armed forces he had sworn an oath of loyalty to Hitler, and had misgivings about betraying him. Fromm also feared Hitler's revenge if the plot should fail. Without Fromm's help, using *Valkyrie* to overthrow the Nazis would be considerably more difficult.

Still, the plotters were not deterred. Stauffenberg threw himself into the task of recruiting allies. He referred to the conspiracy as "Secret Germany" after a poem by German writer Stefan George,

whom he greatly admired. Many officers joined him, but many more wavered. Most were disgusted with Hitler, but like Fromm they felt restrained by their oath of loyalty or feared for their lives.

Briefcase bomb

By the summer of 1944 time was running out. The Gestapo was closing in and the longer the plotters delayed, the greater the chance of being discovered.

They had decided to kill Hitler with a bomb hidden in a briefcase. Stauffenberg attended conferences with the German leader and volunteered to plant the bomb. In order to give him time to escape, the explosives would be detonated with a ten-minute fuse. This device was quite complex. To activate the bomb a small glass tube containing acid needed to be broken with a pair of pliers. The acid would eat through a thin steel wire. When this broke it would release a detonator to set off the bomb.

Stauffenberg refused to let his disabilities affect his life. He adapted these pliers to enable him to activate the fuse on the briefcase bomb with his three remaining fingers.

Stauffenberg intended to kill Hitler with a bomb hidden in a briefcase, which would be placed next to the German leader during a military conference.

Action stations

Their chance came on July 20, 1944, when Stauffenberg was summoned to Hitler's headquarters at Rastenburg, East Prussia. Together with his personal assistant Lieutenant Werner von Haeften he collected two bombs, drove to Rangsdorf airfield south of Berlin, and flew 650km (400 miles) to Rastenburg. Arriving in East Prussia at 10:15 they drove through a gloomy forest to Hitler's headquarters. Surrounded by barbed wire, minefields and checkpoints, the base – fancifully known as "The Wolf's Lair"– was a collection of concrete bunkers and wooden huts. It was here, cut off from the real world, that Hitler had retreated to wage his final battles.

Two bombs

The conference with Hitler was scheduled for 12:30. At 12:15 Stauffenberg requested permission to wash and change his shirt. It was such a hot day this seemed perfectly reasonable.

He was directed to a washroom but went instead to a waiting room and was joined by Haeften. Together they began to activate the two bombs. Stauffenberg broke the acid tube fuse on one, but as he reached for the second they were interrupted by a sergeant sent to look for Stauffenberg, who was now late for the conference.

Stauffenberg (left) with Hitler (right) at Rastenburg. The German leader thought Stauffenberg was a very glamorous figure and had a high regard for his abilities.

One bomb would have to do. But there was further bad news. Stauffenberg had hoped the meeting would be held in an underground bunker where the blast of his bomb would be lethally concentrated by windowless concrete walls. But instead he was led to a wooden hut with three large windows. The force of any explosion

here would be considerably less effective.

Inside the hut the conference had begun. High ranking officers and their assistants crowded around a large oak map table, discussing the war in Russia. Stauffenberg, whose hearing had been damaged when he was wounded, asked if he could stand near to Hitler so he could hear him properly.

Hurried exit

Placing himself to Hitler's right, Stauffenberg shoved his bulging briefcase under the table to the left of a large wooden support. Just then, Field Marshal Keitel, who was one of Hitler's most adoring disciples, suggested that Stauffenberg should give his report next. With less than seven minutes before the bomb exploded he had no intention of remaining in the hut. Fortunately the discussion on the Russian front continued, and Stauffenberg excused himself from the room, saying he had to make an urgent phone call to his Berlin headquarters.

Keitel, already irritated by Stauffenberg's late arrival, became incensed that he should have the impudence to leave the conference, and attempted unsuccessfully to detain him.

There were less than five minutes to go. Stauffenberg hurried over to another hut and waited with General Erich Fellgiebel, the chief of signals at the base, and one of several Rastenburg officers who had joined the conspiracy. The seconds dragged by.

Detonation

Inside the conference room an officer named Colonel Brandt was leaning over the table to get a better look at a map. His foot caught on Stauffenberg's heavy briefcase so he picked it up and moved it to the opposite side of the heavy wooden support. Seconds later, at 12:42, the bomb detonated.

At the sound of the explosion Haeften drove up in a staff car and Stauffenberg leaped in. The two had to escape to the airfield quickly, before the "Wolf's Lair" was sealed off. The hut looked completely devastated, and as they drove away both felt confident no one inside could have survived.

Luck of the devil

They were mistaken. Brandt, and three others had been killed, but in moving the briefcase to the other side of the wooden support, Brandt had shielded Hitler from the full force of the blast. The German leader staggered out of the hut, his hair scorched and trousers in tatters. He was very much alive.

Fellgiebel watched in horror. Hitler's demise was an essential part of the plot. Still, shortly before 1:00pm he sent a message to the War Office in Berlin, confirming the bomb had exploded and ordering Olbricht to set *Valkyrie* into operation. He made no mention of Hitler's fate.

Disastrous hesitation

Olbricht, uncertain whether Hitler was dead, hesitated. Until he knew more he was not prepared to act. Meanwhile Stauffenberg, flying back to Berlin, was cut off from everything. During the two hours he was in the air, he

Wolf's Lair Conference Room

Keitel

Hitler

Killed

Colonel
Brandt
killed

Killed

Stauffenberg places
briefcase bomb here.

Bomb moved to other
side of table support.

Bomb explodes
12:42.

Killed

Standing next to the oak map
table which saved Hitler's life,
a Nazi officer inspects the
devastated conference room.

expected his fellow conspirators to be engaged in a frenzy of activity. It fact, nothing was happening.

At Rastenburg it did not take long to realize who had planted the bomb. Orders were issued to arrest Stauffenberg at Rangsdorf airfield. But the order was never transmitted – the signals officer responsible for sending it was also one of the conspirators.

Only after 3:30 did the Berlin conspirators reluctantly implement their plan. Home Army officers were summoned and told that Hitler was dead, and that Operation *Valkyrie* was to be set in motion. But General Fromm was still refusing to cooperate, especially after he rang Rastenburg and was told by Field Marshal Keitel that Hitler was alive.

Stauffenberg arrives.

None the less, at 4:30 the plotters issued orders to the entire German army. Hitler, they declared, was dead. Nazi party leaders were trying to seize power for themselves. The army was to take control of the government.

Stauffenberg arrived soon afterward. He too failed to

persuade Fromm to join the conspiracy. Instead the commander in chief erupted into a foaming tirade. Banging his fists on his desk Fromm demanded that the conspirators be placed under arrest and ordered Stauffenberg to shoot himself. The plotters regarded him with icy disdain, and he lunged at them, fists flailing. Subdued with a pistol pressed to his stomach, Fromm allowed himself to be locked in an office. Other officers loyal to the Nazis were also locked up. Stauffenberg now began to drive the conspirators with his usual energy and verve. For the rest of the afternoon they worked with desperate haste to

implement their plan. Stauffenberg spent hours on the phone trying to persuade reluctant or wavering army commanders to support him. From Paris to Prague the army attempted to take control, and arrest all Nazi officials. In some cities such as Vienna and Paris there were remarkable successes, but in Berlin it was another story.

Not ruthless enough

The plotters were damned by their own decency. They had

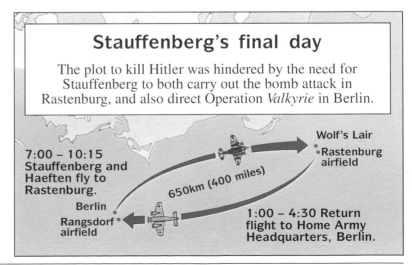

Stauffenberg's final day

The plot to kill Hitler was hindered by the need for Stauffenberg to both carry out the bomb attack in Rastenburg, and also direct Operation *Valkyrie* in Berlin.

7:00 – 10:15
Stauffenberg and
Haeften fly to
Rastenburg.

Wolf's Lair
•Rastenburg
airfield

650km (400 miles)

Berlin
Rangsdorf•
airfield

1:00 – 4:30 Return
flight to Home Army
Headquarters, Berlin.

revolted against the brutality of the Nazi regime and ironically, only a similar ruthlessness could have saved them. If the conspirators had been prepared to slaughter anyone who stood in their way they may have succeeded.

They also failed to capture both the Berlin radio station, and army communication points. As the plot ground to a halt their own commands were constantly contradicted by orders transmitted by commanders loyal to the Nazis.

Surrounded

By early evening it was obvious to Stauffenberg that they had failed, yet true to his character he refused to give up. He insisted that success was just a whisker away, and he continued to encourage his fellow plotters not to give up hope. But the end was near.

The War Office was now surrounded by hostile troops, and inside the building a small group of Nazi officers had armed themselves and set out to arrest the conspirators. Shots were fired, Stauffenberg was hit in the shoulder, and Fromm was released.

Fromm's revenge

There was only one possible course of action for Fromm. Although he had refused to cooperate with the plot he had known all about it. No doubt the conspirators would confirm this – under torture or by their own free will. Fromm had to cover his tracks. He sentenced Stauffenberg, Haeften, Olbricht and his assistant Colonel Mertz von Quirnheim to immediate execution.

Stauffenberg's assistant and fellow conspirator Werner von Haeften.

Stauffenberg was bleeding badly from his wound, but seemed indifferent to his death sentence. He insisted the plot was all his doing. His fellow officers had simply been carrying out his orders.

Execution

Fromm was not convinced. The four men were hustled down the stairs to the courtyard outside. It was just after midnight. By all accounts they went calmly to their death. Lit by the dimmed headlights of a staff car, the four were shot in order of rank. Stauffenberg was second, after Olbricht. An instant before the firing squad cut him down Haeften, in a brave but pointless gesture, threw himself in front of the bullets. Stauffenberg died moments later, shouting "Long live our Secret Germany." There would have been more executions that night, had not Gestapo chief Kaltenbrunner arrived and put a stop to them. He was far more interested in seeing what could be learned from the survivors.

The remaining conspirators were arrested, but the Gestapo torturers had been cheated of their greatest prize. Stauffenberg and his fellow martyrs were buried that night in a nearby churchyard. They had failed, but with so much at stake their bravery in the face of such a slim chance of success was all the more heroic.

Keeping a secret

The plotters took great pains to avoid being discovered by the Gestapo. Documents were typed wearing gloves, so as to avoid leaving fingerprints, on a typewriter which would then be hidden in a cupboard or attic. Stauffenberg memorized and then destroyed written messages and left not a scrap of solid evidence against himself. Such was his good judgment that not a single German officer approached to join the conspiracy betrayed him.

"An das

Der Führer,
Parteiführer

ue von
pfern
nen

Blackbeard meets his match

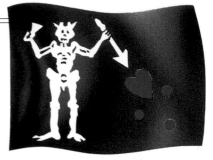

W as there ever a villain more villainous than Edward "Blackbeard" Teach? Was there ever a calling more suited to his outsize personality than piracy? A whole head taller than most and built like a bear, Teach's nickname came from his huge black beard. Stretching down to his chest it was usually braided with bright ribbons, and obscured a face that was in constant communication with a large bottle of rum.

Teach was not without a certain roguish charm, but the succession of women who married him (14 in all) usually came to regret their decision – especially when he insisted on sharing them with his fellow pirates. He was certainly never dull company. Once, during a lull in plundering, he suggested to his crew that they make "a hell of our own" and see who could last the longest in it. He and three foolhardy

competitors duly had themselves sealed into the ship's hold with several pots of blazing, foul-smelling sulphur. Teach won of course, and emerged on the deck to announce they ought to have a hanging contest – to see who could last the longest dangling from a noose.

Straight from hell

But Teach was not all fun and games. He usually went into battle with several slow-burning fuses woven into his hair. His already terrifying features cloaked in a haze of smoke, he resembled a demon from the deepest pit of hell and frightened his opponents witless.

Captured crews who had put up a fight could expect no mercy.

Above. Blackbeard's flag. Pirates played up their evil image for all it was worth, and the crews of many of the ships they attacked were too frightened to defend themselves.

Below. Edward "Blackbeard" Teach. Originally a slave trader from Bristol, England, he became one of the most feared pirates in history.

The Golden Age of Piracy

The years between 1690 and 1730 have been described as the "Golden Age of Piracy". Vessels following trade routes from Europe to North and South America and Africa were regularly plundered by pirate ships, which were mainly British.

"A merry life and a short one shall be my motto" wrote pirate captain Bartholomew Roberts. The risks were great – death in battle or public execution – but the rewards were extraordinary. A successful pirate, who in

everyday life might struggle to earn a pittance as a sailor, millworker or miner, could make as much in a year as a wealthy aristocrat.

Many of the merchant ships they attacked were easy pickings. Hoping to make as much profit as possible, greedy traders manned their ships with small, badly paid and badly armed crews. Faced with a horde of ruthless pirates many were not willing to defend their cargoes with their lives.

Teach even cut off the nose of one Portuguese captive and made him eat it. His own companions sometimes fared no better – he was reputed to have killed one of his crew just to remind them how evil he was.

This was all above and beyond the call of ordinary piracy, but it served its purpose. As his reputation spread, few of the merchant ships he accosted in the coastal water of North America dared to oppose him. Teach's plundered wealth also brought him friends in high places, who alerted him to the movements of government forces, and allowed him to trade his goods in coastal settlements.

Too expensive

By 1715 his activities, and those of other pirates in the Caribbean and Atlantic coast of America, were having dire economic consequences. Merchant ships were having to travel with naval escorts and the cost of insuring their cargoes became astronomical. Clearly something had to be done, but who could be found to fight such a formidable foe?

Alexander Spotswood, Governor of Virginia, put up a reward of £100 (then nearly ten

Pirate dagger. Pirates usually carried daggers, swords and several pistols – their standard tactic being to swarm aboard a ship and engage the crew in hand-to-hand fighting.

years wages for an ordinary seaman), hoping to attract someone whose lust for wealth or glory outweighed his fear of this most evil of pirates. He also called in the Royal Navy, and financed a search party of two ships from his own coffers.

Maynard RN

So, on November 17, 1718, Lieutenant Robert Maynard, commander of *H.M.S. Pearl,* set sail from Virginia, together with a smaller ship *H.M.S.*

Below. From the 1690s to 1720s piracy was rife in Caribbean and North American waters. At the time America was still a British colony, and merchant ships were defended by the British Royal Navy.

Lyme. Altogether there were 60 men under his command. Maynard had been told that Teach had based himself in Ocracoke Inlet, North Carolina, and his small search party arrived there just before dusk four days later.

Maynard soon spotted Teach's ship the *Adventurer,* alongside a captured merchant vessel, and weighed anchor. He would attack the next morning. That night the pirates' drunken curses and coarse carousing drifted across the water between the two ships, and Maynard's anxious crew wondered what manner of men they would have to fight on the coming day.

Bad start

The initial attack was not promising. Ocracoke Inlet is shallow, and no sooner had Maynard's ships moved against the *Adventurer*, than they became stuck in sandbanks. Only when several heavy weights had been thrown out of the vessels were they able to proceed.

Teach watched the approaching ships with ill-tempered amusement. When the *Pearl* was close enough he called across the water,

Doubloons and pieces of eight from a Spanish ship. Pirates regarded gold and silver coins as the greatest plunder of all.

demanding to know what they wanted. Maynard knew all about Teach's reputation, but was determined to inspire his frightened men with a display of bravado. "You may see we are no pirates," he called, and boldly announced he was coming to seize Teach and his crew. The despotic pirate erupted furiously. "Damnation seize my soul if I give you mercy, or take any from you," he bellowed.

Battle begins

Teach's crew were only 19 strong but they were all seasoned brigands, determined to fight to the death. As the *Adventurer* moved closer to the Navy ships it swung around and fired its cannons. *H.M.S. Lyme* caught the full force of this broadside. The captain and several of his crew were killed and the ship floundered helplessly in the water. The *Pearl* pressed on to face its foe alone.

Worse was to come. The *Adventurer*'s next volley hit the *Pearl* with similar ferocity. So intense was the fire that 21 men were injured and Maynard ordered all hands to take cover below. Teach's ship came alongside the deserted deck and his men tossed aboard blazing bottles stuffed with gunpowder, buckshot and scrap iron.

Hand-to-hand

Smoke shrouded the shattered *Pearl*, and Teach thought he had won an easy victory. His

pirates swarmed aboard, but at that moment Maynard unleashed a counter attack, and lead those of his crew who could still stand out onto the deck. Bayonets flashed and pistols cracked amid the horror of hand-to-hand fighting.

Maynard fought his way toward Teach, and both men fired their pistols at point blank range. Teach's drinking got the better of him, and only Maynard found his target. But

Lieutenant Robert Maynard and Teach in combat aboard the *Pearl*. Maynard's victory marked the end of piracy in North America.

the bullet that struck the huge pirate seemed to cause him no concern, and he lunged forward with his cutlass. Maynard raised his own sword to deflect the blow, but to his horror it broke in two. Teach towered over him with a rabid leer and raised his sword to cut Maynard dead. But the blow never fell.

Saved by a seaman

One of *Pearl*'s crew, rushing to defend his captain, slashed at the pirate's throat. Yet even this was only a distraction. Spurting fountains of blood, Teach drew another pistol from his belt and aimed again at Maynard. But then a strange, faraway look came into his eyes. He swayed, and toppled over like a felled oak.

The death of the mighty Blackbeard was the turning point of the battle and the rest of the pirates were soon overcome. Ten of *Pearl*'s men lay dead, and all but one of the crew had been injured.

Poor reward

Although his victory over the fearsome Teach marked the virtual end of piracy in North America, Maynard was poorly rewarded. Alive, Blackbeard had a price of £100 on his head. Once he was dead the authorities refused to pay up. Four years of legal wrangling followed as the Navy lieutenant tried to secure a fair reward for his crew. He was eventually given £3 for his trouble, and those who fought with him were allocated half that amount.

Teach's head was cut off and hung from the *Pearl*'s bow. Such was his fearsome reputation that his body, which was thrown overboard, was reported to have swum several times around the ship in brazen defiance.

Rubble and strife in battlefield Beirut

A car bounced down the rubble-strewn airport road and into the suburbs of Beirut, Lebanon. Inside, insulated only slightly from the stink of open drains and dank December weather, was English surgeon Pauline Cutting. The year was 1985.

Experienced in accident and emergency work, she had been sent to Beirut by her new employers, the charity Medical Aid for Palestinians. It was turning out to be far worse than she ever expected.

Ruined city

A decade of civil war had ruined the once beautiful Mediterranean city, and 50,000 had been killed. There seemed to be no solution to the savage fighting, which flared up or died down unpredictably.

The car passed a block of bomb-damaged apartments. One side had collapsed. Crumbling concrete floors and stairways hung precariously over the road, spilling out tangled wiring and seeping streams of water. The other side of the block was still inhabited and Cutting could see people peering uneasily from cracked or broken windows.

Deeper into the bustling city the buildings closed around them, a maze of dark streets and dirty alleys. Clustered on corners were small groups of young men brandishing machine guns and grenade launchers. Occasionally the sinister silhouette of a tank could be glimpsed, skulking behind a burned-out factory, or lurking in a side street.

Pauline Cutting.

Chaos reigned. Here government had no control. There were no traffic signs, no policemen, no laws. Beirut was a battlefield.

Bourj al Barajneh

Cutting was taken to the Palestinian camp of Bourj al Barajneh. It was not really a camp, more a shanty town of tiny alleys.

In the middle of Bourj al Barajneh was Haifa Hospital, a five-floor concrete building where Cutting was to be in charge of the surgery

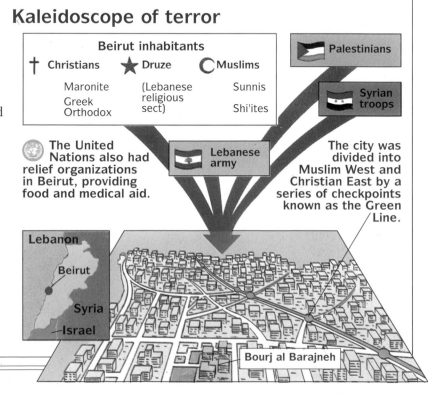

Kaleidoscope of terror

The civil war broke out in 1975, when Christian and Muslim groups fought to decide who would have the most political power. Beirut is a city of many cultures and religious views, and the situation soon became extremely complex. When Cutting arrived there were various major factions (see right), each with their own soldiers, known as *militias*.

Throughout the conflict, alliances and feuds between the militias were constantly changing. Cutting described the situation as being like a kaleidoscope, where one small twist creates a completely new pattern.

Beirut inhabitants

† **Christians**   ★ **Druze**   ☾ **Muslims**

Maronite	(Lebanese	Sunnis
Greek	religious	
Orthodox	sect)	Shi'ites

The United Nations also had relief organizations in Beirut, providing food and medical aid.

Palestinians

Syrian troops

Lebanese army

The city was divided into Muslim West and Christian East by a series of checkpoints known as the Green Line.

Lebanon
Beirut
Syria
Israel

Bourj al Barajneh

department. Like all the other buildings in the camp, it had been seriously damaged in the fighting, and the top two floors were beyond repair. The entrance hall was littered with homeless families and their belongings, and children milled around the muddy floor.

Cutting spent the first few days in a daze, wondering if coming to Beirut had been a terrible mistake. Equipment was primitive, and the staff was demoralized, but she had so much responsibility, and so much to learn there was barely time to worry about it. Most of her work involved treating day-to-day illnesses, and diseases caused by the camp's damp living conditions and dirty water. On top of this there were the casualties of the war. Cutting was used to handling terrible hospital cases such as car crash victims, and now she had to learn to deal with injuries caused by bombs, shells and bullets.

Unwanted refugees

Working in the camp Cutting learned more about the plight of the Palestinians. Driven from their homeland following the creation of the state of Israel in 1948, they lived as refugees, unwanted and in great poverty in bordering Arab states. Cutting had known little about this when she agreed to come to Beirut. After a few months at Haifa she could see the difference her work made to the lives of the people she treated, and she became determined to stay and help.

In early 1986 the situation grew worse. Violence simmered among rival groups, but most troubling of all were the kidnapping and murder of American or European residents. One United Nations worker was hanged, and his kidnappers released a video of his execution. Cutting saw the tape and was haunted by the fuzzy pictures of a hooded body swaying from a tree.

Ben Alofs

But not everything was grim. Cutting made many friends during her stay, especially a Dutch nurse named Ben Alofs, who also worked in the camp. He was tall and amiable, and was tremendously well informed about Beirut politics. Their friendship grew and one day he gave her Ernest Hemingway's *Farewell to Arms* – a novel about a passionate romance between an ambulance driver and nurse during World War One. It was something of a hint. Alofs was transferred to another part of Lebanon soon after, and left a note for Cutting saying he was falling in love with her.

Mortal danger

It was around this time that Bourj al Barajneh began to be attacked again. The camp was surrounded by Amal militia men (one of several armed Shi'ite groups) who wanted to drive the Palestinians from their city. Anyone venturing outside could be kidnapped, or killed. Inside, sniper fire and shelling became a daily danger.

On May 26, Amal soldiers stormed the camp. As the Palestinians fought to defend their territory a steady stream of injured and dying men was brought into the hospital, and Cutting and her staff struggled to save the wounded.

Haifa hospital was very poorly equipped. Many of the surgical instruments Cutting used she had brought over from England.

The next two days were just as bad, and children too were maimed in the fighting. This was Cutting's first experience of all-out battlefield surgery. Apart from the daily danger of being killed, she had to make heartbreaking decisions about who to save and who to leave to die, and cope with only the most basic supplies and equipment. There were no experts to consult, and no backup facilities, and at times she felt very alone.

Worse was to come. On May 31, as Cutting lay asleep, a shell exploded above her room. The blast hit her like a punch in the chest and thick black soot and rubble filled the hospital. The Amal soldiers attacks on Bourj al Barajneh were not succeeding, so now they subjected the camp to a week-long bombardment. During this terrifying time Cutting became close to two

Belgian doctors, Lieve Seutjens and Dirk van Duppen. They noticed how she read Ben Alofs' letter every time she lay down to sleep, and offered to teach her some Dutch, so she could speak to Ben in his own language.

At the end of June, after discussions between the warring factions, the shelling stopped. Syrian and Lebanese army soldiers surrounded the camp, to prevent more attacks by Amal soldiers.

There was other good news. Ben Alofs was back in Beirut, working in another camp. Now that Cutting was less busy she was able to spend some time with him, and also travel to England for a break.

The Camp War

She returned to the camp in late August, to be joined shortly after by Scottish nurse Susie Wighton. Another round of

fighting was brewing, and the next few months were going to be extremely difficult.

At the end of October Amal soldiers attacked Bourj al Barajneh and other Palestinian camps throughout Beirut, in a campaign that became known as "The Camp War". It became impossible for Palestinians to enter or leave Bourj al Barajneh. The fighting grew fiercer, and electricity to the camp was cut off. The hospital had to rely on diesel-powered generators, and ingenious improvisation was called for. Headlight bulbs and batteries were removed from cars and rigged up to provide light in the darkened building.

The hospital became a target for the shelling. On several occasions Cutting found herself trembling with fear as direct

One of the routes into the battered buildings of Bourj al Barajneh.

hits shook the building to its foundations. After one near miss she was partially deaf for three weeks. One shell shattered a water tank at the top of the building and water trickled down the walls, collecting in deep pools in corridors and rooms throughout the hospital. On top of all their other troubles the hospital staff had to cope with having constantly wet feet.

By mid-November the Lebanese winter had taken hold, and in her rare moments of relaxation Cutting fantasized about sitting in front of a burning coal fire, eating stew and dumplings. Ben Alofs, braving sniper fire and shells, and loaded with supplies of cakes and custard, crept into the camp whenever he could.

As the bombardment increased, the staff moved their living quarters to the basement, sleeping in a tiny room next to the operating room. It was warmer here, and everybody was friendly, but the strain of having no privacy was difficult to endure.

Surprising successes

Despite the hardship, hospital staff worked wonders. In November a little boy had been brought in with a terrible head wound. He was so disturbed that when anyone roused him he would cry like a cat. After a few days he started to speak, but would not open his eyes. Cutting was deeply moved by the courage children showed coping with their injuries. This boy had begun to have English lessons and every morning when she visited, he would greet her with a formal "Good morning" and say "I'm fine, thank you".

Bourj al Barajneh

Once 30,000 people had lived here. When Cutting arrived only 9,000 remained. Amid the alleys there were little shops selling food and clothes, hardware stores, a hairdresser, and a garage.

Haifa Hospital

400m (1300ft)

Waste ground

Amal positions

He went on to make a full recovery.

On another occasion a Palestinian fighter was brought in close to death. Cutting and her team struggled all day to save him, removing 500 shell fragments from his body. He too survived. Such successes strengthened Cutting's resolve to stay in the camp until the siege was over.

Collapsing hospital

But the hospital was collapsing around them. Fuel was running out and the generators could only run for four hours at a time. In the cold, damp building the winter wind howled along corridors from one broken window to another, and black fungus crawled down the walls.

By the end of December the third and fourth floor had collapsed under the shelling. The drainage and sanitation system had been destroyed, everyone had lice, garbage piled up in every corridor, and rats scurried underfoot.

But there were still happy moments. January 19 was Cutting's birthday and Ben sneaked into the camp to present her with a siege survival kit – clean socks, soap, toothpaste, two candles and a packet of cigarettes. It was the best present she had ever had.

Cutting also found the people of Bourj al Barajneh were exceptionally kind. Most days a little boy would bring her food from his family. When she said he was being too generous he told her "When I have a little, I will bring you a little. When we have nothing, then I will bring you nothing."

When electricity to the camp was cut off, car headlights were used to illuminate the hospital.

The camp was being starved and bombarded into submission. Worst of all was the fear that if Amal soldiers did break into Bourj al Barajneh, they might massacre its inhabitants. Palestinians had been slain in their thousands when rival militias had entered other refugee camps, and Cutting began to have terrible nightmares about such killings.

It seemed that nobody was prepared to help them, so Cutting, Ben Alofs and Susan Wighton prepared a formal statement to the international media to try to draw attention to the situation in the camp. A declaration detailing the dreadful conditions of everyday life for Bourj al Barajneh's thousands of inhabitants was transmitted over the hospital two-way radio.

Identifying themselves like this took a great deal of courage. They knew the American and European media would be more interested in the siege if they knew westerners were suffering too. But this also made them a target for Amal gunmen.

The declaration was broadcast on Arab radio stations, but it caused little international interest. The situation grew worse. Starvation in the camp became so bad that the people were eating rats, dogs, cats – even grass.

Their spirits at rock bottom, Cutting and her staff radioed out another declaration calling for the siege to be lifted. This time the BBC World Service broadcast their statement.

Worst day

Friday February 13 was the worst day of the siege. A bomb

The basement operating room at Haifa. Cutting would spend at least 18 hours a day here.

181

landed among a group of people who had ventured from their shelters and many were terribly maimed. With the barest amount of equipment and supplies the starving doctors operated on two patients at a time throughout the day.

As Cutting lay exhausted on her bed at 11:00 that night, she was roused by a message on the hospital radio. A BBC World Service reporter named Jim Muir, whose voice they all instantly recognized, was trying to contact her. Over a crackling radio link they talked about conditions in the camp, and then to Cutting's great surprise her mother and father spoke to her. The BBC had arranged a radio link up so they could talk to their daughter. Muir came back on the radio and asked if they wanted to be rescued. Cutting was determined not to leave her patients. "I'm not coming out until it's finished," she replied.

More journalists began to take an interest, and Cutting learned that other factions in Beirut were beginning to side with the Palestinians against Amal. The increasing news coverage that followed their declarations had generated

By February 1987, conditions in Bourj al Barajneh had become almost unbearable.

some support in Beirut for the camp's inhabitants.

On February 17 a cease-fire was negotiated, and a few trucks full of food were allowed into the camp. Women were permitted to go out for a brief period each day to buy food, but they were still shot at by snipers and subjected to brutal treatment by Amal forces. "We know all about Pauline Cutting, and we are going to cut her to pieces" they told the women who passed through their checkpoints.

By now television crews and newspaper journalists were frequent visitors to the camp and the plight of Bourj al Barajneh's inmates had become a focus for the world's media. On April 8, prompted by an international outcry, Syrian troops arrived to patrol the perimeter, and for the first time in five and a half months there were no casualties admitted to the hospital. The International Red Cross arrived, along

with new medical staff for the hospital. After 163 days the siege was truly over.

Home at last

It was time to go home. After many sad farewells, Pauline Cutting, Ben Alofs and Susie Wighton made their way out of the camp. Cutting was still uneasy about Amal death threats so at least 50 people surrounded her to make sure she was not seized as she left. As she got into the car she turned to look back at the camp. All the hundreds of people who had turned out to see her off were smiling and waving. It was a heartbreaking sight. She was walking away. They had nowhere else to go.

The next day they took a ferry out to Cyprus, where they were met by TV crews and journalists. All of a sudden the whole world wanted to know about these three medics from Bourj al Barajneh. In their hotel that evening they celebrated their survival with a bottle of wine and entertained themselves by turning the water and lights on and off. It seemed unreal to be somewhere where anything and everything actually worked.

Safely home and surrounded by relatives, Susie Wighton (left), Pauline Cutting (middle), and Ben Alofs (right), meet the world's press at London's Heathrow airport.

Stakhanov – Soviet Superstar

During the First World War the Russian Empire collapsed into chaos, and revolution swept away the old regime. In 1917 Russia's new rulers renamed their country the Soviet Union. They set up a communist society where citizens were supposed to have more equality and the state controlled farms and industry.

A publicity shot of Stakhanov.

Yet a decade later Russia was still very poor. Dictator Joseph Stalin, who controlled his people with an iron grip, was determined to transform his country into a powerful nation. He gave orders for huge factories, steel works and coal mines to be built. In Stalin's plan, workers on these projects, fired with patriotic zeal, would produce record levels of materials.

But most workers in these new plants and factories were peasants. In the 1920s and 30s 17 million of them moved from villages and farms to towns and industry. They were ill-disciplined and apathetic.

Execution or imprisonment was Stalin's usual method of motivating people, but on this occasion he had another tactic. If other countries made heroes of film stars or royalty, then the Soviet Union would have heroes of industry. His henchmen were dispatched to find a suitable candidate.

Stakhanov's triumph

On September 1, 1935, Soviet citizens woke to read in their morning papers that coal miner Alexei Stakhanov had dug out 104 tonnes (tons) of coal in a Donbass mine during the night shift of August 30-31. This was 14 times the amount a miner was expected to produce in a single shift. The message was clear, said the papers. If an ordinary miner could perform such superhuman work then "there are no fortresses communism cannot storm".

Stakhanov was overwhelmed with attention. He spoke on the radio, starred in newsreels, appeared in propaganda posters, and was awarded the *Order of Lenin*, the Soviet Union's most prestigious medal. He moved to Moscow where he became the figurehead for the so-called "Stakhanovite" movement, which encouraged other workers to follow his example.

Inspired by a speech

How could one man do the work of 14? Stakhanov told the Soviet people he had been inspired by a speech of Stalin's, which he heard on the radio the evening of his heroic shift. The truth was his feat was a con trick set up by the Soviet authorities. Two other miners had helped him dig the coal. A team of workers had carried it from the coalface, and done other jobs a miner would usually do himself. Stakhanov was not even an exceptional worker. He had been selected for hero status because his handsome face would look good in photographs, and he was a docile, easy going fellow, unlikely to question what he was being asked to do.

The "Stakhanovite" movement created other heroes, from steel workers to milk maids whose cows produced record levels of milk. ("Storm the 3,000 litre level" ran one slogan.) They starred in newsreels and were celebrated in biographies. "Stakhanovites" were rewarded with extra pay or smart apartments. But many were unpopular with their fellow workers, who felt their exceptional workmate showed them in a bad light. Some were attacked or even murdered.

And what of Stakhanov himself? The Soviet superman who swapped the Donbass coal fields for a desk in Moscow proved to be a poor organizer. When other workplace heroes sprang up to replace him he was quietly dropped from his post, and vanished into obscurity.

Soviet poster depicting industrialization as a heroic task.

ИНДУСТРИАЛИЗАЦИЯ ПУТЬ к СОЦИАЛИЗМУ

Cosmonaut number one

Outer space; an airless, endless realm, host to lethal radiation, meteor storms, and perils unknown to science. Devoid of life and unimaginably bleak.

In the dead of night, April 12, 1961, on a windswept plain in the central Soviet Union, a towering green rocket named *Vostok 1* sat pointing at the sky. Its task, to hurl a man up into the deadly environment of space.

Technicians swarmed around the concrete launch pad and huge steel gantries that connected and supported a mass of electricity cables and fuel pipes. These snaked into the thin metal casing of the rocket, which creaked and groaned as liquid oxygen boiled away from access vents and into the cold night air.

Capsule to space

As the first rays of the sun caught on the rocket's pointed tip, a small bus drew up beside it. Several figures emerged, including one dressed in a hefty orange protective suit and a large spherical helmet. The technicians paused from their work as this man made a brief speech, raising his hands to acknowledge their applause.

Then he boarded a platform which took him to a small instrument-packed capsule at the top of the rocket. Here he was strapped into a couch, and 30 nuts were screwed in around an exit hatch to seal him in. One by one the technicians retired to the safety of nearby concrete bunkers, leaving him alone with his thoughts. The waiting began.

The man cocooned in this tiny capsule was former jet fighter pilot Yuri Gagarin, the Soviet Union's designated "Cosmonaut* number one". The amiable 27-year-old son of a carpenter and dairy maid had been selected from over 3,000 volunteers to be the first man in space. No one on the project doubted he was the best person for the job – a cool and clear thinker, with great stamina and personal courage. If anyone could survive the dangers of space it was Gagarin.

Like the great seafarers who first explored the world's oceans three centuries before, he was venturing into the unknown. They had feared storms, sea monsters or savage tribes. The fears Gagarin faced were far stranger.

Weightless puzzle

The extreme environment of space was complicated by the phenomenon of weightlessness. On Earth gravity holds everything in its place. In space it does not exist.

Vostok 1 thunders into space, April 12, 1961.

Yuri Gagarin, the first man in space. This photo of him in a jet pilot uniform became a popular Soviet pin-up.

Although animals had been sent into orbit and lived, many scientists still wondered whether a man would be able to survive without gravity. Would blood still flow around his body? Would he choke on food? Worst of all, would his mind become so disoriented by this alien sensation that it would cease to function? (At the time it was a commonly held fear that space voyagers could return from space as burned out zombies.)

Big bang

There were other more obvious worries. A space voyager would travel at speeds no human had experienced before. The physical damage this might cause could only be guessed at. Most importantly, the business of sending a vehicle into orbit by igniting thousands of tons of highly volatile, explosive fuel was never going to make space travel a particularly safe activity. In 1961 rocket science was in its infancy, and the seven months prior to Gagarin's flight had seen some terrible disasters.

One rocket, aimed at the planet Mars, had blown up on

*The Russians called their spacemen cosmonauts. (From Cosmos meaning the universe, and nautes, a Greek word for sailor.)

the launch pad, killing the Soviet's space project director Marshall Mitrofan Nedelin, and scores of his best technicians. More ominously still, several unmanned flights in the *Vostok*-type craft that Gagarin now occupied had ended with the capsule locked in an eternal orbit, or burning up on its return to Earth.

Cold War

The world Gagarin was about to leave had settled into an uneasy peace following World War Two, which had ended 16 years before. Its two principal victors – the United States and the Soviet Union – were now hostile rivals. Each side taunted the other, stopping just short of coming to blows, and vied with the other to demonstrate their superiority to the watching world. Space had become the new front line for this contest, and there was intense competition to see who would be the first to put a man into orbit.

Blast off

For three hours Gagarin sat waiting, as rocket engineers ran through final checks. Then, at seven minutes past nine, it was time to go. Four metal gantries which supported the rocket unfolded, its engines ignited and *Vostok 1* rose slowly into the air. In his capsule Gagarin heard a shrill whistle and then a mighty roar. As the rocket built up speed he was pressed hard into his seat. After a minute the acceleration was so great he could barely move. Technicians monitoring his physical reactions noted his heart rate rise from its usual 64 beats a minute to 150.

Gagarin's pioneering spacecraft

Vostok 1 had two sections. Only the spherical upper module containing the cosmonaut came back to Earth.

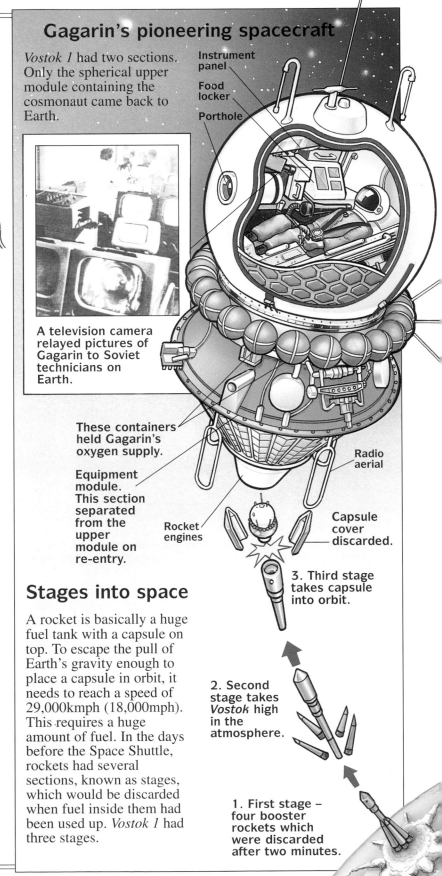

A television camera relayed pictures of Gagarin to Soviet technicians on Earth.

Instrument panel

Food locker

Porthole

These containers held Gagarin's oxygen supply.

Equipment module. This section separated from the upper module on re-entry.

Rocket engines

Radio aerial

Capsule cover discarded.

3. Third stage takes capsule into orbit.

2. Second stage takes *Vostok* high in the atmosphere.

1. First stage – four booster rockets which were discarded after two minutes.

Stages into space

A rocket is basically a huge fuel tank with a capsule on top. To escape the pull of Earth's gravity enough to place a capsule in orbit, it needs to reach a speed of 29,000kmph (18,000mph). This requires a huge amount of fuel. In the days before the Space Shuttle, rockets had several sections, known as stages, which would be discarded when fuel inside them had been used up. *Vostok 1* had three stages.

The crushing sensation began to lessen as *Vostok 1* gradually escaped the clutches of gravity, and entered into orbit around the Earth. Gagarin was now flying at 8km (5 miles) a second.

Rising in his chair as far as his harness would allow he immediately became aware of the sensation of weightlessness. At first he found it unpleasant, but adapted very quickly. It was not nearly as disorienting as scientists had feared. He unbuckled his belt, and hung in the air, between floor and ceiling. It felt as though his arms and legs did not belong to him, and his map case, pencil and note pad floated by. The whole sensation was very dreamlike. Strangest of all was the way in which liquids behaved. Water leaking from a drink container took on a spherical shape and floated in midair until it reached a solid surface where it settled like dew on a flower.

Gagarin kept detailed notes of what it was like to be weightless. He was fascinated by the way water floated into spherical droplets.

High altitude report

Up in orbit, there was very little actual flying to be done. Flight corrections were made automatically. The discarding of stages, the flight path and speed of the capsule, even the conditions inside the cabin, were all controlled from the ground, or by computer. This left Gagarin free to concentrate on what he saw and felt. He quickly realized that weightlessness was not going to affect the way he worked, so he began to jot down observations and report what he could see.

The orbit of *Vostok 1* took it between 181km (112 miles) and 327km (203 miles) above the surface of the Earth. From here coastlines, mountain ranges and forests could easily be seen, as well as the curve of the Earth. Along this curve the pale blue atmosphere gradually darkened in a series of incredibly rich hues – from turquoise to blue, violet and finally black. Above this beautiful sight hung the dark eternity of space. For Gagarin, who was brought up on a farm, space looked like "a huge black field sown with star-like grain."

Cat out of bag

Once he was safely in space, the Soviet authorities decided to release the news to an unsuspecting world. Radio Moscow interrupted its usual schedule with a burst of patriotic music, and a solemn voice which announced: "The world's first spaceship with a man on board has been launched in the Soviet Union on a round-the-world orbit." Throughout the country, factory, farm and office workers listened intently, scarcely believing that their nation had performed such a scientific miracle.

Day to night

The sun looked very different. Without the Earth's atmosphere to soften its rays it seemed a hundred times brighter. It reminded Gagarin of molten metal, and when it shone directly into his capsule he had to shield his portholes with protective filters.

Suddenly *Vostok 1* plunged into pitch dark as the capsule flew out of the rays of the sun and behind the shaded side of the Earth. Below, Gagarin could see only blackness, but concluded he must be flying over an ocean.

Although the cosmonaut was neither hungry not thirsty he

Around the world in 90 minutes

Vostok 1 made a single orbit before returning to Earth.

Blast off. Baikonur cosmodrome, central Asia.

Landing. Smelovka, near Saratov.

Soviet Union

ate a small meal – carefully sucking pulped food from a tube-like container, and drinking a little water. He had to be careful transferring both food and liquid from container to mouth, in case it floated off and attached itself to his instrument panels.

Soon *Vostok 1* emerged again into the light, the horizon blazing from bright orange through all the colours of the rainbow. Having reported carefully the new sensations and sights he was seeing, Gagarin's mind began to wander. Alone in his capsule, more remote and out of reach than any human ever before, he thought of the bustling streets of Moscow, where he had visited his wife and two daughters a couple of days before the flight.

Back to Earth

In less than 90 minutes *Vostok I* had orbited the entire Earth, and now it was time to return. This was the most dangerous part of the flight. If something had gone wrong at takeoff, there was a small chance of ejecting to safety. If anything went wrong now, the first man in space could be marooned forever, or burned to a cinder. Until this time, Gagarin had had every faith in his spacecraft, but now he began to wonder if it would work properly. Was there some unforeseen danger lurking on the return journey?

On board equipment oriented the capsule in the correct flight path, using the Sun as a guide, and *Vostok 1* began its giddy descent. As it plunged inexorably down into the upper layers of the atmosphere the outer skin of the craft began to glow red hot. Fiery crimson flames flashed past his small portholes, as Gagarin was once again pinned to his seat.

Coming back was much more unpleasant than going out, and when his ship began to tumble around he became intensely worried.

Near disaster

Things had in fact gone seriously wrong. Before re-entry his small capsule was supposed to separate from a connected equipment module (see diagram on page 185). Unknown to Gagarin this had not happened correctly, and both craft were still attached by electrical wiring. Fortunately the heat of re-entry burned away the wire cables, the two craft separated, and disaster was averted.

The rotation finally stopped, the descent parachutes opened to slow down the speeding capsule, and Gagarin realized that the worst was over. He had risked his life for the glory of his country and he was going to live to tell the tale. Overcome with joy he began to sing at the top of his voice.

There remained one final, dangerous step. 6,000m (20,000ft) from the ground his couch ejected from the capsule, and he floated back to Earth by parachute. Soviet rocket engineers thought that landing inside the capsule would be too jarring, and parachuting down separately was safer.

At 10:55, less than two hours after he had taken off, Gagarin landed in a field near the village of Smelovka, watched by two startled farm workers. They walked toward him, eager to help, but slowed uncertainly as they approached. His unfamiliar bright orange spacesuit and large white helmet clearly frightened them.

One, a woman named Anna Takhtarova, asked "Are you from outer space?" Taking off his helmet Gagarin reassured her that he was a fellow human, but, yes, he had come from outer space. Then other farm workers arrived. Unlike Takharova, they had been listening to their radio. "It's Yuri Gagarin! It's Yuri Gagarin!" one shouted, completely astonished to be meeting the remarkable man he had heard about minutes before.

Then, elated astronaut and the excited farm workers embraced and kissed like long-lost relatives. This was indeed an extraordinary moment. For the first time in history a man had left the planet and returned safely to Earth.

Above. Gagarin is acclaimed by Soviet leader Nikita Khrushchev. Left. Medal of Pilot-Cosmonaut of the Soviet Union.

Heroes on film

Around half the stories in this book have featured in films which you can still see from time to time on television, or rent from a video store. Here are some of the best.

Reliving her ordeal

Odette Sansom's work with the French Resistance, and her subsequent capture and imprisonment, was portrayed in the 1950 film *Odette*. British actress Anna Neagle played the French secret agent.

The film was partially shot at Fresnes Prison, Paris, where Odette herself had been held prisoner. She worked as an advisor on the project, but seeing the film's actors relive her worst moments was a painful experience.

Anna Neagle in *Odette*. Here, feigning kindness, a Gestapo officer offers a cigarette prior to a torture session.

From psycho to sympathy

Geronimo has fascinated film makers for most of the century and scores of films featuring him have been made. The first picture about him, *Geronimo's Last Raid* was shot in 1912, only three years after his death.

As the years passed his depiction on screen changed from that of a bloodthirsty savage to a much-wronged hero. In 1939 the poster for *Geronimo!* proclaimed "Ten thousand Red Raiders roar into battle!" *Geronimo*, made in 1993, on the other hand, takes a much more sympathetic look at the Apache people and their tragic demise.

Wes Studi plays the Apache warrior in *Geronimo*.

The Right Rocket

Chuck Yeager's assault on the sound barrier was captured spectacularly in the 1983 American film *The Right Stuff*. Based on Tom Wolfe's best-selling book of the same title, the film also depicts America's first efforts to place a man in space. Yeager worked as a technical advisor on the film, and also made a brief appearance as a bartender at an inn near Muroc airbase.

Chuck Yeager with actor Sam Shepard, who plays him in the film. Behind them is a plywood mock-up of Yeager's X-1 rocket.

Owens' Berlin victory

Jesse Owens' Olympic triumph was captured on film by eminent German director Leni Riefenstahl in *Olympische Spiele 1936*.

This sinister but beautiful film is seen by many as a hymn to Germany's racist Nazi regime, but Riefenstahl made no attempt to play down African-American Owens' victories over Germany's athletes.

In this still from Leni Riefenstahl's *Olympische Spiele 1936* the Berlin Olympic Stadium is encircled by columns of searchlights. Spectacular visual displays such as this were also used to great effect during Nazi Party rallies.

Maynard written out

In the 1952 American film *Blackbeard the Pirate* Robert Newton played the infamous plunderer, charging around waving pistols and rolling his eyes with immense enthusiasm. The plot takes great liberties with the known facts. Instead of Lieutenant Maynard, reformed villain Sir Henry Morgan is hired to rid the high seas of the evil pirate. Morgan still has something of a wicked streak in him and Blackbeard comes to a suitably gruesome end. Buried up to his neck on a sandy beach he is slowly drowned by the incoming tide.

Robert Newton in *Blackbeard the Pirate*. Newton was employed to roll his eyes in much the same way in another pirate film, *Long John Silver*.

After the event

Chernobyl

(Terror stalks Chernobyl, p.142)

To prevent further radiation escaping, a huge concrete casing was constructed around the ruptured number four reactor. However, local scientists are concerned that an earthquake could cause this to collapse. For 30km (20 miles) around Chernobyl, farmland lies in ruins, and deserted towns slowly crumble and decay. 135,000 people had to evacuate the area, never to return. Today, illnesses caused by exposure to radiation from the explosion continue to claim lives.

Pauline Cutting

(Rubble and strife in battlefield Beirut, p.178)

In 1987 Cutting was awarded the OBE (Order of the British Empire) by the British government in recognition of her work in Bourj al Barajneh. She is a member of the board of Medical Aid for Palestinians, and returned to Beirut in October 1995, while reviewing the charity's projects in Lebanon.

She now works in a hospital in Amsterdam, and is married to **Ben Alofs**. They have two children. **Susie Wighton** was awarded an MBE (Member of the British Empire) in 1987. She still works as an emergency relief worker and spent much of 1995 in Rwanda.

Yuri Gagarin

(Cosmonaut number one, p.184)

Gagarin's 1961 spaceflight made him an instant celebrity, and he spent the next five years touring the world, even visiting the Soviet Union's arch rival the United States. He was an excellent ambassador for his country, and his amiable modesty made him hugely popular with the thousands who turned out to see him.

In 1968 he began to train for another spaceflight, but was killed when a jet he was flying hit the ground as it swerved to avoid another aircraft which had flown too close. A massive funeral ceremony was held in Moscow, and Gagarin's remains were buried in the Kremlin wall.

Bob Geldof

(Boomtown Bob's global jukebox, p.132)

Live Aid raised £40 million ($70 million) for the Ethiopian famine and remains the most successful charity concert ever staged. Half the money was spent on food, and half went to long-term projects such as road building, irrigation, farming, and sanitation schemes.

Geldof lives in London. He still records and performs from time to time, and also runs the *Planet 24* television company. He returned to Ethiopia in 1995, to make a documentary with BBC television, marking the tenth anniversary of Live Aid. Recalling the impact of the concerts on those who donated money, he told British magazine *Radio Times,* "There was an absolute awareness that you were not powerless in the face of massive events. The individual could make a change."

Ethiopia is still a very poor country, although the civil war, a major cause of the famine, ended in 1991.

Geronimo

(Geronimo's final stand, p.150)

Geronimo spent his last years coming to terms with the society he had fought so hard to resist. He tried farming and Christianity, but was expelled from his church because he refused to give up gambling.

If anyone was going to exploit his notoriety, Geronimo was determined it was going to be him. He sold his photograph to those who flocked to shows and circuses to see him, for a then exorbitant two dollars.

The US Army, in a curious compliment to their old enemy, adopted his name as a warcry. During World War Two paratroops yelled "Geronimo" as they plunged from their aircraft and into battle.

Geronimo is the main attraction in this 1904 poster advertising "Pawnee Bill's Wild West Show".

Chico Mendes

(Brazil's rainforest hero, p.155)

Following the 1989 election Mendes' friend **José Lutzenberger** became Brazilian Minister for the Environment. Further road building into the Amazon was cancelled, and strict laws limiting burning of the forest were enforced. Vast areas of forest were set aside for conservation, including a 800,000 hectare (two million acre) region named in memory of Mendes.

Jesse Owens

(Owens' Olympic triumph, p.146)

When the Games ended, the athletes' Olympic village was turned into an army training camp, and anti-Jewish propaganda reappeared in the German media. Hitler fantasized that following the Nazi conquest of Europe the Games would be held in Germany forever, and black athletes would be forbidden to compete.

Jesse Owens' long jump record remained unbeaten until 1960, but his fame did not bring him happiness. Deluged with show business and business offers, Owens displayed his athletic ability at sideshows and exhibitions, where he would run against racehorses, or play with the novelty basketball team *The Harlem Globetrotters*. The money he made was invested in businesses that collapsed.

After the Second World War his life improved. He worked for children's charities and went around the world as a goodwill ambassador for the United States. He died in 1980.

Owens' friend and Olympic rival **Lutz Long** was killed in 1943, fighting with the German army in Sicily.

Odette Sansom

(Odette's ordeal, p.160)

Following her release Odette returned to England. She had several operations on her injured feet before she was able to walk without discomfort. In 1946 she became the first woman to be given the George Cross, Britain's highest civilian

award for bravery.

In 1948 she married **Peter Churchill**, the man she had suffered so much to protect. But after eight years they parted, and Odette married Geoffrey Hallowes, another former secret agent. In later life she co-founded the British "Woman of the Year" award, worked for charities, and spent many hours writing to thousands of people with problems, who had contacted her for advice or inspiration. She died in 1995, aged 82.

Mary Seacole

(Mother Seacole's Balaclava boys, p.166)

Seacole returned to England ruined by the collapse of her trading business, and set about writing her biography to make some money. "*Wonderful adventures of Mrs. Seacole in Many Lands*" was published in 1857, and its success brought some financial security. She spent the rest of her days living in Jamaica and England and became friends with members of the British royal family, who called on her medical skills to treat their ailments. She died in 1881 aged 77.

Stauffenberg

(Stauffenberg's Secret Germany, p.170)

Had Stauffenberg and his conspirators succeeded with *Operation Valkyrie* the war in Europe might have ended much earlier. As it was, it continued for almost another year.

Hitler described the conspiracy as "a crime unparalleled in German history" and reacted accordingly. Although Stauffenberg, **Olbricht, Haeften**, and **von Quirnheim** were dead and buried, Hitler demanded

that their bodies be burned and the ashes scattered to the wind.

Following brutal interrogation the main surviving conspirators were hauled before the Nazi courts. They refused to be intimidated and knew the regime they loathed was teetering on the brink of defeat. General **Erich Fellgiebel**, who had stood with Stauffenberg as the bomb exploded at Rastenburg, was told by the Court President that he was to be hanged. "Hurry with the hanging Mr. President," he replied, "otherwise you will hang earlier than we."

Gestapo and SS officers investigated the plot until the last days of the war. Seven thousand arrests were made and between two and three thousand people were executed.

Stauffenberg's personal magnetism continued to exert an extraordinary influence, even from beyond the grave. SS investigator Georg Kiesel was so in awe of him he reported to Hitler that his would-be assassin was "a spirit of fire, fascinating and inspiring all who came in touch with him."

Chuck Yeager

(Punching a hole in the sky, p.138)

News of Yeager's top secret X-1 flight was released to the world in December 1947. Showered with awards and accolades, he continued working as a test pilot, pioneering supersonic flight.

In the 1960s he returned to active service, flying bombing missions over Vietnam. After retirement Yeager spent his time hunting, flying (anything from gliders to high speed jets), and making regular appearances as an after-dinner speaker. "I'm not the rocking-chair type," he remarked in his 1986 autobiography *Yeager*.

Further reading

If you would like to know more about some of these stories, the following books contain useful information.

Ablaze – the story of Chernobyl by Piers Paul Reid (Secker 1993)
Animal Heroes by Yvonne Roberts (Pelham, 1990)
Bury My Heart At Wounded Knee (An Indian History of the American West) by Dee Brown (Vintage, 1991)
Children of the Siege by Pauline Cutting (Heinemann, 1988)
Is That It? by Bob Geldof (Sidgwick & Jackson, 1986)
The July Plot by Nigel Richardson (Dryad Press Ltd, 1986)
Odette by Jerrard Tickell (New Portaway, 1949)
Odette Churchill by Catherine Sanders (Hamish Hamilton, 1989)
Jesse Owens by Tony Gentry (Melrose Square Publishing Company, 1990)
The Pirates by Douglas Botting (Time-Life Books, 1978)
The Space Race by Jon Trux (New English Library, 1985)
Wonderful Adventures of Mrs Seacole in many lands by Mary Seacole (Oxford University Press, 1988)
Yeager – An Autobiography by Chuck Yeager and Leo Janos (Century, 1989)

Acknowledgements and photo credits

The Publishers would like to thank the following for their help and advice:

Dr. David Killingray, Reader in History, Goldsmiths College, University of London; Medical Aid for Palestinians and Pauline Cutting; Doug Millard, Associate Curator for Space Technology, Science Museum, London; Mark Seaman, Imperial War Museum, London.

The Publishers would like to thank the following for permission to reproduce these photographs in this book: Band Aid Trust, London (133 bottom); David Brenchley/Cornish Photo News (165 inset); Coldstream Guards (by permission of the Regimental Lieutenant Colonel) (158 bottom); Edwards Airforce Base, California – History Office Flight Test Center (131 top left, 139, 140, 141); Gedenkstätte Deutscher Widerstand, Berlin (170 bottom right, 172, 174); Hulton Deutsch, London (147, 160, 166 bottom, 173 top right, 178, 184 top, 187); Imperial War Museum, London (168 bottom); David King Collection, London, (183 bottom); The Kobal Collection, London (188 top, Herbert Wilcox, 188 bottom, Columbia, 189 top, Warner/Ladd (Irwin Winkler, Robert Chartoff) 189 bottom left, Leni Riefenstahl, 189 bottom right, RKO (Edmund Grainger); London Express News & Features/Evening Standard/Maurice Conroy (136 middle); London Features International – Frank Griffin (137 bottom) Mansell Collection, London (167); Mirror Syndication International, London (132 top); National Archives Still Picture Branch, Maryland (152-3, 154); Peter Newark Historical Pictures, Bath (150, 177 middle, 190); Novosti, London (142 middle, 183 top, 184 bottom); Novosti Photo Library/V. Samokhotsky (143); Ronnie O'Brien, (149); Ohio State University Photo Archives (146, 148 top); Popperfoto, Northampton (170 bottom middle); Punch Magazine, London (168 middle); The Quaker Oats Company, Chicago (158 top); Range/Bettmann/UPI, London (138, 148 bottom); Rex Features Ltd, London, (134 bottom, 135, 137 top, 137 middle, 156, 157, 181, 182 bottom); Rex Features/Sipa Press (145, 156, 182 top); Frank Spooner Pictures, London (144); Frank Spooner/Gamma (132 bottom); Frank Spooner/Gamma/Sigla (155); Frank Spooner/Gamma/Françoise Demulder (180); ©T. Stone – all proceeds from the use of these photographs go to the Multiple Sclerosis Society (165); Topham Picture Source (164); Wiener Library, London (162-3 bottom, 170 top, 170 bottom left).

Picture research: Charlotte Deane

The illustrations of Band Aid and Live Aid symbols which appear in this book are used by permission of the Band Aid Trust, London.

Every effort has been made to trace the copyright holders of material in this book. If any rights have been omitted, the publishers offer to rectify this in any subsequent editions following notification.

Index